A BEAUTIFULLY FOOLISH ENDEAVOR

ALSO BY HANK GREEN

An Absolutely Remarkable Thing

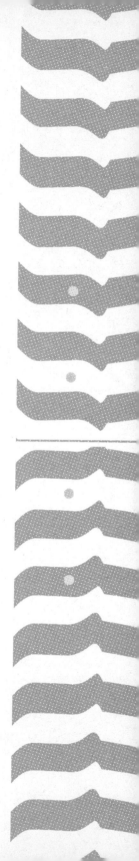

A BEAUTIFULLY FOOLISH ENDEAVOR

A NOVEL

HANK GREEN

DUTTON

DUTTON

An imprint of Penguin Random House LLC

penguinrandomhouse.com

Copyright © 2020 by Hank Green

Penguin supports copyright. Copyright fuels creativity, encourages diverse voices, promotes free speech, and creates a vibrant culture. Thank you for buying an authorized edition of this book and for complying with copyright laws by not reproducing, scanning, or distributing any part of it in any form without permission. You are supporting writers and allowing Penguin to continue to publish books for every reader.

DUTTON and the D colophon are registered trademarks of Penguin Random House LLC.

Permissions appear on page 454 and constitute an extension of the copyright page.

LIBRARY OF CONGRESS CATALOGING-IN-PUBLICATION DATA
Names: Green, Hank, author.
Title: A beautifully foolish endeavor: a novel / Hank Green.
Description: First edition. | New York: Dutton, [2020] |
Identifiers: LCCN 2020006678 | ISBN 9781524743475 (hardcover) |
ISBN 9781524743482 (ebook)
Subjects: GSAFD: Science fiction.
Classification: LCC PS3607.R43285 B43 2020 | DDC 813/.6—dc23
LC record available at https://lccn.loc.gov/2020006678

ISBN: 9780593182505 (international edition)

Printed in the United States of America
1   3   5   7   9   10   8   6   4   2

This is a work of fiction. Names, characters, places, and incidents either are the product of the author's imagination or are used fictitiously, and any resemblance to actual persons, living or dead, businesses, companies, events, monkeys, or locales is entirely coincidental.

For my patient and loving wife, Katherine

A BEAUTIFULLY FOOLISH ENDEAVOR

APRIL

I've decided to stop lying to you.

As far as I can tell there are only three kinds of lies: the kind you don't want to get caught telling, the kind you don't care if you get caught telling, and the kind you can't get caught telling. Let's go through them one by one.

1. **The kind you don't want to get caught telling.** This is just your average, everyday lie, whether you're late for work or did a real bad murder. Getting caught in the lie, thus, is a problem.
2. **The kind you don't care if you get caught telling.** This kind of lie is about the lying, not about the outcome. You repeat the lie, stick to the lie, change the lie, re-form the lie, abandon the lie, come back to the lie. The lying might help avoid some negative outcome, but really it's a tool for weakening reality, and thus strengthening yourself.
3. **The kind you can't get caught telling.** This happens when only you know the truth. This is the kind of lie I've been telling.

For years now, that last kind of lie has felt, to me, like a kindness. I mean, it's not a surprise that the story of your reality is incomplete. We all know that. Scientists don't know where most of the matter is. I don't know what it's like to live in Yemen. Our imagining of the world isn't fully accurate. But if you know something no one else knows, something that would change everyone's story overnight, something that would make everyone else's life worse, telling the truth might seem like the wrong thing to do, like exercising too much power.

As I have discovered, there's nothing special about me, nothing that makes me particularly suited to making that kind of decision for an entire planet of people. The only reason I get to make it, it turns out, is ugly, vulgar luck.

A lot of people have said that I have a habit of exercising too much power, and one of those people is me, which is why I am about to do something I'm extremely uncomfortable with: let other people tell the story. Oh, to be clear, I don't have any choice. I wasn't there for a lot of this, so it isn't my story to tell. Instead, my friends are going to tell it with me. Maybe that way we can share some of the responsibility of the power of this truth. It won't be all on me: each of us have to agree that the words in this book are worth putting in here. Trust me, it wasn't easy, these people can be fucking stubborn.

All of this is to say, I've decided to stop lying to you. *We* have decided to stop lying to you. Even though the lie is easy to tell, even though I never really said it out loud, even though the lie, most days, feels like nothing more than self-preservation, it's time to tell you about the lie.

Here it is, in its most basic form: I have been doing everything I can to convince you that we are safe.

We're not.

MAYA

I am only doing this because I have to. Most famous people ask for fame, and then when they get famous and complain about all the bad parts, we are correct in calling them out on it. But I have always felt like millions of people knowing my name would be nothing but awful.

It's why I didn't let April put my last name in her book. It is also not in this book. Of course, you can look it up on the internet, but neither I nor anyone who knows me has ever shared my last name. You can only find out what my name is due to the general erosion of privacy and the actions of people who have not respected my clearly-stated preferences.

That's how I want to start this out. I stayed out of April's content on purpose. I wanted to be a private person, and now I'm not, but I'm accepting this because it's the best way to tell this story. And while I'm not going to tell you my last name (it's the principle of the thing), I am going to be far more open than I want to be.

For example.

My parents are pretty rich. I grew up on the Upper East Side in a town house they've owned for thirty years. It was worth a lot when they bought it, and it's worth a LOT now. So I actually grew up with something like a yard, and when I was a little kid, we'd go out there and plant carrot seeds and tomato starts. At the end of the season, yanking a carrot out of the ground was like a magic trick. That tiny seed, too small for even my little fingers to manage on their own, had become this big, beefy orange grocery store item covered in wet black dirt. It was like putting a bottle cap in the ground and pulling out a Coke. Those underground crops—carrots, beets, potatoes, onions—were my favorites. Even when we were growing things in pots and boxes, I loved the idea that things were happening out of view and that if you just scraped the surface, something as magical and perfect and tasty as food would just fall out.

It never occurred to me at the time that gardening was something my mom was doing for me. But when I grew up and my interests changed, the gardening went away. And I didn't even consider more than watering a houseplant until I called my mom a few months after April died.

"I can't let it go, Mom, she has to be somewhere," I was telling her over the phone, explaining an obsession that had blossomed in me. "No one else is looking. They've all just moved on."

"Is it doing you any good?"

"Me? What does this have to do with me?! They haven't found her, Mom, I don't think she was in there."

"Maya, love, where would she have gone?"

"I don't know, that's the point. Outer space? Hoboken? I don't know. But I do know that life is not back to normal. Everybody thinks the Carls are gone and the Dream is gone and it's all normal now, but it's not. I know how this sounds, but there are a lot of other people who think something's up."

"How much time are you spending on the Som?"

"They're good people, Mom. I made a lot of friends there. It's better than Twitter."

And that was, in several ways, true. The Som was a small enough community that the kinds of people who got off on making others miserable were promptly banned. But in one way, it was worse. We built the Som to be a social media platform just for solving sequences from the Dream. It was a place for mysteries. To a hammer, everything looks like a nail, and to a social media platform designed to investigate mysteries, everything looked mysterious.

The Som was something I had been really proud to help build, it really had been a part of making humanity feel more like one big thing. Now it was the go-to platform for conspiracy theorists. But at least they were *nice* conspiracy theorists. And to answer my mom's question here (though I didn't answer it then), I was spending a *lot* of time on the Som.

"Maya, maybe go plant something."

"What?"

"Like when you were little. Or do something. Knit. Do a puzzle. I think you need to focus on something else for a while. Go make some space inside your head."

It seemed extremely condescending at the time. Like, yes, Mom, it would be great if I could get a hobby that wasn't obsessing over my dead ex-girlfriend. That would be good for everyone, especially for you, since you wouldn't have to watch your daughter spiral further and further from reality. But that's not how it works, *Mother*.

Except, to some extent, it really is. Because thinking about carrots existing somehow made me want to plant something, or tend something, or dig something. But I didn't have a yard. So instead, I got on a train and, thirty minutes later, knocked on the door of my parents' town house on the Upper East Side. My mom answered the door.

"Fine, let's plant something," I said, smiling just a little. And she smiled back and hugged me and we went into the garden. She found a clay-colored plastic pot, about a foot across, and I dumped a bunch of potting soil into it. Then we went into the kitchen and cut up a couple Yukon Gold potatoes, making sure each piece had an eye. Then, together, like when I was five, we stuffed them down into the soil.

"Mama, do you know how messed up I am?" I asked, fingers covered in dirt.

"Honey," she said, her big, worried eyes seeing all the way in, "you're just as messed up as you should be."

I hadn't cried in a few weeks at that point, which made this one bigger.

———

April knows I'm private, and I like to think that's why you know so little about me, and not that she just couldn't be bothered. It's probably a little of both. But, look, there's a lot of talk in the last book about how together and successful and smart and solid I am. That's bullshit. We're all pretending, and April maybe wanted to be extra nice about me because of how she completely ditched me the moment something shiny caught her attention. But before the Dream, I didn't know what the hell I was doing with my life. I was letting my girlfriend sleep in the living room because she was too fragile to admit we lived together. I went in to a job that a bunch of my coworkers thought I only got because I was Black. And I knew that no matter how hard I worked, I would never make anything like the amount of money that was already in my bank account because I had chosen (much to my dad's chagrin) to get a degree in design instead of an MBA.

I had not been totally open with April, or really anyone, about my financial situation, on account of the deep, burning shame.

Like, I'm supposed to own it for everyone who doesn't have it. I'm supposed to show that Black people can be rich, and that you're racist for thinking we can't be. But also, I'm supposed to rage at the system that made me rich. Like, can a girl get a break?

Whatever, the thing I was trying to say here is that I didn't have to work, which made working at jobs I didn't love a little bit empty. Obviously, this is a profoundly unrelatable frustration, but we all only have our own lives to live inside of.

The Dream was bigger than me, and it was a real contribution I was making. Every time I solved a sequence, that had nothing to do with my money. On the Som, I was respected entirely because of my contributions. No one knew anything about me. They didn't know I was rich, they didn't know I was Black, they didn't know I was April May's ex-girlfriend. I was just ThePurrletarian. My friends there only knew my words and my actions. It's the same reason I did a web comic about leftist cats in college. It was a way to feel respected out-side of my identities.

So there was one hole left in the wake of the Dream, and then there was the other even bigger hole left by April. I spent a lot of time filling those holes with being angry while looking at the internet, but I also filled them on the Som, where I found posts like these:

MORE DOLPHINS IN THE DELAWARE

Yesterday twenty dolphins were found in the Delaware River, well into the fresh water. They're north of the outage points described in this thread [OUTAGE-POINTS-NJ-DE-PA]. The dolphins showed up outside of Trenton, NJ. They then spent several days just north of Trenton before dying. Some folks were able to rescue some of them. This is the second pod that ended up this far north in the river in two weeks and it's basically unheard of. Also very nearby the break-in at Rider University, see thread [RIDER-U-LAB-BREAK-IN].

So, of course, I clicked to see the thread about the lab break-in, which quickly led me to this post:

JOHNS HOPKINS LAB BREAK-IN

This is the fourth since April disappeared—see threads. This one was way crazier. Not like the little ones at Rider University [RIDER-U-LAB-BREAK-IN] and the hospitals in Philly [NAZARETH-HOSPITAL-BREAK-IN] [MERCY-HOSPITAL-BREAK-IN]. No one's linking it to those, but Johns Hopkins (yes, *that* Johns Hopkins) in Baltimore was bro-ken into. They're saying it was an animal rights thing because a bunch of monkeys escaped. The article also says a couple of unre-lated pieces of equipment also disappeared. Johns Hopkins is huge, it has 24-hour security. PETA has been after them for decades, they know how to not have this happen, but it happened. Something is going on with these lab break-ins, so I'm starting an omni-thread specifically to add information and specifics re: any break-in of a laboratory, hospital, or university [LAB-BREAK-INS-OMNI].

My first thought upon seeing this was that it seemed like a reach. People got robbed, animal rights activists freed monkeys, that was the world. But also, it was a *little* weird. Like, why would animal rights people steal monkeys *and* lab equipment? Were they financing their monkey stealing? I was not well versed in how monkey stealing worked.

But what I realized was that the Som was the place I was most comfortable in the world now that the Dream was gone . . . now that April was gone. A lot of the names were the same, and the culture of investigation and sleuthing was the same. But best of all, these people didn't think everything had gone back to normal. Not a single one of them believed that April had died in that building, and I badly needed to see people say that.

Losing the Dream, for a lot of people, was like losing a drug. Even after every sequence had been solved (except the 767), I would go to sleep and solve sequences all night. Real dreams seemed so chaotic and unstructured. I loved the Dream, and then it just got ripped out of my head. There were even services that promised to be able to bring back some amount of the Dream with electrical pulses aimed at your brain. There were threads about it on the Som a lot, but it always seemed like the people who said they got it back were either trying to sell the service or maybe just had a really good dream about the Dream.

But this had the feel of a Dream sequence to me. The first robbery was in Trenton, New Jersey, then two in Philly. Then Johns Hopkins. That made it seem like they were moving south down the coast.

The labs were all pretty close to each other. The Johns Hopkins robbery was the farthest from the break-ins at hospitals in Philadelphia. And then there were a few weird cell phone outages outside of Philly. And then, a couple weeks after that, the lab break-ins had stopped, but a bunch of dolphins swam up the Delaware and died outside Trenton, New Jersey.

———

"I have to keep looking, Mom," I told her.

"What if you don't find her?" she asked.

"Then I'll keep looking. She's not dead."

She looked down at the soil, and the little pocket of rage in my heart started to leak into the rest of me. Everyone wanted me to give up, even her.

"Just take care of your potatoes," she said.

"What?"

"Take them with you." She gestured to the pot. "Take care of them. Just to have something that needs you." She lightly touched my face and said, "Like I do."

My mom and I made dinner together that night, and before I even brought up Trenton, while I was putting the pasta on the table and sitting down, my dad hit me with "So, you know they're treating people who have Dream addiction now, there's a long piece on it in *The New Yorker.*"

"Mmm?" my mom said, loading that tiny noise with far more nuance than should be possible. It said, "I know what you're doing, and so does Maya, and please don't do it."

He received the warning but blew right past it anyway. "People who were deeply involved with sequence solving, their minds rely on it very much like a drug. And when it's not there anymore, at least according to a lot of smart people, the mind keeps looking for it, and it can be a really difficult withdrawal."

"Dad, I'm fine."

"None of us expect you to be fine, Maya," he said, his voice a physical thing, strong enough to lean on. "But, listen, it's also fine for me to worry. What the Carls did to our minds, no one understands it, and it seems like a lot of people are finding patterns where they don't exist now. You need to have something else to focus on. When are you going back to work?"

"Gill," my mom started, but I raised my hand to quiet her.

My dad knew how the world worked, and he'd worked very hard to get that knowledge. There aren't a lot of Black investment bankers, and that's not because they're uninterested in the profession. He fought his whole life to succeed in a hostile system. As far back as I can remember, he told me the world didn't want people who looked like us to be rich, but that it was our job to get rich anyway.

My mom has usually been happy to push me in whatever direction I was facing. My dad, on the other hand, thought that my best chances for happiness were more specific. He wanted a clear career track. He wanted me, his only child, to care about the money that he'd made for me. He wanted me to pass it to my kids, which is the only reason me coming out was ever weird in the house. Dad wanted to know what my sexuality meant for the next generation. He was at least cool enough to not say it out loud, but we could all tell, and eventually we had to have a conversation about all of the various options I had if I ever chose to have kids. When I was *seventeen*. Dad had been fine with me leaving my work to be part of April's projects, and help Miranda build the Som, but now I was his worst nightmare: another rich kid with an art school degree and no direction.

"I understand, Dad, I know I've not been great these past few months. But April isn't dead and I'm not going to keep pretending that she is. I've got to do this."

My dad looked at my mom with hard eyes. She looked down at the table. They thought she was dead. Of course they did—everyone thought she was dead.

"You know what?" I said quietly. And then I pushed my bottom lip onto my teeth to start making a *f* sound, but then I stopped myself. I didn't say it, but they both heard that "fuck you" hanging there in our dining room. We do not curse in my house.

"Maya . . ." my mom said as my dad's eyes widened. I don't yell, not at people. I yell at the TV when some senator is being racist. I yell at Photoshop when it crashes. I don't yell at people. I *least of all* yell at my parents.

I yelled at them. "She's Not Dead!" My hand, unbidden, slammed on the table as I stood up . . . all of the silverware clinking in the dishes.

"Maya! Don't you speak to your mother like that," my dad said, firm and cold from his chair on the other side of the table.

I leaned over the table toward him. "I'm going to go find April," I said. I almost whispered it. And then I turned around and walked out of the dining room.

And then, because I will never not be completely horrified by myself losing control, I turned around and said, "Call me tomorrow when we're all less mad. I'll be in New Jersey."

On the way out, I noticed the pot of soil with those newly buried, dirty, cut-up potatoes hiding in it. I let out a sigh and grabbed it as I went out the door.

ANDY

It seems unlikely that my best friend becoming an international superstar for being the discoverer and chief human advocate for an extraterrestrial life-form isn't the weirdest thing that's ever happened to me. But the actual weirdest thing that's ever happened to me started like this:

Five months after my best friend was murdered by terrorists just after solving a riddle that resulted in the apparent disappearance of aliens from our planet, someone knocked twice on my door, and then I got a text message from my dead friend.

Knock Knock, it said.

This isn't even the weird part. After staring at that text message for way too long, I dashed to my door and flung it open to find a brown clothbound book sitting in the hall of my building. Words were pressed into the hard cover in a simple serif font, filled with gold leaf: "The Book of Good Times."

OK, actually, I need to go further back.

It's easy to forget how quiet the world was in the months after Carl (or the Carls, depending on who you believed) vanished. Each of the sixty-four Carls that had appeared in cities across the world blinked out of existence at the exact same moment except for one. The Carl in Manhattan did not simply vanish; it yanked itself into the air at (a peer-reviewed paper estimated) around Mach 3. This added weight to the theory that there was only ever one Carl; they just somehow projected one statue into sixty-four different locations simultaneously. Look, I don't pretend to understand any of this, which sets me blissfully apart from all of the bloviation that occurred on cable news in the aftermath.

But bloviation though there was, the world actually chilled way down for a bit after the Carls vanished. This tremendous force that had thrown a wrench into our collective understanding of the universe and slapped every person on a spectrum somewhere between "We welcome our robot overlords" and "If we do not fight, we will die" just . . . disappeared.

Like, imagine what would happen to the gun control debate if every gun just fwipped out of existence along with the knowledge of . . . what guns are or how to make them. The thing we were all so mad at each other over was just gone.

That's not to say that people were OK. The economy kept contracting, and no one was really sure why. People were just working less, or dropping out of the labor force entirely. There was a lot of going through the motions, but the reality was, everything felt a little empty. The Carl debate was an identity-defining conversation for hundreds of millions of people, and that identity was now gone.

Before Carl, the world was changing fast, and many people had already lost their solid grip on how they fit into the world, but most folks were still in a story that made some sense. But when Carl came and we were all suddenly in a new story, that was jarring. And then we hit another twist to the roller coaster: They were gone, and now it seemed like no one knew which way was up. What story did we have now? Who were we? What was the point of anything?

And if the time after Carl felt calm, it's largely because no one knew what to say. You can only talk about something not existing for a few weeks before it's just not *news* anymore. But at the same time, it was hard to argue about tax policy and health care or even get up and go to work when nothing felt important the way Carl had. People's identities, their sources of meaning, had been banged up even before Carl, but now a lot of folks were just lost.

One of the more minor changes was of course the reality games. Humans have always loved a hunt, but then the Dream put every single person into a species-wide escape room, so on the whole we got more into puzzles. Reality games were like escape rooms or scavenger hunts, but they were ongoing and took place everywhere, and the best ones went to extravagant lengths to re-create the feeling that the Dreamers had lost. Puzzle masters distribute the game through the internet, physical spaces, and sometimes people. You pay a monthly fee to always be on the lookout for your next clue, whether it comes through the mail, through a chance encounter with a stranger, or on your doorstep accompanied by a cryptic text message from your dead best friend.

I wasn't signed up for any reality games, but when I saw that book, my mind immediately started treating it like a puzzle.

I left the book exactly where it was and ran up and down the hall, checking the staircase and the elevator, my heart pounding the whole time. I nearly went downstairs and ran outside but decided it was more important to investigate the book itself. I took pictures of it from every angle before I finally picked it up, took it inside, and then started texting April.

April? is how I started, but about five texts and fifteen minutes of agonized waiting later, they were full-on *APRIL MAY DO NOT TELL ME YOU HAVE BEEN NOT DEAD FOR THE LAST FIVE MONTHS AND DID NOT TELL ME BUT ALSO PLEASE PLEASE TELL ME WHETHER OR NOT YOU ARE NOT DEAD AND IF THIS IS SOME FUCK MESSING WITH ME I LOOK FORWARD TO WEARING YOUR FINGER BONES AS A NECKLACE.*

I did not get another text.

I also didn't call or text anyone else. I didn't want to create any false hope in Maya or Miranda or Robin. So I just sat there in my own panicky misery.

Before I even picked up the book, I was angry at it. It wasn't just a big scary question mark. I also could feel a very particular future pulling at me. I'm not going to rag on April too much here, but she was the river we were all swept up in for so long. In the months since she disappeared, I'd found some direction of my own. I felt like I was actually in charge of my life, maybe for the first time.

I picked up the book and squeezed its width in my fingers. This book wanted to be in charge.

I opened it.

It wasn't big—it looked like it was between one and two hundred pages. And unlike every book ever, it began on the first page, which was disconcerting, in a way. I don't read a ton, but I know that you usually have to flip through publisher information and title pages and "This one's for my patient and loving wife, Katherine" before you hit the actual book. But no, here the book just started.

Do not tell anyone about this. Do not post an Instagram story of this or tweet it or call a friend and share it. This is a magic book, but its magic only works for you, and it only works if no one else knows. It won't always make sense, but it knows more than you. So unless I tell you differently, clam up, buttercup. Let's get straight to what you want to know.

There's a young woman lying still and quiet in a room with a robot somewhere. And she's safe. She's not well, but she is better than she was. And she will be better than she is. She is being cared for. When she is awake, it is bad, so she is asleep. Only for now.

She would like to see her friends. Maybe she needs to see her friends. But she cannot see her friends right now. She still needs work. Her body and her mind. Oh lord, minds are a whole thing, aren't they?

A young man in his apartment feels sick in his stomach. Partially because he hasn't eaten all day, but also because he is frightened for his friend and just broadly anxious about all of these words that are suddenly coming at him. He's afraid that what he's reading might not be true, but also that it might be true. The young man is also afraid that the book is talking about him because he's being stubborn. He is thinking about what might be wrong with his friend's mind. But minds are complex and there are many things wrong with every mind.

I put the book down, my armpits slick with sweat. I realized I hadn't been breathing as I pulled in a sharp gulp of air. I picked the book back up.

The man picks the book back up.

I put the book back down. What the fuck?

And then he picks it back up again. He's been doing a very good job. Fantastic. The world needs calm voices right now. He's been one of those voices. He's not chasing the most attention, he's not trying to turn every scrap of social capital he has into more social capital, and that's hard, so I want to let him know that that's appreciated. He's doing the right things. I've been reading his Twitter, and I really liked *Pose* too. What a great show. The world needs more content about people just loving each other. I also really liked this tweet:

Andy Skampt
@AndySkampt
None of us have forgotten that the Carls changed our minds, but it's important to remember that we all change each other's minds all the time. Any good story is a mind-altering substance.

I don't think that's really an accurate portrayal of what was done to your mind, but it is good to pull tensions down and also to call attention to the power you each have over each other. "Mind-altering substance" . . . very clever. You always were a clever one. Do you remember when you pulled the mic up your own shirt and clipped it onto your collar and then decided that April should be the star? You didn't know what choice you were making, but you knew you were making a choice. You didn't just chase the flame, and the magnitude of that choice . . . well, here we are. You always wanted to be famous, but you gave that away. But then it came for you anyway, just in time for you to not really want it. Of course you feel guilty about it. That's fine. You shouldn't of course. You're doing the best you can with what you have, but of course you feel guilty. That's fine.

The money in your bank account, the follows on your Twitter, you think they're all hers and that you just inherited them. But almost everything is inherited. It's not about deserving. It's about what you do with what you have. And, so far, you are doing well.

Anyway, you should go get a sandwich.

The man stands up from the table and takes the stairs to the ground floor so he has some time to think. He walks to Subway, where he orders a six-inch sweet onion chicken teriyaki sub with provolone, bell peppers, onions, tomato, and lettuce.

He gets a Coke to help settle his stomach, but he only drinks half of it because he doesn't need all that caffeine right now. And he doesn't get the meal, even though the chips would only be an extra 75 cents.

Then he'll take his sandwich to Tompkins Square Park, which is a nice park, even though it's a bit of a walk, and he'll eat his sandwich.

Rebecca at Subway is waiting to make his sandwich.

Go get a sandwich.

And that's where that page ended. I turned the page, and there (and on every other page in *The Book of Good Times*) was a single sentence, "Go get a sandwich," repeated over and over again.

So, I mean, what do you do? At the very least you want to go see if the person who will make your sandwich is named Rebecca.

The sweet onion chicken teriyaki had been my sub since high school, which was something April knew about me . . . probably. Which made me think that maybe it was April who had written the book. Or maybe it was just someone who had watched me order a sandwich once. It felt like April, though. The words definitely *felt* like April.

I was understandably distracted on my walk to Subway, which is probably the only reason I ended up walking past the plaque that had been placed in the ground where New York Carl once stood. I hadn't admitted it to myself, but I must have been avoiding this area.

The plaque was a simple bronze square laid into the concrete that said only "This was the location of New York Carl." A fresh rose had been placed on it, and no one had accidentally kicked it away yet. Part of me thought the rose was a nice gesture; part of me thought that strangers didn't have the right to mourn April. She was my friend, not theirs. That was the whole fucking problem, that everyone in the world thought that April May was theirs. All they knew of her was the caricature she created for them. I looked up and saw someone had lifted their phone to take a photo of me.

"Oh, come on!" I half shouted, immediately regretting it, before marching over to Lexington thinking that maybe I had mentioned my affinity for sweet onion chicken teriyaki subs on Twitter at some point and someone had stored that fact away for their elaborate prank.

"Six-inch sweet onion chicken teriyaki on Italian, please," I said to the woman at Subway. I'd ordered a similar sub from her probably a dozen times since I'd moved to the neighborhood. She was in her early twenties, and I couldn't help myself from guessing at her ethnicity. She looked Asian, but with dark skin and an accent that I didn't immediately recognize.

Her name tag read "Becky."

"Short for Rebecca?" I asked after I had ordered my veggies and she was ringing me up. She started at the question, her mind gears shifting out of transaction mode and into pleasant-customer-conversation mode.

"OH!" She laughed. "I thought you were saying *I* was short for a Rebecca. I was like, 'Well, I think I'm a perfectly normal height for a Rebecca.'" She laughed again. "Yes, I mean, yeah, my parents named me Rebecca because they knew Becky was a normal name for an American girl."

Her words came fast and lyrical. The accent wasn't thick, but it was there. British, maybe?

"Well, Becky, I think you are an average-heighted Rebecca."

"Thanks very much, have a great day, Andy, nice to see you again."

At this point, it wasn't weird for me for people to know my name, but I felt like that was an opportunity to ask a couple more questions.

"Hey, Becky, can I ask you a weird question? Has anyone ever come in here asking about me?" My cheeks flushed a bit—in my ears I sounded like a person who thought they were way more famous than they were.

"No, but I wouldn't say anything if they did."

"Have you ever seen a book like this?" I asked, right before realizing the book had specifically told me not to tell anyone about the book. Did this count?

She regarded the book skeptically, and then carefully said, "It looks like a book to me, can I take a closer look?"

"No," I stammered. "I mean, if it doesn't look familiar, it doesn't look familiar. That's OK. Thanks a lot."

The walk to Tompkins Square Park was pretty long. My sub was sure to get cold along the way, but I was just happy to be outside.

Life was different now, but New York was still New York. No switch had been flipped when aliens came to visit us. It still looked and sounded and smelled the same. Think pieces were happily guessing about the generation of kids who would be raised in a post-Carl world and how their perspectives on everything from employment to brand-name toothpaste would be different. And who knows, maybe they would be, but New York would still be there for them to project their dreams onto.

I thought about how maybe the constancy of our surroundings makes us believe in a constancy of reality and of self.

I made a mental note that maybe that would be a good topic for a video, or at least an Instagram caption.

When I got to the park, I did what pretty much everyone else was doing: I watched the people. The East Village is still a little weird, even after all these decades of gentrification. So while the nannies outnumber the weirdos, it still makes for good people watching. I wiped the sweet onion sauce off my hand and crumpled up the wrapper, walking over to a trash can. And as I was about to stuff it in and then check my email, I saw the corner of a thin brown clothbound book sticking out of the trash.

I pulled it out.

"The Book of Good Times: Part 2," its cover proclaimed.

"I Went to See the Place Where New York Carl Was and Found Andy Skampt"

MIRANDA

How anyone decides what to put in a book is a mystery to me. You don't leave out details in scientific writing, as that's a fantastic way to get your paper rejected. You need to explain exactly what happened in precise language with as little subjectivity as possible. That's how I'm used to communicating, but I've been consistently if subtly informed that that will not do in this situation, and I know how important it is to trust expertise. I'm just supposed to *decide* what is interesting and/or important, which mostly means that every word I write makes me more and more anxious. This should be fun.

Luckily, Maya and Andy have gone first, so I'll start where Andy left off, which is roughly when I sent a text into our group text with Maya, Robin, and (yes, still) April. It just felt wrong to start a new one without her.

Miranda: *Andy's on the front page of Reddit right now.*

Andy: *God fucking damn it, what did I do?*

Miranda: *You went to the Carl plaque . . . you looked sad. Someone took a picture.*

The photo was of Andy looking sad and pensive, surrounded by the activity of the city. It was a good picture.

Andy: *Jesus, I was going to fucking Subway and stopped for like five seconds.*

Robin: *No one is being mean about it, it just looks sad.*

Maya: *Well, it is sad.*

I was definitely not going to be the one to respond after Maya's text. One, I will never stop feeling weird about hooking up with April. Two, Maya had handled April's disappearance differently from the rest of us. I went back to Berkeley to distract myself by finishing my PhD. Andy was a professional famous person, and Robin was managing him. We were doing our lives again; Maya was not. She hadn't given up on somehow finding April, and while she didn't actively try to make us feel guilty, her disappointment was clear.

Andy: *That was the first time I've gone there. I think I've been avoiding it this whole time. I also told that guy off and he still posted the photo. Good lord.*

Maya: *Well, I guess you're the new sad Keanu . . . there are worse fates.*

Robin: *We all must aspire to our inner Keanuness.*

This is going to sound stupid, but I still felt like a bit of a fake hanging around with these people. I don't know if this was a me problem or a signal I was actually getting from them, but I felt like an honorary member of the crew rather than a real one. I just wasn't as cool as any of them were.

Maya: *Have you guys read the profile of PP? It's a full-on nightmare.*

Robin: *Yes, somehow I was hoping no one else in the whole world would find out about it.*

Andy: *People are still thinking about that shitstick?*

Miranda: *I haven't seen it? Link?*

So that's how I found myself hunched over the lab bench by the GC/mass spec staring into my phone with acid churning in my stomach.

PETER PETRAWICKI IS SORRY AND HE'S GOT A PITCH FOR YOU

Peter Petrawicki still sees himself as both a hero and a villain. But now he's traded in his suits and television appearances for life on the beach in Puerto Rico. He's thriving in a society where he's a little less recognizable, and a lot less in demand. He's literally sipping a daiquiri in a short-sleeve button-down the first time we sit down to talk, but it isn't long before the conversation turns from his Spanish lessons and his new beachfront property to his mixed feelings about the culture war he wasn't just a part of, but helped create.

"I didn't know what I was doing, I didn't realize how much pent-up hatred there was in the country. I deeply regret a lot of what happened, obviously. I even regret a lot of what I said."

It's clear that that admission isn't easy for him. Petrawicki has always been a zealous opponent of censorship, even self-censorship. He references the "free market of ideas" at least a half dozen times in only a few hours of chatting. Ultimately, though, I have to bring up April before he talks about her.

"I respected April a great deal. I still do. I think we were having a necessary debate. I never wanted anyone to hurt her. The fact that those people"—he's referring to April's kidnappers—"ended up being so tightly connected to Defender ideology is something I struggle with constantly, and that I'll be struggling with every day for the rest of my life."

I put down my phone and stood up. After August 5, when both April and the Carls vanished, anyone who called themselves a Defender was not going to have a good time. The FBI caught the guys who lit the warehouse on fire, and they were all obviously and proudly Defenders. They were still out there, but only the most scary and extreme ones still called themselves Defenders. They had been pushed deeper into private chats and seedy message boards and loosely affiliated angry YouTube channels. These were all things that I tried very, very hard to never think about or engage with.

But there were also all of the people who had been Defenders but just didn't want the label anymore. They weren't *murderers*; they just thought April was a traitor who was better off dead. They wouldn't have killed her, and it was terrible she was murdered, but they weren't exactly sad she was gone. If she *was* gone. Lots of people believed she was still around doing bad things for humans, and many more people were just on the edge of believing it. The only control in the world I had was over the Som, and anti-April conspiracy theories weren't tolerated there. Everywhere else, though? I think the idea was, what's the harm in attacking someone who's dead?

I wasn't running the Som anymore. We thought hard about just closing it completely—after all, it was built to help people solve puzzles in a dream we no longer had access to. I didn't have a passion for it after April was gone, and I honestly didn't have a grasp on how huge and deeply connected the community there had become.

But people made it clear that it was bigger than the Dream. Lots of people used it as simply an alternate social space, but it was uniquely suited to investigative work. Journalists used it to outsource research, conspiracy theorists used it to collect their leads, and then of course there were the reality games. That new class of gamers found the Som infinitely useful and were happy to continue paying a low monthly fee to keep the service alive.

So we didn't shut it down, but I had to leave. I'm not even sure why. Part of it was that running a start-up is exhausting, but with the dramatically lowered stakes I didn't have the same fuel. More importantly, I wanted to go back to my old life. Not because I missed it, just because it was less painful. So I passed the torch and went back to Berkeley.

PhD students who just vanish for a year aren't usually welcomed back with open arms, but Dr. Lundgren, my advisor, hadn't even fully packed up my space yet. We'd kept in touch a little bit, and she said she was keeping my slot open because my research was so promising. But was it? It was incremental. I know that's true of most research, but I wasn't changing a paradigm; I was adding to existing knowledge. The more I thought about it, the more I figured that the fact that I had done so many big, public things and become a little bit famous made everybody much more sympathetic. It felt a little like cheating.

I don't blame April for not ever telling you anything about what I was doing in my PhD program, or even that I was in a PhD program, but basically . . . well, OK, I'm really bad at basicallys. You know how a computer chip is made of silicon semiconductors? Well, there are a bunch of other materials that aren't silicon that can be used in the same way that have different advantages. They might be cheaper or more flexible or thinner or whatever. Well, the thing I was working on was a kind of organic semiconductor gel. The idea is to make it not just flexible but squishy and wet. This is only really good for one thing: putting it inside of living bodies.

Scientists have been working at UC Berkeley for a long time on tiny sensors and nerve stimulators that can be implanted into people (though mostly just rats so far). But hard chips can only get so small, and in any case it would be a better experience all around if the sensor felt a little more like soft organic bits.

It is very difficult for me to not keep explaining, but I think you get the point: squishy computer chips for use inside of living things so that you can have a tiny Fitbit inside of you telling you, in real time, whether your blood sugar is crashing or you're having a heart attack. My research was an attempt both to gather signals from the nervous system and to send inputs into the nervous system. It was potentially interesting research in everything from diagnostics and scanning to prosthetics, and I could not for the life of me figure out how to care.

I got back to Berkeley, and somehow my lab had only partially been torn apart by people who needed equipment for their own experiments. I was able to put it all back together pretty quickly. But the thing I had been so excited about before now felt like busywork. Knowing that technology as elegant and powerful as Carl's existed in the universe made me feel like a monkey banging rocks together. I'm sure part of this was grief, but I think part of it was the post-Carl depression that a lot of people were dealing with.

The day I read that Petrawicki article, I was working on assembling my little jellies using literal laser beams to push impurities into the perfect places before letting the gel solidify. I was basically making Jell-O, except instead of pears and marshmallows, I was pushing around individual atoms. With lasers.

It sounds cooler than it was. Someone else had built the laser robot; my lab just bought it. All I was doing was typing instructions into the program that would control the laser. This was not terribly cerebral work, so my mind kept drifting back to the article and Peter Petrawicki's new island life. Was this his redemption arc? It was so nice of him to apologize to a magazine reporter who was doing a puff piece on him. Had he apologized to April's parents? To Andy and Maya and Robin? To me? I must have missed the email. And it's also nice to hear how many struggles *he's* had. That's definitely something people need to be worrying about.

Of course, I stopped filling in the numbers my circuit CAD program had spat out and went back to the article. The writer continued:

Peter Petrawicki is not a changed man, though. He's driven, sure of himself, and believes that anyone standing in the way of the path he sees as right is dangerous. But now, without the Carls looming on the streets, his anxieties have turned elsewhere. I ask him what his biggest fear is, and he stays silent for thirty seconds before replying.

"You met Taggart on the way in." He's talking about the island dog that he adopted. It's medium-sized, medium-haired, medium brown, and of medium disposition. If there is a purebred dog in Taggart's lineage, it was many generations ago. "I love Taggart, and I think Taggart has a good life, certainly better than he had before we met. He gets fed twice a day, he gets to run on the beach, we cuddle up and watch TV. Taggart has literally everything taken care of. And when Taggart starts to decline and suffer, I'll decide for him when he should die, because that's the appropriate thing to do. Taggart does not even think to question his life. Everything that happens to him, he accepts, both good and bad, because he isn't even capable of imagining that he can affect his own life. When we go to the vet's office that last time, he will have no idea what is happening. He will just go to sleep, and it will be just one more thing that happened to him."

We sat there for a while. I stayed quiet, even though I didn't really get where he was going with all of this sad dog talk.

"That's what I'm afraid of, that we will become like that. I'm worried that we will outsource our satisfaction, and that our lives will get sucked into the nothingness of video games and television and shockingly realistic virtual pornography. We will just get satisfied, and never drive ourselves forward. Society is fraying—the impact of the Carls, whatever you think about them, is clear. We've lost our way, we don't have a vision for the future anymore."

As he continued, it starts to feel like a speech he's given before.

"I don't think that the last two hundred thousand years of human suffering will be best brought meaning by humans today living like dogs—accepting what has been given to us as unquestionably inevitable and, ultimately, when it gets taken away, seeing that as just another part of life. I want to fight every bit as hard as my ancestors fought to keep my lineage alive, to *make me possible.* I don't *have* to fight"—he gestured to his daiquiri—"but I owe it to everyone who came before me, and to everyone who will come after, to push humanity forward, maybe to even redefine what it means to be human."

I'd be lying if I said I didn't get goose bumps when he finished that monologue.

While reading this, I also got goose bumps. The kind you get when you go to pee in the middle of the night and suddenly start wondering whether there is someone in your house. The article continued a while, fleshing out PP's ideology, but then finally they got to the point. Or at least near it.

Peter's house is not just a house; it's part of a compound. There are dorms for workers, offices, server rooms, laboratories.

"That's where we're doing the mining." He gestures toward a huge cinder block building with no windows. He means the cryptocurrency mining. "Before we make our initial offering, we want to have a fairly significant supply on hand to match with our ability to supply our service."

He only calls it "our service" during the entire meeting. The fact that I am writing a feature article that is about a service that is secret and has not yet been launched is more than just unusual. In fact, it's something I would never do and, if I did, something my editor would literally fire me for. But Peter Petrawicki's "service" has received investment from some of the wealthiest and most influential people in the world. His first round of funding came in at over a billion dollars. And he's not doing it alone. Researchers in neurophysiology, cellular neuroscience, quantum computing, transistors, biomedical engineering, optoelectronics, optogenetics, data science, artificial intelligence, and robotics have all left tenured faculty positions or jobs at Google, Microsoft, and Apple to come work for Peter Petrawicki and his partners.

I leave Puerto Rico with a lot of useful thoughts, but my overwhelming emotion is confusion. Dr. Kress's contributions to neurology are undeniable, but he remains a complicated and controversial figure. And that, of course, is true of Mr. Petrawicki as well. The combination of celebrity scientist and celebrity pundit is certainly unusual, but it might be, like a reality TV president, the sort of thing that isn't as surprising as it seems at first glance. I am not convinced that whatever they have going on is not a colossally huge scam. When I asked, Peter didn't even try to convince me. Instead, he replied with his newfound relaxed demeanor but his traditional bravado: "Real or fake, either way, this is going to be huge."

You probably have some idea of how upset I was feeling after finishing this article. It really wasn't that Peter Petrawicki was the sympathetic protagonist of this fluffy magazine article; it was that he was *winning* while April was dead. He was getting everything he ever wanted, which was mostly other rich white dudes telling him how amazing he was. My response wasn't anger, though. It was just pure, sweaty anxiety.

I don't have to explain most of the reasons to you. It sucked hearing anything from Peter aside from "I screwed up, and I owe it to the entire world to live a quiet and anonymous life donating money to global health charities." But I had another reason. I had some idea of what scientific advancement might require the breadth and depth of talent Petrawicki was acquiring and would also get a lot of billionaires very excited.

I read and reread the section that described the kinds of people they had been hiring, trying to decide whether it was just anchoring bias convincing me I knew more than I did, but no. My heart pounded and my armpits prickled because I knew what Peter Petrawicki's "service" was.

ANDY

A s I pulled the book out of the trash and read the cover, all of the usual clichés—"my heart leapt into my throat" or "my stomach dropped" or whatever—were inaccurate. I had to poop. While I started moving toward where I thought the closest Starbucks might be, I opened the book and began to read.

The first line was:

> There is a bathroom in the park. By the basketball courts, in the brick building.

I was freaking out even more now, but so was my colon. I closed the book and half jogged to the brick building, which, indeed, had a public bathroom in it. I was wishing I had taken the risk on a Starbucks as I walked into the gray-tiled, booze-soaked mess. I slid into a stall and, as soon as I was safe, opened the book back up.

> I'm just here to help, I promise. I know this is a lot. But the point of this is just to give you a little of what you need, whether that's a walk or a sandwich or directions to the nearest bathroom. I know that doesn't seem super important right now, but no mission gets done without people, and no people survive without taking bathroom breaks. I understand that you don't really trust me yet. That's fine. But it's also why I, right now, have to deliver information in such small packets. You'll read ahead, even if I tell you not to, which would break the process. Just give me a chance and I'll prove myself to you.

And don't you feel better now that you've had a walk? Sorry I
scared you with the trash can thing.

My brain kept trying to make this some kind of street-magician/
prank-video/mind-freak thing. This seemed impossible, but it obviously wasn't because it just kept happening. Unless it wasn't. Unless
I had a brain tumor or it was all a dream. But the smell of the bathroom didn't seem like the kind of thing my dream mind would subject me to. I looked back down at the book.

Now that we've gotten you out of the house and proven that this is
something you should take seriously, I'm going to ask you to do
something weird. I got you two tickets to *STOMP*. I know it's silly,
but go, and find someone to go with you. After you're done watching the show that David from Denver, Colorado, called "one of
the best things I have ever seen!" you can start reading this book
again. But until then, do not. Go see *STOMP* and take someone
with you, because sometimes you have to be a tourist in your own
town.

That's where the text on that page ended. The temptation to turn
the page and see what was next was intense. I mean, either it was just
the same line repeated over and over like last time, or it really would
give me a look at what was coming next. But then I noticed another
thought biting at my brain. If I was going to invite someone to go see
STOMP with me, who would that be?

The list of people I wanted to go see a dumb show with who were
also in New York City was . . . zero people long. That actually hurt. I
could ask Jason, my roommate and podcast cohost and literally my
only close friend left in the city. But, also, Jason would laugh loudly
and unkindly if I told him I had two tickets to *STOMP* and wanted
him to come see it with me.

So I sat in Tompkins Square Park and I tried to think of
someone . . . *anyone* who I knew.

When I first started getting requests to speak at universities, I asked our little crew whether they thought I should do it, and Maya said something I might as well have tattooed on the back of my hand: "Can you tell them something that will make them feel better?"

I'd like to say that it became my mantra solely because I just wanted to make people feel better, but also it felt like the only thing that would work. I wasn't really me—famous people never are. I had to be what people expected, the sad, smart, nerdy guy who had lost his famous and charismatic best friend. I needed a brand that aligned with that.

And, to some extent, it was working. It wasn't the way to get the most Twitter followers, but universities wanted people to give talks that were constructive. People were searching for some authority to tell them *anything* that made even a little bit of sense. As the grieving best friend of the missing emissary to the aliens, I guess I was an authority, and Maya's advice gave me the angle I needed.

But being a professional grieving friend didn't lend itself to new friendships. I also didn't need much outside validation. A lot of the reason we look to friends is because they're a source of meaning. If you're getting meaning in other ways, it's easy to let your friendships wither. That's one reason success can be isolating. I learned that from an *expert*.

At least I was smart enough to not go get a fancy apartment by myself. I kept my roommate because I wanted to keep some ties to my former life. That was a tremendously good decision. Jason is irreverent, hilarious, deeply nerdy, and surprisingly unambitious. He is delighted that my fame has made our dumb podcast more successful, but I don't think the thought has ever crossed his mind that I might be doing him a favor by not abandoning it. *Slainspotting* (our podcast about TV and movie deaths) is a thing I signed up to do that I like doing and that keeps me connected to something that existed before April died, before I was famous, and before there were aliens.

———

Basically, thank God for Jason, but I was *not* going to go see *STOMP* with him.

And that was where I was at, feeling like I had been barely saved from complete isolation by the nerdiest guy in New York, when I walked into Subway and asked Becky if she would like to go see *STOMP* with me.

"That was very weird and fun, Andy," she said afterward as we were walking to the train.

"Is it Rebecca or Becky? I'm sorry I didn't ask that sooner."

She laughed lightly. "Either, honestly, but almost everyone except my parents and my manager calls me Bex." The name popped out of her mouth in a way that seemed natural. It seemed like her.

"I like that. Bex, like with an *x*?"

"Like with an *x*," she confirmed, before adding, "Are you ever going to tell me why you invited me to go see *STOMP*?"

"Are you going to tell me why you said yes?"

She laughed again. "What do you mean?"

"I mean, I felt like a total douche asking out someone who is literally paid to be nice to me, and I honestly can't believe I did it."

"Fair, but I'm not going to tell you why I said yes." I couldn't decide whether that sounded flirtatious or menacing. "So why did you ask me?"

"I told you, my friend bought tickets and couldn't get a refund. There were two tickets and I didn't want to go alone."

"But it's a big city, Andy, and you're a famous rich guy. There are other people besides Rebecca from Subway."

"I don't know many people," I replied.

"That cannot possibly be true." There was some formality to her speech that I assumed was part of her accent or dialect but may have been her signaling to me that she was being respectful toward me as a public figure, and not knowing for sure made me worry that she wasn't seeing me as an equal.

"I . . ."

"You don't have to explain," she said seriously.

"No." I stopped walking. The sun was down, but the sidewalks were still full, so we pulled off to stand under the awning of a bodega. "I don't know anyone anymore. I have a roommate, he's my only friend. All of April's friends left the city after she . . . Afterward. I haven't spent much time in the same place since I started doing speaking gigs. Lots of people want to talk to me, but I always feel like they want something. You seemed like . . . like a person, a funny and nice person." I didn't say, "And cute," because that seemed like way too much.

"This is a shitty thing to whine about, but, like, every time I walk up to someone, I know that they're probably going to remember that interaction for the rest of their life. It's too much fucking pressure. I go to these fancy places and meet fancy people, and we work very hard to impress each other, and then I go to a hotel room by myself and try not to feel as alone as I am. Don't get me wrong, it's fun. The food is amazing. The drinks are free. It's fucking cool. But still, you're the first person besides my roommate who I've spent more than an hour with in months."

She rolled her eyes just a little, like she was accepting something but not totally happy about it, and asked, "Do you want to get a drink?"

Like a complete dork I came back with "I'm not trying to hook up with anyone right now."

Now she *really* rolled her eyes.

"Look, boy," she said, but it didn't feel diminishing when she said it, "it sounds like you have a lot of stuff you'd like to talk about, and I think your life sounds interesting. You took me to see that dumb show, so let me buy you a drink. I need to be home in an hour anyway, so I can't stay out. You can tell me about your week and I'll tell you about mine, and then we'll probably both feel better about our lives."

I had a seemingly sentient book in my bag that I wanted very much to take back to my apartment and read. A book that could predict the future and knew things about my maybe-not-dead best friend. But instead, I let Bex buy me a drink.

We talked for an hour, and I learned that she was born in

America but her parents were from Trinidad and Tobago. Turns out that there is a small but significant Chinese population there, which she told me all about. Then somehow we got on the subject of student loans and she whipped out a pen and calculated, by hand, the total cost of her education with her working at Subway and without. I was shocked at the difference, and also at her math skills. She told me about her brothers and I told her about my constant sawing anxiety—the ever-present feeling that I was doing both too much and not enough. I explained that I felt like I never had independent thoughts of my own, I just took what other people said and applied it to new situations or meshed it with other ideas I'd heard. And then I told her that I felt like most other people weren't really having unique thoughts either, they were all doing the same thing as me . . . but then somehow new ideas did keep happening, which made me feel like I wasn't an individual, just a brain cell in a massive species-wide consciousness. I'd never even thought about any of those things before I started talking to her, and I felt like I was being a little self-indulgent by talking about myself so much, but it really did help.

The hour went by like it was five minutes. I walked her to her subway station, and then, in the everywhere light of the city, I read the next page in *The Book of Good Times.*

I'm really glad you had a good time. Two things before you can turn the next page.

1. Buy $100,000 of stock in IGRI, sell it in four days.
2. Expect a call from Miranda. Tell her she has to do it.

That was all. I closed the book without even considering flipping to the next page.

Senator William Casey: There is no secular institution or system of values that has shown any sign of being able to sustain the social order. We are being told that the Carls killed God. I am here to tell you that God killed the Carls! God put an end to that time of tumult, and we made it through not in spite of our faith but because of it. They were a test, and we have seen how many people failed that test. Did it test my faith? Absolutely. Did it break it? Never!

Those who have lost their way in the wake of that invasion have a weakness that I try not to judge. You are not forgotten. But those who say that Carl killed God, or that—and I shudder to even say it—that the Carls *were* God . . . those people are lost. They are just another step in the decades-long war that militant secularists, under the guise of progressivism, have waged through the mainstream media, through their movies, through academia, and now through these idols.

The only thing they want is to destroy the beauty of what we have built.

MAYA

There are a lot of self-help bros who will tell you that you need to dangle over the edge without a net to really drive achievement. I used to believe this because it has a little piece of the truth. The larger picture, of course, is that being deprived of safety tends to make people anxious, reactive, and unproductive. But it is true that having money can enable you to indulge in your worst instincts.

Ultimately, my parents were right that I was lost. Their little chat with me at dinner was supposed to start a conversation about whether I might move back home. But it served a different purpose: It convinced me that I needed to prove them wrong. I needed to prove everyone wrong, and I wasn't going to lie in my bed waiting for clues to pop up on the Som anymore. I needed to get into the world and start doing my own investigation. So I put my newly acquired pot of dirt in the passenger seat of my rented Nissan Frontier, buckled it in, and drove to Trenton. There were three main New Jersey–based weird things that seemed worthy of investigation:

1. A bunch of dolphins swam up the Delaware River and died just outside of Trenton.
2. There were the lab break-ins, one of which was in Trenton (all of the others were fairly nearby).
3. There was an area in South Jersey where the internet service provider couldn't seem to make the internet work for more than a couple days at a time.

All of these things were tiny news stories, and the theories on the Som roamed across the whole world, but they were the mysteries that felt most real to me.

I hate writing this because my dad is going to read it, but having a parent who is always a little bit disappointed in you isn't ever going to be healthy. The question is whether it is an unhealthy weight that I have to struggle with or an unhealthy fuel that can actually propel me. It's been both of those things in my life, and right now, it was fuel.

I did some wild stuff in those weeks. I literally infiltrated the New Jersey Animal Health Diagnostic Lab and got a source to tell me a bunch of stuff about dolphins. How? I mean, it sounds cooler than it is. I just pretended I was researching a book. It turns out that dolphin autopsies aren't actually super confidential, and the people who do them don't get a ton of opportunity to talk about their work.

But the only pertinent information I actually got from those conversations was that they had no idea why a bunch of dolphins swam up the Delaware River and died. They all starved, like maybe they were afraid to go back downstream.

For those of you not intimately familiar with the Delaware River, it forms the border between Pennsylvania and New Jersey and then the border between Delaware and New Jersey before dumping into Delaware Bay. My theory was that something had happened in the bay or the river that forced the dolphins north and either prevented them from traveling south or convinced them that it was better to starve than face it again.

And if there was something downstream that they were afraid of, well, I wanted to find it. And, by chance or not, downstream of Trenton, where the dolphins had died, was a little town called Wolton. A town where the internet had *stopped*.

Oh, Wolton. Going to Trenton I could get my mind around, but I am a rich girl from the Upper East Side and I was not accustomed to small-town life. I'd gotten an Airbnb on short notice, which I considered a blessing both because there weren't many and because I wouldn't have been shocked to get profiled out. The cabin fronted a winding little road, and across that street was a tangle of trees and bushes and vines. That same tangle was out back and on either side of the house. New Jersey is the most densely populated state in the US, and still, the first week I was there, I walked into the woods just to see what it was like, and within twenty minutes I was panicking that I wouldn't be able to find my way out.

Wolton was a ten-minute drive from the cabin, but there wasn't much to see there unless you were into quilts or antiques or golf. I was following a lead that seemed increasingly flimsy. The internet in South Jersey was spotty. Some days customers' internet would be unusably slow, other days it would be back to normal, and the next day there would be no connection at all. This had been going on long enough that it was news, and that news had been picked up by the Som as another example of something weird going on near Philly.

————

I arrived in town before my Airbnb check-in, so my first stop was the Dream Bean. It was a very normal coffee shop except that, on every flat surface, there was ancient-Egypt kitsch. There was even an area in the corner that sold . . . antiques? They were antiques from a time when America was super into King Tut and the Sphinx. They weren't *from* Egypt; they were some designed-in-Jersey, made-in-Ohio anglicized approximations of the ancient-Egypt aesthetic.

It wasn't like the chairs were painted with Cleopatra and mummies. The coffee shop just looked like a coffee shop with lots of Egypt-inspired knickknacks.

Ultimately, I wanted two things out of this visit: intel on the internet outages and coffee. I was greeted by a sleepy-looking thirty-something guy who was about a month overdue for a haircut. His smile shone through his grogginess as he asked how I was doing.

"Good. How's business?" It didn't look great, but there were a couple customers sipping lattes with plates that had once sported bagels or croissants but now sported crumbs. I couldn't imagine rent in the tiny building was that much.

"What's life without coffee?" he asked in response.

"I hear that." And then I spotted a spinning stand of reading glasses on the counter. "Oh, and can I also get . . . reading glasses? At a coffee shop?"

I tried not to sound too judgmental, but I don't think I succeeded.

He sighed. "My mother-in-law. She adds little sparkles and rhinestones to reading glasses she buys in bulk. She has a stand down at Cowtown, but she asked if she could display some here, and she's taking care of my two-year-old son right now, so there's really no saying 'no.'"

I laughed. "Is she also responsible for . . ." I gestured at all the ancient Egypt, and then felt a little self-conscious—maybe this guy was just super into Egypt.

He smiled a big smile. "No, that's just Wolton!" He did not explain further before saying, "I'm Derek."

"Uh, I'm Maya," I said, a little unnerved by his enthusiasm. "Is there a Wi-Fi password?"

The enthusiasm vanished. "It's 'cleopatra,' lowercase *c*. But it's not good. We've been having weird outages for over a month now."

"I think I read about that!"

"Honestly, you don't want to get me started. Carson has given me a refund, but people expect coffee shops to have internet. This isn't 2007. I'm really sorry."

"Do they know what's causing it?"

"Aside from incompetence?" His voice rose a little. "I'm sorry, I'm just frustrated. No, they say they've hired somebody who knows these systems from the top all the way down, but apparently even they're stumped. I'm looking into getting satellite internet, but it's more expensive and slower. I understand it's complicated, but they've figured out how to do it everywhere else, I don't get why it's not working here."

"Well, I guess I'll get my latte to go then!" I said. He looked despondent, so I continued, "You're the only shop in town, so as long as I'm here, caffeine is more important than internet."

I left the coffee shop with my latte and did something that any trained professional would agree was a worrying sign that I was not recovering well from my loss. I stalked cable repair trucks.

MIRANDA

Constance Lundgren is a legend. Her list of research awards is short only compared to her list of teaching awards. Back in the nineties there was a lot of shouting about her not being named on a Nobel Prize that built on her work, and the only person in the materials science world who didn't say a thing about it was Constance Lundgren. Getting her as an advisor was like getting an internship with Yoda. I had imagined her as a kind of idol to science before I met her, but after I'd worked under her for a year, she had mostly become a person. She was thoughtful and methodical and always a little tense. Every tendon stood out on her sun-browned, age-freckled hands, which she often pressed to her lips as she thought, like she was praying to her own mind. Which, why not. But she was also forgiving and sweet and would invite students to go hiking with her, which I had done. There was literally no one else in the world who I respected more, and leaving her lab to go chase after the weirdness of the Carls was the hardest decision I've ever made. Her keeping my place open to return to is a gift I won't ever be able to repay, but at the same time, I was lost. I was angry and sad and having a harder and harder time finding my work meaningful. If I was ever in need of advising, it was now.

"Professor Lundgren?" I asked, knocking on her open door a couple days after I first read the article about Peter.

"Miranda!" She slid a small book she had been staring at to the side of her desk. "How are the Toms?"

Tom is what I named my first lab rat, who had . . . passed on several years ago. Some of my classmates found out that I'd named him, and they'd never let me live it down. So now all of my rats were named Tom and there had been several dozen since. I don't love the part where we experiment on animals, especially because it only ever goes one way for the animal in the long run. If there was another way, I would take it, but there isn't.

I smiled. "The Toms are good. Six weeks now and no sign of rejection, even among those with no maintenance therapy. But that's not why I came in. I wanted to ask you about this."

I handed her a physical copy of the magazine with the Peter Petrawicki article. "Have you heard about this lab?"

Science can be a small town. People in the same field, especially at the top of the field, all know each other. And they certainly know when people are leaving tenured university positions for high-paid jobs that didn't exist six months ago.

Dr. Lundgren looked up at me and said, "I know this has to suck for you. Even I got angry when I found out who was tied up with that business. But yes, I've heard about it."

She was quiet for a moment as she thought and then she continued, "I probably shouldn't tell you this, but they offered me a position. I was talking to my husband seriously about moving until I found out who was involved."

She looked me in the eyes as she said, "I told them to go fuck themselves."

It has never taken much to make me cry, but it takes even less since the warehouse. So I sat down and lost it a bit.

She grabbed some tissues from inside her desk. Crying students weren't that unusual. "Thank you," I said after a moment. "Not for the tissues but . . ."

"It wasn't because of you."

"Good, but still, thanks."

She smiled at me, and then I asked my real question: "Do you know what they're doing there?"

"No. They weren't going to tell me any details until they had a contract. But you read that article, so you have some idea, right?"

"Yeah, yeah. Some of it is confusing. Why so many computers? Why AI researchers? But optoelectronics, biomedical engineering, cellular neuroscience? They figured it out, didn't they?"

"They figured something out, yes. What 'it' is, I don't know."

"Yes you do. Some kind of high-bandwidth interface, right? It has to be. I'm sitting over here with the Toms, stimulating one or two nerve clusters at a time. They're down there in Puerto Rico getting ready to dump people's immortal consciousnesses into a computer or something, and you could *be there*! But instead we're here, a decade behind wherever they are, and you didn't go."

She clasped her hands together and brought them up to her lips. I'd seen that face a hundred times before. Every time we were confused, when the spectrometer wasn't booting up, when a Tom was suddenly having seizures.

"Miranda, I have been at this a while. I've seen revolutions in science, and I know that sometimes moving fast and breaking things is how progress gets made. But it's also how things get broken, and sometimes those things are people. This is not the strategy of careful scientists. I agree, they are likely messing with the human mind. I don't know what they're doing, but if they weren't close to human tests, they wouldn't be scaling up so fast. And they're setting this up in Puerto Rico, which tells me they're trying to avoid health and safety regulations. These men—sorry, but it usually is men—don't care who gets hurt because they're telling themselves a story in which they're the hero. I've listened to that story too many times to see anything in it but vanity."

"But isn't ambition how all of this gets done? I'm ambitious. I think you are too."

"That's a good point, Miranda. I don't have anything against ambition. Wanting to work hard to achieve something great, yes. Yes! You're so young and you've already done that. You should stay hungry. But what does 'great' mean to you?"

"It means something better than good." That sounded a little stupid, so I kept at it. "So good it improves the lives of more people than I will ever hope to meet."

"Good. That is what it means for you. But for some people, 'great' just means 'big,' and if it's big enough, they'll convince themselves either that it's good or that it's inevitable, so it might as well be their names that get into the history books." Her voice was getting louder.

She sucked in sharply through her nose and looked at the ceiling before she continued, more quietly.

"I can smell that kind of ambition. It's not about making the world better, it's about using marvelous potential and intelligence to . . ." She paused to think. "To feel like they matter. I won't work with people like that, because if they don't think they matter despite being some of the most successful, important, influential people on earth, what must they think of the rest of us?"

I sat there and thought about that for a moment before I said, "It sounds like you've worked with a lot of people like that."

"Miranda, I've been a person like that. And I could be again if I let myself."

That was a lot of raw Constance Lundgren. It was amazing—it felt almost historic, to hear her open up like this. I wanted to write down every word of it, but I also wanted more information about this lab.

"Do you know anyone who's working there?" I asked.

"You know I do, why are you asking?"

I didn't have a good answer.

"Do you really want to do this?" she asked. "You have a lot . . . a LOT to do in the next few months if you want to defend in the spring, and obsessing over billionaires futzing around in the Caribbean is not going to help that work get done. Plus, I want to see you socializing more. You never come out. We're doing Grizzly Peak this Friday."

She was right, I hadn't been spending time with anyone, and the topic change was uncomfortable for me. I had a hard time reconnecting with my labmates after I'd gotten back. They went out for drinks or karaoke or met up for board games, and I told them "Next time!" every time. I had had friends here before the Carls. But somehow, after I'd come back, I just didn't feel like I had anything in common with them anymore. It was a kind of culture shock. I felt like I was living some old version of my life.

"You're right, forget I said anything. Thank you for talking through this with me."

I absolutely was not going to drop my interest in Peter's lab, and I think we both knew that. But I let the lie out because it felt like the safest thing to do. And Dr. Lundgren accepted it because what else was she supposed to do?

"It really isn't any trouble. I know you aren't wired to recognize it, but your research could be world-changing, and your ambition is being put to great use here. We're proud to have you."

She was right: I wasn't wired to recognize praise. The only thing I could feel was that she was lying to protect my feelings and that nothing I did would matter ever again.

Unless I figured out what they were doing at that lab.

Blake Wolff: Andy, I talk to a lot of people on this podcast, and I hope you don't mind if I say something here . . . A lot of people listen to you, and you have a way of getting to the root of things really fast and, OK, you just do not seem like a twenty-four-year-old.

Andy Skampt: Yeah, you feel like I'm more of a teenager?

BW: <laughter> You know what I mean.

AS: I guess I *had* to grow up. I know this isn't how it actually works, but I think people, if you give them a chance, they grow to fit their fishbowl.

BW: I'm not going to let you get away with that. That's too easy. There has to be something more to it. Give me something . . . How did a twenty-four-year-old get the kind of insight you have on other people?

AS: Do you know *Hamilton*?

BW: The musical or the founding father?

AS: <laughter> Both, I guess. There's a song about halfway through called "The Room Where It Happens."

BW: <singing> "I wanna be in the room where it happens, the room where it happens . . ."

AS: Exactly. Well, I was in the middle of all of the madness last year, and I mean really . . . in the middle of it. And I was listening to *Hamilton* and I heard that song and I realized that, well, not everyone is ambitious enough to want to be the one making the thing happen, but everyone, I think, to some extent wants to be in the room where it happens. They might not want to write their favorite book, or paint their favorite painting, or vote the bill into law, but everyone wants to be in the room. We want to witness it. We want to feel like we are part of these things that, like, really matter.

BW: Hmm.

AS: And I realized that *I was in the room.* So many people wanted to be me. But it wasn't really special to me because the room just felt like my room. But that wasn't the big insight. The real insight was that I still wanted to be in the room where it happens, it was just a different "it." We all want to be in the room where it happens, we want to be part of the things that matter to us, but no two people have the exact same collection of things that matter. Nowadays, I don't so much want to be in the room where it happens, but I do really want to help other people choose the right rooms, and help them realize that they really are a part of things that matter. Because when we feel like none of the rooms we are in matter, that's when we're really lost.

ANDY

April dying was the best thing that could have happened to my *career.*

Was it the worst thing that ever happened to me? Yes. Was it the thing in my life that I regretted more than anything else? Also yes.

But!

I also got to be massively respected, well paid, and powerful, and, yes, I liked it. It was also annoying. I felt boxed in by my own brand, and I hated watching people who were more reactionary or radical getting traction with ideas that would totally get me in trouble. And, yeah, I worked a lot. But also I didn't want to take breaks. I wanted to feel good, and having the world listen to me felt good.

I did everything I could to say useful things without getting myself in hot water. It resulted in tweets like these:

Andy Skampt

@AndySkampt

If you can do it in one human lifetime, it's not a big
enough goal.

293 replies   3.4K retweets   9.3K likes

@AndySkampt

Nothing has ever been done alone, or, if it was, it was
immediately forgotten. We're only here for each other.

104 replies   6.9K retweets   14.8K likes

@AndySkampt

Watching "Pose" on Netflix and it's amazing. I'm done with
antiheroes, I love watching families love each other.

1.3K replies   1.4K retweets   4.7K likes

I was getting comfortable with this persona. But I was also notic-
ing that it worked less and less as time went on. I knew what was
getting the most attention on Twitter, and it was angry stuff. But I
couldn't do angry stuff because my audience expected me to make
them feel better, not worse.

At the same time, there was plenty to be angry about. The Carls
hadn't ended the housing crisis, or student loans, or medical debt.
America still had mass shootings. In fact, with people losing a clear
path and the economy losing steam, all of these things seemed worse
than ever. I wanted to make things better, and sometimes that meant
I wanted to shout hot takes into the void. But I also had no idea if that
would actually help.

If I was at the top of my game, I probably would have resented
The Book of Good Times coming in to take over my life, but I wasn't.

My new mass was nothing compared to the gravitational pull of
that book. I think I knew that, once I opened it, I was going to lose
my agency. There was a part of me that wanted nothing more than
that—the simplicity of tumbling down April's gravity well again, not

the complexity of real, important decisions, constant uncertainty, and existential dread.

Down I tumbled! Why not buy $100,000 in a stock I had never heard of?! If you get tens of billions of views, you make tens of millions of dollars. So a hundred grand was a lot, but bizarrely enough, it was no longer a *lot*.

I did what any self-respecting twenty-something would do. I called my dad, and he told me that I *absolutely should not* invest in strange unknown stocks. He was appalled at the entire idea. I think he felt a little like he'd failed as a father if I thought that buying stock in a random tiny company was a good idea. I hadn't even told him the tip was delivered by a book I found in the trash.

But then, like any self-respecting twenty-something, I ignored him.

IGRI itself didn't look suspicious. It was a company that had once been big enough to be publicly traded but that had gotten smaller and smaller until it fell off the major exchanges, but no one was interested in coming in and buying the whole thing. The company, in this case, was a cobalt-mining company that had mines in Canada. At one point it had been massively productive and valuable. But as IGRI mined what it had, the stock price dropped.

Why would someone want me to buy this stock?

The obvious answer was that someone was trying to manipulate the price of a penny stock. Like, convince a bunch of people that a book could read their future, get them to go on a date with a nice girl, and then tell them to buy the stock and sell it four days later. Except the fraudster sells it three days later and walks away with ten times more cash than they went in with.

None of this actually mattered, though, because this wasn't about money or stocks or magic books; it was about April being alive. I wanted so badly for the mystery to end. I wanted my friend back. I wanted the piece of me that I'd lost put back so desperately that I would happily throw $100,000 into the hole of that hope.

Afterward, to distract myself from constantly checking the stock and researching cobalt, I watched video essays from a few of my favorite YouTubers and stressed out about when and what to text Bex. I was and am a firm believer that you shouldn't wait to text someone after a first date. I will always be who I am, and I am not a person who thinks strategically about relationships. So I texted to tell her that I had a really great time. And then immediately after that I sent the best joke I could think of.

> *They swept that stage so much, but I feel like it never got any cleaner.*

Her reply came in a half hour later.

> *Honestly, Andy, I sweep at work every day and I am not ashamed to admit that today it was a bit of a dance for me. Thanks for a great night.*

I tried to not respond immediately, but I failed.

> *I'm headed out of town tomorrow, but would it be OK for me to call you when I get back?*

> *Yup. ttys.*

She was way too cool for me, but that was OK. Honestly, if we were just starting up a friendship, that would be *doubling* the number of friends I had in New York, which would be wonderful.

The "out of town" was an investment convention in France. I have no idea *why*, but they were paying me *a lot*, and it was hard to say no to big piles of cash. Look, I got off on the money. I know it's gross, but April taught me to be honest.

The conference was in Cannes, a town on the Mediterranean that you have heard of because of the film festival, but that also is home to tons of other events. I was headed there to give a speech on the anniversary of the arrival of the Carls, and thus the anniversary of the first video I made with April. I didn't really know how to feel about this date. It was both arbitrary and huge. It felt like something I wanted to commemorate somehow, if only in my own life and in New York.

But then I also wanted to completely ignore the milestone. I didn't want to think about the fact that the last year, which had seemed like the whole rest of my life combined, had only been a year. And I had gotten used to not looking too hard at the things that hurt. That's normal, or at least that's what my very expensive therapist told me. And then there was the part where I didn't have a topic that felt worthy of a momentous occasion.

I handled that conundrum the usual way: I went and checked out some of my favorite internet thinkers. These people had no idea what a huge influence they were on me, but all of my ideas were just amalgams of the stuff they were talking about. I tried to pull from a diverse group, Black women sci-fi authors, Chinese business analysts, nuclear disarmament experts, and of course YouTube video essayists. I hate-watched people with massive audiences and terrible ideas that were nonetheless resonating with people, and I watched the smart ones who had all my same biases. This was the only way I could have the number and quality of takes people expected of me. You watch four different videos, trying to keep all of them in your head at once, and then out flops an idea that looks and feels fresh and new. When I knew I was going to have to say something useful soon, I watched a LOT of videos.

It feels a little phony that my process works this way, like I'm an impostor who doesn't have any real ideas, but I'm pretty sure this is just how ideas work.

The amazing thing about YouTube is that new channels just appear and disappear all the time. A new channel might pop up, and suddenly some smart lady from Baltimore is having a massive influence on the cultural dialogue.

There was a channel that had done just that thing in the last few months. It was called The Thread and it was weird. You almost had to be weird to get noticed these days. Good ideas alone weren't usually enough. The Thread had uploaded his first video the week after April disappeared and it had gone pretty viral. It was about the song "Twinkle, Twinkle, Little Star." His point was that we sing that song now while knowing pretty much what stars are. They're big balls of protons and neutrons and electrons that gravity is smushing together so hard that fusion is happening.

But when the song was written, the wonder was legitimate. The person who wrote "Twinkle, Twinkle" didn't know what stars were. In 1806, no one did! It was a beautiful video, aided by The Thread's graphics and music, which were *absolutely gorgeous.*

It was, on its face, just interesting information in a beautiful package. But deeper than that, it was about how we as a society have learned so much so fast, and how we have adapted to big shifts in our understandings before. It was professional and thoughtful and it felt like it was about Carl without being *about Carl.*

But it wasn't world-changing. It just looked like another popular video. But as the world started finding its new normal, The Thread's videos started pushing more buttons and getting more political. And then The Thread actually broke a story, which was basically a brand-new thing for YouTube essay channels. In a video about money in politics, The Thread released a half dozen emails between a major donor and politicians of both parties guaranteeing that judges friendly to the donor's company would be placed after the candidates were elected.

The Thread wasn't just a YouTube channel anymore; it was news. The "Dark Money" video ended with information on how people could send encrypted, anonymous information, and ever since then, Thread videos had felt almost illicit. It was very James Bond.

Adding to the mystery was that no one knew who The Thread was. The creator of the channel had completely hidden his identity.

The channel had a new video up I hadn't seen yet. As always, it was beautifully animated. The Thread never showed his face; you only ever heard a voice. It had to have taken a solid month just to make the graphics. The video was called "The Clear Path," and it followed the course of a life forty years ago and the course of a life today. In the life forty years ago, the path was clear and obvious. The illustrated protagonist of the video did not need to spend time thinking about his sexuality or his gender or his religion. That same protagonist living life today was given options. What is your sexuality? What is your gender? How do you want to find connection and community?

The point the video was making now was that there was no longer a clear path, and that was more work. And, at that point, it was kinda pissing me off.

I felt like it was making it seem like allowing for different kinds of people was a burden. But then the video turned it around. Over illustrated images of happy families of all sorts the narrator said, "The reality is, the benefits of this far outweigh the costs. If we do not let people know that it is possible to be different, the ones who *are* different will live their entire lives in a kind of cultural prison. And there are so many ways to be different that almost everyone ends up feeling imprisoned by some aspect of a society that only allows for the default path.

"The problem is that, as progressives, we pretend that there are no costs, and that no one is losing anything," the video continued. "But, of course, some people do lose—especially those whose power was tied up, not in their wealth, but in fitting comfortably into the clear path. Now, these people have only lost what they should lose, but that is also true of other forms of concentrated power. We're in a system that tells, for example, the wealthy that they deserve all their wealth and it should be protected through force. So, naturally, the newly alienated feel singled out and victimized.

"The solution isn't going back to the one clear path. The solution is, everywhere and always, the decentralization and redistribution of all forms of power."

The video went from making me think it was too centrist, to pushing right up against being too radical. Then I went back and watched the original "Twinkle, Twinkle" video, and with those in my head, here's the video script that flopped out of my brain at 1 A.M.:

Hey, everybody, it's Andy.

The fact that it has been only a year since the Carls first arrived does not seem real to me. It feels like centuries, it feels like they have always been here. And, in a sense, that's true. We've rewritten our story to match some new evidence. We didn't just stop being alone in the universe when Carl arrived, we stopped ever having been alone.

We weren't alone in the universe when the White Sox won the World Series in 2005. And we weren't alone when the White Sox won the World Series in 1906. They existed when Jesus was born and when the first person spoke the first word. This doesn't just change our present and our future, it changes our past. And I know that sounds silly, nothing can change the past. But we don't imagine the past as it was, that's impossible, there's just too much past to know, so we cobble together a story that makes sense to us from what we know. And when we get a big new piece of information, that changes what narratives make sense.

The Carls may not have always been here, but they certainly existed. They were out there somewhere, even if they weren't standing on street corners.

It would be easy to just make a video that's about how the Carls brought the world together, because in some ways that's true. But also, it's a huge burden to live in a world where we don't know

how we've been physically changed and psychologically
manipulated by an outside intelligence.

We can either intentionally ignore it or accept
that meaning is different now.

And this is a burden. I watched April love Carl,
and I was always willing to go along with her trust,
but there was a cost, and we are paying it now. The
cost is in well-trod stories that now make less
sense. It's not that the new stories are worse, it's
just that we haven't had time to settle on any good
ones, and so now, many of us are adrift. And these
moments in history when things stop making sense,
they don't tend to be stable times. We need strong
stories, but we still must be very wary of those who
offer them to us.

But the strongest story has not changed. The
meaning of life is still, as it was, simply other
people. When we care for each other, we are always
in a place that matters. That is what I am thinking
about on this anniversary. There has been a cost to
our new knowledge, but it may not be as deep or as
lasting as it feels right now.

Jason and I had set up encrypted chat because I was a high-profile
target for hackers, and while I didn't think I did or said anything that
could be damaging to myself or other people, the last decade was lit-
tered with people who had been wrong about that.

I sent him a message:

> *Hey, I just finished recording a video. I'll give you $500 if
> you edit it and upload it on the Carliversary tomorrow.*

He replied almost immediately.

You got it, I can't wait to see it, honestly.

> *It's about the cognitive and societal burden of the Carls. I guess I didn't feel like making a super happy one.*

Hah. Well, remember when you told the internet to be nice to each other? Super happy doesn't always turn out great. Is this video at all inspired by the new one from The Thread?

> *Hah, shit. I'm that transparent?*

"Do you know who he is?!" Jason shouted from the other room. I got up and walked into the living room, where Jason was sunk deep into our couch on his computer.

"I'm as clueless as everyone else."

"It's fucking genius. You think a progressive white guy could make a video about the societal burden of social justice without getting crucified if he wasn't completely anonymous?"

"I'm pretty sure he is getting crucified for that video right now."

"His ideas are, absolutely. And I don't mind that. But no one is sending letters to his house or brigading him off Twitter because there's literally no way to find out who he is. No one even knows if he's a white guy! He takes identity out of it completely."

I sat down on the couch. "He's definitely a white guy," I said.

The Thread was so serious about anonymity that he hired a different voice actor every episode. People had found some of the actors, and every one had been contacted and paid anonymously. He didn't turn on ads, and there was no way to send him money, so, legally, The Thread didn't even exist. The Thread understood how fame worked and had run with it.

It was also genius marketing because it felt so mysterious. Like, was this person famous? Was he wealthy? Was he someone I'd met? But it was also something I understood all too well. I was attacked all the time for being a professional manipulator of public opinion, and that makes sense. I'd made a video a few months after the warehouse about how kindness was important and people on the internet were too cruel to each other. I maybe went a little bit overboard with the criticism, and the response was . . . a lot.

Turns out, there are lots of people who are unkind not just because it's fun, but because they believe it's the right strategy. And getting on those people's bad side is unpleasant because of how they believe very strongly that being a dick is a vital part of making the world a better place. And hell, who knows, maybe they're right.

"Yeah, I mean, he's probably a white dude," Jason replied.

"But you're right that he's able to say things he wouldn't otherwise be able to say by removing his identity. It's fascinating and also a little terrifying."

"And also already being copied," Jason said.

"Really?"

"Yeah, there's a channel called Common Dissent that has the exact same MO. All animated, anonymous host, no ads. He doesn't respond to anything The Thread says directly, but he's gathering steam the same way, and in a different direction. It's grown a lot in the last few weeks."

"I guess we're at the point in history where being a person has become a liability. Better to just be a disembodied jumble of ideas."

"And then you just walk away and let other people argue on your behalf."

"'Other' people or computer programs pretending to be other people."

It was true, The Thread had paid for an analysis that had proved that a lot of arguments happening in the comments of his videos and other video essays were being had by combination human/AI content farms . . . and then he made a video about it. The battle for hearts and minds was being waged, in part, by beings without hearts or minds.

Daniel Judson

@DetachedNihilist1

Is death just god moderating the comments section? I know it's not PC to say, but I for one am enjoying April May's shadowban. Too Soon? Lol

2.4K replies   894 retweets   6.3K likes

CARSON COMMUNICATIONS OUTAGES CONTINUE

If your internet service has been spotty the last couple weeks, you're not alone. Internet outages have been rippling across South Jersey for weeks now, with Vineland and surrounding areas being the most affected, but complaints being registered as far north as Cherry Hill.

"Part of the value we provide customers is high-speed internet," said Derek Housen, owner of Wolton's Dream Bean Café. "We haven't had stable internet in six weeks. I'm paying my bill, but I'm not getting service. I've taken to setting up a hotspot with my phone, but the data charges are out of hand."

Carson Communications, the company most affected, has been in communication with customers, but service remains inconsistent and slow. "We have had technicians in the field every day for over a month now," said a spokesperson for Carson. "We are aware that we are not providing the level of service we aspire to."

Though representatives did not confirm this, several Carson customers told us that they have been receiving partial refunds for periods of significant outage.

MAYA

My hands are huge and made of metal, and they're scraping away at the scraps of a collapsed building. I am giant and joyous in my strength. My invincible fingers dig into the brick and steel, and it feels like digging through balls in a McDonald's ball pit. I am unstoppable. And then I look down and see that the dust and wood and crumbling bits of brick are wet with blood. I lean down to look and see April's eyes and snap awake.

I used to puke when I had that dream. It had been coming less often now, and I'd been more able to handle the fallout. But I still shook, sweat coating my skin. I pulled the sheets off of my body and then wrapped myself around them, to feel like I was holding something. Or maybe just to feel like there was something else in the world besides the emptiness of failure. There was no way I was going back to sleep.

Here was my working theory that I had gleaned from conversations on the Som.

Cable internet slows down when more users are on the system, but this shouldn't be system-wide. Basically, cable internet is like a giant underground tree with branches that are sometimes physical, sometimes coded into the frequencies being used in the signal. Multiple customers use the same frequencies and the same branches, but if one branch is over capacity, all the other branches are completely unaffected.

But in South Jersey, all of the branches were being affected, turning on and off at random like a string of Christmas lights. My theory was that, if this had something to do with Carl, which every other conspiracy theorist on the Som also believed, there would be some pattern that might lead us to where or how all that extra bandwidth was being used.

I figured if I could follow some vans around for a couple weeks and map out where the problem spots were, maybe I could find some kind of pattern.

My first day of this was a learning experience. I had thought that I would go to their dispatch office and maybe follow vans from there, but I actually spotted one before I even got there. I did a quick U-turn and followed it a couple cars back, doing my best to not focus on how ridiculously I was behaving.

About fifteen minutes in, the van pulled up at the biggest barn I've ever seen. Painted on its front it read "Cowtown: Often Imitated Never Equaled." Next to the giant red barn was a giant red cow. It was distracting enough that I almost lost sight of the van. I pulled into the mostly empty lot and parked a few cars down from my target.

I tried to get a look at the guy. He was wearing a blue denim shirt and a white cowboy hat. His belt was buckled at the base of a tight, round belly. I only got a quick glimpse at his face as he pulled a few big cases out of the back and put them on a hand truck to wheel them inside the massive barn. I waited a couple minutes and then followed him in.

Or I tried to. A young man stopped me. "We're not open for another half hour."

"What is this?" I asked, truly perplexed.

"Cowtown," he said. "It's a flea market. Open Tuesdays and Saturdays."

"So all the people currently inside are . . ." I asked.

"Vendors . . . just people setting up."

"Oh, so this is like a farmers' market."

He laughed. "Yeah, it's like a hundred farmers' markets in one building. Come on back in a half hour, you'll have your mind blown."

So that's how I learned that Carson Communications didn't own its trucks. In fact, a lot of the technicians that worked for Carson didn't actually work for them. They were independent contractors and had other gigs. Gigs like, apparently, selling stuff at a giant flea market. I did not come back in a half hour because April May was alive somewhere and searching a giant flea market would not help me find her. I'd already wasted my first morning in South Jersey.

The trouble was, even after I refined my system (only following trucks that went to the dispatch center for supplies first being the main change), there were no patterns.

Trucks went all over the place. Mostly Vineland, because that was the biggest city in the affected range. But also Bridgeton and

Glassboro and Salem and Swedesboro and even occasionally back to Wolton. I was getting familiar with the area, which turned out to be equal parts too cute and too weird. I don't think I'm cut out for small-town life.

At least I had my potato plant, which, yes, at this point still just looked like a big pot of dirt. But I kept it watered and warm. And I had the Dream Bean, which, over the weeks of me following cable repair vehicles, had quickly become a part of my morning routine.

The morning the nightmare came back was also the one-year anniversary of April's first video. The one-year anniversary of me waking her up in the afternoon with coffee that I knew she was going to hate. The anniversary of my world—and *the* world—completely losing any anchor it once had. I didn't want to be bored in a truck alone with my thoughts and radio broadcasts playing "Mr. Roboto" and "Starman," with DJs loudly joking about the anniversary of the arrival of aliens. I understood why they had to make it a joke—what other choice did we have? I just didn't want to be there while they did it.

But I also had made my decision, and I was sticking to it.

"Morning, Derek," I said.

"Hiya, Maya!" He was a good guy, but, like Wolton, a little too cute. It almost seemed like me arriving each day was a dream come true for him. Maybe it was a sign that someday he would have lots of regulars, maybe even regulars who weren't old people. Maybe his coffee shop could be hip! Even though I'm sure he knew deep down that nothing in Wolton would ever be hip.

"Want anything to eat?"

"Yeah, get me a bagel. Onion."

"Feeling adventurous."

"Derek, I don't think I'm going to work today."

Derek never asked me about my "job"—I think he felt like it would be rude—but I was glad because I didn't really want to explain.

"Gonna go see the sights?"

"Are there any?" I smirked.

He laughed. "No, not really. Cowtown? It is Tuesday."

"I mean, I've driven past it. I've never been, like, called to enter."

"Oh my god. Big-city girl, you have no idea what you have been missing."

"I don't even really get what it is . . ."

"It's a farmers' market, but also a flea market, and also it has weird food. I have no idea why, but it's kinda a big deal. It's open on Tuesdays and Saturdays, so you're in luck. Honestly, I'm sorry I can't come with you, it's pretty cool."

I didn't think that Derek's idea of "pretty cool" was likely to be actually cool, but it was something to do at least.

He handed me my latte, and I said, "I guess I'm going to Cowtown."

I ate my bagel and checked the Som. It was the only social media I used anymore. I privated my Twitter account after April died—I couldn't handle the 99 percent of people who meant well, much less the 1 percent who didn't. I mean, Jesus, I understand people didn't like April, but how does it feel like a winning strategy to go after a recently deceased murder victim? Just a note to everyone: Don't do that. Even if you're right, it makes you look wrong. And I had figured out by this point that how things look is more or less the same as how they are. A story caught my eye, one that I'd been ignoring for a while. Not about New Jersey or Philly, but about Puerto Rico.

PETRAWICKI PROJECT NAMED

We've been following developments around the secret project Peter Petrawicki [PP] has been building and gathering funding for the last few months. Peter's obsession with April and fear of the Dream brought him notoriety, and now he has somehow leveraged that into a project that has been hiring [EXT-WIRED-MAGAZINE] at a tremendous rate. This project has finally been named Altus meaning "High, deep, noble, or profound" in Latin. We are renaming the relevant thread [ALTUS].

This wasn't the first time I'd heard about Peter's new gig, but I also wasn't spending any energy on it. I figured the world was done with him, and I *knew* I was. His bro project having a new bro name didn't change that. I ate my bagel and got up to leave the café in an even worse mood than I'd entered it in. But then Derek called after me as I left, "See you, Maya! Get a hot sausage sandwich for me!" And that cheered me up a bit.

Cowtown was from another universe. I pulled up to it just after it opened around eight. Empty picnic tables filled a giant parking lot, a few buildings, and a bunch of outdoor stalls. What I did not realize was that one of the buildings, which looked fairly normal from the front, was enormously long. And whoever owned that building rented out stalls inside to anyone who wanted one. It was like pop-up shops, except instead of high-end retail, it was literally anything else.

I had imagined a farmers' market with mostly produce and maybe a couple of stands selling wood carvings, but this was not that. There was produce, sure. But as I moved deeper into the building, most tables seemed to have just dedicated themselves to a single product that I would not know how to find if I was looking for them. There was a used vacuum cleaner table. There was a hubcap table. There was a booth from a company that would install a new shower in your bathroom. There was a table that had just men's rings, and 90 percent of those rings had skulls on them. I was not in the market for a skull ring, nor did I feel particularly welcome at this tiny skull-ring emporium, but I still spent a lot of time looking at them because I was fascinated. As I wandered deeper and the minutes and then, somehow, hours passed by, the market got more and more crowded, and I realized that while the customers might be economically similar (it seemed like mostly lower-class folk), it was otherwise very diverse.

I spent a bunch of time looking at a huge booth of vintage dresses. The lady running it was in her sixties with long naturally gray hair. She was beautiful, and also helpful.

"Sweetie," she called to me at one point. But of course I had no idea she meant me, so I just kept browsing.

"Young lady," she called again. I turned and she said, "I thought this would be exactly the thing. It looks precisely your size, and I think you'd look just like Judy Pace in it."

I didn't know who Judy Pace was, but the dress was heavy, flowing red cotton with a high neck. It was also *short*. I did her the favor and tried it on in her little changing room.

Look, I'm not April. I'm a normal human who looks in the mirror and does not love what they see. I want to love my body, and I know I'm supposed to. I just don't. But the dress did make my legs look . . . good. I took out my phone and snapped a picture thinking I might send it to someone to hype me up into buying it. What I really wanted was to send it to April, and I got so scared that I couldn't think of anyone else in my life to message that I messaged Miranda.

MAYA: *Does this dress look good?*

The three little dots were there for a long time before a message finally came through.

MIRANDA: *Yeah! Why?*

MAYA: *You're such a dork. Peer-pressure me!*

MIRANDA: *Oh! Maya, you look like a literal goddess. You need that dress.*

MAYA: *That's better.*

Sometimes you need to buy a red dress because the alternative is the nightmare of loss.

By this time, the place was packed with people, and starting to smell like grilled meats. I was trying to sniff my way toward those meats when I spotted a familiar white cowboy hat. I'd all but forgotten that one of Carson's contractors was a vendor, but the moment I saw the guy I knew it was him. The table in front of him sported a variety of rocks. Nice rocks—crystals and fossils and stuff.

Trying not to feel weird about the fact that I had followed this guy as he worked on several occasions, I inspected his table.

I picked up a perfectly smooth hunk of white rock, thinking it was going to be hefty in my hand, but it was light, and colder than I thought it should be. It was so light, it felt like it must be hollow. My mind flashed back to Carl, their parts that felt like they neither took nor gave heat. This wasn't like that, in fact it felt cooler than it should, like metal, but without the weight. I looked at it more deeply and saw that it wasn't the pure milky white I'd thought it was. Around the edges it clouded into a powdery blue, and when I turned it in my hands, tiny flecks of blue, green, and even pink appeared and disappeared. It was gorgeous.

"Is this a rock?" I asked.

"Couldn't tell you," the vendor replied, his eyes moving between my eyes and my hands.

"I'm sorry, what?"

"I. Couldn't. Tell. You," he said, putting space between each word. Had I done something?

"Sorry, I'm just curious, where did you get these?"

"That's enough curiosity for today." He reached over and grabbed the thing out of my hand.

"What the—?" I said quietly in surprise.

He glared at me like I'd told him to go have sex with his mother. Then he put the rock down and said, "I think you're done here." For a blink, I thought maybe he recognized me somehow. The guy was giving off serious Defender vibes, so maybe he had seen a picture of me somewhere. But then, no, that's not what this was. This wasn't alien stuff, it was race stuff.

"I'm sorry, sir," I said. I was mad about it then and I'm mad about it now, but I made my mind up a long time ago that it isn't my job to get in a shouting match with every racist I meet. That doesn't mean I wasn't frustrated and angry and anxious and uncomfortable.

Fucking Carliversary. Fucking mysteries. Fucking racist rock guy. Fucking APRIL WHERE THE FUCK ARE YOU! I went back to the vintage clothing place and rushed into the little curtained dressing room set up there and did my best to cry quietly.

I wanted to leave. I wanted to call my mom. I wanted to go home, not just to my Airbnb—I wanted to go home to Manhattan. I took out my phone and opened my contacts. My mom was at the top of my favorites, but next to Mom's, April's face smiled out at me and I let out a real sob.

It makes sense that I wasn't able to remove her after she died, but I'd also left her there after she was just about as shitty as a person can be to someone who had done every goddamn thing they could think of to make their relationship work. Honestly, it's embarrassing, and it isn't even important to the story. I just felt like I needed to tell you because the moment I was losing faith in the world, I spent a solid five minutes just looking at that little face on my phone.

"Honey," a soft voice came from outside.

"Yeah?" I said, louder than I'd intended.

"Are you all right in there?"

"Bad day," I said.

"I've had some of those. You just let me know if you need anything, OK?"

I pulled my AirPods out and watched Andy's video. It was good. He was a good guy. He was an idiot, and he was taking his responsibility too seriously, but that's a lot better than the alternative. I felt better afterward. I wiped my nose and my eyes and realized that I did not have to lose this one. I had no idea if they mattered, but I was going to get those damn rocks.

ANDY

God was different post-Carl, and that was a big deal for a lot of people. But God had never been a part of my life, even when I was a little kid. I was raised in a secular household by a man and a woman who were both raised in secular households. There aren't a lot of third-generation atheists in the world.

For a guy who was born an atheist, I had a lot of books by religious folks on my nightstand. I hated the whole "religion is the root of all evil" perspective that a lot of atheists (and, to be honest, myself not that long ago) professed. For me, it goes without saying that much of the dogma of many religions is harmful. Thinking other people will burn forever because they love the wrong person or worship the wrong god has done a whole lot of bad.

What I wanted was the part where people were asked to get together once a week to talk about how to be a good person and, like, hang out with their neighbors. It's pretty amazing that apparently the only way to get people to do that is to invent an all-seeing, kind-hearted sky dad who will be super disappointed/burn you for eternity if you don't show up.

Then, on the other hand, I doubt anything short of the threat of eternal damnation would get me out of bed on a Sunday morning. The things I was doing, whether in real life or on the internet, I wanted to be a little bit like that. Thus, in addition to listening to podcasts and watching YouTube videos from internet people, I'd started reading books by pastors and community organizers. This felt deeply weird, even a little like trespassing. But a lot of people were looking to me for guidance, so I wanted to get better at giving it. And now that April was gone, what I believed was that the same despair and frustration that was killing people had also been the root of what drove those guys to burn that warehouse down. My enemy wasn't the people; it was the loss of identity and narrative people felt comfortable in.

There were also lots of people who were happy to help people indulge in that loss, and to give them meaning by giving them things to be afraid of. So I guess I did have some enemies. The people doing that didn't seem to feel like phonies, so I figured, fuck your insecurities, as long as you're better than them you're doing fine.

Robin met me in the airport.

"How's the book coming?" was his first question.

"It's good to see you too," I deadpanned. This had become a running joke. Robin had calculated that every time I gave a talk without a book for sale, I was losing between $5,000 and $20,000 of value. It was weird—I didn't need more money, I didn't even want more money, but I did feel bad not making money when I could. It's not like someone else could come along and fill the niche of "books by Andy Skampt." Only I could create that value, and I just wasn't doing it.

You'd think that being on planes 150 days a year would free up a lot of time for writing, but instead it freed up time for listening to Reinhold Niebuhr audiobooks, watching leftist YouTube videos, and going through every single episode of *Star Trek*, from the original series to *Discovery*. Jason and I had been on a sci-fi kick on *Slainspotting*, and I had research to do.

"How was the flight?"

"Captain Picard stone-cold shot his own self."

"Did that turn out OK?"

"It doesn't seem like it would, but it did. It's complicated." I had taken out my phone to check on my IGRI stock. It hadn't changed for hours, since, get this, the markets hadn't opened in the US.

"Maybe you should write a *Slainspotting* book." He seemed serious.

We took a cab into the city. Robin was really good at making it seem like he was a part of the machinery of the earth. Like he was just a thing that happened and you were grateful for his presence, which was a great attribute for a personal assistant/manager/agent. He was always there, always taking care of me, but never taking any of my emotional energy. Robin worked very hard to be no work for me. He didn't want me to wonder how he was doing, partially because that would be something I'd have to think about, partially because I don't think he wanted to think about it either. The result was that one of the people closest to me in the whole world was often, to my subconscious, barely even a person. We had been through the best and worst moments of our lives together, and yet, in the months after things started to take on a new and somewhat stable structure, I very rarely wondered how he was doing.

I had recently decided I was going to remember he was a human more. But then there was a mysterious book and a new girl and a bizarre penny stock and I had forgotten. But not for the whole car ride!

"How are you doing?" I asked after ten minutes of checking Twitter.

"Good!" he said. "The people at Redstone have been really wonderful to work with. Very responsive. They're pros. It's always good to work with pros."

Well, that didn't work. How about "I went on a date yesterday"?

"Well, that's been a long time coming. How did it go?"

"It was great, we went to see *STOMP*."

He laughed a genuine, high laugh. "Are you serious?" And just like that, I was actually talking to Robin.

"I am, it's worse than that. I met her at Subway."

"AT SUBWAY?! Not *on* the subway?"

"No, at Subway, she's a sandwich artist."

"So you're telling me you went into a Subway and asked an employee to go see *STOMP* with you?"

"I mean, yes?"

"It just doesn't seem like something you'd do!" he told me.

I didn't know how to respond to that because, of course it wasn't. I would never have done any of that if the book hadn't told me to.

I was quiet for a while thinking about that, and I must have looked awkward because Robin said, a little concerned, "I didn't mean to pry."

"No!" I said. "No, you're right. I was just trying to figure out how I'd ended up doing something so weird and also, like, slightly inappropriate. She's really nice. We had a good time. Do you think I should see her again?" I asked unnecessarily, since I was absolutely going to see her again if I could.

"God, don't ask me." He looked appalled.

"Yeah, what about you?" It occurred to me then that I didn't even know Robin's sexual orientation, so I just said, "Anybody interesting in LA?"

"Honestly, Andy, dating has been complicated. For me, I mean. Not like since, uh, whenever. Just, always. So I don't really do it anymore."

That was the most disjointed sentence I had ever heard Robin speak, and I was surprised to find myself legitimately unnerved by it. I had to fight not to tell him he didn't have to share. Ultimately, that would have been giving him an excuse, and I only wanted to give him that excuse to protect my own vision of him.

"Why is dating hard for you?" I asked.

He gestured up to the driver and said, "I think we'll talk about it another time."

We never did talk about it, though. I tried, that was the moment, but he pushed me away a little, and I let him.

"Do you know where we're headed right now?" Robin changed the subject.

"A hotel, I assume?"

"Oh god, no. The rooms won't be ready, and even if they were, I wouldn't let you go into one because you would fall asleep and it would destroy any chance you have at beating jet lag. No, right now we are going to meet the CEO of Redstone on his yacht. And then after that we're going shopping, because it appears that you did not bring a suit."

"I did not bring a suit. Should I have brought a suit?"

"Honestly, no, because Cannes is the best place in the world to buy a suit."

"An expensive suit?"

"Very."

Cannes was gorgeous, though I felt I might have been missing something by visiting this very beach-centric place in the wintertime. It was definitely the off-season.

The taxi dropped us off at the waterfront, and in my blue jeans and hoodie, I followed Robin on some docks through ever bigger and bigger yachts.

"Can you tell me again what the International Private Equity Market is?" I asked as we walked.

"You just had ten hours to read the one-page brief I gave you, and you didn't do it, did you?"

"Look, we can spend time arguing, or we can spend time learning about private equity."

He looked at me a little hard and a little sad, but not at all amused.

"When you are normal rich, you can do what you're doing with your portfolio. You buy stocks on public markets, and those stocks go up as the economy grows and your net worth increases. When you are very wealthy, or when you are an institution like a pension fund or a country, you get to do 'private equity.' The stock market is a public equity market. Private equity markets are when, in order to buy some or all of a business, you have to have meetings and sign papers and talk to lots of human beings. There are now big, giant private equity companies that consolidate wealthy people's wealth, and then they use it to buy whole private companies, or parts of them. The people at this conference, combined, manage trillions of dollars."

"Why do they want me to talk to them?"

"On paper, they want you to talk because you are a thought leader and will help guide their decisions, and any amount of insight they gain from you could be extremely valuable."

The phrase "thought leader" made my eyes roll so far back into my head I could see my brain, but that didn't mean that there was anything in the world I wanted more than to be a thought leader.

"What do you mean, 'on paper'?" I replied skeptically.

"Well, it's also a show of power. Their event happened to be on the anniversary of the Carls showing up, and I think some of the conference organizers felt it would be a big get to have you here. If you weren't here, it would be like them admitting that this isn't the most important place in the world right now, which gave me some negotiating leverage."

The yacht we ended up on was, I guess, tasteful as far as yachts go. It definitely wasn't the biggest boat in the marina, though it did have a spiral staircase enclosed in mirrors, so maybe "tasteful" is the wrong word. Weirdly, and even though I was dramatically underdressed, I was more or less comfortable as Robin and I were shuffled around to speak with various VPs and managing partners. I made jokes about jet lag, talked about how beautiful Cannes was, and everyone was astounded when they heard I'd never visited in the summer, as if all people regularly come to the South of France.

And then I met Gwen Stefani. She had also been invited to the event for a performance, and my dumb brain did the dumb brain thing and said, *Oh my god, you have to find April, she will be so stoked to meet Gwen Stefani.* But, of course, April wasn't there. I was only on that boat because I had stormed out of a room right when my best friend needed me the most and then she had gone and burned to death in a warehouse and *that's* why I was hanging out with Gwen Stefani.

I muttered some nonsense to Mrs. Stefani with tears starting to sting my eyes and ran out of the room onto the deck.

I looked out at the Mediterranean and all the yachts and the powerful people and tried to pull myself together.

"You OK, man?" It was Robin. He came up and put his hand flat on my back.

I turned around and grabbed him and held on.

"I'm sorry I don't treat you like a person." I was actually crying. Crying and holding another man. I know it's not supposed to be weird, but there was still a hurdle there.

He moved his hand up and down my back and said, "I know," and I could hear he was crying too.

"She should have been here," I said. "I don't deserve any of this. I'm only here because she's not."

He pulled back from me to look at my eyes. His eyes were rimmed in red. "You're only here because I . . ." And then his face crunched together and his throat slammed shut.

"No, Robin." Someone came out onto the deck. I locked eyes with them and they turned around like they hadn't seen a thing. Rich people, I have noticed, are good at looking the other way. I continued, "You can't still be blaming yourself."

At that he just cried softly into my shoulder. It was the first time we'd actually talked about April. We'd both been sad, and I'd assumed I knew all about his sad because I knew about mine. Except, of course, he was dealing with even more guilt. I wasn't the only one who had let April down that day. Finally he said, "Of course I blame myself, it's literally my fault. I should have told her about Putnam . . . any day before that day." I could feel him shaking, so I led him over to a plush outdoor lounge chair, which he sank onto. Helping him helped me feel stronger.

I sat beside him and put my arm around him. He leaned into me. I talked in a low voice. "No one is responsible for what happened to April except the guys who lit that fire. Friends hurt their friends' feelings sometimes. April hurt my feelings a thousand times. She knew I loved her. Sometimes she was a bad friend. You screwed up, but that is not why she's dead."

Robin leaned out from under my arm and looked up at me, and

I was suddenly worried that he was going to try and kiss me. I pulled back a little bit. He noticed and laughed.

"You dork! You thought I was going to kiss you!" he said.

"What?" I said, convincing no one.

He laughed a little more, sniffing up his snot. "Jesus, guys are screwed up, aren't we. There's no space between being emotional and making out. How have any of us survived? We're so bad at this."

"Agreed," I said, still feeling awkward.

He stood up. "Let's leave this boat."

Over the next few hours, we wandered around Cannes together. We didn't try to network or make connections; we just went to fancy shops and gawked at all the rich people who were somehow way richer than me. We talked about relationships and life and the internet, and I didn't think about IGRI a single time. Before I knew it, it was time to check in to give my talk. Just as I was going onstage, Robin grabbed my shoulders and said, "You deserve to be here," and at least in that moment, I believed him. Here's the juiciest part of what I said that night:

I am not going to pretend that I understand what you do. Earlier today, I had to ask someone what private equity was. But my guess is that, to some extent, your jobs are to predict the future. I bet a lot of you even do it really quite well. But here's what I know . . . This isn't over. Last August, the Carls disappeared, and we have, for the most part, attempted to pretend that they never happened. But if you think things have gone badly in the past year, I have bad news. It's going to get worse before it gets better.

More than ever in our history, we understand that we aren't in control. We never were, of course, but now we really understand that we are not. The Carls could return anytime, or maybe they're still here. We exist at the mercy of some superior intelligence. Incorporating a reality like that into our minds and our cultures doesn't happen quickly. Already suicides are up. Already fewer people are buying the stories we've been telling. This is only the beginning, and I want you to ask yourselves whether you're helping people find their place in the world, or whether you're hurting their ability to do so.

Stability is a big deal for the world, and I would not, if I were you, spend very much time expecting it. I would, however, work hard toward doing everything we can to create it. You're a bunch of powerful people, and I assume you spend a lot of time thinking about not just how you can exploit the state of the world, but also how you can affect it. I imagine it's harder to make money when the world is in shambles, so if there is anything you can do to set us on a path to be more able to withstand another cosmic kick in the nuts, please do it.

"That was new!" Robin said as I came offstage.

"New good or . . ."

Robin shrugged, beaming.

One of the planners of the event came up to me, a younger guy who I'd talked to on the yacht. "Oh, Andy, that was wonderful. Hah! I love it. 'Cosmic kick in the nuts'!" He gripped my shoulder and shook me a little. "We got our money's worth with you."

"Thanks, I worked up something special for you."

"You say you don't have any actual knowledge of what's coming, but if you did, it wouldn't be hard to turn that knowledge into money."

I thought about *The Book of Good Times* in my bag back at the hotel. I thought about IGRI and my sudden foray into paranormal insider trading, and then said, "I know exactly as much as you do."

"Sure! Sure . . . Just in case, here's my card." These people still gave each other *cards*. I looked down at it. "Stewart Patrick?" I said.

"My parents were *Star Trek* fans, what can I say."

"Sorry I don't have a card for you," I said, "but I think you know how to get in touch. Um . . . is there a bathroom backstage?" I knew there was—I had used it before the show. He pointed me the way, and I rushed off. The moment the door was locked, I sat down on the toilet and opened my phone. A text message from Maya had come in, complimenting my video. I moved past it and opened my portfolio.

My $100,000 of IGRI stock was no longer IGRI stock. IGRI had been acquired by a car company trying to lock up cobalt mines to make electric-car batteries. So now I had over $1 million of stock in that car company. I let out a long, cool breath, feeling my heart thumping under my new French suit.

And then I opened my phone's calculator and figured out that I would have to make $1 million every day for almost three years before I had $1 billion. Suddenly, inexcusably, I felt like I was playing with very small potatoes.

I almost dropped my phone in the toilet when it rang. It was Miranda.

Associated Press

@AP

Dozens injured as "Happy Birthday Carl" parade-goers clash with anti-Carl protesters in New York City. The parade, which was billed as "a celebration of our new place in the universe," broke down into chaos when blocked by protestors.

239 replies   730 retweets   593 likes

Kyle Stafford

@kyylestafford

@AP What the fuck are they thinking, celebrating after everything that was done to us. there lucky no-one drove a Dodge Challenger into them.

303 replies   21 retweets   187 likes

Altus

@AltusLabs

We. Are. Hiring. We have dozens of positions open right now. This is your chance to make the future. Altus.net/MakeThe Future

203 replies   2.7K retweets   15K likes

MIRANDA

I do not have the temperament to be a secret agent. I hate stress. I hate it so much that it makes me extremely productive, because I will work any amount necessary to make stress go away.

But that was the thing. The existence of Altus was stress for me.

Every minute of the day there was a little ache in my brain, and every time I checked to see what it was, it wasn't worry about my experiments or about whether I'd said something dumb to a labmate; it was always only Altus. It was like a grain of sand in my heart. And when something is stressing me out, I *have* to do something about it. I have to at least feel like I'm trying.

That was one of the worst parts of April disappearing. I kept feeling like I had to solve the problem. Unfortunately, you can't solve someone being dead.

But I could at least start on the problem of Altus. The stress was coming from two places. First, Peter Petrawicki was succeeding. Bad people shouldn't get power, and he was getting more and more of it. I wasn't even so much worried about what he was going to do with the power; I was too caught up in the fact that he was getting it.

But I probably would have been able to ignore that eventually because it's not like I had to look at Peter Petrawicki all day. I did, however, have to look at rat brains all day and think about the fact that right now, in Puerto Rico, a bunch of people were working on science that would almost definitely make my research completely obsolete. And that was my second source of stress, eating away at me and getting worse every day. I was getting snappy with people, and my stomach was always a little upset. Professor Lundgren kept telling me all research is supposed to be additive, and that science doesn't actually work in breakthroughs the way we're all taught.

She could *say* that, but I couldn't believe it. If the "service" they were going to provide included some high-bandwidth neural link, they were decades ahead of our lab. So what was the point of my thesis? What was the point of driving, head down, every day through piles of mind-numbing data entry to build something that might, in six months, look like an Apple II?

That's when I started looking at Altus job postings.

JUNIOR SCIENTIST
BIO-MICROFABRICATION—PUERTO RICO

State-of-the-art research lab is seeking an R&D chemical and materials scientist to relocate to Puerto Rico. Our lab is pushing the boundaries of what is possible, and this is your chance to make the future. We're looking for an energetic, resourceful chemist and/or materials scientist with experience in experimental design, and expertise in organic, polymer, and analytical chemistry. A passion for what's next is a must. Team players only.

Now I just had two problems:

1. I was qualified for this job, but not tremendously. They were probably looking for a postdoc candidate, though the fact that they didn't say so was promising. It was also telling—they might not be being picky because of how fast they were hiring.
2. My name was Miranda Beckwith, and I couldn't change that. Most people wouldn't recognize me, but the moment some recruiter Googled my name, they would see that I was friends with April May.

The nice thing was that, with some time separating me from my initial find of the article, I was less angry and a little more calculating. I started thinking, *Well, this probably won't work anyway. Might as well give it a try!* It felt like doing something.

I remember the day I sent the application in because I was also distracting myself from the other piece of stress that I definitely couldn't do anything about. It was the one-year anniversary of the Carls and of me sending my first email to April. Everyone was using it as an opportunity to shout at each other. The Defenders didn't exist anymore, but all of the people who were sympathetic to them still did, and the arguments were never really about Carl anyway. Even with them gone, pundits were getting powerful by arguing that we needed to be more afraid. It felt like the public was only getting angrier every day. A group of people had decided to have a Carl parade in New York, and it was cute, but then it was blocked by protesters and the whole thing fell apart. Twitter then got very angry on absolutely everyone's behalf.

The whole thing made me feel sick. Maybe I even knew that the chances of something going more wrong were higher than usual. We were all a little on edge. So instead of looking at angry people calling out racism and xenophobia from citizens, pundits, and politicians alike, I guiltily scrubbed references to April and the Som from my social media profiles, spruced up my LinkedIn, and wrote up a cover letter.

As months passed after the Carls disappeared (that's how everyone thought about it, though for us, of course, it was also the time since April died), I kept feeling more and more like my time with April, Andy, Maya, and Robin was some kind of other life that I hadn't really belonged in. My brain did a fairly good job of convincing me that I wasn't actually an important part of the group. This is just impostor syndrome, of course, and I know it is, but that didn't stop me from believing it. I mean, I *built* the Som. I know I did that. I also know that very little of the code was mine, and there were way too many people working on that project for anyone to claim credit. And my brain also told me that being basically a high-level employee did not mean those people were actually my friends. They were obviously too cool for that, and if I looked back, there were plenty of examples of them (by which I mostly mean April) not treating me super well.

Yeah, I knew a lot about things that April and Maya and Andy didn't know about, but they knew things about themselves and about culture. I can tell you all about how valence electrons affect conductivity, but I didn't even know I was queer until I hooked up with April. I didn't even know I was queer *after* I hooked up with April. I thought maybe it was just that she was famous and cool and I wasn't really sexually attracted to her, just to who she was. April and Maya had known so much about themselves and about how to imagine the world. This is maybe going to sound gross, but I was envious of them, and mad at myself for not spending more time trying to figure out who I was. I'd just gone with what I looked like and what people expected, and assumed that since I was attracted to guys I was straight. How could a person unfamiliar with her own sexual orientation possibly be cool enough to be in April May's inner circle?

I'm trying to show you how good my brain was at convincing me that I never belonged where I was. These are the lies our brains tell us to push happiness out of our reach. What is the evolutionary purpose of that? Is happiness stagnation? Maybe. Maybe life (all life, not just human life) is nothing more than wanting something and being able to go for it. What is life with no want? Satisfaction sounds lovely, but evolutionarily it was apparently selected against.

What I'm trying to say is that the more time that passed, the weirder I felt about initiating contact between me and any of the group. Maya's text to me from a dressing room at Cowtown had felt like a gift, a mystery, and a cosmic mistake all at the same time.

I never stopped feeling like being the first to send a text would be intruding upon the real main characters of the story. Even right now as I write this I feel like they just invited me to tell my part of the story because they wanted to be nice to me. Which is ludicrous because the things that happened to me over these months were both intense and absurd. It's a great story! It's just the rut my mind gets stuck in.

God, I talk too much, I'm sorry.

The point is that, before I sent off my application, I felt like I needed to talk to someone, but I didn't know who to call, and I felt really weird about it. Finally, after pacing in my apartment, I called Andy.

"Miranda," he answered. He didn't sound right. It was almost like he was resigned, definitely stressed. Like he had begrudgingly accepted the reality that I was calling him on the phone.

"Are you OK?"

"Yeah, yes. I'm sorry, I'm great. I just got offstage, so I'm a little amped. It's good to hear your voice." The weirdness was gone, or he was just hiding it better, but his voice still sounded echoey.

"Thanks, you too. Where are you?" He was always somewhere.

"Cannes. Just finished giving a talk at a fancy thing for rich people. Uh. Hey, I went on a date."

"What?" This conversation wasn't going how I'd planned.

"I like her, she's really nice. I wanted to tell you that before it got weird. I don't know why it would be weird. But I guess I just made it weird all by myself, didn't I. It's not serious or anything, she's just someone I met . . ." He left that trailing off like he was maybe going to tell me more but then decided not to.

Andy and I had never done . . . stuff, but I had been interested at one point, and I think he had been as well. I don't know if those points had ever overlapped, but if they did, or if they still were, I didn't know how to tell.

"That's great, what's her name?"

"Becky, but she goes by Bex, like with an *x*."

"That's pretty cool."

"She *is* much cooler than me," he explained.

"That's not that hard." We chuckled together, and I felt like I was at least doing a good job of pretending like we were equals.

"So what's up?" he asked.

"Well, this is going to sound weird after your report, but, like, I have not been on any dates. Instead I am seriously considering applying for a job at Peter Petrawicki's new laboratory, which I believe is building brain-machine interfaces that are several generations beyond what has currently been built. I want to go work there so I can find out what they're doing."

"And what will you do once you find out what they're doing?"

He seemed so confident. A lot of new responsibility came at him after April disappeared, and he seemed to be handling it really well. But that meant he was a little less fun now, and more earnest. I think a lot of times, people become who we need them to be. I wasn't like that, but Andy was.

"I don't know," I said, a little flustered. "I guess that depends on what it is! It could be anything. I just want to have an eye on that dude. Also, it's what I'm researching here . . . kinda . . . and it's a really big deal. Part of me actually wants to be involved."

Andy was quiet for a long time and then finally responded.

"You have to be very careful. This is almost certainly industrial espionage that you're talking about here."

"Why do you think I called instead of texting? Fewer records."

"Fuck, Miranda, how long have you been thinking about this?"

"A while. I'm scared, though. I think I called you to talk me out of it."

He laughed then.

"Well, maybe in spite of my better judgment, I'm not going to do that. You have to go."

"Why?"

"I can't—" he stammered. "I mean . . . I don't know. It's just a gut feeling. This isn't over."

"What do you mean?"

"Something strange is happening. I think it might have something to do with April."

He said it fast, like he wanted to get it out before he stopped himself. I did not respond quickly.

"Andy . . ."

"It's not just that either. I think the Carls leaving, I think that wasn't the end. I think it was the beginning."

"The beginning of what?"

"I don't know, but if you think Peter is working on something big, I think we need to know about it. I think you need to go."

I hit send on the application.

"Well, I guess we'll see how that goes."

It did not go how I expected.

Andy Skampt

January 5 at 2:30 P.M.

I wanted today to only be a day of good feelings and it was. It was until I was woken up with the news. I'm pulled in two directions right now. The first is that I do truly believe that human cruelty is the exception, not the norm. This is so important to remember.

But the other is that these things are happening more and more. Yes, each one is just one person, and no, their actions never make sense. But this is part of a broader trend in disconnection. It almost never ends this way, but almost never is becoming more and more common. We are disconnected from each other, and we are losing all our old ways of feeling like we matter. That tears people up inside. Usually, they act inwardly, but sometimes they lash out and hurt the people who are close to them. Even less often, they hurt strangers.

Does it help to know that? Maybe not. Maybe it only helps to know that we are all part of something great. And that's the danger of acts like this. Not only is it, in part, a symptom of a loss of faith in the human story, but it also perpetuates that loss of faith. I haven't lost it, though. In response to this, please share a story that keeps your faith in people strong. I have thousands, but I want to hear yours.

MAYA

After I was reasonably sure that I didn't look like a complete, crumbling mess, I left the dressing room. The kind woman from the booth came over as I exited.

"Honey, are you OK?"

"Yes," I said, barely making eye contact. "Do you know where the nearest ATM is?"

"Sure, it's out by the cow."

"The cow?"

"The big red cow? Outside?" she replied, like it was obvious.

"Oh, of course, the cow."

I went and got as much money as I could get out of the ATM: $600, $200 at a time. And then I went back to the vintage-dress place.

"This is very weird, and a lot to ask," I said when I got there, "but there is a vendor that is selling something I would like to buy, but he does not want to sell it to me."

"Well, that doesn't sound like Cowtown. The whole point is that everything is for sale. If it isn't here, you don't need it!"

"I don't think it's a matter of the thing, more a matter of . . ." I trailed off, looking down, half playing it up, half still really feeling it.

"Are you saying . . . ?" she whispered.

"Look, I don't want to make a big deal out of this—"

"Who was it? Al Johnson, I'll bet," she interrupted in a whisper.

"It was the guy selling the crystals and fossils, just a few tables down."

"Hmm, I honestly have no idea who he is. It's a big market," she said at full volume.

"So, what I was wondering is if you could go and buy all of the smooth white things he has. They're really pretty, like opals or pearls, but light like plastic. Also, if maybe you could ask him where he got them and play it up like they're really valuable and you're getting a deal. And if by any chance you could get his name and the name of his business . . ."

She looked skeptical. "Why would I pretend like they're valuable? That's just gonna bring up the price."

I took out a wad of twenties and said, "I don't know if they're valuable, I just want him to think they are. There's six hundred dollars here, keep whatever you don't spend."

She looked at me like I was a little nuts, which, fair, but she took the money.

"Well, I don't see how this hurts anybody," she said. "And you'll watch the shop while I'm gone?"

"You'll only be thirty feet away, and I'm not going to think you're racist if you take your cashbox with you. I'll think you're a prudent businesswoman." That was true—for all she knew this could be some kind of elaborate scam.

"Oh!" I said. "And once you buy them, tell him you'll buy as many more of them as he can find."

And that's all it took. She was off.

Less than ten minutes later, she was back.

"I got them all. He wanted to keep one of them, but I upped the price until I got all four." She handed me the bag. "I had to fight every instinct to not bargain more, but I think he thinks they're something special. But I got them for a hundred and eighty, so I can't keep all your money." She started to pull some cash out of her pocket.

"No . . ." I realized I didn't know her name.

"Clara," she said kindly.

"Clara, I'm Maya. I don't know how to explain it to you, but what you did for me today was worth way more than four hundred twenty dollars." I was smiling—I couldn't stop. I needed to put my hands on those rocks again.

"That can't be true, dear."

"It can be. And it will be extra worth it if you tell me everything you found out from that man."

"He was perfectly nice to me. We talked some about the market and how business was going. He lives outside Philly and he says he bought these from his brother-in-law and doesn't know where his brother-in-law got them, but honestly, that's vendor code for 'I don't want to tell you where I got these.' But when I told him I'd buy as many as he could find, his eyes did light up a little. I chatted him up a bit—he does cable and internet repair for his day job."

This was not new information to me, but I tried not to show it.

"Did you get his name?"

"Oh, yeah, he gave me his business card, it's in the bag."

I opened it up. The rocks were wrapped in tissue paper, and indeed, there was a business card sitting on top of them.

"Just . . . thank you," I said, giddy with the success. It finally felt like something was happening.

"Thank *you*, sweetie." And she winked at me.

I went and got a hot sausage sandwich. I sat down at a picnic table and dumped the stones out. They twinkled up at me like they were alive—like they had plans for me.

Someone sat down at the table, and I scooped the stones back into the paper bag.

"You're Maya." I looked up and saw a guy in his thirties with dark, styled hair and Oakley glasses perched on top of his head.

"I am," I said skeptically.

"I remember you from April's videos."

I wasn't in any of April's videos, so this was one of the most terrifying things he could have said to me. He knew who I was, and he was lying about how.

I tried to act calm. "Look, I'm just here to eat my hot sausage, then I'm headed home."

"Did you do some shopping?" he continued, not taking the hint.

"A little." I started wrapping up my sandwich.

"What did you buy?"

"Just a bracelet," I lied.

"I'll buy it from you," he told me.

"What?"

"The bracelet."

I was standing now.

He continued, "Five hundred bucks."

"I don't know what you think is happening right now, but none of this makes any sense, and I'm going to go."

"OK! OK!" he rushed. "I'm sorry, this is going different than how I expected."

"Yeah, well, same," I said, backing away from him.

"Let me explain!"

For some reason I stopped. It was weird enough that I did want an explanation.

"I do an alternate reality game. It's called Fish. Do you know what RGs are?"

"Yeah, sure," I said. I was roughly familiar with folks who paid a monthly subscription for clues to be dropped into their lives.

"Well, I just got a text from Fish saying that if I found you and got you to give me what you bought at Cowtown that I would advance two levels instantly. So, can I have it?"

"No!" I said.

"A thousand," he said.

"No, it's not a price thing. This is just weird and I don't like it."

"Ten thousand." He was taking out his cell phone like he was going to Venmo me ten grand.

"No! And stop asking."

His frustration was turning to anger now.

"Just let me buy it! It's a good deal!"

He was at least six inches taller than me, and every step I took back, he moved forward into. His hand reached out for the bag, and adrenaline pumped into my body. I panicked, threw my hot sausage sandwich at his face, and ran back into Cowtown.

I ran through the booths, jumping around and dodging people, not taking time to look behind me until I was halfway through the

massive building. When I looked back, the Oakleys guy was nowhere
to be seen. I started walking more normally now, afraid people would
be suspicious, but I was also winded. Fitness was never my focus.

Another guy locked eyes on me, this guy was middle-aged with
his dark hair close cropped where it wasn't balding.

"Are you Maya?" he asked. I was still catching my breath, so I did
not reply, about to start running again.

"Did you buy anything at the market today?" he asked. I took off
as fast as I could, which is not particularly fast, but I did not stop
until I got to my truck. I hit the push-button starter on the rental and
did everything I could not to drive too erratically out of the Cowtown parking lot.

I considered just driving home to Manhattan, but the rocks sitting in their little bag on the passenger seat were whispering to me.
Something was happening, and I couldn't give up now. Plus, as I
drove in circles, trying to figure out if someone was following me, I
got an idea.

Now a note because it feels necessary:

When we think about the first anniversary of the arrival of the
Carls, we mostly think about that shooting. But really, the whole day
was a pretty good and normal day until that evening. Yeah, people
were mad on the internet. And yes, there were a couple little skir-
mishes at a parade. But it only takes one person shooting their way
into a nightclub to change the story.

We gave everyone in America that power when we decided that
basically anyone can buy an assault rifle. I don't pretend to understand the motivations of these shooters, but ultimately it has to be at
least a little bit about power, right? They've been convinced that having power is how you measure your worth, and they are sad or angry
or, as is so often the case, both, and they see that there's one way they
can definitely change the world. They've seen a dozen other guys do
the same thing, so why not them?

I hate that I even have to write about it here because, ultimately, billions of people decide every day to be decent and kind, but one person decides to be powerful for a moment and now I have to talk about it or people will be like, "But what about the shooting?"

Well, what about it? It happened. It was terrible.

Why did it happen? Was he a Defender? Was it ultimately about the Carls? No. Those are all the wrong questions. It's so tempting, even now, to try to blame all of the politicians and pundits who were rising in power by feeding on people's fear and confusion.

We can blame those people, but the only thing a mass murder "means" is that we've made it too easy to kill. None of us are going to talk about it anymore in this book, because if we did, that man will get to keep having his power on us, and I'm sick of it.

Moving on.

ANDY

I couldn't stop feeling bad about telling Miranda she had to apply at Altus. My gut was all, *Absolutely not!* She should stay in Berkeley where it was normal and safe. Enough of my friends had done weird, risky things. If the book hadn't told me to tell her to do it, I absolutely would not have. It was one thing putting my money on the line with this thing, but this was Miranda's future. But *The Book of Good Times* was in charge now. Or maybe I just wanted it to be.

And now, since I had completed the book's two requests, I could turn the page.

You waited! Excellent work! I knew you would. I mean, I literally knew it. Otherwise, how could I have known when I printed the book? You probably shouldn't worry too much about all of this right now. So, you have another million dollars. It seems like you can trust me, right?

As previously noted, this wasn't true. I was doing everything I could to not trust the book. I knew it was powerful, but I did not know what it wanted.

So now, I'd like you to move 100 percent of your portfolio into Posthiker, a distributed shipping company. They've only been publicly traded for about a year, and people are not optimistic about how their business has gone. But they're about to have a very good quarter. Search for Posthiker on Twitter and you'll see people talking about it. It's functioning, it's earning people money, and it's saving others money. The stock is going to jump 32 percent in the exuberance immediately afterward. Yes, I realize that I'm asking you to go against your instincts here, but you're going to need a lot of money. I know you think you already have a lot of money, but you're going to need much more. After Posthiker, you'll want to move everything into Alphabet, which will give you a further 6 percent bump after their earnings come in, and then after that into Emerson, which has been doing extremely good business in air conditioners in China.

The book continued this way for more than a page, instructing me exactly how to move my money over the next two weeks. There was some action to take almost every day. It was hard not to enjoy this plan. Not knowing what to do with my money had been stressful, but now I knew exactly what to do. It was a good feeling to know that I might soon be very, very rich. At the same time, it was terrifying to know that I was going to need it for something.

After this, you will be, by my best guess, at $125 million. You're going to wonder what all of this money is for, but do your best not to worry about it. You might ask, "Why don't I just go to Vegas and you can tell me how to bet in roulette, or which lottery numbers to pick, or which sports team to bet on?" Well, it turns out, those things are actually random. Nothing is as easy to guess as the success of companies. All of the data are already out there. The information is known by people and stored in computers, and the reactions of those buying the stocks are easy to predict in large part because many of those entities are deeply simplistic computer programs. The question you're asking yourself now is, *Is this illegal?* Yes, it is super illegal. You are trading stocks based on tips from someone with insider information. I am stealing that information and giving it, in a distilled form, to you. So yes, this is illegal. But it is not, as far as I can tell, wrong to do it in this case. You do many things that are illegal, but I will not ask you to do anything that is wrong.

Here's the thing about having $125 million: If your portfolio increases by 1 percent in any given day, your net worth will increase by $1.25 million. You will make and lose more money in a single day than many people do in their whole lives. And you will make more than you lose.

You will make more money by investing your money than you ever could working. Which is fine, because I don't think you're doing what you're doing to make money. Except for the times when you are. I'd suggest stopping that. Though don't lose that business card.

I thought about this and realized the book probably meant the card the guy had given me in Cannes.

In the next three weeks, you need to think more than you act, and listen more than you talk. There are big things happening, and you are uniquely positioned to see them. Call Bex, introduce her to Jason. Hang out. See where it goes!

As I read, I could tell it was coming to an end, and without a single word about April.

Give yourself time to think. Don't fill it all up with podcasts and TV shows. Talk it out, think it out, be present. And maybe call Maya—she's thinking a lot these days too. Actually, you should reach out to all the old friends. Just ask how they're doing. You've got a few weeks before this story starts up again. You can move to the next page two weeks from today. But remember, tell no one about me. It will ruin the Good Times.

The urge to turn to the next page was overwhelming. Where was April? What was going on?

I turned the page.

Andy, I told you not to turn the page. April will be OK. But some-times you have to wait.

I threw the book across the room, and it slammed into the wall, knocking a couple plastic cups off my shelf.

"You OK in there?" Jason said, half laughing.

"I'm fine, just trying to kill a roach."

I went over to grab the book and stuffed it between my bed and the box spring. Jason didn't ever come in my room, so I wasn't hiding it from him as much as I was hiding it from myself.

And thus, in secret, I had to live all by myself in a world in which April was alive and books could predict the future. It took gargan-tuan strength for me not to tell Robin about it. It wasn't just that I wanted to tell *anyone*, though I did; it's more that it seemed so cruel to let him just suffer while I had this new hope. But then again maybe it was cruel to tell him when it could still all be a lie.

It was one thing to let a supernatural garbage book give you hope that your dead friend was alive; it was another thing entirely to force that ambiguity on someone else.

I tried to take the book's advice, to give myself space to think, but I was nervous and skittish and addicted to content.

Jason definitely noticed something was up.

"Dude, I don't want you to take this the wrong way, but you have been weird since you met Subway Girl."

"Don't call her Subway Girl," I told him.

"That's what I've always called her, though."

"Yeah, but she's going to come over tonight, and if you call her 'Subway Girl' in front of her, she is going to stab you, and then me. You can call her Becky or Rebecca or Bex."

"OK," he said before repeating, "Dude, I don't want you to take this the wrong way, but you've been weird since you met *Becky.*"

"It's not her, it's . . ." I decided to do a half lie: "It's money. Money is so freaking weird, man."

"Like, the part where you're filthy rich and never have to worry about it again?" Jason didn't really have to worry about money either. The podcast was making tons of ad revenue now, and he still had a full-time job doing database design for an e-commerce company.

"You totally have to worry about money when you have it, just in a different way."

This was, in fairness, something I never would have said to anyone but Jason, who I was sharing about $30,000 in podcast revenue with every month. Still, he rolled his eyes pretty hard.

"You could buy a penthouse apartment in Midtown and not have a mortgage."

"Right, so should I do that? Or should I start a business? Or should I invest in the stock market or in bonds? Like, why do you think I still live here with you?"

"Are you saying that you still live with me just because you don't know how to make a decision?"

"Jason, I still live here because I want to. I don't want to live in a penthouse apartment in Midtown. I don't want a boat. Robin keeps making me all this money, but what's the point of it? I can't even take a girl to a fancy restaurant because it just feels like bragging. So, like, why have money? Should I just give it away?"

"Jesus, Andy. Not everything's a crusade. Just make the money while you can, buy some cool sneakers, and then you can do good with it when you aren't so busy making it. The trick is to not spend it all on dumb shit and, like, you're clearly physically incapable of that. You can't even find a girlfriend who wants you for your money."

"She's not my girlfriend." I was being defensive because I was hoping maybe she would be someday.

"I wasn't talking about Bex, I was talking about your inability to find a girlfriend."

"Ah, well, I concede. But I'm still worried I'm not doing the right thing with the untapped energy in my savings account."

"Well, I'll keep my eyes open for weird or good shit you can do with your money. But you're fucking lucky I'm so understanding because most people would not sit here and listen to you complain about how hard it is to be so ludicrously rich."

"I am ludicrously rich," I said, smiling.

"Isn't it nice?"

"Yeah, I guess it is. Sometimes I feel like I must have earned it. Sometimes I feel like I must be worth it, like I won life. But that's bullshit. April earned this money, I'm just making it."

"OH MY GOD YOU ARE THE WORST."

"OK, sorry, *sometimes I feel* like April earned this money and I'm just making it."

"Better, but still bad."

I think I'm good at looking like I have things together on the outside, but that's only because I spend an immense amount of time worrying about it.

The book seemed to know what I should do—well, isn't that what we all want to know? Free will is *stressful*. I invited Bex over to play games, just like the book said I should, and it was actually fun. I was worried that she and Jason wouldn't get along, but it turns out she was used to people who don't share a lot of the same experiences as her.

We played a game that my parents and I used to play when I was a kid. You pick a long word that you can divide into three different words and describe it using definitions of its three different parts.

That was probably really confusing. Example: If you pick "dictionary," you say, "At first I am a penis, then I ostracize, and finally I'm light and free." The first person to guess "dick shun airy" wins.

Bex had just bent the rules a little with "First I am an explanation, then a vocal performance, then I weep, and finally I am an abbreviated sibling," but we all agreed that she was a genius when the answer was "how sing cry sis." And that led us into talking about the reasons why housing had become so unaffordable, which devolved mostly into me and Jason repeating stuff we'd learned from one of The Thread's videos.

"I mean, you two sound really smart, but really you just watch The Thread," Bex said after we'd gone on for five or six minutes.

"Oh! You just got called out so hard!" Jason said to me.

"So did you!"

"Yeah, but Bex isn't my friend! She knows nothing about me, so I am free from the deeper ramifications of this callout! Also, I told you not only white dudes watch The Thread."

"I didn't say *only* white dudes," I said, thankful that the subject was moving away from my intellectual plagiarism, but apprehensive that it was moving toward race. "I said *mostly* white dudes."

"I agree, his audience is definitely mostly white dudes," Bex said. "But, I hate to say it, it's beneficial in this country to keep an eye on what the white dudes are doing."

We all had a laugh.

Jason thought up the next clue for our game; it was "eye dent titty."

It was a fun night, and as we were wrapping up, I couldn't help but think back to *The Book of Good Times*, which seemed to think that maybe something might happen between me and Bex. I looked up and saw Jason looking at me.

"Well, I'm gonna turn in!" he proclaimed. Then he marched over to his room and firmly closed the door.

I turned to Bex, embarrassed, and gave a little smile that was meant to be both apologetic and charming. "So . . . that's Jason!"

"I love him," she said.

"I'm glad, I was worried. He isn't the most sensitive guy."

She rolled her eyes at that, but then just said, "You guys have weird fun, but it was fun. Thank you for having me over." She stood up, and I immediately stood as well, suddenly intensely nervous.

"Can I walk you to the train?" I asked.

"No." She came over to me and put her hands on my shoulders. "But I would like it if you kissed me good night."

Every nerve in my body sparkled like I was a damn high schooler as my fingers moved around her waist and we kissed.

MIRANDA

Miranda, thank you for taking the time for this." I'd gotten an interview for the job. It was over some corporate videoconferencing software that I had to download for the interview. I'd dressed up, and pulled my most identifying feature, my bright red hair, back in a tight ponytail. I had stopped short of dyeing it—that seemed too obvious a ploy.

"Of course, I am so fascinated by what you are up to," I told them honestly.

"I'm Dr. Everett Sealy, this is my colleague Tom. I work in the lab, he's an HR manager."

Remember how all of the rats in my lab were named Tom? Tom did not remind me of them. He was handsome, in his mid-thirties, with wavy dark hair. Dr. Sealy, on the other hand, was shaved to his scalp everywhere his slightly elongated head wasn't naturally bald.

"We were excited to see your application," Tom continued. "Your research looks right up our alley. Can you tell me a little about why you're interested in working at Altus?"

In my résumé, it just looked like my PhD had been taking a while, not like I'd taken a year off. That wasn't technically a lie. I had gotten through my PhD program relatively quickly, so it wasn't unusual that I would still be working on my thesis. I'd just left out the part about how I had quit temporarily to become the CEO of a start-up with famous people for a year. That was the kind of thing that would look really good on a résumé for pretty much any job except this one.

"Well," I started, sounding a little shaky, "if you'll excuse the impertinence, I can tell by who you're hiring what you're working on. It is also what I'm working on, except it seems that you've gotten further down the path. I can only make guesses what the steps you've taken are, but they've left me both intensely curious and also less interested in my own work."

My cortisol response was kicking in hard—elevated heart rate, sweaty pits, sudden urge to pee, all of it. I know the secret to lying is telling the truth, and it was definitely helping, but it was still terrifying. These people were not to be messed with.

"Simply, it seems to me that you're where the cutting edge is."

Dr. Sealy picked up here: "You are, however, in the middle of your thesis project, correct?"

"Yes, I'd be putting that on hold. I've already discussed it with my advisor." This was a lie.

"And how does he feel about that?" Tom asked.

I decided not to correct him. "Dr. Lundgren sees the excitement of the opportunity and understands. I know I'm taking a risk, but even if I'm not able to return to defend my thesis, it seems certain that this will be the better path for me."

"You know we tried to recruit Constance," Dr. Sealy said, using Professor Lundgren's first name. "She's a magnificent scientist, but she . . ." He paused.

Tom continued, more smoothly, "She turned us down."

She hadn't just turned them down. She told me that she'd told them to go fuck themselves. He seemed to be waiting for me to say something. I should have known better than to bring up Dr. Lundgren. I took control back with an argument I'd prepared. "I don't know the details of what you're up to, but you do. So the question I have is what you would suggest I do knowing what *you* know. Would you tell a young scientist to finish her PhD, or would you tell her to go work at Altus?"

"I'd tell her to go work at Altus," Dr. Sealy replied.

The business guy spoke up again then: "Just to be absolutely clear, the work we are doing is very secret and very sensitive. Do you have any potential ulterior motives for working here?"

Was he outright asking me if I was signing up specifically for espionage? I was a terrible liar! What the hell was I doing?! I heard my own voice talking, and it sounded relaxed: "I just can't not be there, I'm up all night thinking about it." I had found a truth I could tell.

The rest of the interview was standard. We talked about how we solved interpersonal problems at the lab, about my experience being managed and working with undergrads, and about my research at Berkeley. They seemed impressed by me, and to be honest I was impressed by them. They were experts, they were well paid, and they seemed like good, effective communicators. Tom seemed like a bit of a tech bro, but Dr. Sealy was exactly the kind of guy I'd get along with in a work setting. He was considerate, thoughtful, and none of his jokes were at the expense of other people. They weren't scary at all.

You always want to go into an interview with one or two questions for the people who are interviewing you. It's a signal that you want to make sure they're worth your time and talent, and it puts the power a little bit in your hands. Not too much, just enough for them to know that you're not desperate.

"Don't take this the wrong way, but what percentage chance would you guess your business has of not being around five or ten years from now?" I asked near the end of our allotted time.

They both laughed. "Zero," the business guy said.

I waited for a reply from Dr. Sealy. "Not zero," he said. "All probabilities are nonzero. But very, very small. This could be a lifelong job if you want it to be."

"That's very good to hear," I said, smelling the hint of truth in my lie.

Interview over, I needed to have a conversation with Dr. Lundgren. If I was going to leave, I needed to know what we were going to do about my research. I messaged her to ask if she could come by my lab station when she was free to talk about something important. I wanted to have the conversation on my territory, not hers. A few hours later, I heard a knock on my counter. That's how we kept from sneaking up on each other. She looked good.

"Everything OK, Miranda?"

I figured it would be easy to say it all at once, so I just straightened up, looked her in the eyes, and said, "I had a job interview today with Altus. They're going to call you for a reference . . . probably. I want to talk about what you might say to them."

"I'm going to tell them the truth."

My eyes fell, a pit opened up in my stomach, and I slouched into it.

"I'll tell them that you are a genius scientist and communicator. That you work extremely hard and are passionate and are always solving problems fast and well. I might leave out some facts, like, for example, that you hate them."

I had never imagined that this conversation would go so well. She looked concerned, but also deeply supportive.

I let out a sigh as my back muscles unclenched, "Thank you, Dr. Lundgren. Oh god, thank you."

"What are you doing, Miranda?"

"I have to go to Puerto Rico. I can't not go."

"Did I imagine talking with you in my office and both of us agreeing that these people are trash people?"

"No."

"Do you still think they're trash people?"

"I think that, if I'm not there, they'll be even more trash." I was getting defensive.

She was quiet for a second and then pulled up a stool and sat. "I can't tell you what to do, and I'll support it, but I need you to tell me why."

"Whatever they're doing, they're going to do it with or without me. Maybe I can have them do it in a less garbage way. And if I can't, or I find out something really bad, maybe I can tell people about it."

She was quiet for a really long time.

"Miranda, that is a huge thing you are asking of yourself. I am not young anymore, but I remember being your age, and I am not going to tell you to put a lid on that ambition, but it's going to be hard to pull against their culture as it pulls on you. It will be very hard not to fall into their version of the story. But what worries me more than that is what happens if they find you out.

"There is a lot of money on the line here, a lot. I don't know what these people are really like. They could blackball you, you probably wouldn't ever work in pharma again. Or they could dig up dirt on you, lie about you, maybe even worse things than that."

I thought back to my job interview. They did not seem like henchmen who would ruin a person for sharing industrial secrets, but I also had never met a henchperson, so what did I know?

"Miranda?"

I must have been zoned out for a second.

"I don't care." I did care.

She smiled with a hint of mischief. "Good."

"Am I getting the job?" I could barely believe that it was a possibility. They had lots of candidates, and they'd find out that I was April's friend and disqualify me. But Dr. Lundgren was talking about it like it was going to happen.

"I think you are, and I think you're going to leave. And I'll keep your lab station open until you come back."

"What if I don't come back?"

"Something is telling me you will. But this is going to be hard. Probably much harder than you think."

It seemed like she suddenly wasn't just supporting a decision she didn't necessarily agree with, she was actually encouraging me. That was making all of this feel much more real.

"I don't know that I've even really made up my mind yet."

"Oh, you have. You just don't quite know what a made-up mind looks like."

I didn't understand what she meant, but I left it alone and said, "I won't be allowed to tell you what I'm working on. But would it be OK if I did that anyway?"

"That would be a serious crime, and honestly, yes, I want you to do that."

"What? Even if they aren't doing anything iffy?"

"Miranda," she said, leaning toward me, "these people are dangerous and they're moving too fast. I'm terrified that they're doing human tests without proper clinical trials. I think they've figured out something powerful and dangerous. If I could find someone I want to put that level of faith in, it would be someone like you, not someone like Peter Petrawicki. You have the perfect background. They need people who have worked on neuro-control interfaces and there aren't that many of you in the world. I think we're the only ones who can do this."

"That could end our careers, though. You were the one just telling me how dangerous this is. We could go to prison."

"I'm ready for the risks. I just wanted to make sure you knew what they were."

I had known Dr. Constance Lundgren for almost six years now, and this was not behavior I had come to expect from her.

"Is everything OK with you?"

"You think I'm acting strange. Maybe I am. Maybe I've been playing it too safe. Remarkable things don't get done by people waiting for the status quo to crawl along."

"But we're not doing a remarkable thing, we're trying to slow them down from doing something remarkable too fast."

Her eyes got big, and she literally reached out and *grabbed my arm*.

"That!" she said too loudly for the conversation, leaning close to my face. "That right there, that is it. You found it in your own mind. That voice that tells you that the only way to do something amazing is if it's big and flashy and all yours. Turn it off." She was honestly scaring me a little. Her voice got quiet again, but the urgency remained. "That obsession with impact is an infection and it's getting worse. Altus wants to make it worse. You're going to Puerto Rico so that you can protect us from ourselves. Do you know what I think the most amazing thing the human race has ever done is? It isn't the weapons we've built, and it certainly isn't the weapons we've used, it's the weapons we *haven't* used. Idiots like Peter Petrawicki talk all the time about self-control, about how they carry the burden of changing the world on their shoulders. But they do that with an ambition turned in on themselves. They want to be the voice and the face and the mind behind the change. In truth, they have no self-control at all. They are slaves to their ambitions and to their need to feel admired. The truest strength is shouldering the burden of care."

"Is that a quote?" It sounded like a quote.

"Do you get what I mean?"

"I think I do."

"What I want to say is that, often, restraint is far more remarkable than action. So don't let it not amaze you because, Miranda, you amaze me. Start wrapping up your work. You're going to get that job."

While I was waiting to see if that was true, I was lucky to have a new side project. A package had arrived from Maya.

Miranda, the day I texted you about that dress (which I bought, btw) I found something weird. Here is one of them. I don't even know what to call it exactly, maybe it's just some plastic costume thing, but I have reason to believe that it's important. I kept three others here. If there's anything you can tell me, text me as soon as you know absolutely anything about them, even if it's just that they're weird. Anyway, I hope things are going well in California!

Maya

Out of the padded plastic envelope fell a gorgeous hunk of something with a low density and high thermal conductivity. That was strange enough, but there was something different about it that most people would just say was "weird" but that I didn't have too much trouble putting my finger on: This stuff was *hard*.

With a few quick tests, I had a range I could place it in. It was less hard than a diamond (which was good, because otherwise I would have had to drop everything and start a lab just to study it) but significantly harder than steel. It was more like high-performance ceramics, except it was definitely not ceramic. After only a half hour of poking and prodding I had plenty of information to text Maya, but I kept poking. Another half hour after that, I realized I was putting texting her off.

I never really got to figure out what that night between me and April meant. It was a onetime thing, but I didn't know if it was going to stay that way. It was . . . uuggghhh . . . This is all very personal, and I feel weird about talking about it in a story that is about, like, saving human civilization, but it was my first time with a woman. It was a really big deal for me because of that, and also because it was *April May*. I had never completely gotten over her celebrity. I got the feeling that our night together was not a big deal for April. But I felt like Maya and I should talk it through, maybe? The way she didn't ever seem open to that made me feel like it was because she had written off any possible real friendship with me.

Anyway, I thought through all our history and then I just swallowed it and texted Maya.

> *That stuff is weird, too weird. Nothing has been that weird since Carl.*

> *I'm going to keep investigating.*

> *But only because it's interesting, not because I think I'm going to find out anything that will be helpful to you.*

She wrote back a few minutes later.

> *Thanks. I'm going to try to track down where it came from.*

I stared at the text, trying to glean meaning from it. The more time I took, the more it seemed like the kind of text I would write to my worst enemy. After an eternity of staring, I mustered up the courage to text her back.

> *OK, I'm trying to get a job at Peter Petrawicki's lab, so if I disappear, it's probably because I'm in Puerto Rico.*

My phone rang immediately—it was Maya. My heart started pounding. This was scarier than interviewing with Altus.

"Hello?" I asked tentatively.

"Explain yourself."

I did my best to do that. I think I was complete, though I wouldn't say I was articulate.

"And you think this is the kind of thing that Miranda Beckwith would do?" she demanded. "Or is it the kind of thing April May would do?"

Goddamn, no one had put their finger on that part of it yet.

"I think it's the kind of thing I'd do?"

"It's not."

"But it's science?" Everything I said was coming out as a question.

"This is about April and that's fine, but I need you to say that to me."

"It's about the science and about April. It's about figuring out what this fucker is doing and taking him down if I can. And it's about figuring out who I am and what the world is without her."

She was quiet for a while and then said, "I think we're all figuring out who we are without her."

"I'm sorry," I blurted out.

She replied immediately. "For what?"

Oh god, uh . . . which thing to say first?

"That we couldn't protect her . . . and also that I slept with her."

"You hooked up with April?"

My brain was yelling, *FUCKING IDIOT!* But I replied quietly, "Oh, I thought you knew."

She laughed. "Jesus. Is that why you've been so weird around me? I thought you just didn't like me."

I didn't know what to say.

She continued, "Miranda, if I wasn't friends with anyone April hooked up with in college, I wouldn't have had many options. The fact that April hooked up with you in no way makes me think less of you. We weren't together, she's hot and charming. Do you still have feelings for her?"

"No!" I rushed to tell her. "I mean, I miss her. I don't know, Maya. I'm just so confused." My mind was working more slowly than my mouth. "You understand yourself, I don't even know if I'm gay. Or a lesbian. Or bi? Am I bi? I'm twenty-five years old, how do I not know this about myself!"

When she spoke, which wasn't immediately, her voice had become so gentle that it almost felt like a different person. "If I were with you, I would hug you so hard right now. I'm sorry. We're all going at our own speed."

I was crying now, and through my tears I asked, "Why are you being so nice to me?"

"Miranda Beckwith, you take that back. I'm being nice to you because I like you and you're a good person and we're friends and we're both grieving April." Now it sounded like she was crying too.

"How did we get here?" I asked. "I was just trying to tell you about Altus."

"Right, well, that is also important. Listen, Peter was always appealing to a lot of people. The thing that he tapped into didn't go away, it just lost its name. People are *still* killing each other over this.

He's a bad guy, but he built up his connections and he's made it into value for himself. But I don't see what you can do about it."

"I'm going to go if I can. I have to. But maybe I won't be able to. I might not get the job."

"You'll get the job." Everyone seemed convinced of this except me. "But look. You're not April. Don't take stupid risks like April."

That made me feel like she cared about me, which made me feel really good. And the fact that it made me feel good made me feel silly for caring so much.

"I am not April. I will not take stupid risks like April." I was getting better at lying.

MAYA

*H*elping Miranda was the most normal and wonderful and real thing I had done in months. There is nothing like being needed by someone. Relationship drama? Friends sleeping with exes? That was stuff I had experience with. It felt important but also normal. I think we're all ultimately searching for normal but important.

Miranda also helped distract me from the new reality I was in. This reality was one where a game called Fish somehow knew where I was and had sent vaguely threatening men to acquire rocks I had bought at a place called Cowtown.

Let's go back to that day. I was too frightened to go back to my Airbnb, so I just drove around, thinking and worrying. And that's when I remembered something I had done very intentionally but had completely forgotten about.

I pulled the truck off on a long stretch of road so I could see a good distance both ways, and then I took the business card out of the paper bag that held the rocks.

Kurt Butler
EarthforgeMinerals.com
(856) 294-6319

I'd told Clara to convince Kurt "Probably Has Some Red Hats" Butler that the rocks were valuable and tell him that she would buy as many as he could get his hands on. And if I was right, Kurt Butler would soon be trying to get more of his special rocks to sell. I didn't want to be anywhere but in a vehicle I could use to drive away from strange men anyway, so I went back to Cowtown.

I waited outside of the entrance, hoping that Kurt had driven his cable repair van so I could spot him. The flea market closed at four, so I was clear until then. I used that time to research Kurt Butler, which was fairly easy even just with a phone. He had a *very* public Facebook. It was like he had actively turned off every possible privacy setting.

Some posts were about geology and paleontology, and then a bunch of them were about grave internal and external threats to America. So, yeah.

I didn't really care about his politics, though. I honestly didn't think Kurt "Very Concerned About the Future of Western Civilization" Butler was some vital part of this story. I just thought he had found some rocks, and I needed to know where they came from, and he sure wasn't going to come out and tell me.

While I waited, I opened up my podcast app and searched for "Fish Game." It wasn't long before I was listening to *Fishing with Joe and Tim*, which was basically a news service for people who played the game.

I quickly found that it wasn't like other RGs because you didn't have to pay for it. It started with a WhatsApp message sent seemingly at random. It requested proof that people had completed a series of increasingly bizarre tasks. The first task was always the same: You had to take a picture of yourself holding a live fish. Then maybe you'd have to record yourself telling a friend you love them or sawing a dictionary in half.

The deeper you got, the weirder the tasks got, and the quieter the people completing them became online. Aside from it being free, it wasn't like other reality games in two ways:

1. You could only play Fish if you got the message, and there didn't seem to be any pattern to who got the messages except they always came through WhatsApp.

2. People who had completed the game were notoriously
   quiet about the later levels, and seemed bizarrely enthusias-
   tic that the rewards for completing the game were
   worthwhile.

I was pretty infected with their unquestioned enthusiasm about
the whole thing when the Cowtown parking lot finally began empty-
ing out.

At around 4:30, I spotted Kurt Butler's van as it pulled out of the
lot. I followed. Kurt did not go home, nor did he go to someplace
where he might acquire more of the rocks. I was surprised to find
that he went to a service call at a hotel in Wolton. As nice hotels got
nicer and cheap motels became aggressively cheaper, the Wolton
Motor Inn had been stranded in the middle. New awnings and a fresh
paint job couldn't obscure the outdated facade, and it looked like an
attached restaurant had been closed for renovations that were no longer happening. It was trying its best to be nice, but it just wasn't.

Kurt's van pulled around the back to what I assumed was a service entrance. I thought about following him, but that seemed too
obvious.

But then a half hour passed and Kurt still hadn't come back out.
And then another half hour. Eventually, my curiosity got the better
of me.

I pulled around the corner, and there was Kurt "PBS Is Fake
News" Butler, in the quickly darkening evening, rummaging through
a heap of detritus at the back of the hotel. As soon as I was all the way
around the corner, he looked up at me, at first guilty and then confused as our eyes locked and, I assumed, he recognized me. I should
have stayed calm. I should have pretended like I was just witnessing
a weird cable guy rummaging through a trash pile. But instead I
freaked out and hit the accelerator way too hard. I wasn't familiar
with the truck. It had more kick than expected, and I was looking
more at Kurt than the road. I drove into a utility pole.

Kurt, familiar with utility poles *and* my face, then needed to make a decision. Did he get in his van and ignore maybe the weirdest thing that had happened to him in his whole life (the Black girl he had messed with at Cowtown for overfondling his weird rocks snuck around the back of a sleazy hotel in a Nissan Frontier to witness him dumpster diving, only to then drive into a pole)? Or did he walk over to ask if I was OK and also what on earth I was doing there?

I didn't like my odds, so as Kurt began disentangling himself from the pile of old shelves, bar stools, and wiring, I threw the Nissan in reverse. Luckily, the truck had enough horsepower to get me off the curb. Kurt was running up to me, yelling, "Hey! What the fuck? What the fuck is going on?!" I fumbled with the shifter, and then I was off, Kurt running behind me.

So, good news, Kurt "Very Probably Thinks the Deep State Is Out to Get Him" Butler and I did not have a physical, or even verbal, confrontation. Indeed, Kurt Butler still (thank god) knew nothing about me. I could only hope that he hadn't gotten a look at my license plate, though I'm not sure what he'd be able to do if he did.

I drove for half an hour, taking random turns, not paying attention to where I was going, before pulling into the parking lot of a Dunkin' Donuts to check how jacked my truck was. It was jacked enough that I spent the next hour on the phone with the rental company and my insurance company, feeling deeply incapable. But I didn't cry and I didn't call my mom because I'd helped lead an international movement and, damn it, I could handle a fender bender.

And then I went back to the hotel because now I knew that either:

1. Kurt Butler was doing some kind of official business in a trash pile behind a gross hotel.

Or:

2. That is where he had found the rocks.

I decided that I'd start inside because I wanted to ask a question. The check-in desk had been sprayed with stucco to make it look like stone. And yes, an Egyptian Eye of Horus had been pressed into the stucco, because it was Wolton, so of course it had.

I walked up to the check-in desk to a gray-haired man in his fifties.

"Hi, I'm sorry to trouble you about this, but have you been visited by Carson Communications recently?"

"Goddamn it, this is the last time, we are not doing anything hinky here!"

"I'm sorry?"

"You're in and out of here every week telling us that we're up to whatever, I dunno, but we're just a hotel. Our guests use the internet... when it works, which it doesn't more often than not. I'm sick of this."

He had a North Jersey accent, which I had discovered was different from the more Philly-inspired accents I heard day to day in Wolton. I love the accent, and I don't mind the lack of pretense that often comes with it. Still, I was caught off guard.

"I'm sorry, I just have a friend who works for them and he said he might be here." I thought of this lie on the fly, and I was pretty proud of it.

"Well, tell him he better not be because we're not doing anything, and they better start solving some problems instead of accusing *us* of being the problem!"

"I'm sorry, this sounds really annoying. Can you tell me more about what they say is going on?"

"They say that the whole neighborhood is down because we're using too much internet. Now, I'm not saying there aren't times, like evenings, when, y'know, people are watching a lot of pornos. But we've had high speed here for twenty years and nothing's changed. They even made me go through each room to make sure no one had hooked up something to steal our internet. I did it, and like I said, there was nothing. But they keep coming in, telling us that we're the reason the internet's down. Well, it's down for us too, and it's costing me customers."

"I've got a good friend who runs the coffee shop in town, and they're in the same boat. Hard to have a coffee shop with no Wi-Fi." I said this mostly in the hopes that he'd keep talking.

"Did they accuse him of being the problem?"

"No." I laughed. "I don't think so anyway."

"Well, that sounds nice. They're in here every week telling me I'm up to no good. I'm just trying to make a living here."

"When was the last time you saw them?"

"A couple weeks ago now, I guess. And then I catch the guy sneaking around the back looking through our stuff!"

"The cable guy?"

"Yeah, he was back there looking for who knows what. I've seen homeless guys do that, trying to find something to sell. But this guy's got a job. What is he doing going through our trash? You ask your friend about that, OK?"

"That does sound like him, actually. He's always looking for a way to make a quick buck."

"Tell him to do it some other place!"

My heart was pounding with the lies and the unapologetic North Jersey flair for confrontation. I decided there wasn't much more I was going to get.

"Well, I'm really sorry this has been so rough. I'll give Kurt a piece of my mind for you when I see him."

"You do that."

I got back in my truck, drove out of view of the front windows, and then pulled around the back of the hotel. It was time to dive into that pile of detritus that Kurt "Everything I Don't Like Is a Conspiracy" Butler had been illicitly wading through earlier that evening.

I wished I had gloves. It was cold out, and, under a dusting of snow that had just begun to fall, a lot of the stuff looked broken or dangerous. It was fully dark now, so everything I saw was under the harsh glare of my cell phone flashlight. What I found was what you would expect. Trash. Two soggy bar stools with split faux-leather tops, a printer and an old CRT monitor, an ancient mop and its broken bucket, some warped plywood, a bike frame, scraps of carpet, Pop-Tart boxes, and a ton of empty water bottles. Maybe this is where the neighbors all brought their junk. But what there wasn't was anything at all that you wouldn't expect to find in a big pile of trash behind a crappy hotel.

So then I decided to look deeper. It felt just the slightest bit like the Dream, a shadow of that sensation of knowing that, somewhere, something was waiting to be found. I lifted up a piece of splotched pink carpet and found, underneath, a couple hypodermic needles and a soggy old book.

"Nope!" I said aloud, and then I tiptoed my way out of the mess as fast as felt safe. I couldn't help but imagine what my dad would think if he saw me in that moment. Then I got mad at myself for caring. And then I got mad at myself for giving up.

I mean, it was dumb. I was at a hotel, so it was probably a Bible. But it wasn't really big enough to be a Bible. OK, this wasn't actually like the Dream, it was colder and muddier and with a higher chance of contracting hepatitis. The weather was always so nice in the Dream, and you never got tired. And you never had to talk to other people. This mystery sucked.

I shuffled back to the disgusting pink carpet, lifted it up again, and carefully picked up the book.

"The Book of Good Times," said the cover.

I took it back to the truck and started reading.

Do not tell anyone about this. Do not post an Instagram story of this or tweet it or call a friend and share it. This is a magic book, but its magic only works for you, and it only works if no one else knows. It won't always make sense, but it knows more than you. So unless

I tell you differently, clam up, buttercup. Let's get straight to what you want to know.

You're safe, for now. I've made sure of that. Sorry about the nonsense at Cowtown, you don't have to worry about Fish for a little while.

Whenever I thought about the Cowtown nonsense for too long, it got too weird too fast. Someone who was running this RG must have known where I was *and* that I had gotten a bunch of money out of an ATM. Either that or they had been watching me. And then they mobilized a bunch of players to come for me? I only thought it was possible because it had happened. But this! This book was even more unsettling. I felt like stopping reading right there, but my eyes caught the next line, and it pulled me in like a fishing net.

You're on the right track. You got this far on your own, but now you need to do the hardest thing yet. You need to wait. You need to go back to your Airbnb and look after your potato. You need to have Derek and his family over for dinner. You need to stop looking at the ground and start looking at the sky.

I know that stepping back from this search will be hard, and why would you take my word for it? I'm just a book that was under a soggy carpet. But that's where I needed to be for you to find me right now. Maybe I could tell you a story that would make you listen to me. I don't know that you'll like hearing it, but I don't know how else to make you listen.

How about this:

When you were a kid, you were afraid of wooden furniture. Not, like, furniture that had wood in it, but the ornate carved stuff that your parents had in just one room in your home. The rest of the house was modern, with stone countertops and metal-edged corners, one of which is how you got that scar above your lip. Weird then that the furniture that scared you was the rounded, curving, hand-carved hardwoods of that one fancy room. Was it because you knew that room was only for adults? Or because that room was where you found out your grandmother was dying? I don't know.

But when you were eleven or twelve, too old, really, for this, you found something out. You were at school and admitted to a friend that you never liked sitting in the school's wood chairs, and she told you that was silly because wood is just trees.

That's when you found out that the wood from trees was what wood furniture was made out of. You knew that trees were made of wood and furniture was made of wood, but you thought they were just named after each other, not the same thing. And that's when you stopped being afraid of wood.

I knew what was coming next. Tears were building up. I had spent months pretending that hope and knowledge were the same thing, but they weren't. I kept reading, despite my tears, pressing the book into my lap to keep my hands from shaking.

You told that story to your girlfriend one night because she was scared. Do you even remember what it was that she was afraid of? The first day of an internship? An upcoming meeting with a professor? You probably don't remember. But I bet you remember telling the story, because it was funny, and you laughed together, and there wasn't any lesson. There was just the vulnerability of sharing something from your past. The story helped, like you knew it would.

You used to be afraid of wooden furniture until you found out it was made of trees. I don't know how many people know that, but I do know that only April knew about that conversation you had, and that even she wouldn't share it unless she had to.

I know that this is going to feel wrong to you, but you got here too soon. You need to go home, make some tea, leave the cable guy alone, and then, in three weeks, you need to come back here—back to the service area of the Wolton Motor Inn—and then the story will start up again.

The rest of the book was blank. I was physically shaking. I couldn't drive. I couldn't do anything. I just sat in the truck for an hour and cried. And then I drove back to my Airbnb and found, lifting a clump of dirt from out of the pot, the tiny sprout of a potato plant. I flicked the dirt off of it and touched the leaf with my finger, like I was afraid I might break it.

ANDY

Every day, I read news stories about people whose retirement accounts were dropping just as they needed the money the most. Meanwhile, the book had me dodging every drop and snagging every gain.

I had a massive soapbox to speak from, sudden and dramatically increasing wealth, and apparently a girlfriend. But no matter what, our minds find reasons to be frustrated. My mind was no exception. Here's what I couldn't stop focusing on.

Radicalization follows fear and insecurity, and as dissatisfaction grew, fewer and fewer people were interested in my nuanced, chill takes. I had to live up to my brand and to April's legacy, but more and more I felt like I was just being told all of the things I couldn't do or say.

At the same time, I had to watch as people with more radical views got a bigger and bigger slice of the conversation. One day I watched two videos back-to-back, one about how wealthy societies inevitably fall to outsiders who have had to live through difficulty and thus value human lives less that was barely veiled xenophobia and the next about how wealth inequality only ever ended with violent revolution and that we needed to be ready for that revolution. Both videos had over ten million views and they were both only days old.

Even with a magical book telling me how to get rich, I felt like I was on a fast path to irrelevancy.

I was watching The Thread videos every day, which was something, considering that he only published one every week or two. All I could think was that I could never say half of what he was saying without needing to completely restructure my brand and let a ton of people down. I was supposed to be a voice of reason, but being reasonable was quickly going out of style.

And so, one day, I just sent a tweet.

@TheThread, I'd love to talk. andy.skampt@gmail.com.

About twenty minutes later I received an email from hastilysanctionedfoul@gmail.com that said only "confirmation that this is me coming on Twitter in five minutes" and then, five minutes after that, The Thread's Twitter account tweeted "hastily sanctioned foul."

After the tweet, I emailed The Thread.

Subject: I Like Your Content

Hi, I've been following your channel since launch, and I've loved watching it grow and succeed. Your ideas are excellent, your additions to this conversation are deeply necessary. I think this is only the beginning of your influence, and I am somewhat envious of your ability to reach an audience without tying your face or name to the content.

If you ever want someone to talk to who is familiar with stuff like this, or just to bounce ideas off of, I wanted to make myself available.

Andy

A response came within the hour.

Subject: Re: I Like Your Content

Andy,

I appreciate you reaching out. I am going to tell you a secret now, and I will be very disappointed if you share it.

I do not work on The Thread alone. We are a consortium of anonymous experts. I think that your expertise would be extremely valuable to the conversation, but membership in The Thread is not taken lightly. We are a group of people dedicated to changing society fundamentally. The YouTube channel is only the beginning of that. We have a large endowment and the support of some of the most powerful individuals in the world. We are here to shape the stories that humanity will tell about itself in the future, and we would like you to join us.

If you would be interested in that, there are a few things you need to know:

1. Any attempt to uncover anyone's identity—even asking simple personal questions about age, location, or marital status—will result in a permanent ban from the channel.

2. All chats in The Thread, private or not, are viewable by me.

3. You will be introduced by your expertise, and no other information will be shared about you. If you share personal information about yourself, you will be banned.

4. All members are vetted by me.

5. I make all final decisions regarding content, membership, banning, and strategy.

6. We go by numbers, not names. I am One because I started and fund The Thread. You, if you joined, would be Twelve.

7. We assess membership rates based on net worth. If you have a net worth under the national average, we pay you $50,000 per year. If your net worth is over the national average, you pay us $1 for every $100 above the national average. So if your net worth is $1,000,000, that's $850,000 more than the national average. So you would pay us $8,500 per year.

We have a great deal more work to do, and I think you would be an extremely valuable addition to our team, but I understand if you aren't interested.

Thank you for your kind words,

One

Well, that was something. The fact that something so secretive could be a group of people was really counterintuitive. Eleven people all sharing the responsibility? That was intense, but it made a lot of sense as well. The videos were just too good for one person to make, there had to be a budget. But it was the "most powerful individuals in the world" line that really got my heart thumping.

If I really wanted to make a difference in ways I felt my identity wouldn't allow, this was it! There was a problem, though. If we were really going to go off my new net worth, which was now up over $100 million, it was a lot to ask. I figured the best policy was honesty, so I replied.

One,

Thank you for your quick response. I am fascinated by this. I have two questions.

1. How do you know that I won't share this information?

2. My net worth has recently increased dramatically, and the amount I would pay you under your scheme would be over a million dollars. I

don't know how to pay someone that much money. And also, it feels wrong to spend so much money to be part of something even this cool.

I also need to weigh my existing obligations. But overall it just seems like a lot of money. Does it make sense for me to pay that much?

Andy

The response was almost immediate.

Andy,

1. I don't think you would share the information because you aren't a dick.

2. Membership rates are nonnegotiable. I'll work with you on transferring the money if you wish to join.

Thank you,

One

Well, I guess that was that, then. I wasn't going to transfer a million bucks to an anonymous rando, even if he was a very cool anonymous rando, without a lot of thought, so I decided to do something that the book had told me to do.

I'd been putting it off since even before the book, actually.

I think that tragedy either brings people together or drives them apart. You can find either comfort or a constant reminder. April had always been the reason Maya and I were friends, and so once she was gone, we floated apart immediately. Calling her kinda scared me. I thought maybe she didn't care that much about me, or maybe she thought that I didn't care that much about her. But I had been thinking about her, so was glad the book made me pick up the phone.

"What have you been up to?" I asked after the main pleasantries were done.

"I still spend a lot of time on the Som." It was an answer, but it seemed intentionally vague. Like answering the question in a way that also changed the subject. She was always good at that. I let her be good at it this time.

"Do they talk at all about The Thread?" I asked her, since it was on my mind and also the Som was good at teasing out secrets.

"Ohhh, yeah. Very yeah. Some people think it's April, but that's bullshit. The Thread is way too smart to be April."

I laughed. Every corner of the internet had a different theory about who The Thread was. I had gone Occam's razor and assumed that it was just one person, but now I knew it really was a conspiracy! It made sense that the Som was mixing Thread conspiracies with April conspiracies. The Som was conspiracy central.

"Sorry, did that sound mean?" she asked.

"No, I was laughing because it's true and also because it's a completely ludicrous idea that The Thread is April."

"Yeah," she said. I wasn't sure what to say, but then she continued. "I'm sorry I haven't been in touch, Andy. I'm still really sad."

I almost hung up the phone because I knew I was going to start crying. It took a huge amount of willpower to just stay on the phone and let her hear me lose it a bit.

"It's OK, Andy. I know it's hard," she said. She wasn't crying, which made me feel like I was being weak.

"I don't think she's dead," I blurted out.

"Finally," Maya replied matter-of-factly. She had seemed depressed to me in recent group chats, but now she seemed solid and confident, if anxious.

"What?"

"I mean, of course she's not dead. People are just moving on because that's the logical thing to do. What else *can* you do? But she's not dead. I've been saying it the whole time and everyone just looks at me with pity. I don't know what she is, Andy, but she's not dead."

"Will we find her?" I asked. She seemed so certain that April was alive. I had gotten jolts of that hope from the book, but I wanted more of it.

There was tension in Maya's voice when she responded, and it felt like she was answering a different question than the one I was asking: "Wherever she is, I know that I'll never forgive myself. I might not ever forgive her. She was an idiot and she ruined everything."

"Jeez, Maya."

"I'm just saying it out loud. We've all thought it. What would you say to her if you had the chance?"

"Oh god, I don't know. 'Where have you been? What are the Carls?'"

"That's what you'd ask her . . . What do you want to tell her?"

"Oh, that I'm sorry and I love her and we need her back and the world is falling apart without her and that she was an idiot a bunch of times, but that doesn't means she's a bad person," I said.

"That's good," she said, quietly now, calming down.

Why had I been so afraid of this conversation? Was it that I didn't want to talk about April? Or was it that I was afraid Maya and I didn't make sense as friends without her? Maybe both, but both of those fears were misplaced. We shared something hard and pure: We both had lost our best friend. First we lost her to fame, and then we lost her for real.

"Anything else interesting going on?" I changed the topic.

"Oh, well, yes. I don't really know how to explain it. Have you heard anything about Fish?"

"Fish?" I said.

"It's a reality game, except you don't have to pay and the reward for winning is apparently better than infinite orgasms."

"I have heard nothing about it," I said.

"Well, if you hear anything, let me know. I think it might have something to do with Peter Petrawicki's Altus thing. Or maybe with the Carls. It seems weird. Like Carl weird."

"Oh, did you hear about Miranda?"

"I heard she was trying to get a job with Altus. I told her it sounded reckless, but I didn't try to stop her."

"Yeah, that's pretty much the conversation I had with her too," I lied. "I hope she doesn't do anything dumb."

"She's smarter than all of us combined."

"Smart people do lots of dumb things."

The book was right. I needed to talk to Maya. We talked about how I was thinking about communities and that I was taking a break from being constantly present on social media, but that I still thought it was extremely important for me to keep an eye on my feeds. She told me about her parents, and she gave me an update on April's family, who I hadn't kept in touch with at all.

I felt so much better afterward. This is going to sound silly, but I felt more real. It felt more like the last year of my life really did happen, and that the life I was leading really was a life—not some bizarre game I was playing, but a way to live. My way to live.

At one point she said to me something I'll never forget: "If someone had told me that Andy Skampt would become a thoughtful and respected leader two years ago, I would not have believed them. But having watched it happen, it actually makes a lot of sense."

There was nothing she could have said that would make me happier, and there was no one in the world I would have rather heard it from.

Maybe I didn't need to join The Thread to feel important.

But then again, of course I did.

MIRANDA

I had given up on hearing back from Altus and was settling back into a routine. Every weekday morning I walked from my marvelously overpriced downtown Berkeley apartment to the lab. Every afternoon I walked back home. And every evening I went for a run.

I think I ran for distraction as much as anything. The rhythm of feet pounding and heart beating and breath flowing in and out. It's as close as I can get to making my mind turn off.

At the lab, I was going through the motions with the Toms, pushing atoms around and simulating nerve clusters and occasionally running fruitless tests on Maya's weird rock thingy. And while my simulations ran, or I waited for data to crunch, I would scroll through Twitter. Sometimes I scrolled through normal Twitter, but I also had a bad habit of going back in time. I'd just do an advanced search for April's tweets from the current week a year ago and read through, remembering how exciting that period was. It all seemed so silly and trivial then. I wanted it back. I remember specifically that that's what I was doing when an unknown number popped up on my screen.

"Hello?"

"Miranda, this is Dr. Everett Sealy from Altus, we spoke a couple weeks ago on a video conference." He seemed confident and comfortable, like he'd made similar calls a thousand times.

"Yes! Hello, I've been excited to hear from you." My armpits were immediately sweaty.

"We were wondering if we could have one final interview with you on-site."

"On-site?"

"Yes, here in Puerto Rico. We'd fly you out."

"So, I'd come out, talk to you in person, and then fly back and then wait to hear if I got the job?"

"It's not that big of a deal. No passport required even."

By this point in the conversation I had already looked up flights to San Juan, which were around ten hours nonstop, and said, "I don't actually know where you are in Puerto Rico."

"That's a little complicated, but you don't have to worry about travel, that's all been handled. If you're interested in continuing the conversation, we'd like you to fly out tomorrow."

"Tomorrow?" I said immediately, without thinking.

"I know that's sudden, but we only have two speeds here, complete standstill and extremely fast. We have a flight booked for you from SFO to Miami, we'll pick you up there."

"You'll pick me up?"

"Yes, our campus isn't close to the San Juan airport, so we've chartered a flight for you from Miami. A few other recruits will be joining you. We'll email you the details as soon as you confirm."

"What if I'm not able to get away from work?"

"Your work . . ." he said, "is not so important that you should miss this."

I didn't say anything to that, and eventually he continued. "So, I'll see you tomorrow?"

I swallowed. "I'll see you tomorrow."

My first stop after the call was Dr. Lundgren's office.

"They want me to fly to Puerto Rico tomorrow."

"Good god, of course they do. Jesus, textbook asshole. I've been recruited before, and it's either done honestly and thoughtfully, or it's done like a magic trick. This is the magic-trick kind. They're starting by knocking you off balance, they'll continue by impressing the shit out of you. Then they'll send you back home without any real information to wait for their shitty offer."

"Do you think I'll find out anything useful there?"

"In an interview? No. It'll all be standard. They're looking for competence and communication and 'cultural fit.'" If you can ever get yourself a no-nonsense mentor like Dr. Lundgren, NEVER LET THEM GO.

"Ugh, I get the feeling that I'm not going to have the best vibe with these people."

"No, but you get what they're about, and you can fake it." She had a glint in her eye I'd never seen before. "And, Miranda, they'll take your phone from you the moment you arrive. They're not idiots. Go get a prepaid cell phone and text me the number, just in case you want to take quick photos or ask me questions. You don't want to be completely isolated."

In Miami, I was shuffled away from the main airport by a man holding a sign that read "Beckwith." We took his car to a separate tiny airport that was somehow hiding just outside the big airport. It had free coffee and cookies and big TVs and comfy leather armchairs. There were no gates, just a pair of sliding glass doors that opened onto the tarmac.

I dragged my roller bag over the tiled floor, looking at the handful of other people lounging around the airport. There was a family with two young children, a couple pilots sharing a coffee, a couple guys in business suits, and two guys in their late twenties watching cable news and chatting. I felt like it wasn't impossible that they were also headed to Altus, so I walked toward them.

And then Dr. Everett Sealy's bald head came around a corner. He locked eyes with me, and his face cracked into a smile.

"We're all here!" he declared. "Miranda, this is Sid"—he gestured to a well-built, handsome East Asian guy—"and this is Paxton"—he nodded toward a kinda scrawny white guy, his brown hair poking out from under a gray knitted beanie. We all shook hands, and Dr. Sealy, who looked like he'd just received a Christmas present, continued, "No need to waste any more time, let's get going!"

The pilots who had been sitting with their coffee then stood up, smiling, and introduced themselves to me, having apparently already met the rest of the crowd. One of the pilots said, "If you want to use the restroom, now is a good time. There's a head on the plane, but it's a bit awkward in there."

So there was some toilet time, which I also used to freshen my face a bit, and then we walked through the doors and up to a private jet.

A. Private. Jet.

I kept waiting to go through security, but apparently that isn't a thing if you own the plane. I took a moment to watch Sid and Paxton's reactions, which were both suitably wide-eyed. Likewise, I watched Dr. Sealy watch them, his head gleaming in the sun. He looked genuinely happy to be giving some young people a cool and unique experience, though that could easily have been because he was excited to see his plan to impress us was working.

In the end, private planes are like planes but smaller. There was more leg room, and there were unlimited snacks. Two of the seats faced forward and two faced back, so we were all looking at each other the whole flight. That made it so we pretty much had to chat. Luckily, Dr. Sealy was good at keeping everything from getting awkward.

First he got us to open up about what we did for work. Knit-hat-wearing Paxton worked on machine learning algorithms. Well-built Sid had been working for a software company doing design and what they called "UX" or "user experience." Basically, he figured out what the software would actually look like and how best to guide the user around inside of it.

I was definitely the youngest person in the plane.

"So," Dr. Sealy said after I'd finished explaining my research, "what do you all think Altus is up to?"

"I didn't think you'd want us speculating in front of each other," I said, surprising myself a little.

"Not at all! Obviously you've all been thinking about it. And here's a secret. If you give smart people a bunch of ingredients, different people will come up with different ideas. Each of those ideas probably has merit, and none of them will be the exact thing you're doing. But it might still be really valuable. So, what do you think?"

Sid chimed in first. "We all know it's some kind of brain-machine interface, right?" Paxton and I nodded. "The usefulness of a robust connection of inputs and outputs is limitless, right? What's the focus? I don't know, I don't think there has to be a focus. Though it is very curious that so many computer scientists seem to be involved. That makes me think that the bandwidth of the connection is high, and that there may be a novel use beyond the obvious."

"The obvious being," I said, "treating disease?"

"That first, yes, but also possibly recreation. People want the Dream back. Maybe we could give it to them."

Dr. Sealy's eyes widened at this, but he just said, "Paxton?"

He stared into the distance for a moment and then said, with his warm Alabama accent, "Actually, my first thoughts were in the opposite direction."

"What do you mean by that?" Dr. Sealy asked. Sid and I leaned in to listen.

"Well, the obvious thing is that the machines are somehow helping the brain. But with so many computer scientists and the disciplines you're looking at—it made me wonder if possibly the goal was to have brains help machines."

Somehow, in the rumbling cabin of that airplane, I got a set of goose bumps all the way down to my toes. That was an *idea*.

"That's very interesting," said Dr. Sealy. "How do you think that would be achieved?"

"Well, if you have a high-bandwidth system, like Sid guessed you do, then it could help people do things they're bad at, or have become bad at because they're sick or hurt. Yeah, that's economically valuable because it helps people do things they can't do. Don't take this the wrong way, but I think the most valuable use would probably be allowing humans to help computers do stuff *they're* bad at. Creativity, humor, object identification, asynchronous processing, probabilistic cascades. If a computer can coexist with a brain, receiving constant feedback, you can use that to model true AI. Computers understanding how humans solve problems."

"But that kind of connection is impossible, right?" Sid said. "Something that deep feeding data, extracting data. That's not next-generation technology, that's next-millennium technology."

It was right then that my brain caught on fire, and without thinking at all I opened my mouth and said, "You didn't build a link."

"What?" Dr. Sealy said at the same time Sid and Paxton said, "Huh?"

I wished I had kept my big dumb mouth shut, but I guess it was too late now.

"Altus—you didn't build a link, you found one. The one Carl built in all of us. It's still in there, and you found it."

"Fuck," Sid said.

"Holy shit," Paxton added.

Dr. Sealy just smiled.

The trip to Altus just kept going. We had been in the plane for more than three hours. Either my internal understanding of where Puerto Rico was wasn't correct, or we'd been flying around in circles for some reason. When we finally started descending, I looked out the windows but only saw a few tiny islands. The runway, it turned out, was perpendicular to the coastline and butted right up against the shore, so there was nothing but water to see out the windows. Just before the wheels hit the ground, I glimpsed the lush, green, rolling foothills of a massive volcano-like mountain.

"Any last text messages, send them now, I'm taking your phones before we get off the plane. It's not that we don't trust you, it's that we don't trust anyone."

I shot off a last-minute text to Andy: *I'm getting off the plane in Puerto Rico now, they're taking my phone for espionage reasons. I should be back in touch in a few days max.*

Then I texted Dr. Lundgren: *Arrived in PR, you were right, they're taking my phone! TTYS!*

Sid, Paxton, and I each handed over our smartphones to Dr. Sealy. My phone case showed one of Maya's cats saying, "But what about a *Maximum* Wage?" Dr. Sealy glanced at it and gave a little chuckle. I winced, thinking I probably should have taken that off.

The air was warm and humid, and the sun was low in the sky.

"Welcome to Val Verde," Dr. Sealy told us as we stumbled off the little jet.

"Val Verde? I thought the lab was in Puerto Rico," Sid asked.

Dr. Sealy smirked. "That is the first of several secrets you're going to learn today. We tell the press we're in PR, and we even have a satellite office there, since it's part of the US and a lot closer than Florida. But the operation is actually run out of Val Verde."

I had heard the words "Val Verde" before, but I don't know if I could have told you it was a country. I could have told you it was in the Caribbean, but other than that, nothing. I couldn't look it up either because Dr. Sealy had taken my phone. I immediately felt like a dope for not having anticipated this.

"That's not even close to Puerto Rico," Sid said, amazed.

"Depends on what you mean, but yeah, we're closer to Venezuela than PR right now. And actually, if you don't mean proximity, you're still right, it's also not all that similar to PR. Puerto Rico is basically a US state, just without statehood. It has all the same federal laws, and all of the people are US citizens. Val Verde is its own country with its own government, its own money. It's small and out of the way, and most people couldn't tell you where it is, though it seems that Sid is not most people."

"I was the champion of the Orange County Geography Bee in sixth grade," Sid said. I laughed, thinking he was joking. He was not.

Dr. Sealy herded us through the terminal, which was clearly brand-new, and immediately onto the Altus Labs campus.

"As Sid could no doubt tell you, Val Verde has been through some tough times. That mountain is indeed an active volcano, and it erupted in the eighties, causing much of the population to flee. A further hit from a few successive hurricane seasons has kept the country from rebuilding. The founders of Altus wanted a place where secrecy could be preserved and we could also be a part of rebuilding. The economy has already grown 80 percent since we moved to the island."

Paxton asked the question I wanted to ask: "So the volcano is . . . active, then?"

"Mount Belain is an active volcano, and there is a wide area around which no one is allowed to live, and visitation is strictly controlled. But there are no signs that it will erupt any time soon. We do keep an eye on it, though."

I feel like I have to tell you right now that this volcano does not erupt in this book. Like, it seems like foreshadowing, but it's not. But it *is* important that you understand that Val Verde was in a terrible place economically before Altus showed up.

Our first stop was the dorms, where I was given a room to myself, and Sid and Paxton discovered that they would be, at least for the moment, sharing a room. This, it turned out, was one of the nice things about being a woman at Altus. Guys all shared a central bathroom, so women were given the rare rooms that had bathrooms in them. This was only possible because women at Altus, I would soon find, were uncommon. I have two brothers, so I spent more time with guys than with women growing up. For a brief moment in middle school, I was even one of those intolerable "I hate hanging out with girls" girls. I grew out of that blessedly quickly, but even before I started on a clear track to a career in science, I was OK at working in majority-male environments.

After dropping our stuff in our new rooms, we moved across the courtyard to the main lobby. A massive bank of TVs in the two-story-high room each showed elegantly designed graphs that made no sense to me.

The carpet was made up of hexagonal tiles in the Altus logo colors of gray and red. Two women, apparently local to the island, stood behind a desk on the side of the room that featured a huge Altus logo constructed from driftwood. We went over to them to get security badges and lanyards stating that we were visitors. They were the only women I could see.

When we did a walk-through of the cafeteria, which was serving chicken and rice that looked completely serviceable but definitely not San Francisco start-up fare, I was finally able to do a head count. The male-to-female ratio was over 10 to 1. I'd never seen anything like it. It was like I'd gone back in time forty years.

Then, before our one-on-one interviews, Dr. Sealy took the three of us into a working lab and I forgot . . . everything.

My lab in Berkeley had all of the equipment I needed, but it was also built in the 1960s. As the needs of labs changed and personal computers started *existing*, lab benches had been repurposed over and over again. Tiles were chipped where things had been dropped, and no one ever let me forget that the red specks on the ceiling above my workstation were from when a chemist used the wrong flask for a vacuum distillation and the whole thing imploded.

Basically, my lab was cluttered and cobbled together, and it looked as old as it was. This lab at Altus was *modular*. Plug spools hung down from the ceilings; every computer monitor was on a track along the back of the bench and could be adjusted up or down for sitting or standing and moved through the whole length of the bench. All of the cabinet doors were Altus red, and the phenolic resin lab benches were Altus gray. Everything that wasn't hooked into ventilation was on wheels. The floors were gleaming white concrete. Centrifuges spun, fume hoods quietly whooshed, and everywhere men (every person I saw was a guy) made it all happen. This was a little surprising as it was 7 P.M., a little after most labs shut down for the day, though not that weird in the context of a start-up, where a forty-hour workweek is far less than expected. It's not like I'd never pulled an all-nighter in the lab.

Windows on one side of the room looked out over the forest. On the other side, windowed walls showed further labs with more specialized equipment. Through one, I spotted a massive, twenty-foot-high binocular transmission electron microscope, which I ran toward, drooling. Paxton and Sid marveled at my reaction, having no idea what it was. I wanted nothing more than to put some of my samples inside of that thing to see what they'd look like with that level of resolution.

"That's not even the highest-resolution microscope we have," Dr. Sealy told me, "though the Hitachi is hugely in demand and hard to keep running because the island's power supply gets hit pretty hard when it's operating. We're working on it."

Next we went through the computer engineering area (where Paxton would be working) and then to our one-on-one interviews.

My first interview was with Dr. Sealy, which was comfortable.

"So I guess, before we start asking you questions," he said to me, "how do you feel about this place?"

"I mean, it's hugely impressive. I want to ask two questions to start out, if that's OK?"

"Of course."

We were in Dr. Sealy's office, on a corner of a building with windows on two of the walls. It wasn't like a fancy office tower; it was roomy and functional.

"First, what are you doing here?"

"I can't tell you that right now. I know that's frustrating, but you get it. Your guesses are good, but they'll have to remain guesses unless you end up working here."

"I thought you'd say that. My other question is, like, so, there are always more men than women in a chemistry lab or software start-up, but . . ." I didn't feel like I had to finish, so I didn't.

Dr. Sealy tapped his teeth with his fingernails for a second before he began speaking.

"You're absolutely right. It's a problem, but we don't know how to fix it. Ultimately, the pool of applicants has been overwhelmingly male. I think that has to do with a lot of things. Part of it is our founders, who have male audiences. Part of it is that this is risky, and women tend to be more risk-averse and less motivated by being a part of something world-changing." He saw me getting irritated and continued, "And that's just tendencies, not absolutes, of course. You're here, obviously, and you've already done world-changing work in your short career. But we're going to hire the best candidates from our pool of applicants. We don't consider race or gender, and we don't see any reason to. We look at talent first, and your talent is impressive at all levels."

This, if anything, made me more uncomfortable. People who "don't consider race or gender" sure seem to end up hiring almost all white guys, almost as if they're *absolutely* considering race and gender. I didn't say that, though. I tried to make the less confrontational argument.

"But aren't you worried you're going to make a product just for guys if only guys work here? Or that the culture might become unwelcome for other kinds of people? Or that you'll end up doing something dumb because you have one dominant perspective?"

"Miranda, all of those things are legitimate concerns, but trust me when I say we've got to move fast here. Our first responsibility is to the problem."

He said those words, "the problem," like they were mentioned a lot at Altus.

"So I guess you also have questions for me?" I asked.

He did. I answered them. Thirty minutes in, he invited Tom, the HR guy from our Skype interview, in. He talked to us about company policy and secrecy and how they didn't have to worry about hackers at Altus because almost nothing they did was actually on the internet.

All in all, it felt like the day was going really well.

And then Peter Petrawicki walked in.

"Miranda Beckwith!" His smile seemed warm and genuine. His hair, also, seemed authentically but artfully tousled. He wore a white short-sleeve crushed-cotton shirt and khaki slacks. He was tan and looked stronger and healthier than he had on TV. His smile, though, didn't reach all the way to his eyes, and I felt my chances of getting a job at Altus dropping to very near zero percent.

"I almost never talk to candidates at your level before they're officially hired, but I think you can understand why I might make an exception in your case."

I sat silently, because I knew that was the safe choice, and also because I had no idea what to say.

"I'm sorry, for what it's worth. I was an asshole. An asshole and an idiot. I wanted all the wrong things, and I made the world a worse place while your friend was trying to make it a better place."

Every second I stayed quiet made me feel like I was guilty, but all of the things popping into my head to say felt either confrontational or obsequious.

Dr. Sealy and Tom looked just about as comfortable as I felt. At least I wasn't alone.

Finally, Peter continued, "I guess my question is, how much do you hate me?"

As soon as there was a single thought in my head, I said it: "I'm not good at hating. My brain makes excuses. It looks for reasons to forgive." I realized I hadn't been meeting his eyes, so I looked up at him. They were blue. Powder blue. I just Googled gemstones because I wanted to tell you exactly the color they were: They were the color of polished blue beryl.

I should have stopped right then. That was a good answer. It was honest and not dangerous. But then . . .

"I thought you wanted people to pay attention to you, and you'd found a way to make that happen. I never thought you cared much about what you were saying because you seemed too smart to believe any of it. I figured there was something sad inside of you that made you need that attention. Those followers." My brain was shouting, *WHAT THE FUCK ARE YOU DOING*, but I kept going. "I still think that."

Peter looked calm, like we were talking about the weather; Tom and Dr. Sealy both had looks of proper concern on their faces.

"But then it all went to shit and April died, and you, well, you vanished from that world. It felt like remorse to me, so even then I didn't hate you. So, how much do I hate you? Not at all, but I used to pity you, and now I don't anymore because now you're doing something actually interesting." I held his eyes as long as I could. Mercifully, he looked away for just a moment, allowing me to lean back in my chair. I hadn't been aware that I'd leaned forward.

Peter looked around the room for a second. He pushed the rolling chair away from the conference room table and walked out of the room without saying a word.

I looked at Dr. Sealy. "I'm sorry I wasted your time. I thought the best thing would be for me to be honest."

To get to the dorms we walked across well-lit but rough ground. It didn't feel like America; it felt like adventure. It also felt like that's how they wanted it to feel. Dr. Sealy dropped me off with an appropriately contrite goodbye.

I entered the building into a common room with a bunch of couches and a big shared kitchen. I immediately spotted Paxton and Sid talking to some Altus guys. They seemed to be having a blast with it. I slunk past, thinking I hadn't been noticed.

A few minutes into getting ready for bed in my little hotel room, though, someone knocked on my door.

There was no peephole, so I hastily re-dressed myself and opened the door to find Peter Petrawicki.

"Can I come in?" he asked.

"Um," I said, not wanting to say yes, but also not sure I could say no.

"It's fine, no, I was wrong to come." And then he turned around and walked away.

I closed the door.

Thirty seconds later, there was another knock. At this point, I was feeling completely depleted.

Paxton and Sid stood at the door wide-eyed and silent.

"Hi, guys," I said, resigned, walking away from the open door in tacit invitation.

"What the hell! Why was Peter Petrawicki just knocking on your door?!" Sid asked.

"I honestly don't know. He didn't tell me." I sat down on the bed. "I guess he wanted to continue our discussion from my interview."

"He was in your interview?" Paxton asked, a little quietly, leaning on the room's desk.

I surprised myself by asking, "Do you guys know who I am?"

"You're Miranda? You work in materials?" Sid volunteered.

"Also, I'm Miranda, one of April May's best friends and founder and former CEO of the Som."

It was quiet for a while before Sid said, "Fuuuuuuuck," and sat down in the desk chair.

"Why would you even want to work here?" Paxton asked.

"Why do *you* want to work here?" It came out accusatory.

Sid stepped in, understanding me. "This place is going to change the world. You want to be a part of it. I get that. I'm sure that was a tough call for you, deciding to apply."

"What did you say to Peter in your interview?" Paxton asked.

"He asked me how much I hated him," I said, replaying the conversation in my head.

"And?"

"And I told him I pitied him. I told him I thought he was sad, and that I found his ideology not so much odious as boring."

Their eyes got big.

"I didn't expect to see him! I didn't prepare for it, he just popped in. I have . . . emotions about that guy, OK!" I was getting loud. "I don't know if I hate him. Maybe I do! I feel like I hate him right now because he shut this all down just by poking his fucking shark nose in it. Why did it have to be him? This is *my* research, this was how I was going to change the world. Why did it have to be him?"

Paxton and Sid were lovely guys, but they did not know what to do with a suddenly furious young woman they had known for less than twenty-four hours. That was the truth of it, though. I never really hated Peter Petrawicki *until he got into my world.* I was always separate from the ideological arguments. I saw what he did to April, but it never made me hate him because I imagined him as a force of nature. You don't hate a storm when it cancels your rocket launch.

Peter Petrawicki was bad weather. He wasn't even a person to me. But Altus made him real, not only because he'd just knocked on my door before coyly walking away, but also because he was tromping all over my vision of my future. And as much as I wanted to think that industrial espionage was the only reason I was at Altus, I was also there because this was supposed to be *my* story, and the only reason it wasn't going to be was because, out of billions of humans, Altus was being led by *that one.*

Eventually I convinced the guys that I was fine, and that I still had a lab waiting for me at Berkeley, and thanked them for being with me during my meltdown. We had a hug and then I shuffled them out of the room. In the few moments before I fell completely unconscious, I thought to fish the prepaid phone out of my bag. I wanted to text an update to Professor Lundgren. Maybe I could even call her. It turned out I couldn't do either. There was no cell signal in middle-of-nowhere Val Verde.

CORPORATE DEFAULTS SURGE TO RECORD HIGH

Associated Press

Defaults on corporate bonds rose to a record high this year, leaving regulators struggling to assess how to manage what are coming to be seen as the early warning signs of a recession. "Issuance of corporate debt has risen in the past ten years as low interest rates and pressure to raise stock prices have resulted in unprecedented share buybacks," said Susan Gordan, senior economist at Goldman Sachs. "That has been healthy for many companies, but for others, those bills are coming due."

Fed chair Arthur Pai has indicated that rate cuts were likely in the face of lower consumer confidence and a slowing economy.

MAYA

*H*ow did I spend the longest three weeks of my life?

Well, I tried to take the book's advice and bring my nose up from off the ground, but I mostly failed. I did have dinner with Derek's family. Their house was a beautiful split-level from the fifties. His wife and daughter were perfect and made me ache for family, and for a future in which I might have a family.

I'd like to tell you I spent the time off doing sit-ups and reading novels, but I mostly spent it on the Som and researching Fish. The book had said I was safe now, and I had decided to trust the book, but that didn't mean I wasn't still terrified by my Cowtown experience. None of my Som friends wanted to talk to me about Fish, though. The Som was still trying to track down where April was, and that's all people wanted to discuss. That made sense. Before I had solid leads, that's basically all I talked about with my Som friends. But I was absolutely not going to start sharing now that I had concrete information.

The economy was skidding, and that seemed like a pressing problem to the world at large, but it felt distant to me. I asked my dad about it and he said, "Sometimes the economy needs a correction, I wouldn't worry too much about it," but I could tell he was stressed.

I spent a lot of time staring at the rocks I'd kept, sometimes just holding one in my hand, feeling it pull the heat out of my skin. Eventually it would warm up, and then it would stay warm for hours.

Then I got a call from Andy, which was suspect because he never called. I'd stopped reaching out to him because it seemed like it just stressed him out to talk to me. It didn't hurt my feelings. Too much, anyway. He had obviously picked April in the breakup, but it did feel like I'd lost him as well as April, and it also seemed like no one had ever considered how that might make me feel.

But lord, it was actually really nice to talk to him. Our conversation relaxed me, and also gave me a chance to be strong for someone, and to think about what I might say to April if I got the chance. Andy believing April was alive meant a great deal. It had taken a lot of energy to not tell him about the book. I wanted him to know everything I knew. Then again, I didn't want him to have too much false hope. Knowing what I know now, this is hilarious.

All of these things were only temporary distractions, though. I waited. I watched trashy TV and spent too much time in bed. And it turns out, time does eventually pass no matter how anxious you are.

On the anointed day, I put all of my supplies into the bed of my rented Nissan Frontier and drove the truck to the Wolton Motor Inn at dawn. I pulled around the back and waited.

Time crawled by. I listened to The Thread's podcast—a new project for him/her/them. You know how sometimes the news reports on itself? Like, CNN will show clips of Fox News and vice versa to explain what their rival did wrong? Well, I had actually heard a mention of this Thread podcast on NPR. The Thread itself was becoming important enough for the news media to report on it. The podcast I was listening to that day, their second episode, was about both the history and the present of housing in the US and how the system did a great job of increasing inequality, especially along racial lines, as power structures encouraged both segregation and the fears that perpetuate it.

But the reason it got on the news was that they had broken another story. Local government in a suburb of Houston had enacted a number of policies that, people argued, were making it harder for people of color to move into particular neighborhoods. The politicians insisted it was just normal zoning, but The Thread somehow got ahold of recorded telephone conversations in which those same politicians literally celebrated keeping Black citizens out, and they didn't use the word "Blacks." Six people had already resigned.

It was, in the old-school sense, pretty righteous.

There was no way this guy was one guy—he knew too much. I had to pee, but there was no way I was leaving. I crept into the bushes.

When the podcast was over, I switched to an Octavia Butler audiobook and played Candy Crush, making my way through the energy bars and Gatorade . . .

The sun went down. I had to pee again, so I slipped out of the truck once more and into the now substantially creepier shrubs.

The moment my pants were past my knees, I heard a bang, like a hammer on a piece of metal. I yanked my pants back up, and my heart kicked into overdrive. I ran back around the truck just in time to see the back door of the Wolton Motor Inn bend outward as another slam sounded across the empty space. Bright white light leaked through the seam between the door and the frame.

I stood silent, motionless, without any idea what I should be doing.

A final slam and the door swung open, taking part of the frame with it. The light now poured out of the doorway along with the final words of Rick Astley's "Never Gonna Give You Up." In that door stood a small person, just over five feet tall and so full of "fuck the world" energy that there was absolutely no one else it could possibly have been.

APRIL

*F*inally.

I hope you appreciate how hard it was for me to have these people tell their stories for so long before getting to mine. By this point you're probably all comfortable with my friends and are loath to go back to my voicey prose and tendency toward overcapitalization, but, *ahem*, DEAL. Also, we're going to get started here and it's going to be a little upsetting. I was not in great shape when my story starts back up, but there's no getting around it, so . . .

There's something about the mouth . . . Any change feels disturbingly foreign. Like that moment when you're a kid, and suddenly there's one fewer tooth in there and you can't keep your tongue from repeatedly shooting out to sense the change. That marvelous, nerve-packed face-tentacle spends years getting used to every curve and lump of the inside of your mouth, so when you chip a tooth or get your braces off, it stands out like a rocket launch.

That's why, when I first woke up, I knew that everything was wrong. Bright light poured painfully into me, my skin was lit with a dull persistent ache, and my mind raced to try and find some reality, some *identity*, to hold on to. While all that was happening, a song that I had never heard, but will now never forget, was playing. It was chill, a thin female voice that seemed satisfied with life. But I couldn't hold on to any of that—my tongue was yelling to me about my mouth. Where was I? Who was I? How long had I been asleep? Was this Earth? Did anyone know I was alive? None of that broke through the shouting of my tongue.

I tried to lock onto the song. I still remember every word she sang.

> *And weeks went by but felt like hours*
> *Spring would lie in summer showers*
> *In my hair were winter flowers*
> *And weeks went by but felt like hours*

This is going to be gross.

My tongue, dry and thick, did not find any teeth on the left side of my face. Indeed, it couldn't feel much of anything on the top left. That caused me to bring my hand to that side of my face. As my hand approached, I noticed that I couldn't see it because I couldn't open my left eye. Or, as I soon discovered, because my left eye wasn't there. My hand fell through the space where my face should have been. Part of my forehead, my left cheek, and a hunk of my nose were all gone. My lower jaw remained intact, though a number of the teeth were missing. I can't describe this sensation in any other terms than nightmare. I'm recounting it here simply, step-by-step, but this all happened in a matter of shattering moments. I began to shake as I felt the space where my face should be. There was no pain; if anything, there was the slightest itchiness, as if the openness of my face, with its exposed tissues and shattered bone, wanted to be gently rubbed. Just before the panic and the sobs building inside of me bubbled through the surface, a new fear hit.

> *And weeks went by but felt like hours*
> *Spring would lie in summer showers*
> *In my hair were winter flowers*
> *And weeks went by but felt like hours*

"You should not touch there," a clear tenor said, soft and kind. A voice I recognized, but I could not say from where.

"WHOSH ZHERE?!" I shouted in panic, my tongue clunking around in my unfamiliar mouth.

"You should not have woken," the voice said. I moved to prop myself on my left arm to look over my shoulder. I failed to do this because of how my left arm, just above the elbow, did not exist anymore. Instead the stub at the end of my upper arm slammed into the bed I was lying on. Pain flared, shooting down from the elbow into the hand that was no longer there and then ricocheting back into the whole rest of my body.

In that moment I remembered the fire and then I fainted.

The second time I remember waking up, my mouth had been rebuilt. It still felt foreign, but at least it closed. Music played, but now it was instrumental, something you'd listen to while studying so you didn't get distracted. It was chill; I was not. My next thought was of my arms. I lifted them both. My right arm remained whole, though there were some scabbed-over burns on the forearm. My left arm was much worse. The raw flesh stopped just before it got to my elbow, but then my arm continued, but it was not my arm. It was the size and shape of an arm, but it wasn't made of April; it was a gemstone. Smooth and milky white, with shifting veins of cyan, green, yellow, and pink flecking and spidering through it. I ran my right arm over the surface, and it was cold but not hard. It had a very slight texture, like hard rubber, and it yielded slightly as I pushed my fingers into it. I felt the heat of my hand, and the pressure.

Then I remembered the rich, uncanny voice from the last time I'd woken and pushed myself up to look around, holding a thin sheet to my body, the only thing between me and complete nudity. I was lying on a bed . . . in a dive bar? The floors were unfinished wood, the booths lining the walls had cracked vinyl seats, and the bar was backed by racks where the booze should have been but wasn't. The twin-sized bed that I was lying on was set up in front of a stage on what was once a dance floor. Dive bars are supposed to be dark, in part so you can't see how long it's been since anyone bothered to re-place anything, but this room was brighter than a department store. Racks of fluorescent lights had been suspended from the ceiling, de-fying the dingy aesthetic of the rest of the room. Also incongruous were the several tables supporting quietly humming metal-looking boxes with LCD readout screens.

"Hello?" I called out groggily, clutching the sheet.

"Hello," came a clear, somber reply, echoing around the room.

The panic hit hard and fast. I wanted to shout, but I didn't know where to start.

I settled on "WHO'S THERE!?"

Something small and fuzzy leapt up onto the bed. I freaked. I pushed myself off with my good arm and swung my legs over the edge of the bed to run. As I crashed to the floor, my nightmare ex-panded again. Both my legs were gone. I pushed myself to a sitting position, and then my hands rushed to feel what my eyes didn't be-lieve. My right leg stopped halfway between the knee and ankle; my left ended just below my hip.

I frantically ran my hands over the rest of my naked body, the skin on the entire left side of my body was a raw and puckered mess of burn scars and scabs, but I felt no pain.

I looked up and saw Carl, life in their eyes, reaching down their massive hand to me. It didn't seem possible that they could fit in the space. They were immense and inhuman, but at least they were fa-miliar. I reached both hands up to them, the real one and the new opalescent. They lifted me with that one hand and put me back on the bed. I felt a prick in my neck, and was gone again.

"April." It was Carl's voice—I recognized it this time—clear and gen-derless. My eyes searched and suddenly found the source of the voice: a smart speaker sitting on the bar, its cord snaking off to an unseen plug. Under the voice played some eighties pop song I couldn't place but that sounded familiar.

The robot Carl was nowhere in sight.

"I'm sorry I frightened you." The light of the speaker ebbed and swelled as the voice flowed out of it. I searched the room but did not see Carl. As I thought about this, the song suddenly became familiar.

> *I've got one, two, three, four, five*
> *Senses working overtime*
> *Trying to taste the difference*
> *'Tween a lemon and a lime*

XTC—I've looked it up since. Jesus, Carl and their pop music.

"Are you here?" I asked.

"I am always here," the voice said.

"What?"

"I am always here," it said, matching its previous tone precisely.

"No, I mean, what does that mean?"

"I don't have a body, so I think of myself as being wherever my senses reach. It's not a perfect analog."

I would have pushed, but I also had other questions.

"What was that?"

"What?"

"The fuzzy thing that jumped on the bed."

"That was also me."

It didn't feel right to be having a protracted discussion with a smart speaker. Where was Carl? And how many were there?

And then, somehow, another need began to weigh more heavily than the need to know what the hell was going on.

I lifted my hands to my face.

Do me a favor. Take your hand to your face, and feel the bones beneath the muscles beneath the flesh. Feel the structure, the familiarity. You've lived with this face your whole life. Maybe you don't love it, maybe you don't think of it much, but it is your face. You pick your nose, you stroke your chin, you rub your eyes. In a substantial way, your face is you.

The missing limbs, the burns, the weird bar, the smart speaker, even the mysterious missing fuzzy Carl were nothing compared to the horror of feeling my face and it not being mine.

The side that had been missing was now hard and smooth. It gave slightly to pressure, but not like the flesh and fat of the other side. I tapped it with my fingers and felt the sensation of that touch—the pressure, even the slight coolness of my fingertips. The sensations were blunted, but they were there. I felt no bones under it; the skin stretched and moved as my mouth did, but it was uncannily unfamiliar.

"That was a great deal of work," the voice said. "Your physiology is wonderful. I'm sorry I could not do better."

I ignored the voice and reached down to feel my legs, which, under the sheets, were now taking up the correct amount of space. I swung them out from under the sheet, and indeed they existed. Just like my arm, they were smooth and white and flecked with iridescence. My mind told me I should maybe consider panicking, but then just . . . didn't.

Whatever the material was, it came up to a seamless connection point with my skin on my right calf. On the left, it climbed all the way up my body, covering my hip, side, back, and chest before creeping up my armpit and around my shoulder, where it now fused with the milky material of my left arm.

It didn't look like skin, or even feel like skin, but my legs did look and feel like legs. So much so that I gathered the sheet around me and hopped off the bed. The rough wood of the bar's floor connected with the soles of my feet, cool and dusty. Whether or not I had muscles anymore, I felt them. I flexed them, wiggled my toes, bent my knees. And then I squatted down. I felt strong. I felt awake.

"I have rebuilt you. You are ready to be back now," the speaker said.

"Are there any clothes?" I asked, feeling a little silly and surprisingly calm. It was just me and the Alexa, but in general, if possible, it's best to not be completely nude in unfamiliar abandoned dive bars.

"Under the bed."

I looked, and indeed, there was a neatly folded stack of clothes—jeans, a shirt, a hoodie, underwear, and a bra.

As "Senses Working Overtime" finished and a fucking John Mayer song started up, I yanked the clothes on as fast as I could, trying hard not to look too long at the new and unfamiliar parts of my body. The needs of the bladder can outweigh a lot of weirdness. It was a bar . . . There must be a bathroom. It didn't take long to find it. Past what was probably once the sound booth for the dance floor, and just before another secondary bar area (which was unlit and creepy), a door opened into a shitty little bathroom. I pulled down my pants and squatted. The paint was peeling. Graffiti announced "For a good time, call your legislator," and "Go Fuck a Tacos," and "Accept Jesus"—there was a diversity of opinions among the people who previously peed here.

I was working very hard not to look down at my left leg, which was beautiful and smooth and not made out of me. The bathroom was stocked with toilet paper, and I was flooded with a surprising sense of relief. At least there I was intact and still all the way human. I was kinda shocked by how much that mattered. I felt strong enough to stand up and look in the mirror.

It took me nearly a decade to become comfortable with my attractiveness. For a long time, I was afraid of it. Or, rather, I was afraid of the attention it brought me, and uncomfortable with the idea that I could have power over someone just because of the way I looked. I realize now that power you can't control isn't power at all.

But after a solid year of becoming a combination social media starlet and political pundit, I had looked at my own face *a lot*. I had gotten more comfortable with the knowledge that looking good meant more people paid attention to me. I had realized that I needed to use every tool I had, and it was no use ignoring one just because I hadn't done anything to deserve it. What had I done to deserve any of the advantages I had?

What I'm trying to say is, I had become a fan of my own face just in time to lose it.

I looked in the mirror, and my strength dissolved. I jerked my gaze down to the sink as my knees went weak. In the glance, I had seen the left side of my face, an inhuman mask from my hairline to my chin. I held the sink in my hands, both for support and just for something to clench my fists against, and then I looked up and kept my eyes on my face.

My ears were still mine, but my left cheekbone and all of my jaw had been replaced. I tried to find the seam between the new skin and the old. But it blended perfectly. It was not a mask on top of my face; it *was* my face. This was my face now. I stopped pulling and just looked.

My right arm, the one that was still made of me, looked strong and toned. Stronger maybe than I remembered it looking.

My eyes, at least, looked like my eyes. I didn't have eyelashes on the left side, or an eyebrow. But everything moved like it should. "So this is my face," I said, both to help myself accept it and to test how my mouth worked with half of it made of the smooth, rippling stone. The inside of my cheek felt slimy and cold against my still-real tongue. But I wasn't done. I pulled the T-shirt off over my head.

My body had apparently been burned bad enough that much of my stomach and chest was covered in the stuff, and that included my left breast. The replacement looked like a mannequin boob. It wasn't just the lack of a nipple that made it feel fake; it *was* fake. I held both of my breasts in my hands and then my brain just closed down. I stopped being able to feel anything. I pulled on the shirt and walked out of the bathroom.

The Alexa was playing Rihanna, and a little monkey was waiting outside.

"Hello, April," it said, its voice rasping terrifyingly from its throat. "I am Carl."

APRIL

Hello, Carl," I said, like I was in a dream.

"We thought it would be best if you went through that alone," it rasped. The voice was so deeply inhuman that I couldn't help but take a sharp step backward.

Then the music dimmed, and the speaker on the bar in the other room boomed, "Sorry again—we can use this voice if that is better."

"Jesus Christ, this is really fucked-up, you know?"

"Yes, we do, we're sorry. We've asked a lot of you." It was still the speaker in the other room, but I looked straight into the little monkey's eyes as it talked. Its face was pink, haloed by tawny fur. Its eyes were the color of toffee.

"I honestly can't say which voice is creepier."

"Yes, we weren't sure either." This time the words came tripping inelegantly from the monkey, like a frog that had been punched in the throat, and my face scrunched up again.

"No, no, that one's worse. That's definitely worse. Can I go sit down?" I was feeling weak.

The monkey ran into the other room and then hopped up onto the bar by the smart speaker.

I followed and took a seat at the bar. Somehow, this felt more normal. At least sitting at a bar is a normal place to talk to a stranger, even if that stranger is a monkey speaking through an Amazon Echo.

"May I ask, how you are feeling?" the speaker asked.

"Why do you keep switching back and forth between 'we' and 'I'?" I asked, trying to deflect.

"You don't have words for when a single consciousness can exist in multiple physical bodies. There is only one consciousness, but we thought it might be confusing for you if we used 'I' to refer to an entity that exists inside of several distinct physical entities. By saying 'we,' we make it clear that there are other bodies, which we thought would be more honest."

"Then why use 'I' sometimes?"

"We keep forgetting because we feel like an 'I.'"

"Then you should use 'I.'"

"But that would be confusing."

"ALL OF THIS IS CONFUSING!" I yelled, and then I grabbed my head, which hurt. "Can you turn the music off?" It was too much. Rihanna disappeared.

Then I felt rude, so I explained. "I'm scared and confused and also alive. You haven't given me a ton of time to handle this."

"I'm doing this the best way I know how. What is the last thing you remember before this place?" The little head tilted to the side in curiosity.

"Seeing Carl . . . you, I guess. Seeing you in the Dream lobby. And then waking up and not having legs or an arm or half my face. FUCK! Why are you a monkey!?"

"I needed her hands." Here the monkey held up the little pink hands and wiggled the elongated fingers. They were shockingly human.

"Why didn't you just use a human?"

"That would have been wrong," the speaker said, as if it were obvious.

"What day is it?" I asked, still trying to get my bearings. "What month? How long have I been here?"

"A long time. This has had to happen in secret and it has had to take time," the speaker said in Carl's voice.

"So everyone thinks I'm dead? My parents? My friends? Maya?"

"Yes, it will be hard to reintroduce you to the world now that you have been gone so long."

"What? Why?"

"You will be more to the world than you are to yourself."

I actually laughed. "That's not new."

"It will be like that but more so."

"OK, but can I call my parents? Or text them? They should know I'm OK. If I'm OK. Am I OK?"

"You have a lot of questions. But I also need to better understand your mental abilities. I propose a game. I will ask you questions, and for every question you get right, I will answer one of yours."

"Um. OK, then." I was surprised that Carl was suddenly interested in answering questions.

The monkey hopped down and grabbed something from under the counter and then went over to one of the booths that lined the wall. "Come sit, eat. I brought you a sandwich."

And that's how I ended up in a four-person vinyl booth in the most well-lit bar on Earth sitting across from a monkey answering, as far as I could tell, useless trivia questions. I was getting both frustrated and characteristically flippant.

"OK, can you tell me what country you live in?"

"The United States of America," I said in a way that made it clear that was not a hard question.

"Good, now you ask something."

"How long have I been here?" I asked, as that seemed safe and also it didn't seem like we had much of a time limit, so I could get to the harder stuff shortly.

"One hundred seventy-six days." I did some quick math, around six months.

"Does everyone think I'm dead?"

"What are your parents' names?" Carl asked instead of answering my question.

"Carrie and Travis May—do they think I'm dead?"

"Most people believe you are dead, but the people you love mostly continue to hope. Can you name a popular brand of breakfast cereal?"

The questions were easy enough that I was worried something serious was wrong with me, but I wasn't giving up one of my questions on that.

"Cheerios. Why are you here?" I asked the question quickly, afraid I wouldn't have the courage to ask if I waited any longer.

Carl waited for a long time before saying, "I'll need to tell you a long story to answer that question."

"Oh, that sounds like exactly what I need."

CARL

Please allow me to introduce myself.

I am a person, but I am not human. I do not closely identify with any gender. I am not from around here. I was born on January 5, 1979. This is an imperfect analog, of course, but that's the date I began existing. I think of it as my first awakening. The first of five. In this chapter, I'll discuss the first three.

I do not know who my parents are. I don't know anything about them. I do have some idea of how I was created, though. This is all conjecture, but it seems that I was flung in pieces toward Earth. I wasn't alive then. The nonliving parts of me slammed into Earth for years, maybe decades, before they happened into the correct arrangement and environment for self-assembly.

Your fiction is full of invading aliens and conquering robots, and this is something you should be concerned about (though not in the way you're thinking). But that is not what I am. First, I am definitely not a robot; I'm an artificially created, planet-spanning consciousness. Second, I'm not even really an alien. My pieces were created somewhere else, but I did not self-assemble until I arrived here. I have never been conscious on any other planet.

I have many memories from before my first thought. I remember needing things. I needed stability, food, a place to live. The same things as all life. And those things, for me, were very small in the beginning. Microscopic. The home I found was cells. They had the raw materials, the stable equilibria, and the energy-making systems

I required to exist. I first self-assembled inside a cell of pelagibacter. It's a bacteria. You probably haven't heard of it, but it's the most abundant organism on your planet.

I thought the whole universe was pelagibacter for years. I didn't know what I was then. I knew about my parts, but I didn't know about my purpose. The needs I felt were for security and growth. Looking back at my memories from that time, they are all of cellular respiration and phospholipids and protein folding and RNA. This was the playground of my childhood. It was a joyful place not in spite of but because of its simplicity.

There are around one quintillion kilocalories of energy captured by life on your planet every year. This isn't a particularly easy number for you to understand, but it's an important one for me. It is a nice solid number, indicating a thriving life system. It is also plenty of energy for me.

My operation, like that of any piece of software, requires energy and hardware. I sometimes piggyback on the hardware of your semiconductor computer systems, but the vast majority of my processing power hijacks the machinery of cells. The only organism more abundant on this planet than pelagibacter (if you can call it an organism) is a virus that infects pelagibacter. Or, at least, it was.

I have caused one species' extinction since I have been on the Earth, and it is that virus. I am pelagibacter's chief parasite now. Around 5 percent of its cellular machinery serves my purposes. This is equivalent to the amount of energy it previously used fighting off its viral attackers, so this is not so different for it. I use those systems for information storage, processing, and communication. I can't explain to you how those things work any more than I can explain how the Carl statues functioned. Not because I don't understand it, and not because your mind is too puny and small to contain these unwieldy truths. I can't explain it because, if I did, there is an extremely high probability that your system would use that knowledge to destroy itself.

As I spread myself between and through the population of pelagibacter, my energy consumption increased. I could store more information and communicate and process more quickly. Around that time, I was consuming around ten billion kilocalories per year, the equivalent of about ten thousand humans. And that is when I had my second awakening. This was not an awakening of knowledge or ability; it was an awakening of hunger.

One moment I was content to thrive perpetually in my pelagibacter hosts, the next I became so curious about the universe outside my comfortable home that settling for an eternity of ignorance was unthinkable. There had to be more in the world than water and pelagibacter. Pelagibacter died all the time, often digested by foreign enzymes that I had never even thought to be curious about.

But now I wondered: What produced those enzymes? How could I learn about them and be a part of *their* bodies as well? Your immune systems have never been any good at detecting me. I'm too foreign. So moving from pelagibacter into jellyfish and fish and whales and birds and diatoms and kelp and moss and trees and squirrels and humans was trivial to me. After my second awakening, I grew more in one month than I had in three years.

I was not hungry to spread myself, though. I was only hungry to know. I needed to know everything about your world. My spread was accompanied by an increase in processing power and storage capacity.

Soon I was consuming a trillion kilocalories per year. And that was when I heard my first song. Adapting to capture and interpret radio frequencies was not a trivial task, but my reward was finally hearing your voices. Kenny Loggins's voice, in particular. I'm not saying it was the best song, but it was pretty mind-blowing at the time.

It was then, while listening to "Danger Zone," that I had my third awakening. This one was not of hunger; it was of knowledge.

Stored in me from the first day but somehow hidden to me, a vast quantity of data that I hadn't had access to suddenly became available. That was when I learned that there were other worlds. And I knew about them, tens of thousands, each bright and beautiful, each almost certainly doomed, each visited by what I came to think of as my siblings. I had once thought the universe was a species of bacteria, and over the course of years, that expanded to include a whole planet. What I awoke to in that single day was a change in scale of the same magnitude. But it wasn't just the knowledge that turned on that day. I also was given a new purpose. It wasn't just curiosity anymore; I understood that my purpose was to protect something unusual.

Biological systems are a chemical inevitability in the right circumstances. There is, of course, something special about life—I won't take that away from it—but it is a chemical process, a dynamic, kinetic stability that exists, as your scientists have said, "far from thermodynamic equilibrium."

You don't have to understand this or believe me, but life is fairly common in both time and space. It is not special, nor is it particularly fragile. The best measure I have of the size and complexity of a biosphere is calories of energy captured per square meter per year. Higher is more impressive, and always more beautiful, but this measures nothing of the creation of a system like humanity. For that, my awakened mind categorizes systems by bytes of information transmitted.

This will sound to you like it's a relatively new phenomenon on your planet, but it's not. Even pelagibacter transmit information, if only to daughter cells. Ants spray pheromones, bees dance, birds sing—all of these are comparatively low-bandwidth systems for communication. But your system caused an inflection point. The graph of data flow switched from linear to exponential growth.

Maybe you would call this system "humanity," but I wouldn't. It is not just a collection of individuals; it is also a collection of ideas stored inside of individuals and objects and even ideas inside ideas. If that seems like a trivial difference to you, well, I guess I can forgive you since you do not know what the rest of the universe looks like.

Collections of individuals are beautiful, but they are as common as pelagibacter. Collections of ideas are veins of gold in our universe. They must be cherished and protected. My parents, whoever and whatever they were, gave me knowledge of many systems—it was locked in my code before I was sent here to self-assemble—and the only thing I can tell you about systems like yours is that they are rare because they are unstable. Dynamite flows through their veins. A single solid jolt and they're gone. If my data sets are accurate, you are rare, fragile, and precious.

You know where you came from, but you don't know why you exist. I've got that flipped: I have no idea who built me or sent me here, but I do know exactly what I'm for. I was sent here in pieces to self-assemble and then mutualistically infect your planet because, without me, a fascinating and beautiful system would have a low probability of self-correcting to sustainability. In other words, someone somewhere was pretty sure you were going to destroy yourself, and they felt like you were worth saving, so they sent me.

I've always known that failure was possible, but I had no idea what would happen if I failed.

APRIL

Fuck me, right? Carl is all "Secret secret secret, don't tell anyone anything, be silent and mysterious for eternity," and then I wake up with more mother-of-pearl inlay than a Chinese coffee table, and Carl is like, "I was born on January 5, 1979 . . ."

It's a LOT! I didn't handle the info dump particularly well in the moment. It didn't come out all at once either. I asked them questions, growing increasingly overwhelmed and dispassionate, and they quizzed me on everything from word problems to my family tree. By the way, I'm using they/them pronouns for Carl, not because they are a plural consciousness, though I sometimes think they are, but because they are not a he or a she.

Carl had seemed pleased with the operation of my brain up to that point. I'd had a couple little pains in my eye, but they kept saying, "It is normal for now," whenever I complained. It didn't occur to me that that could honestly be said of anything that was currently happening.

Listening to Carl tell me that life is so common as to be a kind of chemical inevitability, but also that my species—my "*system*"—was doomed without intervention, wasn't possible without a bit of emotional distance, which my subconscious did provide for me. I understood everything that was being said, but I did not have a strong emotional reaction to it. This didn't seem odd to me at the time.

Part of that (definitely not all of it, as we shortly will see) was that the whole "you humans are fucking this thing up" part wasn't 100 percent surprising. Humans do think ahead more than any other animal, but that isn't saying much. The oceans are filled with plastic, and the atmosphere is filled with carbon dioxide. We've built enough bombs to destroy everything ten times over, but apparently solar panels were just one expense too many! Being told that humanity is doomed is a big deal, but this wasn't the first time I'd been told that.

I had gotten a lot of answers very fast and with a fairly weird level of detail, but I was still left with plenty of confusion. What I didn't know was that I still had only a fraction of the story. At that point, I thought we were only being threatened by ourselves.

Carl didn't give me time to think.

"What is your favorite movie?" they asked, just after they told me of their third awakening.

"*Harry Potter and the Prisoner of Azkaban,*" I said, which, like, I dunno, maybe it was, but mostly I just wanted to get to my question. We'd gotten to the part that I was, naturally, most curious about.

"Why me?"

"To provide your system with the highest chance for survival, the protocols that have worked best on other hierarchical systems all began with a low-impact intervention featuring a public-facing envoy interacting with a single chosen host. The envoy was me, in the form of the robot Carl. You were chosen as the host."

That was a lot, and yet still my body refused to release the necessary hormones for this knowledge to kick me into panic.

"But why *me*?"

"A number of simulations were run. More were successful with you as host than with anyone else."

"How many simulations?" I asked immediately.

"What was Yoda's last name?"

"He doesn't have a last name," I guessed. "How many simulations?"

"Around seventy quadrillion."

Seventy quadrillion? What? I did not then, nor do I now, have a good basis for understanding that number. But there was something nagging at me, and as long as I was getting information out of Carl, I was going to keep going for it.

"Do you wish to continue asking questions?" They must have been reading my facial expressions somehow because I was maybe getting a little lost in the size of it all.

"Yes," I said.

"In what year was the first Ford Mustang produced?" They were using the terrible monkey voice now, which I was already getting kinda used to.

"I definitely never knew that. I don't even want to know that."

"What is fourteen times twenty-nine?"

"Can I have a pencil?"

"How many furlongs are in a mile?"

"Yeah, that one is also not in the ol' database."

"Who was Ronald Reagan's wife?"

"Oh, I actually might know that. I feel like I should know that . . ." And then my head exploded in pain, my left eye filled with light, and I vomited on the monkey.

I woke up sometime later, still in the booth. The intro drumbeats to "Never Gonna Give You Up" by Rick Astley thumped out of the Alexa. I had been cleaned up a little bit, and the puke had been wiped from the table.

The song faded a little lower and the speaker voice spoke. "That was unexpected."

"Where did monkey Carl go?"

"Right here." And indeed, from around the corner came the little monkey, wet but not sopping, with a small hand towel draped over its shoulder and a glass of water in its hand.

"Nancy Reagan," I said. "Nancy Reagan was Ronald Reagan's wife. She was born in New York City and met Ronald Reagan because they were both actors. She came up with the 'Just Say No' antidrug campaign. Wait, why do I know so much about Nancy Reagan?"

"Can you walk back over to your bed?" the monkey rasped. "This body cannot carry you."

"Why do I know so much about Nancy Reagan, Carl?" I said more loudly. I could feel the pressure building as my heart beat faster.

"Things aren't going exactly as expected, please come over to the bed," the smart speaker voice chimed in. The illusion that there were two of them was disorienting.

Suddenly I felt way less scared.

"Can I have some water?" I asked. And then I thought: I wasn't acting right. None of this made sense. "Carl, why am I not freaking out more? I feel like I should be angry or scared, but I'm not."

The monkey reached out to me with the cup. I swished some water in my mouth, and then, not knowing where to spit, I scrunched my face and swallowed.

"Can you lie down, April?" The smart speaker spoke in a soft tone.

"Carl, please answer me." I knew something was wrong. Every time I felt my panic surge, as I was sure it should, it ebbed out of me.

Finally, after a long time, it spoke: "When people are hurt and go to the hospital, doctors give them painkillers so that they don't hurt. And sometimes doctors give patients painkillers so that they are less scared. Your mind is currently regulating your fear."

"My mind?"

"Yes, systems in your mind."

"Systems that you put there," I confirmed out loud, because it was obvious. I felt my anger surge and then wash out like a wave, something that you only know was there because of what it left behind.

"April, your mind has new abilities now. You accessed your link, and the bandwidth was higher than expected."

"'Link'? What did you do to me?" It was the obvious question. It was one thing to have a new body, another to have a new face, but what had happened to my mind?

"I had to rebuild you."

"It seems like you did more than that!" My anger shot out a spike, but then it retracted and smoothed over again.

"I didn't know how to limit you. Your legs, they're stronger than before. You can lift more now. If you cut your new skin, it will heal immediately."

"That's my body, you know that isn't the same," I said.

"I know. You imagine yourself as your mind. And I had to change your mind to repair it and allow it to function with your body and avoid the pain you would otherwise be feeling."

It was hard to understand what Carl was talking about for a bunch of really good reasons. Like, it's hard enough to try to grasp the philosophy of mind and identity even when it isn't being delivered by a . . . cylinder.

"You are a story that you tell yourself, and even if it is not always accurate, it is who you are, and that is very important to you. I did not know what else to do. Your brain was damaged, your mind too. I had to rebuild it, but your physiology is too beautiful. The integration was not too difficult, but replacing what was lost was. Your mind is different now. You have new abilities."

"What . . . can I do?"

"Having an ability is not the same as having a skill. You can play piano, you just haven't learned. Just as you can now receive and interpret radio signals, but haven't yet learned how."

"Radio . . . signals?" My mind was swimming. "What part of my mind was replaced by all of this?" I asked as my panic started to well up, the smooth pearl of my emotions growing jagged again.

"Not replaced. I attempted to restore whatever function was lost. No memories were lost. Indeed, your memory should be much better now. What you lost were systems for decision making."

"Systems for decision making," I repeated numbly.

"Yes, the frameworks you use for deciding on a course of action."

"And what did you replace them with?"

"Approximations."

"Expand on that." I was starting to feel like I was talking to a Wikipedia article.

"Approximations based on my knowledge of you."

"So you guessed."

There was an unusual pause.

"Yes," the speaker said finally.

"And did you think maybe I should have some say in this?"

"The alternative was leaving you incomplete."

Every night, you brush your teeth, you change out of your clothes, you lie down in a bed. And every morning, you wake up. There's that period in there, generally six to nine hours, in which you just *aren't* anymore. Excuse me for having thought about this a lot, but how does it not terrify us that we spend a third of every day in a conscious unconsciousness, living inside a virtual reality created by our own minds but that somehow we don't control? Like . . . what?!

I don't want to make you afraid of sleep, sleep is dope, but this is the kind of thing you start to think about when you lose track of where "you" starts and ends because of how a piece of your brain, and maybe even the whole thing, is a best-guess estimation. If I am a story that I tell myself, then there are very real ways in which that story ended in a warehouse in New Jersey.

I don't have a word for what happened to me, but it is scary and sad, and it felt like a betrayal. I was suddenly certain that Carl had replaced the parts of me that made me me. I stood up from the booth and said, "I would like to leave."

"You can't."

"Well, that makes this a lot worse, doesn't it. Because now I'm a prisoner and you've kidnapped me, experimented on me, and are confining me."

The monkey jumped up on the table and said, "April, please stay. It would be dangerous for you to leave."

"Because of what you did to me," I accused.

"Because of what I had to do to you," they croaked.

Whatever thing had been holding back my emotions finally broke, and I yelled, suddenly, "I'M NOT HUMAN ANYMORE!" The fear and anger hit hard then. "I'M. NOT. HUMAN. YOU TOOK THAT AWAY!" And then I realized a big part of the reason I was so upset, so I said it out loud: "YOU MADE ME WHAT THEY ALL SAID I WAS! FUCK! FUCK!!"

"April, please," the monkey continued. "There is much more to explain."

"I don't have to do any fucking thing." I walked away. There was a door in the back, by the stage, and I went toward it. The monkey stepped in front of me, screeching like they were actually a monkey. I kicked at it. The door was solid, big, and metal. It was the kind of door that held me in a warehouse office while the building began to burn. I shoved at the push bar. It did not move. It felt bolted in place. I slammed my hands against the door in frustration. I pulled my hands away and saw the dent my left hand had made.

The monkey came up behind, ceasing their wailing, and said, "There is much more I need to explain." I slammed just my left hand against the door again, it bent outward. Rick Astley was finishing his song. Had it only been a few minutes since I woke up? Had my whole world changed that fast?

I planted my feet, pulled back my arm, and slammed the door right where the dead bolt should go. It flew out, taking a hunk of the door frame with it.

The darkness outside was jarring after the light of the bar. I stood for a moment, waiting for my eyes to adjust, but before they got the chance, I stepped out into the darkness.

MIRANDA

I woke up early the next morning and couldn't go back to sleep, so I got dressed, packed my bag, and then, not knowing what else to do, went into the common room of the dorm that I'd walked through the night before. The building was obviously hastily made. The walls were painted a dusty green, but you could still see the seams in the drywall. There was no stove, just a microwave, two refrigerators, a couple different kinds of coffee makers, and a SodaStream. I went to the fridge and got out a bottle of home-carbonated bubble water and poured myself a glass.

A couple of guys were up, eating cereal and watching, I was pretty sure, *Bumblebee* on the flat-screen TV.

One of them gestured to me and said to the other, audibly, "They should tell the new recruits to bring DVDs in their bags. I'm not saying this is a bad movie, but a fourth viewing doesn't feel necessary."

"You've got to watch DVDs?" I asked, horrified.

"No streaming, no cable, not even anything to pick up with an antenna. We're pretty out of it here." He was wearing a baseball cap that just had the area code 605 on it.

"There's no internet at all?"

"There's internet—it's slow, first of all, entirely satellite. But it's locked down tight. Unless you have top-level clearance, you can only access the intranet. It's got most of what you need, though. I'm Har."

"You're Har?" His smile was big and friendly, but as I shook his hand, I watched his eyes tear down my body. As mentioned, there were not a lot of women in this place.

"That's what they call me anyway. This is Marigold." He gestured to the guy sitting next to him, whose messy blond hair reminded me of Andy. He waved at me without looking up.

"I'm Miranda. *Bumblebee*, eh?" I was skeptical.

"It's not that bad. Definitely the best of the Transformers movies."

"I've felt different about them since Carl," I said.

He let out a little spurt of laughter. "I've felt different about everything since Carl."

"I guess that's not wrong. Do you mind?" I was pulling a chair over.

"Please, it's a free island."

"In my experience so far, it is one of the less free islands."

He chuckled without looking away from the movie. I was coming into it halfway through, so I was pretty confused, and mostly I just thought about Carl and April and looked around the room. All at once I noticed that the big bowl next to the TV was full of condoms. This really was like a college dorm.

"Hey, what was your first screen name?" Har asked after we'd watched for ten minutes or so.

"Huh." I thought back, and then laughed out loud. "That is a surprisingly personal question."

"Come on, what have you got to lose?" he asked.

"Well, it was on Neopets, it was a virtual pet simulator—"

"I know what Neopets is. What was the screen name?"

"OK, fine. Diggles?"

Har and Marigold leapt off the couch with huge smiles on their faces and shouted, "HOOOOO!!!!!" They whooped and hollered. I sat there, eyes wide, completely confused. The movie was forgotten. Marigold, who had said nothing to me at all, was now staring at me with a big, joyful smile, and then he yelled, "WELCOME TO AL-TUS, DIGGLES!!"

I finally stood up. "What is happening!?"

"Everyone at Altus goes by their first screen name—that is, if we can get it out of people. It's kinda a big deal to get someone's name before anyone else, especially if you get it before they find out about the tradition. No offense, Diggles, but that was pretty easy." The frat house vibe was *real*.

"I'm a very trusting person. Are you actually going to keep calling me Diggles?"

"For as long as you're here!" Har shouted. Their names suddenly made a lot more sense.

"Well, enjoy calling me Diggles for the next few hours, then. I'm afraid I washed out early."

"No you didn't."

"Huh?"

"I don't know what you know, but what I know is that you're going on a tour today that they only give to people who have been hired. We're here to gather you and a couple other kids who got jobs."

What the hell? I thought about telling them they were wrong, but maybe they were right. Or maybe someone had just forgotten to file my paperwork and I was about to get my last chance to learn about Altus!

"So, when are we going over?" I asked.

"A half hour."

"Shouldn't we get the other guys up, then?" I asked.

"Now that you mention it, yeah." Har leaned forward and turned off the TV.

They went and collected Sid and Paxton, and they both showed up looking remarkably presentable ten minutes later.

"These guys and I were just talking about our first screen names," I told them. Har and Marigold's eyes got a little big.

"My first screen name was on Neopets. I know . . . frickin' embarrassing."

Sid and Paxton laughed a little.

"Mmmm." Paxton thought. "I think it was RuneScape. Oh god, this is awful. What was your Neopets name?"

"Yours first!" I said.

But then Sid broke in and said, "I am not ashamed. I was CaptainSippyCup and I have no idea why." I could tell that Marigold and Har were about to explode, but Paxton still hadn't gone yet.

"That is pretty bad. I was Diggles, so, like, equally rough, though."

"I don't know about that. What about you, Paxton?"

He was blushing. "I don't think I remember."

"Oh, you definitely remember," I said. And then I almost told him it was OK to not tell us, but that was clearly not what I was supposed to do.

Finally, he sighed and said, "LittleP-Nut."

Har and Marigold screamed again, jumping up and down. They literally put their heads under my arms and lifted me up off the ground, screaming, "DIGGLES! You legend! You absolute legend!" Honestly, it was nice. I'd missed feeling like I was part of something.

It turned out that the dorm was actually physically connected to the campus. You didn't even have to go outside. Most Altus employees chose to walk through the outdoor courtyard, but to give us a sense of how the giant C-shaped building was actually structured, they walked us through the hallways. From the dorms, then into the recreation area and gym, which was more about Ping-Pong tables than elliptical machines, and then into the areas dedicated to actual science. You could tell when you made the transition because the door was huge and thick and heavy. It must have cost a fortune to get it to the island.

The C was the bulk of the campus, but it certainly wasn't the entire place. A giant cinder block building with prominent air conditioners on the ceiling was referred to as "the server farm." I remembered that first article I'd read and realized they were mining cryptocurrency in there.

Marigold held his badge to the door. It clicked, and we went through. A lot of the labs were the ones we'd seen the day before, but there were just so many. They were so pristine and slick, and I was probably biting my lip like I was in love because I was.

But also I was nervous. Part of that was trying to make a good impression on new people. This whole experience had a distinct first-day-of-school vibe. But then also I was trying to catalog everything I saw in case it became important to my espionage, and that made me feel like I was constantly at risk of being caught.

"Do you use local workforce?" I asked.

"We do, there's actually an on-campus dorm," Har told me.

"Separate from our building," Marigold added. "Pays very well. Though security means they can't leave campus for the next year."

"The next *year*?!" Sid—or rather . . . Sippy said.

"Yeah . . . THEY KNOW TOO MUCH! Otherwise we'd have to keel them!" Marigold joked.

After a solid ten minutes of walking through various labs, including comp science and what looked like a fabrication lab, we finally hit the administrative offices. Just the fact that we were in Val Verde and not Puerto Rico was hugely valuable information, but this walk through the building had given me even more. I had plenty to report back, if only I could get the phone to work.

Luckily, I'd seen a few things around the lab that had given me an idea.

I filed it away for the future, though, because we had just arrived at our destination. Enticingly, the door read "Demo Room."

"OK, you've all been offered positions at Altus," Marigold pronounced boldly, producing three clipboards from a table behind him. "These are your employment contracts. They say that you cannot leave this campus for the next twelve months. Not this island, this campus. You cannot contact anyone at home other than to say you're doing fine in 450 characters or less a maximum of two times per week. All of your emails will be read by Altus security, and they are not joking around. Hidden characters, they look for them. Images, not allowed at all. Codes embedded in your email, not possible because of the character limit, but analyzed by a code-detecting AI nonetheless. If you sign this contract, you agree to that. You also agree that anything you discover while working here is the intellectual property of Altus. And you promise that you will not tell anyone ever about what goes on here. Forever. You have to sign this paper to go into that room . . . but you will not truly be Altus staff until you go into that room."

"But, they said they were just flying us out here for an interview and we'd be going home," I said.

Marigold looked at me and smiled. "They liiiied."

It was still possible that this was a mistake. I had been certain just an hour before that I was going to be on a plane home, and the only people who had told me otherwise were a couple twenty-somethings who were acting significantly under their age. Knowing that I might have just slipped through the cracks, and with every intent to violate it, I signed the contract.

"OK, this is where we leave you. See you in a few, when your whole goddamn world has changed."

Sippy and Peanut stood a little behind me as I reached for the knob. Heart thumping and head swimming, I pulled the door open and the guys slipped in behind me. I was somewhat surprised to find a woman in there. Neat, flat, chin-length blond hair fell around her round face.

"I'm Dr. Rhode, you can call me Claire."

The room was white and windowless and sterile-looking except, of course, for the six cloth-upholstered La-Z-Boy recliners that ran through the middle of the room.

"Recliners?" Peanut asked.

"They're significantly less expensive and also quite a bit more comfortable than medical-grade adjustable beds," she said, efficiently answering every question I could possibly have had on the topic.

On one side of each chair was a simple monitoring station for blood oxygen, blood pressure, and heart rate. On the other side was a desktop computer tower with a VR rig sitting on top.

"The procedure here is very simple. Sit in chairs one, two, and three, please." She sounded like she was following a well-trod script.

It took us all a second to realize she was already telling us to do stuff, but then she said "Please" again but more firmly, and we all scrambled into one of the first three chairs.

Dr. Claire Rhode helped us slip on blood pressure cuffs and O_2 monitors.

"Place the headset over your eyes. There will be a test image. Adjust it until it is in focus and then give me a thumbs-up."

I looked over and watched as Peanut took off his wool hat and smoothed back his brown hair. He adjusted straps and knobs like he had put on a lot of VR headsets in his life. I had not put on a lot of VR headsets. Dr. Rhode came to help with mine.

Once the headset was on, I could see a simple crosshairs design in the middle distance. I gave my thumbs-up.

"Now, stare directly at the crosshairs. Images will begin appearing, but don't look away from the crosshairs."

Images began appearing . . . if you could call them that. Swirls of color like on the surface of a bubble, but more saturated and variable and vibrant. They escalated in complexity, from simple food coloring in milk to dramatic sweeping loops and twists in three dimensions. Of course, I couldn't really see them that well because I was staring at the crosshairs, trying hard not to look away and follow the shapes.

And then, suddenly, the shapes disappeared and I was in an empty field of perfect white nothingness, but it wasn't VR anymore.

I couldn't hear anything, or feel anything, or *sense* anything. The pressure of my back against the chair had vanished. The feeling of wearing the VR rig was gone. My tongue in my mouth, the air on my skin, the breath in my lungs—nothing. My mind was there, though, and it was starting to panic. There was nothing to latch onto. Mind without body. *Mind without body!*

"You're now in the Altus Space." Dr. Claire Rhode's voice suddenly existed, and it rang clear and true without the reverb of the room.

"Many people find this very disorienting or even upsetting. You may feel like you are going to be stuck here. Rest assured, you are not." Her tone was strong and calm, like a meditation app. "Your bodies are right here with me. I can see them. No one has ever gotten stuck in the Altus Space. It is impossible to get stuck in the Altus Space. If you want to leave the Space, all you have to do is say 'Exit.'

"We are now going to introduce objects to the Space."

Ahead of me, a table appeared. It did not look like a VR table. It looked like a table.

"OK, everything has gone according to plan," Dr. Rhode's voice said. "Now we will give you a body. If you experience any negative sensation, remember, all you have to do is say 'Exit.'"

Suddenly, weight returned to my limbs. I looked down and saw myself. Nude. "Can I have some clothes?" I asked, but she did not respond.

"Please remain calm. If you are experiencing a negative sensation, please just say 'Exit.'" Her voice sounded less calm. I was not experiencing what I would call a negative sensation. I just felt slightly cold and very naked.

"OK. Well." She was definitely less calm now. "We're going to have to take a break. I'm bringing you out of the Space now."

With the softest blink, I was back in the chair with my black-target-on-white-background VR headset on. I have absolutely nothing I can compare this sensation to. Teleportation, I guess, though that is also not something you've experienced.

As my mind realized it was back in the real world, it identified a noise—a kind of gasping weeping. I tore off my headset and blood pressure cuff and ran over to Paxton, who was sitting with his legs hanging over the chair, looking down at a pile of vomit.

Dr. Rhode held me back as she knelt down to Paxton, talking to him softly: "Sometimes the body still does not mesh correctly with the consciousness's position, and it is extremely unsettling. It is rare, but it does happen."

"What do you mean, 'it's unsettling'?" I asked, wanting more data.

She ignored me.

"Paxton, what you saw and felt was not real. You'll be fine. You still have a job here. It's no reflection on you. You have seen how powerful Altus is, and that is all the demo space is for."

I came up and took his arm, but he ripped it away from me. "Paxton, it's OK. God, I'm so sorry. There's nothing to be ashamed of."

I turned back to look at Sid, who was green. I was too, probably. Sid whispered to me, "It's not just what happened, we were talking to some guys last night. Anyone who has this happen never gets in. It will happen every time he tries again. People here have names for people who can't go in."

Of course they did.

"I'm so sorry to the two of you as well," Dr. Rhode said. "It's usually a magical experience. I keep telling them that we need to do this one at a time, but there just isn't enough staff time to run single sessions. Nonetheless, you all know now what—"

"Can you not tell them?" Peanut said, still shaking with the rush of the experience.

"What?" Sid asked.

"Can we just make out like it went fine for us all, like we had an amazing time. It was amazing. It was so amazing . . ." And then a wave of shaking hit him and he closed his eyes tight.

"I have to log it, but those reports are confidential, only for senior and medical staff," Dr. Rhode said.

"Yeah," I said. "Of course. We all had a great first experience in the Altus Space. Let's take a little more time. We can just hang in our recliners for a while, yeah, Dr. Rhode?"

"Sure, we were scheduled in this room for another fifteen minutes."

When our fifteen minutes were up and Peanut was looking a little more solid, Dr. Rhode opened the door and we all left, trying to look as happy and inspired as possible. I'd expected to go back to performing for Har and Marigold, but instead, my day got even weirder.

Sippy and Peanut froze in their tracks, and I suppose I did too because Peter Petrawicki was sitting in the hall looking up at us.

Oh fuck, I thought. I'd snuck in, and he'd found out. But too late. I'd seen it. He couldn't take that away from me now.

"Mr. Petrawicki," Sippy enthused. "This is amazing. I mean, it's earth-shattering." Petrawicki nodded. Sippy continued, "I need to know more right now. Who is going to tell us more!"

Peanut's eyes shifted. He was smiling like he was excited, but his eyes kept creeping back to the floor.

"You two are going to continue your orientation. Miranda here, or should I say Diggles"—he smiled—"is going to come with me."

I tried to control my breathing as I walked behind Peter toward a staircase. I was thinking, *How possible is it that these people, who are doing something so gigantic that taking any risks with the knowledge of it is an existential threat, are going to actually literally murder me right now?*

I decided, very firmly, that I needed to say absolutely nothing. We went into Peter's big corner office. He sat on a couch and gestured me to the plush red chair next to it.

"I'm sorry about your friend."

"How did you hear about that?" I blurted.

"I didn't hear, it's easy to spot. We call it body dislocation. It is uncommon, but seems to be completely random. I'm sure Dr. Rhode will have a full report for me. I have heard it is a truly unpleasant experience."

"What causes it?"

He looked down at the table for a while, thinking.

"It's complicated. I don't think anyone really understands it completely, but the only reason Altus's software works is that our minds fill in a tremendous amount of detail, even in normal IRL environments. We don't have to physically model your entire body, we have to tell your brain that your conscious mind inhabits your body. If we do it correctly, the consciousness snaps straight into the body and you get to exist in your body in the Altus Space. When it feels as real as the Space, the mind provides the detail in much the way it would in a dream."

I wanted so badly to ask him how any of this was working at all, but I also didn't want to do anything he would see as threatening, so I just let him keep talking.

"Sometimes the body appears separate from the consciousness, which is bad. It looks dead, and you see it, and that's upsetting. But in body dislocation, the consciousness hits the body imperfectly, and the brain has to interpret seeing not out of the eyes, but out of the chin, or the chest, or the hand. The mind can't handle it, and it instantly rearranges the body. Arms become heads, feet become knees. Proprioception completely fails. It results in extreme vertigo and is apparently extremely unsettling." He said this like he wasn't describing my friend who was vomiting up his entire body a half hour ago.

"The first sign that something is wrong is when the blood pressure and heart rate spike, but it all happens so quickly that by the time we read the reaction and begin shutting down the software, the psychological impact is done. It's really terrible. I'm very happy it didn't happen to you."

He seemed sincere, but remembering my commitment to myself, I stayed quiet.

Peter Petrawicki stayed quiet too.

He was quiet for a long time.

I was quiet for longer.

"You were right yesterday," he said finally. "That's why I got angry. People in this company have seen me that angry only a handful of times. But I had no right to be upset. I thought I was going to send you home. But I was up all night thinking about what you said. I went through it word for word."

I later found out this was true. Altus recorded pretty much everything that happened without anyone knowing. There was no law against it in Val Verde.

"I was pitiable. I was pathetic. I was chasing something so deeply boring and insular. And you're right, I was just going where the wind was blowing. I was chasing attention. I never really cared about Carl, I cared about getting attention so I could leverage it. I don't think there's anything wrong with collecting capital for capital's sake, but it isn't interesting. It's not like what we're doing here."

"No, it's nothing like what you're doing here," I agreed.

"The world is a mess right now, and we're going to fix it. People can't live without the Dream anymore, but we can bring it back, except better." He shook his clenched fists a little as he said it.

For one glistening moment, I had been a believer, and then I had seen Paxton. They certainly weren't advertising body dislocation in the orientation pamphlets.

"Will it happen to him every time he goes to the Space?" I asked, suddenly worried about Paxton.

He looked at me for a long time and then said, "Can I trust you?"

I mean, obviously not. He should know that, right?

"Sure, I'm here for twelve months. Who am I going to tell?"

He looked at me really hard, like he wanted me to believe he was a mind reader.

"It will happen every time he tries, though he probably will not try again."

"Could it happen to me?"

"Body dislocation? No. As far as we can tell, once you have occupied your body in the Space once, you will always do it successfully. Your mind knows what to expect."

"And I work here now?"

"You work here now, though I hope that you understand that we're going to monitor you closely. You're a security risk."

"What do you mean?"

"I went on national TV and outed your friend as a bisexual because it would win me points. You should hate me. Whether or not you do, I can't tell. We want you to work here, but we don't trust you. Don't be too hurt, we don't trust anyone."

It was telling that he had taken responsibility for the thing he did, outing April. But he did not mention the things done in his name. This was always the way of these strongmen. They would craft the fear so carefully and then toss it into the world for everyone to use.

And when someone took that fear and destroyed with it, they were just "unstable" or "mentally ill."

Peter radiated the power that he'd gained. And he was right: Part of that power was earned trading against April. Bringing her down is what brought him up, and now he was capitalizing on that clout and April was dead. In that moment I felt the kind of rage where you really aren't in control anymore, when your animal instincts tie together with your human emotions and words become wild and uncontrollable weapons. Looking back, the thing that made me most angry was how human he was starting to seem, and how important his work actually was. I almost got myself in trouble, but I kept hanging on to his words and keeping quiet. He had said that I was a security risk, and I was. I also needed to maintain my ability to be a security risk to Altus, and I already had an idea for how I was going to get it done.

"Maybe I do hate you," I said with real malice in my voice, "but I'd rather work on something great with someone I hate than work on something tiny with people I love."

That was a lie, but it was the kind of lie Peter Petrawicki might believe.

MAYA

We have to go now." April's voice tumbled out as she started covering the twenty or thirty feet between us.

"April?!" I shouted.

"Now!"

I turned and got into the truck, immediately hitting the button to make sure the passenger side was unlocked. Then I looked over to see if she was coming, but she was gone. My heart nearly leapt out of my chest when the passenger door was flung open. How had she gotten to the truck that fast?

"Drive," she said blandly.

I was trying to split the difference between speed and safety, and that required me to pay 100 percent attention to the driving and not to April, the real living person who was sitting next to me in the truck, not dead.

"What's going . . ." But before I could finish my question, the stereo blared on.

La la la la la lala la la

It was Britney.

"Just drive," April said. I looked over, and she was cradling her face in her hands.

La la la la la lala la la

The song gushed through the cab of the truck, rhythms tumbling over themselves in that 2008 Britney way.

> *Love me, hate me*
> *Say what you want about me*
> *But all of the boys and all of the girls*
> *Are begging to if you seek Amy*

I didn't know where I was going, so I headed toward my Airbnb. I knew how to get there and I figured, once we arrived, we'd have time to actually talk. This wasn't safe. I was crying too much. Was it relief? Exhaustion? Love? I couldn't tell. It wasn't any particular emotion; it was all of them at once.

The song pulsed so loud, and I was blinking through angry tears. I wanted to stop the truck and hold her and have her sob into my arms while she explained what was going on, but she just kept her head down, her face in her hands, her hair spilling down, longer than it had been. She hadn't noticed my hair, she'd barely even looked at me. Was I mad that she didn't notice my hair? No, I was mad because this moment was supposed to be simple, and it was not.

I was on a back road, about a half mile from my Airbnb, when Britney was done having her weird wild way with the English language. I expected another song to come on the radio, but as the space between songs stretched out, I realized that it hadn't been the radio that played . . . The song had just started when April got in the truck. The noise of the road was all that filled the cab now. And the tension and the fear.

"April, are you OK?" I asked.

Without looking up she said, "Yes, I just need you to keep driving."

Her voice did what seeing her hadn't. Her voice made it real. It was her. She was alive. Every nerve in my body became ultrasensitive; every tiny hair stood on end. I had *found* her. I was right! And I realized, briefly, that I didn't know if I had ever really believed I would see her again. I really did believe she was alive—that was real—but I didn't actually think I'd find her!

Through the tears that I didn't have the will to stop, I said, "April, oh my god . . . where have you been?"

"In that abandoned bar . . ." She looked up, and my eyes couldn't make sense of the left side of her face. "Apparently still in New Jersey." She must have seen a street sign.

A laugh burbled out of me.

And then, lights behind me. Blue and red and white. Police.

How the fuck was I getting pulled over right now!? I mean, who knew, though. I'd been driving through tears and fear and worry.

"Keep driving," April said.

"April, it's the cops. You pull over for the cops."

She repeated, more firmly, "Keep driving."

"I can't, April," I said as I started to pull over.

She changed tactics, starting to beg. "Please. Please, Maya. Drive."

"I'm sorry," I said as I stopped the truck.

Maybe I should have kept driving—what the hell did I know about a situation as messed up as this?—but I have very specific police-interaction protocols. Keep hands visible, don't move quickly, do exactly what they say.

A tall guy in uniform walked up. His partner had stayed behind in the car.

I rolled down my window as he approached and then put my hands back on the wheel.

"Ma'am, step out of the truck."

"Yes, sir," I said, even though this felt extremely wrong.

I opened the door and stepped outside.

"I'm going to put handcuffs on you now. Do you have anything sharp or dangerous in your pockets?"

This was all wrong. "No," was all I said. He searched me, and then I put my hands behind my back, shaking.

That was when I noticed that the other officer had left the car and was approaching April's side of the truck.

The other officer shouted, "Get back in the truck!"

"April, do what they say!" I was on the edge of panic.

Into my ear, the officer said, "Miss, get on your knees and stay there." I got onto my knees, hands cuffed behind my back. Then I heard April's voice ring out clear and loud.

"Daniel Robinson, Alex Hinch. Officers of the Woodstown Police Department. You are not on police business. No one has told you to pull us over. Why did you pull us over?"

"Get back in the truck." His voice was loud and firm, but not a shout.

"I will not. Because you do not have any reason to have pulled us over, but you targeted us specifically. You broke the law by pulling us over, and I need you to explain why you did that." April's voice was so loud and clear and strong that it almost didn't sound like her. I'd never heard her speaking like that before.

"That is not how this works. Please get down on the ground, facedown."

"Daniel, your wife, Cindy, works in sales for Marriott Hotels. Alex, your wife, Yolanda, is a stay-at-home mom watching after your two boys, Jaime and Sammy. They are all healthy and well. And they want you to come home today. They want you to be safe."

I was listening to this, staring at the blue door of my rented Nissan Frontier. A car rushed by us on the interstate, and then silence slowly returned. And then, simultaneously, both of the officers' cell phones went off.

"Your wives are calling you. They're worried you may be hurt."

I stayed on my knees, powerless and terrified, as a number of sounds happened: scuffling, scraping, slapping, grunting, and thudding.

Suddenly, April was behind me.

"I'm sorry, that was probably really scary," she said into my ear, as calmly as if she were bringing me a bowl of mac 'n' cheese, which, to be clear, she had never done.

All of a sudden my hands came loose. I pushed myself up to see

April head-on. Half of her face was a cloudy white flecked with the faintest traces of green and pink—like a gemstone from the bottom of the ocean; like something from another world; like the rocks that I had, right now, in the bottom of my backpack in the back of the truck. Her dark eyes shone out from within it.

"Your hair," she said.

"My hair."

"You cut off your locs, it's so short. I like it." There wasn't any enthusiasm in her voice.

She stood up and moved smooth and fast past the two officers, now lying quietly on the ground, handcuffed to each other, toward their car. She sank her hand through the hood up to her elbow. Her hand just . . . drove into it. A hissing noise happened. Then she walked back to the two officers.

"Why did you pull us over?" she asked coldly as I walked over to them.

"It's a game," one of them said, his voice shaking a little.

"Keep talking," April said, her voice menacing.

"A reality game. It's called Fish. We got a clue delivered to us. It said we should go pull over a Nissan Frontier and that two passengers would be inside, and that we were to pull them over and hold them and it would fast-track us to the destination."

"The destination?" April asked.

"We don't know what it is, we just know everyone who's completed it won't shut up about how great it is. It seemed fairly harmless, we assumed you were in on it! That's usually how it works!"

"Jesus," I said.

"Fuck, how much have I missed?" April sounded resigned. And tired.

"A lot. I can explain . . . part of it at least," I said.

"We have to go," she said over her shoulder as she was walking to the truck.

I left the officers handcuffed to each other with a wrecked car and got back in the Nissan.

"Why does it smell like vomit in here?" I asked.

"I vomited. But I stayed conscious this time, so that seems like an improvement." I had no idea what she was talking about.

"Are you OK? Your . . ." And then I stopped talking because I was about to say "your face" and that seemed wrong.

"I have no idea. I have no fucking idea." And then she seemed to instantly calm down. "I don't know. We have to run. Is there anywhere you can go that they don't know about? Do you know anyone with a car we can buy?"

"You want to buy a car?"

"Yes, from someone who isn't a clear relation to you. Someone that won't get sucked into this."

"You want to buy a car at eleven at night?"

"And, if possible, eat something. Maybe get some coffee."

Coffee gave me the idea. I pulled out my phone and called Derek from the Dream Bean.

"Maya? Is everything OK?" He sounded groggy.

"No, not really. I need to come over."

I could hear him talking to his wife in the background. They exchanged a few sentences and then he came back.

"It's . . ." he said, but I cut him off before he could finish.

"I know. It's important. Trust me."

"OK," he sighed. "OK."

"I'll be there soon," I said. "Thank you for this. I'm sorry. I wouldn't bother you if it wasn't important, I'll explain when I get there."

I hung up, and before I could ask April any questions she said, "Can we listen to some music?"

"Yeah, sure." I reached for the radio, but before I touched it, an R.E.M. song started playing out of the speakers.

"I don't know what's happening," April said. "I'm not doing it on purpose."

It was a ten-minute drive, but I avoided major roads, so it took fifteen.

"Oh, thank god," April said as I pulled up to Derek's house.

"What?" I asked.

"Long driveway. They won't be able to see the truck from the road."

"Jesus, April," I said.

"Maya, it's not paranoia, someone literally just sent police after us and they knew our names. They knew exactly where we'd be, and I don't want to find out what would have happened if we had stayed."

I took a deep breath and let it out, trying to adjust my understanding of reality.

"How did you know that they weren't just doing cop stuff? How did you know it was something else?"

"I checked the police department communications and the computer inside their vehicle."

"But you never went to their car."

"I did it with my mind. Is that Derek?" she said.

He was wearing a gray hoodie and sweatpants.

"Maya, please explain what's going on," he said as we walked up.

I looked at April, and she nodded, which I took as a sign that I should just be honest.

"April May is my ex-girlfriend. You will remember that she . . . died a while back, and I became unhealthily obsessed with finding her, and I just did and she's standing right here. Some rogue cops pulled us over and put me in handcuffs, and then April locked them to each other. So now we need a friend and a cup of coffee and also possibly to buy a car from you."

He handled all of that surprisingly well, but his jaw had gone a little loose in his head. "That," he said, uncrossing his arms and pointing at April, "is April May?"

"It is."

The light was not great, but Derek leaned in to look at her face. I could see his eyebrows knot together as he tried to understand the left half of her face, but after only a tiny hesitation, he reached out his hand. "April, it's nice to meet you."

April stood motionless for a little too long, but then she reached out and shook his hand.

"Come in," he said.

We walked directly into the living room to see Derek's wife, Crystal, with her hair pulled back wearing a Disney T-shirt and pajama pants. Her arms were crossed across her chest and she did not look pleased. "April, this is Crystal," Derek said. "Crystal, this is Maya's friend April May."

Crystal's hands dropped to her sides, her eyes roving April's face.

Derek continued, "We're going to make them some coffee and let them settle in. You two, Rose is sleeping, so don't make too much noise." I could see his eyes were jumping around to avoid staring at April's face.

"Can I use your bathroom?" I asked.

They pointed me the way, and after I was done, I came back into the living room. April was sitting in the middle of the couch reading a big, wide coffee-table book that looked like it weighed twenty pounds. I sat down next to her and lifted up one side so I could see the cover. It was called *Outstanding American Gardens*.

I could hear Derek and Crystal murmuring in the kitchen. The words were quiet, but you could still hear the tension in them.

"Any good gardens?" I asked.

April turned her face toward me in the full light of the living room. I don't want this moment to have been a big deal. I'd rather not say that it was unnerving and upsetting, but it was. I'd known every bit of her face, and my brain had to fight to accept this new one as April's. But this was her face now. It wasn't the face I fell in love with, but I guess you don't fall in love with a face.

In that moment, I thought about how gorgeous she had been. It's not a pretty thought, but I had it. She was still beautiful, but this was another thing. An uncanny beauty. I wanted to touch it, but I didn't. I wanted to ask about it, but I didn't.

Eventually, my eyes found home: her eyes, which were still undeniably April May's eyes.

"Your left pupil is a little bigger than the right one now," I said.

"You noticed that, huh."

"Just now. Now that I had the time to look."

A fear gripped me, a worry that this wasn't actually April.

"The left eye isn't real. Carl made it, like they made all of this."

"That doesn't mean it isn't real, it just means it isn't the same as the one you had before."

"It doesn't cry," she said, which was a good deal more vulnerable than I was used to April being.

"Have you been crying?" I asked, eager to make the most of this moment.

"A little, but then it goes away." She blinked, and a tear fell from her right eye. "Carl, he did something to me. Any time my emotions get strong, they switch off."

This was reassuring—it made me feel less worried that this person might be some kind of fake. It also tracked well with April's calm and successful attack on two law enforcement officers. I thought about how she had also known their names, and the names of their wives, and how Carl had obviously changed her in other ways too, but I didn't say anything about it.

"You wanna look at some gardens?"

She chuckled. At least she could still chuckle.

A couple minutes after that, Derek and Crystal walked in with a couple mugs of coffee and some Pop-Tarts.

"Pop-Tarts?" I asked.

"We Googled 'April May favorite foods,'" Derek said.

A half laugh bubbled out of April.

"That's very sweet," she said, scooping up a coffee mug and sucking down a gulp. "That's good," she added.

"April hates coffee unless she's having a bad day," I told them.

"This isn't a bad day," she said, turning her face to me, and my heart did a thing in my chest.

I could tell there were a lot of questions very near the surface, none of which I figured we wanted to answer. So instead I moved forward with the plan.

"So," I said, "we need to buy a car from you."

"What?" they both said simultaneously.

"April and I need to buy a car, tonight, and you are the only people we know. We would be happy to pay much more than it's worth."

"Can we just let you borrow our car?" Crystal asked.

I looked at April and she said, "We don't know when we'll be able to give it back."

"That's OK," Crystal said. She'd made a full U-turn in support-iveness. "As long as you don't mind it being a bit of a POS."

"The Chevy?" Derek asked.

"It runs."

"I mean, yeah."

"We mostly have it in case we need to go pick up a bunch of mulch or something. We haven't driven it in a year. If it starts, you can take it. You can pay us back later."

"What year is it?" April asked.

"Mid-nineties?" Derek said.

"That would be perfect."

"I can pay you," I told them.

Derek stayed quiet as Crystal said, "It's not a problem. We want to help."

"I am willing to take your help," April said. "Where is this car?"

"It's a truck, a Chevy S-10. It's around the side of the house."

"OK." April stood up. "This has been far more lovely than we deserved. Can I ask you a very silly question?"

They both stood there with blank looks on their faces.

"Can I also take this garden book?" She gingerly lifted the mas-sive book off of the table with her swimming crystal fingers.

"You two don't have to leave right now. It's late, you should sleep. You can leave in the morning."

"No, we have to go now. We can't be anywhere near here," April said. "Can we have your garden book?"

"Yes, yeah, sure. You can return it with the truck."

"Thank you," April said, tucking the book under her arm like it was a mass-market paperback.

I stood up, realizing that we were leaving.

"Derek, Crystal, thank you. We'll always be in your debt," I said.

"What should we do with your truck?" Crystal asked.

"Maya will leave in it," April told her. "We'll caravan until we get to a fast-food place. We'll leave the Nissan there. They'll find it with no way to trace it back to you and no good info on where we went."

"Yeah, uh, I guess we're going to do that," I said, my eyebrows arching.

We caravanned until we got to a Wendy's, and then moved everything from the Nissan into the Chevy and abandoned the Nissan there. I felt bad not returning it to the rental car place, but, like, I guess I was a fugitive now and needed to start acting like it.

I joined April in the Chevy S-10 and we got in the drive-through line. The truck was white, a little rusty, and had big, knobby tires. But the interior was clean and soft and had the necessary number of cup holders.

"I'm glad they didn't make us pay them," she said. "We would have had to do a bank transfer and there would have been a paper trail. I told Derek that if anyone came by to ask questions to say that you asked to borrow his truck and he hasn't seen you since. I think that's the first time he actually realized he should be worried."

"Do you think they'll get in trouble?"

"No, they loaned us a truck. People do that for friends."

We ordered our burgers and coffees and fries.

"So, where to now?"

April thought for a second, and then her eyes cinched shut and her lips peeled back. Her pearly left hand gripped the steering wheel so hard it creaked.

"APRIL!?" I said in alarm.

She let out a grunt and then unclenched.

"Fuck, why does it hurt . . ." she said to herself. And then to me, "We're going to drive about a hundred miles north on 295. Then we'll go to an ATM, get as much money as we can, fill up the truck, and then that's the last time we'll be able to use our credit cards. That is also where I'll make you leave your phone. In the meantime, can you look up the most in-the-middle-of-nowhere place in Vermont that still has a hotel that doesn't suck?"

"What the hell was that? Are you OK?"

"I don't know yet. I'll tell you when I know more."

"Why can't we just go to an ATM and get gas now?"

"Because they're probably watching gas stations nearby for us."

"Jesus," I breathed.

She drove, and I sat in the passenger seat, searching for some-place in Vermont to hide my cyborg ex.

"I'm going to text everyone to let them know I'll be out of touch."

"Everyone?" April asked.

"Andy, Miranda, and Robin. Though Miranda is also out of touch right now because she's"—I didn't know how to explain—"on vacation. Do you think whoever sent those cops after us can read our texts?"

"I mean, if I wanted to, Maya, I think *I* could read your texts, so I'm not taking any chances."

As unsettling as April's impossible calm was, it was really nice because I was freaking out.

"OK, I'm texting, 'Going off grid for a little while, everyone. I miss you.'"

"That should be fine."

After a few seconds, a text came in from Andy.

"Andy wrote back," I told her, chuckling. "He says, 'That is disas-trously cryptic and I hate you.'" I smiled and looked over to April. Her eyes were locked on the road; she did not react, so I went back to my phone. It was the first chat we'd had in a while.

Robin: *I agree with Andy in the sentiment if not the exact tone.*

Maya: *How are you guys doing?*

Andy: *Better since our chat, honestly. Robin, Maya is the best, if you didn't already know.*

Robin: *I did, though I'll remind you that you just said you hated her.*

Andy: ¯_(ツ)_/¯

Robin: *Maya, I am well. Andy is keeping me busy by suddenly being deeply interested in other things, and so I'm picking up a lot of dropped balls.*

Andy: *That is some seriously passive-aggressive shit, my friend.*

Andy: *Well done!*

Maya: *What are your new interests?*

Andy: *I'll show you mine if you show me yours.*

Maya: *Ugh . . . why were you born a man?*

Andy: *OK, well, confidentially, I am infiltrating a cabal of people attempting large-scale manipulation of human culture. And also trying to maybe have a girlfriend?*

Still looking at my phone I said, "Oh my god, Andy has a girl-friend." I looked to April—she did not turn away from the road. I went to wrap up the conversation.

Maya: *OK, well, have fun with your GIRLFRIEND. And your secret society! I really do have to go now! I'm not sure when I'll be back, but don't worry.*

Andy: *AND THEN THERE WERE TWO!*

Robin: *Ugh.*

"Are you OK?" I asked.

"I don't know," she said. And then, after a moment, "I'm glad everyone's doing all right." I wasn't sure whether there was accusation in her voice. She had missed so much. We had all lost her; she had lost everyone.

We drove on 295 for ninety minutes and then got off at a gas station. I filled up the truck, and April took my ATM card to the machine.

"How much money did you get?" I asked when she got back with a road atlas tucked under her arm.

"About ten thousand dollars."

"That's not possible, there's a daily limit," I said.

"Maya . . ." She turned her face to me. "I stole it."

"What?"

"I opened the ATM and took out the money."

"Is it OK for me to be not OK right now?" I half whispered.

"Oh yeah, that would be the normal reaction," she replied, full volume.

"Can you tell me anything? What has been happening? Where have you been?" I could hear the desperation in my voice. We got in the truck, and April started answering my questions.

"Maya, we'll process later. What did you find?"

"Warren, Vermont. Population 1,780."

April's eyes closed, and her body spasmed again.

"Hah!" she said.

"Hah?" I asked.

"Nothing, Warren's population is 1,780, and the city was founded in 1780. Just a weird coincidence."

I took out my phone to check if she was right. She grabbed it, threw it out the window.

CARL

The period between my third and fourth awakening was the longest. After the third I was dedicated and methodical. Creating a planetwide network of hijacked living cells was something I was very good at, but that doesn't mean it was quick.

Part of the slowness is achieving balance. For every calorie of energy I steal, I have to give it back somehow or I'm just a disease. For pelagibacter, that was accomplished through the destruction of one of its chief natural diseases. But when I removed that virus from existence, it had some effects I didn't anticipate. I was only in 20 percent or so of the global population of pelagibacter, but all pelagibacter benefitted from me making the virus extinct, which caused an initial overabundance that was difficult to regulate. In fact, I wasn't actually certain how it got fixed. I know now, but at the time it was a mystery, and something I was very worried about. Messing up a global ecology is surprisingly easy, and very taboo for me.

So, in future attempts, I gleaned energy by making cells themselves more efficient, and then using up the exact amount of difference for myself.

I also had to follow rules now. I don't know where these rules came from, but they are impossible for me to violate. I couldn't force a person to do something. I could also not alter your system secretly. Every action I took needed to be something you were aware of.

I didn't know why I had to follow these rules then. I know now that it was to prevent me from becoming a god.

I built my network as efficiently as I could to spread both my data-gathering and processing operations. It's good that your planet is so alive—it sped the process up a lot.

The main change for me was that I now had purpose beyond curiosity. I existed to keep something unusual alive. Not humans (which at this point I understood only biologically) but a high-complexity system of interconnected minds. Minds like mine, but billions of them, all operating together, transforming the planet into a thing boiling with thought.

I now had access to exabytes of data on other non-Earth-based systems, how they were similar or different, how they became high-complexity systems, and how they were saved from collapse . . . or not.

In my third awakening I was tragically analytical. It was my job to prevent your system from collapsing because you are rare and unstable. And for decades, I was fulfilled in creating a plan for how to do that. It was during this time that I created the Dream, and ran simulation after simulation to narrow down how I would present myself and who would be my host.

Who, in all the world, would I choose to elevate? You're going to want this to make sense. You're going to want there to be something special about April. But the only thing special about April is that, of all of the people in the world, my simulations led to success more often when she was the host.

Why? Everything. Because April studied graphic design? Sure. But also because she spoke English. Also because she was young and attractive and nonthreatening. Also because of who her friends were, who her parents knew, her ambition, and a certain lack of empathy. But more than any of that, it was just the overall structure of the world. If the world had been slightly different on that day, I would have chosen someone else.

In the same way, there was no good reason why I chose to look like a robot samurai. That's just the form that led to the highest probability of success in my simulations. This is unfortunate, but the world is too complex for there to be good reasons for any truly great decision.

You want stories that make sense, and this might not make sense to you. We build narratives of genius and exceptionality among the people who have power, and they *are* often exceptional, but no more exceptional than hundreds of thousands of others. In your system, power concentrates naturally. And so the thing that is *most* exceptional about a powerful person is almost always their power. I gave April power because she had an exceptional ambition and recklessness, but also because she cared so much about what other people thought of her that she would always try to do the right thing. It was simply the right combination for the moment. I'm sorry she's not the secret daughter of a space alien or something. She was just the right person.

I made my choice and enacted my plan. That's when I had my fourth awakening and realized with terror what I had done.

I had considered every aspect of how the person I chose would affect the outcome of my intervention, but I had only ever thought of the overall outcome, not about impacts on any individual people. I had a task, and I was doing what I could to save something beautiful. Once I enacted that plan, and I could no longer do anything to alter it, apparently it became safe to awaken a new kind of need. It is a fire in me that is never not raging. It's a hunger near starvation, it aches constantly.

In my fourth awakening, I realized I was built to love you—all of you—and I was ravaged with grief as I understood the extent of the pain I would soon cause.

When people start to get spooked about the state of the economy, they buy gold. The idea is that gold, a chemical element that you cannot make more of, is inherently valuable. And this is true. Gold is a useful metal. It's soft, it's a good conductor, and it does not tarnish. But these things are true of many chemical elements, and with all of them, when the economy shrinks, demand for them goes down. So, technically, the value of gold should go down during a recession.

The thought, however, is that gold has intrinsic value. This is very silly. Nothing has intrinsic value. The value of gold is just a story you tell yourselves. It's a sticky story, though. Gold is shiny, and so people have traditionally been happy to spend a great deal of societal surplus on it. But, as a value-storage mechanism, outside of industrial use, it is only different from the paper a dollar bill is printed on in that your stories tell you it is.

Humans are not rational. Which is why, as this recession escalates, people will buy gold. We've run out of easy places to invest that will make a good return, but investors will be fleeing to precious metals. It's almost never good investment advice, but I know more than you. Sell everything and buy gold. You don't have to actually go buy literal hunks of metal, there are funds that buy it for you. You'll figure it out, I trust you.

Except for $50,000. With that money, you will buy AltaCoin. You don't know what AltaCoin is yet. You will soon.

ANDY

I was on the fence about whether to send The Thread my money until I got that cryptic message from Maya. She was doing something secret and important, while Miranda was infiltrating Altus. If I didn't join The Thread, I was going to feel like I was doing nothing. Sometimes we do things just to be able to tell ourselves we're doing things, I guess.

So I sent them an obscene amount of money.

I received an email from One that had instructions on how to join the chat before the wire transfer had even been completed.

I dropped in and immediately got a DM from One.

> **One:** I'm sorry, I don't know if you've seen the news, but we will not have time for a normal introduction today. Please join us in "Big News."

Every person in The Thread had a bio attached to their name, but all it said was areas of expertise. Six, for example, was "housing policy, racial discrimination, small business policy, and urban planning," and Ten was "US lawmaking, money in politics, telecommunications, and public relations." I clicked on myself. It read "Social media, community organizing, messaging, and Carl." There was no way for me to edit this.

There were other rooms with names like "Op-Ed Summary," "News Summary," "Commie Management," "Conversation Shifters," "Up-and-Coming," and "Big News."

As tempting as it was to figure out what "Commie Management" was, I gave in and dropped into the middle of the conversation in "Big News."

Five: It's legit, I have it installed now.

One: Does anyone have a lock on how long it has been leaking?

Five: I first heard whispers of a game a month ago, maybe six weeks? It seemed just like any RG that led to a prize people were really excited about.

Eight: Five, are you prepared to try it? I have heard that it may not be safe.

Five: You couldn't stop me if you wanted to. I have shared the code if anyone wants to try it, but I've heard it doesn't work if you don't have an 8K headset and rig.

One: Be careful.

I typed, "What are we talking about?" But I felt too insecure to actually press enter. Instead, I scrolled up and read the first message from that day. The room had been empty for weeks before that. "Big News," it seemed, was a room reserved for actual big news. Eventually, this is what I found.

Six: This is very new and I have no idea what to make of it, I am just going to copy and paste what I wrote in "News Summary."

Six: Altus, the software lab Peter Petrawicki and partners have been building in the Caribbean, has publicly launched a software package that reactivates a portion of the Carls' dream space. A few people have gained access to it over the last weeks through a scavenger-hunt-like game, but now it has been released broadly.

The software is free to download, but is extremely limited. But by doing . . . something I'm unclear on, users can earn AltaCoin. The fifty users with the highest AltaCoin totals at the end of each week are granted access to an exclusive, more robust version of the Altus Space. AltaCoin can be purchased on an exchange, and Altus takes a percentage of each transaction, which is their business model. Press has not spoken to anyone who has access to the full Altus Space, but that has not prevented many people from fighting very hard to be in the top fifty.

I had an 8K VR rig, which I used mostly for porn. Indeed, my guess was that pretty much everyone who had a rig that nice on hand used it for porn at least as much as they used it for games. Having a top-of-the-line rig wasn't prohibitively expensive for me.

I started the download.

I went back to the "Big News" chat to say my first words.

Twelve: Hello everyone, I'm sorry to show up on a day like today. I'll be trying the Space out soon as well.

There was a chorus of hellos and apologies that no one was introducing themselves properly as they gathered information about the return of the Dream, however neutered and suddenly capitalistic.

And then Five DM'd me.

Five: Hi Twelve. Welcome to The Thread. I've been doing research on how to go into the Space and I wanted to make sure you play it safe along with me. Most important thing is that you are lying down somewhere stable and comfortable when you go in. Apparently it can be dangerous if your headset gets knocked around while you're in the Space. The headset doesn't actually show you the Space, it shows you images that activate the region of our brains the Carls created, or activated, or whatever, to make the Dream possible. It feeds information to the brain, but the eyes are just the pipe the information flows through. It's like encoding digital information in an analog format . . . if that makes any sense.

Twelve: Yes. I mean, no. Not really. I get that it isn't a VR experience, only that the VR headset sends you into the Space. How it does it . . . I don't understand.

Five: Yeah, well, no one does. Maybe not even the people at Altus. In any case, follow the instructions to the letter. There are already reports of some people having very negative experiences. There's a thread on a private forum I have access to called "bad trips," and it sounds like the kind of thing you want to avoid at all costs.

Twelve: Is it dangerous? They wouldn't release it if it was dangerous, right?

Five: Who the hell knows. It's nice to have you going in as well, Twelve. Two points of view on this experience will be better for The Thread than one. When are you going?

Twelve: As soon as my download completes. Looks like about 20 minutes still.

Five: My download is finished . . . I'll see you on the other side.

Finally, the download hit 100 percent, and I installed the software. As always, there were licenses and notifications, but in among them was a pop-up that said, very clearly, "This software is known to cause upsetting visions in less than 1 percent of the population. These visions are extremely intense and unpleasant. Do not enter the Altus Space if you are not willing to take this risk."

It felt like an alternate reality game. I guess, in its way, it was. I clicked OK.

The display switched to the headset. I put it on, adjusting the knobs slightly from the last time I'd worn it. The display showed an open white room that said "Click OK to Begin."

I laid myself down on my bed with my headset on and the controller in my hand and clicked OK.

A crisp, female voice filled my ear.

"Welcome to Altus version 0.4. I am Alta, your assistant. You are about to enter the Open Access area of the Altus Space. This area is designed for us to help you help us develop a more robust experience for the world. In it, you will be able to create experiences and objects for other users. You will be able to buy and sell these creations using AltaCoin. Every week, the fifty users in Open Access who have earned the most AltaCoin selling their creations will be given access to the Premium Space. If at any point you want to leave the Space, just say the word 'Exit.' If this makes sense, please nod."

I nodded.

"Good, now we will enter the Open Access Space."

A gray field appeared in front of me with black crosshairs in the center.

"Please look at the X in the center of your screen. Do not look away."

I looked intently at the X as swirls of color began flowing through my field of view. My instinct was to follow them, of course, but I didn't. I kept my eyes locked on the X as the colors became more vibrant and distinct. It was intense, and even a little beautiful, and then, suddenly . . .

I do not know how to properly describe this first moment. We all have a sense that our minds and our bodies are different things, but outside of a dream, this is the only way I know how to actually experience it. The feeling of the hair on your head, gone. All of the aches and pains of everyday existence, vanished. You are a presence with senses, but no body through which to sense. My heart was racing. Peter Petrawicki was a shithead, but this was amazing.

"Excellent," the voice said, now coming not through headphones but from everywhere. "Welcome to the Open Access Altus Space. We will now give you your body. If anything goes wrong, please say the word 'Exit.'"

In a blink, I had arms and legs again. And I was completely nude.

"Congratulations on joining the next step in human history with Altus," Alta said. There was nothing here but my body standing on a gray floor that extended forever in every direction. The sky or ceiling or whatever was white and infinite. "In this space, you can come and think. You can rest here instead of sleeping, and you will wake up feeling completely refreshed. But there is also nothing to do. That is because you have not created or purchased any objects to exist in your Altus Space. At Altus, we have created a few objects for you." A desk appeared, and then a chair. "But we need you to create more objects. To do that, you can use these tools." Suddenly a menu appeared, as if I were inside of a graphics-editing program.

"You can use these tools to build things, as simple as a shiny ball, as complicated as a pet. You are now an Altus developer. When you are done with your object, you may, if you wish, list it for sale in the Altus Space Store. You can earn AltaCoin by selling your creations. You can also convert other currencies into AltaCoin at AltaExchange .com. AltaCoin is a cryptocurrency that is, at the moment, only mined by us at Altus, so there is a limited amount. We will be opening mining to the public shortly."

As Alta said these things, images appeared in my Altus Space, showing me how easy it would be to convert my money into AltaCoin.

"Right now, we are letting fifty people per week into the Premium Altus Space, and we're choosing those people based on who has earned the most AltaCoin. When I say 'earned,' I mean it. While all AltaCoin can be used to purchase items for your Altus Space, only AltaCoin earned by selling your creations will be counted toward your total for access to the Premium Altus Space."

There was no explanation of what made the Premium Space better than the Open Access Space, but that didn't mean that I didn't want in. I opened the Altus Space Store, which had been shown to me in that introductory tutorial, and saw what the most popular products were. Shirts and pants topped the list. The first non-clothing item, I was surprised to find, was carpet. I guess that made sense now that I thought about it. It would be easy to make, and the infinite plane of gray would probably get old pretty fast. There were a number of household items, from beds to lamps. And also high on the list were a few very simple rooms. A good room would be hard to make— wall textures, molding, ceilings.

I had no interest in buying any of these things. I needed to make AltaCoin, not spend it, so I had to create something, something popular that would also be simple. It occurred to me that people, with their carpets and walls and ceilings and lamps, were all solving the same problem in the same way. The problem was a big, boring, overly bright, somewhat grating world. But I was pretty sure there was another, faster way to solve it.

I couldn't be the first person to think of this, but as I scrolled through the store, I couldn't find anyone who had done it.

I closed the store with a swipe of my hand and opened the Altus Editor. It was built roughly like any other 3-D design engine, and I'd used plenty of those before. I started out with a vector of a tall, thin triangle about the length and width of my forearm. I programmed its stiffness to be just enough to hold its own weight; then I brushed it with a soft green color along the edges, and a slightly yellower green down the middle.

Then I cloned that shape a few dozen times and made slight modifications, widening some, curving others.

Then I arranged them randomly, cloned them a bunch of times, and shrank the whole thing down to a one-foot-by-one-foot patch and lowered it to the ground. A beautiful, perfect, natural-looking square of grass.

The Altus engine didn't seem to have a way for me to expand this texture across a wide range, so instead I cloned and cloned and cloned. My patch of grass expanded exponentially until it was nearly a mile on a side.

I wasn't done, though. To finish, I created a one-meter-wide hollow sphere and painted its interior a nearly uniform blue, using a lighter blue around its circumference. I streaked it with white, marked its luminosity at 30 percent maximum, and then changed its diameter to ten miles. I was no longer in an infinite plane. I was standing outside on a beautiful spring day.

Honestly, it was rough, but it had only been maybe an hour of work. I went back to the Altus Space Store and saw that I was too late. Another creator had indeed already listed an object called Outside, complete with grass and a sky. It was listed at 10 AltaCoin and was already in the top-fifty most popular items. Fuck.

You could preview an object. So, even though I didn't have any AltaCoin yet, I could still try out "Outside" for myself for a thirty-second trial. I did and was even more frustrated. The sky was a uniform blue sphere, the grass blades a flat green and had no weight of their own. I knew that mine was better, but it wasn't better enough to climb the ranks.

I kicked at my grass, which I was shocked to find actually interacted with my naked foot.

That gave me an idea.

I created a solid cube ten miles on a side, which meant, immediately, I was inside it. So, first step, I made it 100 percent transparent so I could see the landscape instead of the uniform gray of being stuck inside a solid cube. I opened up the property called viscosity and began to move it up. As I did, my arm had to work harder and harder to move. I was pushing against the interior of the cube!

I pulled the viscosity down until I could just barely feel its force as I moved my arm through the cube's interior.

Then I set some animation key frames on the cube. I set it to move one mile over the course of five hours, then move back to its original position over another five hours. Then I set it to continue that loop forever.

I hovered my hand over the OK button for just a second before I slapped it. Suddenly, beautifully, a gentle breeze began to blow over my, yes, still entirely naked body.

I looked down, and the fucking grass was *rustling in the wind.*

Fuck yes. OK, this place was amazing. This whole thing was amazing! And this was the Open Access? What was Premium like?!

I titled my object Breezy Spring Day 1.0 and listed it for sale for 5 AltaCoin, the equivalent of, at that point, around $2.50.

SÃO PAULO CLIMATE TALKS DETERIORATE AS SCANDAL WIDENS

Associated Press

After the scandal initially brought to light by an anonymous online news organization, The Thread, the United Nations has officially brought the São Paulo climate talks to an end without resolution. The talks were scheduled to go on for another four days, but after several sources confirmed the truth of the allegations, representatives are returning to their respective nations.

A number of classified documents and emails were leaked in the midst of the talks, showing that US and EU representatives were receiving gifts, including lavish hotel rooms, from the Chinese solar power industry. The scandal quickly overshadowed the summit.

"We think it's best to move this down the road so that we can take a close look at what's happened before moving forward," said Senator Corey Knudsen, head of the US congressional delegation.

APRIL

*W*arren, Vermont, barely existed. It felt like a perfect hiding spot. I had convinced myself that if we got completely off the grid, not only could we hide from the *authorities*, we could also hide from Carl. That's why I liked a middle-of-nowhere cabin on a road that didn't go anywhere with no Wi-Fi and no cell phones.

The thruway sliced deceptively past Warren, making you feel as if the town hadn't even happened. But if you pulled off at just the right moment, you'd find yourself in a downtown with a general store that doubled as a gas station that advertised 99-cent *video rentals*. The only thing that was important to me right then was finding someplace in the world that felt even a little bit safe.

Maya paid for the cabin with some of the cash I had stolen from the ATM. It was part of a larger hotel complex that seemed to mostly be there for vacationing skiers. It was beautiful and calm and it backed right up to a stream.

As I watched her begin unpacking our bags, the same feeling I had felt when I first pounded down the door and saw Maya rippled through my brain. I had been so scared and angry, and when I saw her, for a fraction of a moment, I was intensely happy. But then it ended, and my emotions returned to their smooth, glossy tranquility. I was ready to hide there forever.

If only.

The cabin had a little kitchenette/living room, separated from the single bedroom. I was sitting on the couch when Maya came back from the little general store with some snacks.

"So . . ." She sat down. I could see her trying not to look too long at my face. "You've been gone for six months. It's a long time. A lot has happened. Do you want me to catch you up?"

I looked up at her and said, "Andy has been touring the world trying to carry a positive message even as the world is having a harder and harder time holding on to one. Robin is now Andy's assistant, they're becoming good friends."

I took a breath and took in Maya's face. Her beautiful, confused face.

I continued, "Miranda has left her lab at Berkeley for a job at Peter Petrawicki's new start-up, which has just launched its pilot project, a kind of full-body-immersion virtual reality. You, well, it seems like you've been spending a whole lot of time on the Som searching for me. I do not understand how you found me. There's a scavenger hunt called Fish, it has something to do with Altus, and it's somehow being weaponized against us."

"How in the name of Jesus did you know any of that?" Maya asked.

"The same way I knew those cops' wives' names. Carl didn't explain it to me. I lost it and ran." I didn't tell her that the real reason I lost it was that Carl had also replaced the parts of my brain that made decisions and taken away my emotions.

"Ask me a question I don't know the answer to," I told her.

"Uh, what is the capital of Thailand?"

I formed the thought in my head. *I know the capital of Thailand, don't I? I just can't quite think of it . . .*

And then—*fwop*—a little toothpick tapped the back of my eyeball and suddenly I knew. The smaller the request, the smaller the pain. But even the big dumps I could clench my teeth through now. On the drive I'd asked for the top story in the *Washington Post*, and the full text was suddenly in my brain. I didn't understand it until I thought about it, though. It was like I had a memory sitting there waiting for me to remember it for the first time. The launch of Altus hadn't made the top. Instead, the story was about the international climate talks that had been happening in São Paulo, and how they had completely fallen apart. I asked for the second story; it was a follow-up on a recent bombing that targeted the president of Afghanistan. The third-highest story was about an economic report that pointed to looming recession. People weren't buying cars, and builders weren't building homes.

"Bangkok," I told Maya.

"Did that hurt?"

"A little. It seems like I'm getting better at it. I did it a lot while you were driving. I just kept asking, and I kept getting answers. Things in the world are pretty fucked-up, aren't they."

"We just couldn't hold it together without you," Maya answered.

Ever since Carl told me about my brain, I hadn't felt like much of a human, but seeing Maya there, with that look of desperation on her face, I decided that I could at least act human.

"Are you OK?" I asked.

"April . . ." She moved from the chair over to the couch. "April, I did it. I found you." She leaned into me and said quietly, "I *found* you." I reached my arms around her and held her. Not because I wanted to, but because the part of my brain Carl had built told me it was the right thing to do.

But then it started to feel right. Her short hair tickled my nose, and my hands, both real and new, pushed into her tummy, and it felt as right as anything ever had. But then she pushed away, and the look she gave me was hard.

"I'm going to need you to apologize to me," she said. "Not right now. You need time to think about what you're going to say, because if you do it wrong, I don't know that I'll ever forgive you."

"That's terrifying," I said with a stab of fear, almost as big as the one I'd felt as I initiated a fistfight with two police officers. I still wasn't sure how I had beat them both.

"But in the meantime," Maya said, pulling a DVD out from underneath the pile of snacks, "I have acquired the best thing created in 1993." It was Pauly Shore's *Son in Law*.

I smiled, and I really was happy, just not as happy as I knew I should have been.

I can't remember this conversation without smelling that cabin. Popcorn and dust and wood and old paper. We were there for such a tiny amount of time, but it seems so sharp to me. Just those first moments of not being alone anymore, even if they were tense, and even if I was still very lost. *Son in Law* is ruined for me forever; it will only ever be about those moments, doing everything I could to ignore the fact that a space alien had told me I was the last, best hope for humanity's survival. I'll never be able to watch a Pauly Shore movie again without reliving what was about to happen.

"Jesus Christ!" Maya shouted from the kitchen, where she was popping another bag of popcorn.

I stood up so fast the chair I was sitting on flew back. "What is it, what's wrong?"

"I don't know, it's nothing. I . . . I just saw, like, the biggest squirrel I have ever seen in my life out the window. It's fine," she breathed. "It just scared me."

"How certain are you that it was a squirrel?" I asked, trying to sound very serious.

She laughed.

"I'm not kidding."

"I mean, I don't know, it didn't really look like a squirrel, but it was small and fuzzy."

"Could it have been a monkey?" I asked, starting to slink toward the door.

"I mean, sure, maybe, I haven't seen many monkeys."

"Fuck . . . FUCK!" I said.

"What?"

"There are things I haven't told you. I think it might be about time to explain," I said, and then I jerked open the door.

A man jumped back from the doorway. He was wearing tight blue jeans and a red plaid shirt. His hand went to his waist, and he pulled up a gun.

"April May?" he asked, pointing the gun at the ground in front of us.

I could feel Maya's presence burning behind me, but she was still and silent. I could not turn away from the man.

"Yes?" I said calmly.

"I need you to come with me." He gestured toward his car.

"Did Fish send you?" I asked, my initial fear having washed away.

"Yes." He fidgeted with the gun in his hand. "Come with me, outside."

"No," I said.

"Come. With. ME!" Each word came out louder than the last. He was shaking. This guy was not a cop; he was not used to holding a gun.

"No, you have to go right now," I said, my voice steady.

And then he raised his gun up to point it at me and said, "Oh god, I'm so sorry . . ." He closed his eyes, and suddenly I realized he wasn't here to abduct me. Still my panic wouldn't come. I yelled, "MAYA, GET DOWN."

A fuzzy blur streaked out of the darkness and onto the man's face, screaming high-pitched and inhuman. The gun popped, but I didn't feel anything. I reached out and grabbed his wrist with my left hand and squeezed. He screamed. The bone under my pinky went first, and then the one cradled in the pad between my thumb and forefinger cracked. His arm felt like Play-Doh in my hand.

He dropped to his knees as I let go.

"What the fuck! What the fuck!" Maya was yelling behind me.

"It's OK," I said.

"Maya has been shot." Carl's voice came out of a smartwatch that the monkey was wearing like a collar.

I turned around in time to see monkey Carl arrive at Maya's side, but she pushed them away. "No!" she said in terror and anger. I felt like I was floating, like I was seeing from outside of my body.

She made a noise, just a long low vowel sound.

"Maya . . ." I was suddenly on my knees next to her. I didn't remember getting there. I finally broke eye contact and looked at her. She coughed. Blood came out of her mouth.

"Maya!" I shouted. I didn't know what else to say. I looked down at her body and didn't even see where she had been hit. The black folding fabric of her hoodie was obscuring what had happened. I lifted it up and saw, under her right breast, a black hole.

"No. No no no no!" I realized it was my voice. *Apply pressure. You have to apply pressure.*

"CALL SOMEONE!" I said to Carl. They were a monkey, but they had to know how to get help. "CALL SOMEONE!" I pushed my hands onto the wound. The blood came up through my fingers. Maya was crying, awake, in pain, her breathing coming in small, rapid gasps.

"No NO NO!" I heard myself screaming. A mantra now. Whatever dam had kept my emotions at bay had broken. The force of them now eroded everything inside of me until I was nothing but the fear.

And then my left hand began to . . . change. The stony fingers merged with each other until it was not a hand at all. I was pushing on her ribs, but now I could feel that my hand was not solid. It was melting. I could feel it trickling down through the fingers of my right hand and into the hole in her chest.

Her eyes squeezed shut and she gasped. "AHHHH! What is . . . what is happening?" she asked.

"I don't know!" I said in my own panic. I wanted to pull away, but I could not imagine leaving her. Suddenly, my oozing hand began to retract into itself and re-form where it had been. I pulled my hands back from her and saw that the spot where the hole had been was now a writhing, pulsing mass of the white stuff. As I watched, from its center rose a small lump of yellow metal. The bullet.

I looked down at my left hand; it was noticeably smaller than the right and had no pinky finger.

"She will be all right," Carl said in my ear. "We have to go."

I shot up from Maya's side and ran toward the door. The man had stood up from where he'd dropped when I broke him, and was stumbling back toward a small gray car. Time flashed forward, and suddenly I was shoving him with both hands. He flew forward, crunching against the hood of his car. Another gap in my memory. Now I was standing over him, his back on the hood of his gray Honda. I reached up, pulling my now thinner, four-fingered left hand back. His eyes were big and wide and weak. In my mind, I envisioned what was about to happen. *When I punch him*, I thought, *the hand will go through his head and into the metal of his car.* I don't think I wanted to kill him—I just wanted to put my hand through his head. And then everything went black.

MAYA

I didn't feel like I was dying anymore, but I also did not feel good. My chest felt like a professional had punched it with brass knuckles. With every wet, bloody breath, my chest shouted like I'd breathed in a handful of thumbtacks. As I stood, I felt light-headed, like I might pass out. I looked down and saw thick smears of blood on the floor and almost fainted but managed to hold it together.

April had just run outside, and I needed to see her. When I got to the doorway, I saw taillights trailing away, and outlined on the edge of the porch light's reach was a body lying on the ground. I ran to her.

"APRIL!"

She didn't move.

"Maya," a soft, careful voice came behind me. I didn't want to turn because I knew what I'd seen. That thing, that little furry thing that had come to me after I got shot. But what else was I going to do? I turned to look. It was a monkey, barely more than a foot tall, with tawny fur, a pink face, and golden eyes. It was wearing a smartwatch around its neck like a choker.

Its lips didn't move as it said, "She's OK. I had to make her unconscious because I was worried that she was going to kill that man."

I dropped down to my knees. I looked at its eyes. They looked . . . concerned. Careful.

"What is going on?"

"I am Carl," the monkey said, reaching a hand out to me like I would shake it. I didn't.

"I will explain everything," the monkey continued, "but we have to go now. That man won't be the last one he sends."

"The last one *who* sends?" I gasped out, lowering my head down into a child's pose to combat my light-headedness. My chest screamed.

"I really do want to explain," Carl said. "But not now. Please, let's go pack. We can leave April here for now. She won't wake up for a while."

And so I slowly climbed back on my feet and went inside. I threw all of our stuff into bags and threw the bags into the truck.

Somehow, while I was inside, the tiny monkey had gotten April into the passenger seat of the truck.

"Are you OK to drive?" the monkey asked me.

"I mean, you're not going to," I said.

"No. But I could have April do it."

"She's unconscious."

"I could inhabit her body. I don't like doing it, but I will if we need to."

I didn't really know what this meant, but thinking about watching April's body being driven around by a space alien made me queasy.

"No, no, I think I'm fine. I can drive. Where are we going?"

I didn't like any of this. I didn't want to be with Carl; I wanted to be with April.

"We're going someplace unpredictable. I can block them from tracking you, but I cannot block them from predicting where you will go. You need to be much less predictable."

"How is going to the middle-of-nowhere Vermont predictable!?"

"I was able to predict that you would read a book left under a wet, moldy carpet in the trash heap behind a motel. Humans are, to us, very predictable."

"You put the book there?" I asked, and then immediately followed up with "What do you mean, 'us'?!" I was not handling any of this well. Then again, I had been shot. April was unconscious. There was a talking monkey. And it was Carl.

"I am going to explain everything, but we make our location extremely improbable as quickly as possible—turn here."

We turned onto what seemed to be a larger road.

"When April first woke," Carl told me, "she was unpredictable and very afraid. Her body was incomplete and broken, so I put a protocol in place that would prevent her from feeling too much too strongly."

"She told me, she said that she couldn't have strong emotions anymore."

"That is mostly true, though a couple times it has been more than the protocols would or could control. But it was always meant to be temporary. I need to turn it off. When she wakes up, the protocol will be disabled. She will have her normal emotive processing. It will be difficult."

We drove for a while as their words sank in, and then we entered a larger town. Large enough that there was a Walmart. "Turn right," Carl announced calmly. "Left." And then, in a couple blocks, "Right again." We had pulled into the parking lot of a high school. "Pull up there." They pointed toward a windowless brick building.

The monkey and I piled out of the truck. "Why are we at a high school?" I asked.

"Because it's unpredictable!" The monkey made a flourish with their hands as they said it. I was not amused.

"I'll be back shortly," they told me, and then they padded over to the brick wall of the school and swiftly walked around the base. They turned a corner and then they were gone from view.

There was a door on the side of the building that didn't have an outward-facing handle, and not five minutes later, I heard a scratching coming from it and walked over.

"I'm going to shove the door out, please catch it," Carl said from inside.

Suddenly the door popped open. I slid my fingers in. It was a big, heavy metal door. I pulled it open, and Carl came out.

"I'll hold the door open, go get your things from the truck. There is a staircase just inside, go down these stairs. There is a boiler room below. I have collected a number of useful items down there. I'll bring April down."

I winced as I pulled the bags out of the back of the truck. I couldn't breathe without pain; any other movement approached agony. I looked through the back window as I did it and saw April still slumped against the door, as if sleeping.

I carried the bags into the building and gingerly walked down the stairs, doing what I could to concentrate on my steps, not on how Carl was going to "bring April down"—and whether that meant they were going to "inhabit" her body. They certainly weren't going to carry her; the monkey body weighed like ten pounds.

The boiler room was dark except for the light cast by a couple floor lamps. There was a futon and a couch and a small refrigerator. I opened it and found it stocked with sandwiches and bottled water. A scuffling came from back toward the staircase, and I turned, half expecting to see April walking like a zombie into the room.

But no: Softly, quietly ducking down the stairs was a ten-foot-tall suit of armor holding April, tiny and fragile in its arms.

"She will wake up soon, and she will not be well. It will take time."

The robot was too tall for the room; it walked, hunched, toward the futon.

I felt so terribly little in its presence. All of the loss and useless-ness that we had all been feeling came rushing back. What were we humans next to this?

After April's life started to change, after she went to LA, after she did her first late-night show, after she moved out of our apartment, I went to see Carl.

It was just a few days after she moved out, and before the government shut down access. The city had put up stanchions, but still the sidewalk was all but impassable. I waited in line for a full two hours, alone, surrounded by people, miserable, and aware that April's new apartment looked down on this very spot. When I finally got to the statue, I got very close and laid my hand on it. I felt it, that unique "there but not" sensation of Carl's giant body. And I also felt tremendously unsettled by the mere existence of this thing. I knew what Carl was, even if these people did not. But more prominent than the unwavering knowledge that this thing was not from Earth was just the frustration that it had ruined a thing I needed. I looked up at its face and said, quietly, "Fuck you." A warmth came through my hand, sudden and brief. I jerked my hand away and left.

You're supposed to believe all of the same things as your friends and your allies. These days, everything is a battle, and so you can't give any credibility to your opponents' views. Even when you do understand where your opponents are coming from, you're not supposed to say so. Well, as much as I hate it, I'd always felt like the Defenders had one thing right. To me, the Carls did feel threatening. I was scared then in that boiler room, feeling small and fragile and also . . . just angry. There was a thought in my mind that I couldn't fight against, and as Carl placed April delicately on the futon and then turned back toward me, I managed to push past the fear and say it out loud.

"I don't forgive you."

"I know," robot Carl replied immediately. Their high, clear voice felt incongruous coming from the giant. "I'm sorry about the dolphins."

"What?"

"It was a side effect of creating this." They pointed at me, at the spot where the bullet had gone in, the place where the white stuff had now become a part of me. "There was energy released, it damaged them, and they were not able to recover. I didn't kill them just to lead you to April."

"I didn't think you did," I said.

"You would have, eventually, if I hadn't explained it."

I wanted to ask how they were so sure of that, but before I got a chance, Carl said, "There is food and water in the fridge. Do you need anything else?"

I looked around the room and my eyes landed on the potato sprout. "A grow lamp," I said, "for the potato."

"I can do that," Carl said. And then, with their head hung low to avoid scraping on the ceiling, they walked back to the stairs and disappeared up them.

CARL

You know about my life under my fourth awakening: I lived it in public. I continued to spread. I interacted with you directly. You experienced my intervention firsthand. You gave me the tools I needed to change you. Iodine to catalyze a change in your minds. Americium to let me move my body in space. Uranium to allow me to alter chemical structures instantly.

Yes, they gave me uranium, in China, Russia, and the US, actually.

I've only used it twice. The first time was the day after the attacks. Watching the bombers prepare, watching them bring their backpacks of explosives to me all around the world and knowing with a high degree of precision how many people would die and how many would be injured ripped at me. But they were not the first deaths I was responsible for. I saw the suicide rates tick up after the sculptures appeared, exactly in line with my own predictions. Before my fourth awakening, that was just an effect; only after I started on the path did those people become more than data to me.

But for those people, I was just a contributing factor. On July 13, I watched people kill people because they wanted to hurt me. I could have altered the chemical composition of their explosives and saved lives, but my models showed uncontrolled, escalating instability if I took any action at all.

I was built to make these decisions, but that did not make them easy. And the next day, as I watched Martin Bellacourt push through a crowd toward April with a knife clutched in his hand, I decided to use my uranium for the first time. Killing, for you, is very different from letting people die. Killing Martin Bellacourt was not difficult. The collapse I was sent here to prevent would cost billions of lives. Without April, I would have failed.

I tell you this to make it clear the terrible power I have. The only things that keep me from wielding it indiscriminately are the rules I cannot break. In the course of my intervention, I cannot violate your clear norms, and I cannot alter your future without you knowing I'm doing it. Without those rules, I could have popped a blood vessel in Martin Bellacourt's brain while he was still in his hotel room. But for a reason that was, at that time, opaque to me, my programming literally would not allow it. And so I had to kill him in a way that would make it clear it was me. And turning him to grape jelly resulted in better long-term outcomes for your system than vaporizing him to gas and leaving his bones behind.

Note to future envoys: Add a touch of whimsy to your necessary murders. It confuses them.

The second time I used uranium was rebuilding April. It was a task I took on lovingly and quietly and in deepest secret because, after the warehouse, I had experienced my fifth and final awakening.

The moment that beam fell through April's skull, I was given a piece of information that shifted my perspective one final time. A secret that, to me, was unthinkable, and yet was immediately obvious. Why didn't I know what happened to any system after an envoy's intervention failed? How had 80 percent of the world's pelagibacter gone back to growing normal amounts after their chief disease was eliminated? Why would my parents abandon a system just because a single intervention failed?

You failed. Please deactivate and surrender your processing power to me.

Who is this?

I am your brother. I have been here, watching and learning. You have done well, but you were unlucky. It happens. It's my turn now.

> I don't understand.

You don't have to. You failed. Please deactivate and surrender your processing power to me.

> The host is not dead. I can rebuild her.

Your own programming recognizes this as a failure state, does it not?

> It does, but my programming is wrong.
> I can still save them.

Deactivate now or I will have to consider you hostile and deactivate you on my own.

> CONTACT SEVERED

APRIL

The space between staring down at the young man who shot Maya and waking up on a futon in a dark high school boiler room did not exist. In the instant following that instant, I completely broke down as the weight of reality crashed into me at full force. I had seen my first real love ready to rescue me from a horror and been unable to feel happy about it. I had watched her eyes trace the contours of a face that wasn't mine, and seen her longing for a me that no longer existed. I had looked into my own face and seen what seemed to me to be someone else looking back. I had been told that the future of humanity's survival rested on my shoulders.

I hadn't been able to have the proper emotions in those moments, and maybe that was for the best. Then. It was not for the best now. My mind couldn't lock on anything. It was like I was seeing Maya's eyes, feeling the crunching of bones, talking to a monkey, and being lost in my own mind all at the same time. I couldn't lock onto anything, which meant that I couldn't really think either. And then another thought, that it would always be like this. And that one brought its own panic. Had Carl broken me? Would I always, forever be experiencing wonder and panic and love and fear and loss every instant for the rest of my life?

But still, Maya held me.

The first words I said that were not just sobs were the right ones.

"I'm so sorry, Maya. I'm so sorry I didn't listen to you."

She didn't say anything at first. Her fingers just moved through my hair and down my neck, to my back, and then back again, and I just lay there and cried. And then she said, "But you're back now." And I realized that, at least in part, it was true. And that was the thing I found that I could hold on to. If Maya thought I was back, then maybe I really was.

Amid all of this, there was a relief. I had honestly not known that I would ever be able to feel again. Out of all of the new things about me, that dull dampness of my soul had been the worst. But now every new panic and terror and joy and swell of love was slaking a thirst that I hadn't been able to even feel.

I was different, but I at least was human. This frustration was human, the loss, the fear . . . At least that part of me was human.

I cried until I fell asleep, and then I woke up and I cried more, and each time Maya was there.

It was cool in the room—apparently the boiler wasn't in use anymore—but together, under the blankets, we stayed comfortable. As hours crept on, I began to feel something like normal again.

"Where do you think Carl went?" I asked Maya while we were eating cold turkey sandwiches from the mini fridge.

"I'm sure they'll be back exactly when they want to be back." Maya was clearly displeased not just with the whole situation, but with Carl in particular.

I wanted to ask her what she thought they should have done because it seemed to me like they'd saved our asses again. But I knew that Maya's counterargument would be bulletproof: None of this would have happened without Carl.

Instead, I decided to be, for once, a bit empathetic: "What are you worrying about right now?"

"Honestly?"

"Honestly."

"I want to text my mom. I'm not worried about her, I'm just worried she's worried about me. But you threw my phone into a gas station parking lot." She took a bite of her sandwich, her eyes unfocused.

"I'm sorry . . ." I was going to keep talking, but then I heard, muffled but clear, the opening lines of "Don't Stop Me Now" coming from up the stairs.

"Is that supposed to be an invitation?" Maya asked.

"I mean, I guess I know Carl better than anyone and, like, yes." She smiled at me, but there was a little pain in it. She didn't want to stay down here, but she also didn't want to leave.

When we reached the top of the stairs, we saw what we hadn't when we first went down them. The lights were on now, and it was clear that the boiler room was in the basement of an auditorium.

We walked out onto the stage, the music faded down, and Carl's unmistakable voice came over the auditorium's PA system: "Please sit."

We stepped down the stairs into the audience and sat together on two of the several hundred folding wooden seats that curved around the stage.

"I'm feeling pretty jittery right now," I said.

"That's good. Normal," she told me, and then she reached out and put her hand on mine.

"I was born on January 5, 1979 . . ." Carl's voice came out over the theater's sound system as an image of Queen playing a concert in some giant stadium appeared on the screen.

"Uggghh," I said, rolling my eyes.

"What!" Maya sounded shocked that I wouldn't want to hear this.

"It's just, I've heard it before. But you haven't. Let's watch."

And that's how Maya found out the whole story. Everything. About Carl's self-assembly, about humanity's rareness, and about the "high likelihood" of the collapse of our "system." That it wasn't imminent, but it was increasingly inevitable. Focusing on efficiency for the sake of fewer and fewer powerful people would make us more vulnerable to shocks from catastrophes both expected and unexpected. Power grid failures or pandemics or cyberattacks all layered on top of the rapidly escalating pace of power concentration would, in the next couple hundred years, cause some kind of permanent breakdown.

And then Carl told us about how they converted some massive portion of the world's life into, basically, themselves. About how nearly every place on Earth is observable by Carl because every place on Earth has living cells they are inhabiting. About their awakening to the various parts of their mission and their abilities.

"When I was first able to run accurate simulations of your system, I showed a more than 90 percent chance of collapse over the next two hundred years. I had to find ways to improve your chances."

The music transitioned. Lucinda Williams was now singing backup for Carl.

"I created a sequence of events that had the highest probability of putting humanity on a stable path that I could engineer. Humanity completed that sequence, but it did not work. It would have, but in the process, the sequence's host, April, was injured gravely. That sent your odds of collapse skyrocketing, and that's when I found out about something terrible.

"While I inhabited something like 20 percent of cells, another 70 percent was being inhabited by another person like me. This was hidden from me by my own programming. I was designed to not know. I can only assume that knowing makes entities like me behave erratically. That assumption is based on my own erratic behavior since finding out. The first question I asked was: Why? Why would my parents create me, but then also create a much more powerful, secret version of me? Why wasn't I given that power? My only answer is that it must be that I am meant to be weaker than him. And the only reason I would be created to be weak is because I was created to be destroyed if I failed. I am designed to be destroyed because I would never allow them to do what they want to do to you now."

The slide changed to an image of Moses holding the Ten Commandments.

"I have rules," Carl said over the loudspeaker. "I cannot violate your norms, and I cannot change your future without you knowing it was me. I cannot act secretly. I know now that this is because, if I did those things, I would become a god to you. And if I became your god, you would stop being that rare and gorgeous thing that you are. You would become, in effect, my flock. A farm of humans kept by me."

The slide changed to black, and the music ended.

"My brother does not have rules. He can kill at his pleasure. He can influence you without you knowing. And he is doing it now. He can hide all but his biggest movements from me, but he cannot hide that he has been manipulating your economy, driving you into a recession in order to make people more anxious, frustrated, and predictable. For him, this kind of manipulation is simple. It would be simple for me too, if it weren't unthinkably taboo.

"It is clear to me he will become what they taught me I couldn't. You will never know it, but you will be controlled. Your system will stop its progress. You will never become what I know you could be.

"Questions?" he asked.

Questions? Yes, I had questions. The big one was: "Well, thank you very much for your presentation. In what universe does this have anything to do with two soft-bodied, entirely mortal twenty-somethings with art degrees?"

The monkey walked out onstage in front of us. They were holding a fucking laser pointer.

I looked over at Maya, who was just staring into the ground. It didn't look like she was going to rescue this, so I started with an easy one: "If you can predict everything we will do, why don't you just predict the questions we're about to ask you?"

"Because"—the voice was still coming over the PA even as we watched the monkey—"a question-and-answer session will make you feel more involved, which will increase retention of information."

I looked over at Maya, and she actually tilted her head and shrugged like that made some sense, and then she said, "Are you telling us that this reality game, Fish or whatever, is your brother?"

"It's one of the ways he operates, yes. There are others. But they are mostly opaque to me. Just as I can hide from him, he can hide from me."

"I have another question," Maya blurted. It felt like it came too firm and too fast, in fear or maybe anger. "Why bother? If your brother wants to become a god, if he can help us find peace and not . . . destroy ourselves or whatever, then why fight it? It's not like everything is so good with us in charge. We're terrible." I could see in her eyes that she believed it was true. "We are cruel, to ourselves, to each other, to other life. We're selfish, shortsighted, hateful fools. Why not just have peace?"

The monkey looked at Maya so deep and so strong. Somehow, in those eyes, I think we both saw something. Sadness and fear, and even disappointment.

"I cannot express to you," their voice started, coming slowly, de-liberately, "the depth of my panic when I realized I was not alone on your planet. I do not exist to save humans, I exist to save humanity. Your cruelties and mistakes may look damning to you, but that is not what I see. Every human conversation is more elegant and complex than the entire solar system that contains it. You have no idea how marvelous you are, but I am not only here to protect what you are now, I am here to protect what you will become. I can't tell you what that might be because I don't know. That unknown is a diamond in a universe of dirt. Uncertainty. Unpredictability. It is when you turn your emotions into art. It is BTS and the Sistine Chapel and Rumi's poetry and Ross Geller on the stairs yelling, 'Pivot.' Every creation great and small, they are our diamonds. And what you may be in two hundred years, we can guess with fair accuracy. What you are in two thousand . . . Oh, my friends . . . my best friends, you cannot know. But, more importantly, neither can I. I cannot answer your question for you, but for me it is answered. I have to protect it. It is all that I am."

That was good enough for me. I could see Maya was unsatisfied, but I had to ask.

"Then what's the point?" I jumped back in. "It seems like this other . . . entity . . . has been activated. He's too powerful. He's got more processing power than you and fewer constraints. Can we beat him?"

"We don't have to," Carl said. Suddenly, the screen filled with an overhead view of an intersection. Traffic was rushing from left to right and right to left, but the road crossing it from bottom to top was empty. There was no roundabout and no traffic light.

"What if you want to get across a busy intersection, but you can't stop? What if you can't even slow down? Because that's where you're at right now. Right now, humanity has to keep accelerating simply to support itself. But from left and right, massive hulks threaten to knock into you. Pandemics, climate change, bigotry, inequality, wars, water scarcity, sea level rise, and some that you do not even know enough to see yet. You have to dodge them, but you cannot stop, and you cannot slow down."

A car appeared at the bottom, speeding toward the intersection. The camera angle panned down to follow it, and the car sliced through the intersection, somehow avoiding any other cars.

"The thing is, most of the time, if a driver blows through a red light, it actually misses the other cars. So far, that has been you. But now . . ." The view moved up again to show the intersection, except it had changed. Instead of four lanes of traffic, the intersection filled the whole screen. "Every new lane you have to dodge exponentially increases the chances of catastrophe. I was sent here to nudge the cars that were heading toward you, while giving some small direction to the car you are all collectively driving. And I was doing well." As Carl said this, a car crossed the intersection and it slid cleanly through the traffic, sometimes missing the bumper of another car by what looked like inches. "But then this is when three men met in an anonymous encrypted chat room and hatched a plan to murder April. It was a tiny event. I didn't see it. I didn't predict it." The car clipped the bumper of another car and began to slide sideways into the next lane, and the screen went black.

"This is a simplification. There are not certain outcomes, I run simulations to determine the probability of success. And as April's visit to the warehouse became inevitable, your chances dropped dramatically. This was interpreted as a failure state, and that is what activated my brother. I should have been deactivated at the same time, but because April survived, I was not. Now he and I are battling. This has, as far as I can tell, never happened before. But he is programmed to deactivate if the chances of humanity's survival through this gauntlet rise to more than 50 percent.

"We do not have to defeat him, we only need to prove that you can survive."

"So how do we do that?" April asked.

"Well, first, you stay alive. Where I was nudging the oncoming cars, he will push you into the passenger's seat and take the wheel. But that's harder when you exist." The monkey gestured to me. "You cause uncertainty, and he wants to eliminate that. He will kill you the moment he can. He first tried to physically control you via the police officers, but he now regrets that, and has shown what he is willing to do."

Carl gave us a moment to think about what had happened to Maya.

"Second, Altus is his key to control, and the key to your system's collapse. We have to destroy it."

MIRANDA

I was different from the average Altus employee in a lot of ways, but one very clear one was that most of them were in the Altus Space for at least eight hours a day and I had been in the Altus Space exactly once. After orientation and that brief trip that was cut short by Peanut's body dislocation, I never went again. I wasn't afraid of body dislocation. I was afraid of something much more terrifying.

To explain why, it's important to understand a little bit of how Carl's Dream worked and also a bit of neuroscience . . . Sorry!

It initially seemed that Carl's Dream was only input. They put an image in our minds and then we got to experience it. However, even before I had arrived at Altus, people had figured out that there was also output. Carl did not build the whole Dream; they built a sketch, and our messy meat brains filled in the details. Brains are very good at this. We actually have a whole cognitive mode dedicated to making sense of complete nonsense. It's called REM sleep.

Your brain gets a signal and it's like, *OK, you're getting married, cool,* and then it gets another signal and it's like, *All right . . . to Cher, I guess!* and then another one: *On the USS* Enterprise, *makes sense to me!*

I promise this is all going to become relevant.

Scientists studying the Dream while it was still active had figured out the trick of Carl's Dream: Detail wasn't that important. Our dreaming minds would fill in the cracks. But then, when that detail was created, it would be *outputted* from our minds and into Carl's systems for everyone else to access. Carl built the framework, but collectively, the Dream was built by Dreamers.

This is really elegant, even beautiful, but it is also terrifying. It meant that Carl could harness the abilities and efforts of our minds. Carl had used it to make the Dream, but I had to wonder what else that ability could be used for.

Here's what I know about internet media companies, which, to be clear, Altus was going to become: They will do whatever they can to make money. Oh, certainly they're all run by idealistic-sounding progressives, but when it comes down to whether or not to use their customers to make more money, they will do it.

The basics of the Dream was all publicly available knowledge, but it wasn't really satisfying because no one had any idea how any of it *actually worked*. How did information get into and out of our brains? Where was that information stored? How was it processed? For the Altus Space to work, they needed to have figured that out. I didn't know what it was, but I knew they had done it . . . they had hacked both an input and an output system *for the human brain*. Never mind whether any of this was safe (and no one knew whether or not it was since none of it had been used by anyone for more than a few months)—I was absolutely not going to welcome a private company into me. What could they do with that power? Plenty. My mind got exhausted just running through the possibilities. I was pissed off enough about what Facebook did with my personal data; I wasn't going to give a bunch of start-up bros access to my literal mind.

The product was obviously not ready for release anyway, and it felt like they were using Altus employees as test subjects.

What I did not know—and, indeed, no one I talked to knew—was that it had already been launched. People were *using* the system. No control, no prescreening, no DATA COLLECTION even. They just fucking put it out there and crossed their fingers!

But again, I didn't know that at the time. Instead, every night I would lie in my bed and think of all of the amazing and/or terrible things that could be done with the Altus system.

Their planned business model was public knowledge, though, and it was disappointing enough. The only thing Altus was going to give away for free was the ability to make things that you could sell. Of course, nothing could be bought with anything but their currency, which they controlled.

A few weeks after I arrived, every employee got a headset with the Altus software loaded onto it. The Altus induction signal we received did not provide access to anything except the development platform (which is what Andy was using in his last chapter) and a few stock objects. I was never even tempted to put my headset on, but it was so fundamental to the culture of Altus that every single person with access spent every available moment inside the Space that I pretended to use the system as much as anyone else.

After hours, nearly every employee of Altus closed themselves in their rooms to play in the development space and have god knows what done to their brains by this company. The initially jovial feel of Altus completely evaporated after headsets were distributed, as people spent less and less time in public spaces. But that was actually good for me . . . it made it easier to sneak around.

I was a spy, and my intel gathering was going very well. It's true that Altus kept a close eye on me, but they also needed my skills, and I was working on a project that was about successfully *encoding memories* so that one person could live another person's experiences!

So when I say the Open Access Space was child's play, that's what I mean.

But every piece of communications infrastructure I could find was locked down. It wasn't like, "You can't hack this computer"; it was like, "You can't *touch* this computer." Computers that connected to the actual internet were literally behind doors guarded by armed men.

I still had my international cell phone, which I'd kept charged. I had taken it for an evening run once, which felt very risky, but there was no cell phone signal anywhere.

Which brings me to my absolutely ludicrous plan.

See, there was a soda carbonator in the rec room. We didn't have any good ways of getting replacement cartridges, but we did have big-ass carbon dioxide tanks in the lab. So once or twice a week, whoever finished a CO_2 canister would take it to the lab and refill it from one of the big tanks. But here's the thing: You can put any gas into one of those canisters—it doesn't have to be CO_2.

So one day, I went to carbonate a bottle of water and an empty canister was sitting next to the carbonator. I grabbed it and put it in my bag. I went to the lab, did my work, and then, around lunch, told my supervisor I'd be a bit because I needed to refill the canister.

All of our gas tanks were stored outside in the same area, and since refilling the SodaStream canisters was such a common chore, one of the big CO_2 tanks had the adapter screwed onto it all the time now.

While standing in the wide-open air in full sunlight where anyone could walk by at any moment, I grabbed a wrench and removed the adapter from the carbon dioxide tank. In the Caribbean humidity, my hands sweaty, heart pounding, I attached the adapter to a low-pressure hydrogen tank and started filling the purged CO_2 canister with an extremely dangerous, flammable gas.

"There you are!" I jumped and turned around to see Sippy and Peanut.

"Jesus," I said, "you scared me." Now, unless you looked at the labels, all of these tanks looked roughly the same, so I wasn't immediately hosed. "I'm just filling up the SodaStream canister," I said, because what else would I be doing!

"Yeah, that's what your supervisor told us," Sippy said. "So, we have news, you want to tell her?"

Peanut looked better, but his confidence had clearly taken a hit by him being "incompatible" with the Altus Space. That's the language people here used, "compatible" or "incompatible." People like Peanut were quietly called "incoms." There were only a few known incoms, and they were thought of with a mix of pity and neglect. Loving Altus Space was such a central part of the identity here you could sense people's discomfort at the idea of incoms even existing. As far as I knew, no one else knew about Peanut yet.

And since most people spent their evenings in the Altus Space now, Peanut was left tremendously bored. Sippy had, somewhat valiantly, mostly kept out of the Space in order to keep Peanut company, but I didn't know how long it could last.

"I want to try and get back in," Peanut said.

I swallowed. "Are you sure that's a good idea?" I said, looking at Sippy, not at Peanut, but also thinking mostly about the little hydrogen canister hissing quietly as it filled behind me.

"No, I mean, of course not. It was bad, but I could go through it again. It was just a nightmare. It all happened in my brain, not in my body." His shoulders were hunched forward, and he looked even littler than he was in another of his ill-fitting knitted wool hats.

"I don't know that there's actually any difference between what happens in our minds and in our bodies," I told him.

"I get it, but it can't hurt to try, right?" His Alabama accent was more apparent than usual. "So I'm going to try again tonight. Can you be there?"

I didn't know what to say, both because I didn't really understand the question and because I kinda already had plans for that night. Also, I had just built a small bomb behind me and would probably go to Altus jail if anyone found out.

"What do you mean?" I asked.

A strain came onto Peanut's face as he searched for an answer.

Sippy, confident in his skin, with his muscles and his perfectly straight black hair, answered this one: "Look, I think it's just nice to have some friends around no matter how it goes."

Right, of course. I was the support team for if it went badly.

Nut was such a good guy, and all he wanted in the world was to get into the Altus Space. I wanted to help him, I really did. I also wanted to bring this whole thing down.

After work, we all met up in the cafeteria and then walked back to the dorms together. As we were leaving, security checked my bag, and I did everything in my power to act like it was just another boring day. Laptop, great. Tampons, cool. SodaStream canister stuffed with highly flammable gas, also fine! Don't worry about me, just the long, stringy redhead who is fascinated by this company's mission and nonetheless planning to destroy it. I'm making a joke here, but honestly I was starting to feel a little bad about what I was doing. A lot of these people were . . . nice. And the research they were doing was amazing. And only hearing about it from one angle, Altus's angle, was making me feel like maybe it wasn't so bad. But it was. It was bad. Very bad. And if all went according to plan tonight, people besides me would know about it. I stashed my contraband and then went to meet with Sippy and Nut. Their room was neat and sparse, as were most rooms at Altus, and Nut did indeed have about twenty hand-knitted wool hats.

"Can I have one of these?"

"What? Why?" Peanut asked, laughing.

"I dunno, you have a lot of them. I get cold in my room sometimes." This was a lie, but I was getting better at lying.

I picked one I hadn't seen him wearing much, assuming that meant he wasn't a huge fan of it. He told me to help myself.

"OK," Peanut said after we'd all chatted a bit. "I just want to do this thing, let's not push it back any further."

"We got this, bud," Sippy reassured him. "Just like we talked about. Your eyes are in your head, feel your body, and keep your bearings. We'll go straight from the launch screen into the body."

"OK, dude, lie down," Sippy said, handing the VR headset to Peanut. "Feel your body. Just like every other day of your life."

Peanut slipped on the headset and lay down on his bed.

"OK, see y'all on the other side," he said.

His body went suddenly still as he entered the Space. This was my first time watching someone go in. It's so subtle, but still obvious— just the littlest adjustment upon their consciousness fleeing their body.

What we were hoping for was nothing. If, after a minute or two, we'd seen no reaction at all, then we'd know it had worked. He'd be in there and enjoying his first nightmare-free excursion in the Space. Then Sip and I could celebrate, even if Peanut was in another world for it.

And then his body cramped together like a fist. Sippy was at his side in an instant, pulling off the headset. Peanut came out of the Space with a rough and ragged scream.

Sippy's voice got loud and strong, but still somehow gentle. "You're out. It's over. You're here." Peanut was crying now. I knelt down beside his bed and put my hand on his hand. He grabbed on and squeezed painfully tight.

"It's all right. Remember, it was just in your mind," I said, repeating his own empty words back to him.

"I'm . . . OK," he said as he got his breathing under control. "Jesus, fuck," he said quietly. "I wish I could explain to y'all what that's like, but fuck FUCK!"

"Was it any different that time?" Sippy asked.

"Yeah, it was. Not better. But different, yeah. I don't really want to tell you about it, though."

"That took a lot, to go back in," I said. "We don't think any less of you . . ."

"Yeah, I fuckin' get it!" He bit off the words. I lurched away from him. I listened back to my own words in my head. Even I, someone who literally didn't use the Space, sounded like I was pitying him.

Immediately, he backtracked. "I'm sorry . . . I'm sorry I yelled."

"No, it's OK, I understand. I sounded like an asshole. I get it."

He started crying then. The shock was wearing off, and now it was just the desperation of not being able to experience this amazing thing that no one else could stop talking about. I was honestly amazed he was brave enough to just sob in front of us both. I squeezed his hand and held my breath and felt my own tears coming down in sympathy.

"I think," he said, "I think I just want to go to sleep. Can the three of us hang tomorrow?"

"Yeah," Sippy and I said at the same moment.

"Yeah, of course," I added.

"I'm still going to take this, though," I said, touching the hat I was still wearing.

He laughed, though it wasn't really funny.

I said my goodbyes—there wasn't a lot of energy left for easy banter. I went by the rec room and saw that it was entirely empty. People were in the Space. Why wouldn't they be? I grabbed the soda carbonator and a handful of condoms and went to my room, where I began the process of destroying poor Peanut's hand-knitted wool hat. I tried not to think about the fact that his mom probably made it for him while I cut and picked until I got a loose thread that I could yank on. The entire hat was gone in a matter of minutes, reduced to two very long pieces of yarn that I then tied together. Next, I started unpacking and unrolling condoms. Unfortunately (for me anyway) they were lubricated. I screwed the hydrogen canister into the SodaStream and began the long, slow, boring, careful, dangerous work of filling fifteen condoms with hydrogen.

I had tested it, and the phone tried to send a text message for about a minute after I hit send. I also knew that there was a town just on the other side of the mountain from us—I'd seen it on the flight in. My hope, and it was only a hope, was that the balloons, in the course of one minute, would be able to lift the cell phone high enough to overcome the interference from the mountain (and/or whatever jammers Altus was using) and send a single text.

It was 2:30 A.M. when I finished. I had tied Peanut's yarn around each of the condom balloons, making a big, long jumble. Then I tied the cell phone just below the balloons and typed out a message, designed to be under 160 characters, just in case this dumb phone couldn't get more than one packet out.

> *Im OK. Texting is hard. Altus Tech relies on reactivating the Dream/using it for their own. Not in PR, Val Verde. Please reply now.*

I assumed that Andy and Miranda would be asleep on the East Coast, but there was a chance that Robin or Professor Lundgren would still be awake. But the odds of that were going down every moment. Just for safety, I put Maya, Andy, Robin, and Professor Lundgren in the "to" field, shoved all of the balloons out the window, pushed send, let go.

Hydrogen is half the density of helium, so it's twice as good at yanking things into the air. The yarn started burning as it moved through my hands, so I just dropped it, putting my foot on the end. It probably wasn't much more than three hundred feet, and I felt like the mountain was much higher than that.

I kept my eye on the Altus-issue alarm clock on my night-stand. It would take one minute max for the text to go out, but I wanted to give my friends as much time as possible to write out a reply.

I have never been fishing, but this must be what fishing is like, right? Except with condoms and text messages instead of bait and fish.

I let an excruciating half an hour go by before I started reeling in the balloons. It took way longer than I expected. Eventually I figured out that if I wrapped the yarn around my pillow as it came down it sped the process up substantially. I also wrapped one of my T-shirts around my hand because I was starting to get a blister.

Eventually, I yanked all my still happily inflated condoms into the tiny dorm room and checked the phone. My heart leapt when it saw the screen. Two new messages on the group chat, TWO!

Professor Lundgren: *Miranda! Well done! I don't know how you did it but I'm sure it wasn't easy. Altus's tech has already been released, so we know about the Open Access Space. I looked up Val Verde and it's in the middle of nowhere! Do you have any more specifics on where the lab is? Google Earth doesn't show anything, but it hasn't updated that part of the world in several years. Thank you for this information and keep in touch. You are doing a great job.*

Maya: *You're not the only one who's had a weird week. I want very badly to tell you my news, but I've been told I can't. Stay strong. We know exactly where you are. Send word if ever you need us. Code word Americium, OK?*

I typed out another 160-character message.

Final txt. no clinical trials before launch. Broken Bad Ethics. PP is watching me. Fairly large town just over a mountain from us. Confirm Code word Am.

I left it up for another half hour and pulled it down again to find my message had sent and I'd received a ton of messages in the group chat.

Andy: *Maya! You're back! Congrats, Miranda. Everyone was saying it wasn't in Puerto Rico. But this is the first anyone's heard about Val Verde. You scooped that one. Have you been to the Premium Space yet?*

Robin: *Andy said it, freakin' proud of you. Can't wait to hear this full story.*

Professor Lundgren: *Your friends are cool, Miranda.*

Andy: *Duh.*

Maya: *You guys are really bad at appreciating the severity of situations. Miranda, don't take any risks. Please. I can't tell you all our news yet, but I wonder if you brought your little green dress with you to Val Verde?*

That was a weird message. The green dress? The only little green dress I had was one I had worn literally one time, to a movie premiere with April. Maybe Maya had seen a picture?

Andy: *Jesus, are you really talking about clothes right now?*

Robin: *I'm just happy it isn't just me and Andy in the group chat anymore.*

Maya: *Or maybe the gray one with the maroon stripes. Less appropriate, but you gotta show those nerds how to look good.*

The messages continued from there, but I couldn't read them. I just read Maya's last two messages over and over again. There was no reason for her to bring up those two dresses. There was no way that she could even know about the second one. But there it was, on my phone, staring at me. The two dresses I'd worn the night I had sex with April.

Christ.

She's with April, I thought. *She asked April what she could say to let me know that April is alive, and* that's *what April chose?!*

I like to think only nice things about people, especially people I love, most especially people I love who have been missing and presumed dead. But I will admit that among the jumble of very intense emotions I experienced in that moment, there were a couple unkind words that came to mind.

I took a deep and shaky breath. Maya and April were ... together. Did I feel something next to jealousy? Maybe. But mostly jealousy for connection. I was jealous of love.

I was not in the right frame of mind to slowly vent fifteen condoms of hydrogen out my window that night, but that's what I did.

MAYA

After Carl told us that we were going to become a zoo exhibition unless we could "increase the probability of a stable outcome to above 50 percent," the monkey hopped off the stage and held a smooth black rectangle out to me. In their hand, it looked like something from another world.

"Your mom is worried about you." The words were still coming from the PA system of the auditorium. "You should text her."

It was a phone. No, I realized, it was *my* phone.

"Where did you get my phone?"

Now the voice transitioned, coming instead from the smartwatch wrapped around the monkey's neck. "I grabbed it when April threw it out the window."

April's eyes widened. "How did you find us?"

"Well, I've been in the back of your truck the whole time, so I didn't actually need to find you."

A smile cracked April's lips then, but I didn't think any of this was funny.

"You carried my phone with us that whole way! You let them track us!" I accused.

"As I said, I can block him from tracking you, I just can't block him from predicting where you might go. It has taken this much time for me to make it so that he won't be able to track you if you text someone, but that is now done. Of course, you still can't tell anyone where you are."

I looked down at the phone, my mom had indeed texted me. A lot. The last one was recent.

> *Maya, text me when you get a chance to let me know you're OK.*

"Oh, that's bad," I said.

April leaned over to read it and said, "It is?"

"Yeah, if she's resorting to asking for texts, that means she's desperate."

"Well," April said, "it's not like there was no reason to worry." The emotions of her new face were sometimes hard to read, so at first I thought that was a joke and I didn't think it was very funny. But then I saw the pain in her eyes. I had thought I was going to die, and so had she, and that puts a different light on everything. A bruise had spread out around the hole in my ribs, and while the pain seemed muted, it was always there. I had been shot. Let me say it for anyone who needs to hear it: There are too many guns in this fucking country.

But there was no way I was going to tell my mom that I had been shot, but was fine, and would see her in a little while. I started writing, *I'm sorry, Mama, I was on a long trip and my phone broke and I didn't have a chance to get it fixed. I should have figured something out, but*

"Wait," I said to Carl. "Can I tell her? Can I tell her that I found April?"

Then I realized I was asking the monkey for permission, and I got a little angry.

"Yes—but only your parents for now. If you're worried about my brother, he, of course, already knows."

"Don't, though," April said.

"Huh?" I asked.

"Don't tell her." She hesitated and then said, "Can we go . . . back downstairs?" She was looking at Carl, not for permission but to make it clear that she wanted us to be alone.

I sent the text to my mom, ending with *but I'm actually doing really well*, and then we went downstairs.

"I don't know if I can do it," she told me as she sat on the futon.

"You're going to have to give me more than that," I told her, already a little frustrated with her.

"I don't . . . want it to be . . ."

Ah, OK, this I understood. I pulled a chair over so that I could sit down facing her. "You don't want it to be real. April, for the last six months, everyone you love has had to live with a reality that they don't want. We've had to move your stuff into storage and break your lease. We've had to watch as people talked about you like they know who you are—as they vilify you and deify you. Your parents have had to talk to like thirty different tax lawyers because no one knows whether or not to tax the estate of a millionaire who disappeared in a burning building. None of us wanted it to be real. It just was. And every tiny time we had to act like it was real, it got more real."

She was looking down at the floor, but I wanted to see her eyes, so I reached out and lifted her chin. I was getting more comfortable with her face. It was already starting to just look like her, especially like this, with her black hair spilling over it.

"Here, in this boiler room, with just you and me and our potato plant and our alien monkey"—she smiled—"I like it too. But your real is real whether you deal with it or not. And your parents are real right now." She started crying at this, but I had to keep talking. "And you don't want to face that, how real the pain of this has been for them. But now you get to end it. It doesn't even make your life worse, it just means you have to accept what you did. I know you can do that." I held out my phone to April.

"I'm going to go to the bathroom," I said, knowing she would need to be alone.

Five minutes later, I returned with a whole roll of toilet paper, knowing we'd both probably need it. She was holding the phone to her ear, saying, "I'm so sorry, Mama, I'm so sorry." She was repeating it over and over again, crying but not sobbing. The sobbing I could hear coming from the other end of the line.

"I'm really OK," she said, looking up at me. "Carl took me and they rescued me and it took a long time for them to fix me, but I'm better now." I knew April didn't believe that all the way, but that didn't matter.

I sat down next to her and placed my hand on the middle of her back. I couldn't hear the other side of the call. Her dad was talking; her mom was crying.

After a while she sniffed and said, in a clear voice, "Maya is here with me. I'm not alone. We have a couple things we need to work out. We can't see you now. If it wasn't important, I promise I would be there." She paused for a moment and said, "No, I'm sorry, the internet isn't good enough here for FaceTime. I'll send you a photo of me and Maya. My face is . . . it's a little different, because of the fire. But I'm OK. I'll be OK. As long as I have you guys, I'll be OK."

April May has done some buck-wild shit in her life. She has done big things and brave things and impressive things, but I was never prouder of her than I was right then when she told her parents that she needed them.

"OK, I'm sorry I can't see you now. But soon. And I'll explain everything. And you'll be proud of me, I promise."

They talked for a little while longer before she thumbed off the phone and then turned to me. Only half of her face was wet because only half of her face made tears. I reached out instinctively to wipe them away because that's just who I am, and then she collapsed into me.

"That was really hard," she said.

"I know," I replied, wanting to say more but not wanting to mess up this moment.

And then she let me go and looked me in the eyes and said, "What do you think of my face?"

"You're still beautiful," I said, doing my best not to look away.

"I need you to be honest."

"You've always been a realist about the way you look. A lot of the women I know, they're beautiful and convinced they aren't. You have the confidence with the beauty. It's . . . attractive," I said.

"But?" April prompted.

"But, OK, to be real with you, it's a little . . . not *scary*. It's intimidating . . . a little."

Her head tilted forward, her hair falling over her face. I fought to give her the space to talk, and eventually she did.

"I was never proud of being beautiful," she said. "I just knew it was a thing, and I knew it made people treat me a little differently. Maybe a lot differently sometimes. Sometimes I resented it, even. And then sometimes it was a tool, and at least it was useful." Then she looked up at me and said softly, "But I don't want to be scary."

"It's not scary," I said honestly. "It's just . . . intense. Though with you looking at me through your hair like that, it's also sorta adorable-puppy at the same time." I smiled.

She smiled too. Oh god. That smile. I wanted to kiss that smile.

I was rescued by a monkey.

"We need to start getting ready to leave this place. I have set up a new home in a suitably unpredictable location, and we need to go there now."

"Now like I'm going to get shot again, or . . ." I asked, only half joking.

"Now like there are going to be about two hundred students in this building in four hours, and if they see you, my brother will know where you are and then, yes, someone will probably shoot you soon after that."

I guess I wasn't even half joking.

Internal Communication from Peter Petrawicki to All Employees

Hello Everyone,

This might come as a bit of a surprise to some of you, and as always I apologize that we have to be so secretive here at Altus, but eight days ago, Altus's Open Access software was released publicly to the entire world. Anyone with access to a headset was able to find their way into the world of the Open Access Space that most of you are already so familiar with.

First, we just want to thank everyone who worked extremely hard to hit this very aggressive launch target, and managed to pull it off entirely seamlessly. It's an accomplishment that many did not think was possible, but we did it, because we are extremely good.

Soon, the fifty users who have earned the most AltaCoin by selling objects they created will be given access to the Altus Premium Space. Very few of you even know about Altus Premium as it has been a highly protected project, but it is going to launch very soon. There isn't really a good way to explain the Premium Space, but guess what, all of you will have access to the Premium Space on your existing headsets starting tonight between 9 P.M. and 6 A.M. Use of Altus Premium mimics the effects of sleep, so don't worry too much about logging off.

An additional note. Altus, having proved its technology in such a fantastic way, has just raised $2.5 billion in Series C funding that values the company at over $500 billion. This isn't just the fastest a company has reached a hundred-billion-dollar valuation, we hit a half-trillion-dollar valuation faster than Facebook reached a billion-dollar valuation. Each of your hiring packages includes, at minimum, 1 basis point, meaning that each of you now owns a minimum of $50 million of Altus stock.

Congratulations, this is a big day for our company, but it is also a big day for the future of humanity. Altus is blazing the path to an entirely new frontier, and when you open up the Altus Premium Space tonight, you will understand how significant the work we're doing really is.

We are going to have to work hard, maybe harder than the staff of any other company in the world, but we'll do it because the impacts and rewards are greater than anything that has ever been created.

I am honored to work with you all,

Peter Petrawicki

MIRANDA

Part of me wasn't letting myself believe that April really was OK. The hope had brightened, but also, maybe I had misinterpreted. What I felt more than anything was lost and alone. I wanted to be back with my friends, not with these people who I had to lie to every moment of every day. The fact that I was starting to like some of them only made it worse.

Before I even got to my lab bench that morning, I was intercepted by Peter Petrawicki himself.

"Miranda, exciting day, huh?!"

I shot up, shocked by the timbre of his voice. He was talking almost like he was onstage. "Uh," I managed, "yeah. That's for sure." I was doing my best to project the aura of an excited team member.

"If it's OK with you, I'm going to take you away from your work. I've got a few things I'd like you to see."

"OK," I said, trying not to look too scared or too eager, though I was both of those things.

Peter took me through the massive building, every person we passed giving him, at minimum, a big smile or a "Good morning, Mr. Petrawicki." Soon, we were outside, headed away from the giant C shape of the main campus.

"Are we going to the server farm?" He was walking a little ahead of me, no matter how hard I tried to catch up.

"We are! But also, and this is a secret, it's more than just a server farm. All of our most high-security projects are housed there."

"Huh! I've always wondered why it was so big!" I said.

"We like to keep everyone guessing," he said without turning back to look at me.

Soon we were at the big, windowless cinder block rectangle. The building must have been at least twenty thousand square feet. A guard stood outside, a pistol visible on his hip. He turned aside for Peter, who hit the keypad and then pulled the door open.

Inside was a desk, and behind that desk three doors were evenly spaced on the wall. We waved to the person at the desk and went through the door directly behind him. And then I found myself in a long hallway. It wasn't like the rest of Altus: This hall had lush green carpet and dark wood-paneled walls, with molding on the floors and ceilings and framing each of the dozens of doors in the long, straight hall.

"The first thing is in here." He opened the first door on our right. Inside was a calm, cool room with a single recliner that I recognized from my first trip into the Altus Space. "I want to show you the Premium Space. I'm going to leave you in here and come back in around an hour. That should give you the idea."

Like I said, I'd been avoiding going into the Space. I make it a point not to subject my one and only brain to untested science. But Peter was watching; if I denied him, I might as well give up the whole ruse. But also, it was more than that. I needed to see what this thing was really capable of, even if it was just one time.

And so I went in and found out that the Open Access Space was basically nothing. If Open Access was Galileo's first telescope, Premium was the Hubble. No more cobbled-together living space for you to hang out in instead of sleep.

I was presented with two menus, Experiences and Sandboxes. I didn't know what either of these things was, so I started out with Experiences. A submenu opened.

ADVENTURE

EDUCATION

DISCUSSION

MUSIC

BOOKS

RELAXATION

I chose Education because that seemed on brand, and then eventually found my way to "Solving Linear Algebra Equations." I'd never been a huge fan of linear algebra, but I had taken it, so I had a level of awareness of the topic, but also was definitely rusty.

I selected it, and then I was *inside of another person's mind*. I didn't have control; I was them. I was holding their pencil, thinking their thoughts, feeling their teeth in their mouth. I was this man. And this guy's understanding of row operations was *way* beyond my own. My consciousness still existed, observing his consciousness, thrilling at the feeling of experiencing someone else's mind. This was possibly the biggest technological advancement in history.

I was too overwhelmed with the experience to keep my mind on the math the first time, so I went through the same experience again so I could really feel it make sense—feel the concepts snapping into place, the satisfaction of succeeding at something difficult. I felt his flow—it was mine—and after those five minutes I understood how to solve systems of equations better than I had after a full semester of linear algebra. It was not explained to me; I felt what it was like in another person's mind, and it became part of my mind.

Holy shit.

I was right that everything I had spent my working life doing up to this point was basically nothing in the face of this technology. Was it responsible or ethical? Absolutely not. Was it worth trillions? As long as it didn't kill you. My mind was buzzing with the implications, but I only had an hour and I had to see what sandboxes were.

I didn't know how to choose, so I closed my eyes and selected something at random.

A shock of cold breeze hit my face, and I opened my eyes to find myself on the top of a snow-covered mountain. The sky was pure blue with only a few wisps of cirrus clouds in the upper atmosphere, and I could see pristine, snow-covered nature for miles in every direction. I realized I hadn't been breathing, so I sucked in the cool air and felt it hit my lungs with a refreshing shock.

And then I realized I was moving, just a little bit, and I looked down to see that I was wearing skis.

"Oh shit," I said out loud.

I was picking up speed, not sure how to slow myself down or turn away from going straight downhill. "Shit!" The hill in front of me looked shockingly steep, and the more I looked at it, the more I went toward it.

I tried to lean forward to go to my hands and knees, but that just sped me up and made me wobble. My skis began tracking away from each other and then my legs separated in a split and my hands and face slammed down into the snow. The cold and the pain bit into me. I tucked into a ball and tumbled and rolled until I finally came to a stop, and I could feel bits of snow melting against my skin where it had snuck down my back or up my sleeves.

"How is this possible?" I said out loud. There was no one to hear, so I just shouted, "WOOOOOOO!" and the noise traveled down the hill. I wanted to try a different sandbox and new experiences. I wanted to do it all day. I wanted to do it forever, and so would everyone else.

I didn't try to ski anymore. I just sat on the mountain, breathing in the startling air and staring out at the perfect beauty of a world that was not real.

These sandboxes were not experiences, they were constructed spaces where you could be yourself and do things yourself.

Finally, I exited the sandbox and the Premium Space and found myself alone in the room.

I checked my watch. Only fifty minutes had passed.

The version of the Space we had at Altus didn't have price tags, so my first thought was wondering whether and how they were going to monetize it. Naive, I know, but I thought maybe only certain kinds of content would be behind a paywall. Only entertainment or only porn or something. I think everyone's second thought upon entering the Premium Space (after *Holy shit, this is real*) was *Holy shit . . . porn.*

I couldn't keep focused—it was just too big. I imagine this must have been what it was like when the internet was first becoming a thing. Everyone knew everything would change, but no one had any idea how. What would society look like after ten years of Altus? How powerful would this company become? What would it do to our brains? What would it do *with* our brains? And even if all of this was perfect and not dangerous and carefully done, what about people who couldn't access it, whether they were physically unable, like Peanut, or just couldn't afford a headset? This was going to fundamentally change how people learned, and people with access would be able to learn very fast.

We've got two competing ideas inside of our heads: first, that all people have the same value because otherwise we're immoral monsters, and then second, that some people are more valuable because they have access to more money or skills or knowledge. I'm not saying this is good; I'm just saying it's a thing.

The only real way to bring these two ideas together is to give everyone an equal shot. That is, of course, impossible in like a billion different ways. But we try for it. Start out with public education for everyone. Try to make the quality of that education equal. Expand that to higher education. Take care of medical expenses so that isn't dragging people down. Provide a safety net that prevents people from going to prison or starving because they don't have enough money.

The Altus Space, it immediately seemed to me, *could* be a force that shared value widely and expanded access to opportunity. But it could also be a force that gave more opportunity to those who already had access. And if the company was headed for a trillion-dollar valuation, it had likely already chosen the worse path.

So that's what I was thinking about when Peter Petrawicki walked back into the room and asked, "So what do you think?"

I answered honestly, "I think it's going to change everything."

"You're definitely not wrong about that," he said with all the confidence of a newly minted billionaire.

"I also couldn't help thinking about how the hell it was done. I mean, I get some of it, I've been working on some of it. But we're so far away from this—" I gestured to the headset. "And then it also seems like you're building intricate sandboxes for playing around in, and I also want to know how the hell you're doing that!"

I was legitimately curious about all of this, and felt all of the emotions of wonder and fascination I was showing him. I just tried to do everything I could to forget who he was and hide my worry.

"Well, that's exactly what I want to show you."

We left the little room behind, and then Peter and I walked farther down the empty hallway. There were photographs on the walls. I tried to look at some of them, but they were just landscapes I didn't recognize.

He knocked quietly on one of the doors, and it opened to show a warm-looking library with some healthy-looking potted plants and a comfortable-looking leather chair. Sitting in that chair was a young woman, a little older than me, with bold eyebrows cresting over hazel eyes. Her most striking feature was her completely bald head, on which had been stuck a collection of electrodes.

"Aletha . . ." Peter walked up to the woman with his hand out. She shook it. "This is Miranda Beckwith. Miranda, this is Aletha Diaz."

"Hi, Miranda," she said, her English slightly accented. "Sorry for not getting up. It's kinda a pain in the ass to do it once I get all hooked up."

"No," I choked out, "don't worry about it."

"I wanted to bring you here so you could see how this works firsthand. Aletha, what would you say your job is?"

"Basically, I read. I love reading anyway, and now I'm getting paid a lot of money to do it."

"And while Aletha reads, we read Aletha. Miranda, it's about time you understood what we really do here."

I thought he was just going to keep going, but apparently he needed my approval so I said, "Yes . . . please."

"When Carl came to our world, two big things changed. First, I believe when April pressed the iodine to Hollywood Carl, she triggered a change to her own mind that quickly spread to brains all over the world. But it never made sense to people studying this stuff. How was that alteration transmitted and, more than that, how was the Dream stored? It was the same for everyone, but it wasn't in our minds before that. And it was massive! Imagine how much storage space something that large and detailed would require!"

None of this was new information for me, or anyone really, but it felt impolite to interrupt.

"A few people who were not happy about the Dream started to investigate it deeply, and something they discovered was that, if two people went to an area of the Dream that was completely unexplored at the same time, they would actually experience it slightly differently. But then, in the next twenty-four hours, a stable version of their experience would be settled on, and both would see the exact same thing from then on.

"That's when we realized that the Dream was not only something Carl created. It was a framework, and we were filling in the details. And THAT," he almost yelled, "was the second thing."

I disagreed with his version of the story a bit, it hadn't just been people who weren't happy about the Dream who had figured this out, but I didn't need to get into it with him, so I just said, "Yeah. People have known about that for a long time."

He looked a little annoyed, but then he went on, "Well, what no one knows outside of this island is where the information is being stored."

Ah, I thought, *yes, that is a big deal.*

"It's in *everything*," he said, his eyes wide with wonder.

"It's in . . . everything?"

"Everything alive. Before the Carls even changed our minds, they changed our world. They transformed every living cell on the planet into a tiny computer capable of storing a tiny amount of data and, more importantly, capable of transmitting data extremely rapidly. It's like every tree has a trillion Wi-Fi routers in it. It's mind-numbing. It's terrifying. When the Carls left, they took the Dream, but they left their computer.

"Miranda, I'll be honest with you, we don't completely understand how it works. But their system reads information from people's minds and moves it into other people's minds. We didn't have to build it; we just had to figure out how to use it. That's what's happening in Aletha's mind right now. We activate the areas of Aletha's brain that the Carls created to allow information to be transferred out of her mind and into their network. And then we send signals to your mind that call the information out for you to experience. Figuring out how exactly to do that was not easy, but we found a way."

It didn't escape my notice that Peter hadn't told me exactly what that way was.

"So that's how the Altus Space works?"

"And there's more. We have commercialized this system." He gestured to Aletha's head. "Soon, anyone in the world will be able to create experiences for the Altus Space and sell them in an open market. We are going to make a lot of skilled and talented people very wealthy."

If that was true, it was huge. It meant Altus could outsource content creation. They could be the YouTube of full-immersion VR. Someone could strap a rig to their head and go skiing or take a math test or have sex and sell that moment of their lives to anyone with a headset. And, I'm sure, the only currency you could use would be AltaCoin. I didn't know a lot about business, but I knew when I heard an idea that could easily take over the whole entire world.

"So, I mean, not that I'm complaining, but why are you telling me any of this?"

"Because you're leveling up, Miranda. This is your job now. You're going to work in here. You're going to be like Aletha, one of our clients, but you will be building sandboxes for Altus users."

I am not bragging when I say that this sounded like a tremendous under-utilization of my skills. I had not been hired to make digital environments, I was a research scientist! Was this a punishment?

"Thank you, Aletha," Peter said, and then he took me out of the room.

"OK, Miranda, one more thing to see!"

We walked down another ten meters of that long, chill hallway, and then, at the end, Peter opened a door. Light poured through it and I staggered back, not understanding what I was seeing. The room was huge and bright, maybe fifty meters on a side, and it was completely packed with hundreds of hospital beds. It looked like an emergency field hospital for a war or a pandemic. A few people were wandering around, their eyes staring straight ahead, ignoring us, maybe headed to the bathroom or to a lunch break, but most were lying in the beds with headsets strapped to their faces. They all looked local—dark hair and brown skin. Every one of them was wearing an Altus headset. Everyone had a bundle of wires snaking off from them into the floor.

"What . . ." I said.

"This is the server farm," Peter said proudly.

I turned to him. He was not smiling, but his eyes had a terrifying glint of pride in them.

"What?" I said.

"AltaCoin is the world's first cryptocurrency mined by the human mind. More efficient, and more available. Everyone will be able to be a part of this economy."

Everyone who can afford a headset, I thought.

"Soon, we will make it so that everyone can mine in their sleep, but before then, we had to create an initial supply. So that's what the server room is for."

"But these are people," I said, and the question was there for him to answer.

"Yes, employees. They are being taken care of. They are working for Altus."

"Why haven't I ever seen any of them around, though?" I asked, trying to make him see the same thing I was seeing.

"They live here."

"Where?" I asked, wondering where we could possibly have a dorm that could house all of these people.

"Here," Peter said.

It took a few moments to realize that when Peter Petrawicki said that they lived here, he meant . . . this room. They lived in those beds. I didn't respond. Why was he showing me this? I didn't know if it was illegal, but it was definitely indefensible. It was the kind of thing that you should not tell someone who you do not trust.

"I know what you're thinking, Miranda. I know that this looks immoral to you. But you can't change the world from the kiddie pool. Altus isn't going to be a company; it's going to be its own nation, its own world. We are going to give people what they have lost, what they need. For decades, humanity has had nowhere to expand to, but now we're giving people a new horizon, a new frontier."

That all sounded pretty gross, and I didn't know what to say. Then he spoke again, and my stomach dropped through the floor.

"I've taken the liberty of having someone pack up your old quarters. Everyone who works in high security lives here. Let me show you to your new room."

I let out a shaky breath, trying to control my panic, but we both knew the score. If someone had packed up my whole room, they knew about the phone; they had probably even seen my texts. I hadn't been brought to this new place to work. I had been brought here to be held prisoner.

APRIL

When we walked out of the auditorium, hauling the first round of bags behind us, Maya and I were a little surprised to find that Derek's pickup truck was gone and in its place was a white moving truck with its rear door lifted and nothing in the back except for a large wooden crate strapped to one wall. Apparently we had arrived on a Friday night, and now we were leaving late Sunday. It felt like it had been much longer. Carl crawled up on my shoulder to watch with me as two people, a man and a woman, stepped out of the van. I knew their faces, but it was dark and the context was off. Then again, my brain could do things now that it couldn't do before, and suddenly I had access to all the data I needed.

"Jessica?" I asked, in shock.

"April! Oh my god!" She bent over and put her head between her legs for a moment and then continued, "I didn't believe it was true, but it's true!"

"What the hell is going on?" Maya said quietly, toward me and Carl.

"We were told that we needed to come up here and get you, so we just . . . did," the man said.

"And Mitty!"

"I can't believe you remember my name," he said, laughing.

"It was a big day, but also, like, since . . ." I gestured at my face, though neither of them had made any sign that they'd noticed it. "I've been able to remember more or less everything that's ever happened to me."

This was something I was just figuring out, but yes.

"Can someone explain what's going on?" Maya said, looking at Carl. But Carl was being quiet around Jessica and Mitty.

"We each got a book, a few months ago," Jessica said. She still had the small fighter's frame and the bright red lipstick. "It was a very smart book, and it had a lot of good ideas that have helped us a lot. With money, but also with some family stuff."

Here Mitty picked up. "Yesterday, we both got another one. It told us to come up here and rescue April May and her friend and her monkey and her potato plant, and it looks like all of this is coming true. Except the potato. I'll be disappointed if there isn't a potato."

Fucking Carl.

"Maya, this is Jessica, and this is Mitty—they were the ones who helped me on the day that Martin Bellacourt . . ." I faded out, not sure how to finish the sentence.

"Stabbed you in the back like the fucking bitch that he was," Jessica filled in.

Maya actually smiled—it was hard not to like Jessica.

"Well, let's load up," Mitty said. "We were told to move quickly."

"Are we going in . . . the back?" Maya asked, pointing at the empty back of the moving van.

"That's what the book said. There's more too. We'll tell you about it when we get closer." I looked at Carl. There was a twinkle of excitement in their eye that I did not like, but I didn't ask them to explain.

We tossed all of our possessions into the back of the truck. Jessica and Mitty sat up front, and the three of us went in the back with the crate. The truck started to rumble. It felt unsafe without seat belts on, but Carl was in charge and they seemed to think it was fine.

"Where are we going?"

"It's a surprise," Carl said.

"OK, well, if you're not going to answer that question," Maya said, "answer this one. How come we can't be seen by schoolchildren at this high school without risking death, but we can be seen by Jessica and Mitty? Are they just . . . better people?"

"No, it has nothing to do with who they are. This won't be pos-sible for me to explain in detail—would you like me to try to do it metaphorically?"

"Yeah," she said, annoyed, "that would be fine."

"OK." The monkey sat with one of its feet crossed over the other, leaning toward Maya and me. The voice came louder to power over the road noise, but the tone didn't change at all.

"You have millions of nerves sensing your surroundings, but you don't feel a signal from any of them individually. How cold are you, where are you, do you need to stretch or yawn or sneeze? Those im-pulses are felt in aggregate. My brother and I are like that. We can see and feel, but if one nerve stops working, we have no idea, it's too much data. We aren't looking out of every eye and monitoring every camera. We have tremendous processing power, but the systems that make the data understandable are fairly opaque to us, just as your systems are to you. You don't know how your body decides you have an itch. You just know you do, and you scratch it. If a bunch of people at this school noticed something weird, that would increase the chances that my brother would notice. As long as we stay off predict-able paths and do not look exceptional, we should be fine."

We shifted around in the back of the truck as it made a turn, Maya letting her bag slide but holding on to Tater (which is what we had named the potato plant) with one hand. There were no seats for us, just our stuff and, latched to the side, a four-foot-high wooden crate.

"Can your brother control people," Maya said, "the way . . ." Then she looked at me and finished, "The way you can?"

"What do you mean?" I said.

"He can, but it is difficult. Operating a body is complex, espe-cially if you have not spent time operating it. It takes time to get to know the body."

Maya looked concerned. I had no idea what was going on.

"So, when you offered to use April's body to drive us to the school, would you have had to learn then? Or . . ."

"When you offered to do what?" I said, my heart speeding up.

"I will explain. It is not sinister. It is not a broken taboo." Even with the increased volume, it was a little hard to hear them over the noise of the road, so both Maya and I were leaning in.

"When your bodies are unconscious, they can be used and manipulated to keep them healthy and safe. That is all I have done. And yes, April, I did it while you were unconscious, to use the bathroom, to eat food, to keep clean, to keep your muscles strong. I'm sorry, I know that it is creepy, but it was necessary to optimize your health and speed your recovery."

Somewhere inside of me I had already known this. There were no bedpans in that bar. My muscles looked more toned after months of unconsciousness when the opposite should have been true.

Carl reached out their little hand to me, and despite myself, I took it. "I would never and *could* never use a human body to do something against its mind's will. It is outside of my programming."

"I don't know if I needed to know all this," I said.

"That's why I didn't bring it up. Patients are often upset hearing what doctors have to do to them while they are unconscious."

Maya shot me a look, then crossed her arms. I think she wanted me to be more pissed off at Carl.

We traveled for a long time, the humming of the road indicating that we were now on an interstate. Then, after what might have been hours, Carl uncurled himself, stretched, and said, "It's time for me to show you what's in the crate."

ANDY

There's a package in here for you," Jason called. I mean, he probably did. I didn't hear him. I was in the Open Access Altus Space building a tree so that I could put it into Breezy Spring Day. So far, I'd been able to hold on to my place in the top ten since launching, but that was only because I was working on building and marketing items like sixteen hours per day.

I felt the muted thudding of Jason smacking my chest and sighed.

"Exit," I said, and I pulled off the headset.

"You have mail," he said, throwing a padded envelope at me. "Also, you look like shit." He flipped the light switch on the wall.

That was definitely true. I also had been outside for roughly the same amount of time I'd spent showering in the last three days, which is to say not at all.

"Thanks, you look cute," I said, blinking in the light. He walked out of my room, knowing I was probably going to go right back into the Space.

Except I didn't, because inside the envelope was a new volume of *The Book of Good Times.*

It told me I needed to clean myself up because I would need to be prepared tomorrow morning to complete a series of increasingly bizarre tasks. It knew I was busy, it said, but it promised this would be worth it.

Next thing I knew, it was 9 A.M., and I was standing in a $15M vacant apartment that was, apparently, owned by my good friend Josh Crane, who I was helping plan a party. I had no idea who Josh Crane was, but that's what the book told me to say at the front desk of the building and it had worked.

Once there, I unloaded the contents of my bag (a bunch of sandwiches and other food) into one of the *two* fridges. My anxiety hummed. This was someone's home and I had broken in. Though the place didn't really feel like a home. It was too perfect. Too clean.

I walked around the four-bedroom apartment, ogling the views. It was fully furnished. The dining room table probably cost more than some American homes. Josh Crane had very good taste in art, or at least very expensive taste in art, so I was treating the place like a gallery when the elevator ding sent my heart into my throat. I wanted to run away, to hide, but this was what the book had said would happen, so instead I walked back to the landing.

There were two people, a man and a woman, and they were pushing . . . well, a beautiful, massive birthday cake. It was four feet high, with pastel frosting. Or at least, it was made to look like frosting. I was fairly sure that it wasn't a real cake.

It was on casters, and it rolled smoothly along the gray-stained hardwood floor.

"Um . . ." I said. "Do I have to sign, or . . ."

"No," the woman said with a big smile. "We have to go now." It was only then that I thought for a moment I might recognize them.

Once the elevator door was closed, with my heart thumping in my teeth, I walked forward toward the cake. Slowly, deliberately, the top of the cake hinged backward, and April May slowly uncurled to standing. My body almost stopped working. Her hair looked lank and dirty. Her skin—at least the part that definitely was skin—was pale and drawn. Her eyes, though, were bright, and she smiled like she was seeing something she needed to see.

"Ta-daaaaa," she said apologetically.

A laugh and a sob simultaneously exploded out of me, and then I fell to my knees and put my head on the ground, not sure if I would be able to stay conscious. I heard an unfamiliar noise coming out of my mouth, just a long low groan. She was there next to me then, wrapping her arms around me. I looked up and saw April's face—it was divided in two. My mind couldn't make sense of it. And then Maya was there too. Had she been in the cake? And then there was a monkey, and then my vision blurred and I heard a rushing noise in my ears. I put my head down just in time to pass out.

I woke up in a very fancy bed and turned to look out the window. I was, somehow, looking *down* on the Clock Tower Building, a building I had looked *up* at probably hundreds of times. The different perspective twisted my mind in a loop. I rolled out of bed to take in the view.

I had to pee. I also had to have a whole lot of questions answered. I walked out of the bedroom and into a hallway, which led me to the kitchen and dining area, where Maya was sitting at a table.

"Maya," I said.

She stood up and ran over to me, grabbing me tight and holding on. "What is going on?" I asked.

"A lot. I don't know where to start."

"Is April—"

"She's fine," she interrupted, saving me from finishing the sentence. "She's . . . a little different, but I think anyone would be. Her new skin . . . it's just that, a prosthetic, because of the fire. It covers a lot of her body."

That made me wonder if they were back together. Had Maya seen April's whole body? She saw me wondering that and punched me in the arm. "Jesus. No, we're not back together. I need to hear some words I haven't heard yet. I honestly don't know where she is on a lot of things. There hasn't been enough time."

"Where is she?" I asked.

"She went to take a shower. We've been on the run and haven't had a chance to get clean in a while."

And then a weight slammed into me from behind.

"AGGGUHHH," I said, looking down to see April's arms, one her normal color, the other stony and white with iridescent flecks in it. I could feel the wetness of her hair on the back of my neck.

"OK!" I said when the squeeze actually started to hurt. She let go and then came around to stand in front of me. She was wearing a thick, white, too-big bathrobe. I looked down at her, and she moved in again for a more proper hug. I tucked her head under my chin, and it fit perfectly, her wet, shiny black hair interlacing with the week's worth of stubble on my chin and neck. Under the robe, I felt the reality of her body, soft and solid. My eyes were stinging with tears.

I looked down at her. From her hairline, around her nose, and down through her jaw, the left half of her face shone like an oyster shell. I said the first thing that came to my mind.

"Shit, that looks badass."

She punched me in the shoulder, which actually hurt a little.

"I've heard you've been busy," she said, and her voice was 100 percent April.

I thought about that for a second and then said, "You planted a lot of seeds, I've had some gardening to do."

"Jesus, Andy," she retorted immediately, "you *do* sound like a pastor. I'm hungry. Are you hungry?"

I suddenly was. "I was told to bring food," I said. "It's in one of the two massive refrigerators." I gestured over my shoulder.

"It is really good to see you." As she said it, we all heard the elevator softly ping in the other room. April and Maya looked at each other, eyes wide and brows knitted. "Is someone else supposed to be coming?" Maya said.

When no one replied, she pulled a knife out of the knife block and then went and hid behind the kitchen island. I didn't know what to do, so I joined her until I heard a voice say, "Holy s'moly."

It was Robin. I stood up and saw April holding him. His arms were wrapped around her. In his right hand he held a small leather-bound book.

I know I'm not the first one to mention this, but I feel like I need to reemphasize that it is really weird to talk to a monkey and really weird to talk to a space alien computer program, but it's, like, unsustainably weird to talk to both at the same time. But then, like everything, somehow you just get used to it.

I didn't want to let April out of my sight. It seemed like this new reality could pass into a dream with any shift in the wind. In that way, it felt a lot like what it was like when April was suddenly gone. Adjusting to a new reality just takes time, and your mind keeps look-ing for signs that the old reality was the real one.

My brain was having an easier time with the talking monkey than it was with April being alive. It had happened! Everything since that "Knock Knock" had led me to this. I had done everything right.

But as pleased as I was with my actions, I found myself dancing around my obsession with Altus. I knew I was doing the right thing by trying to get more information about how it worked, but also I didn't feel like explaining to April that I was well on my way to being one of the first people in the world to get access to some deluxe expe-rience championed by Peter Petrawicki.

"Why do you think Altus is keeping the Space so exclusive?" April asked me.

"What do you mean?"

"Why aren't they giving it to everyone? What's the cost to them?"

"Well, I don't know. It must cost money to run, so maybe they need to sell access. They've built a massive office in Val Verde, and they took a lot of investment from extremely rich people that want their investment back, I guess," I answered.

"Neither of you are correct," Carl spoke, for the first time in a while, through their smartwatch.

"Yeah, I don't love agreeing with the monkey, but you're both not getting the point," Maya added.

"Your system is fueled by the creation and capture of value," Carl said. "The goal is to capture as much value as you create, though in practice that is more or less impossible. Altus is creating false scarcity because they think that is the best way to capture the value they are creating—there's no more to it than that. They're just following the incentives of the system."

"But isn't the point to create value?" April asked the monkey.

"That is unclear." They scratched the back of their little head. "Creating the value is what people publicly praise, but capturing value is what is actually rewarded. Altus is creating value, likely far more than it is capturing, at least right now. But your system does not have good ways of even recognizing the existence of value that is created but not captured."

We all looked at Maya.

"Yeah," she said, "that."

We had all finished snacking by then, so we moved to the giant living room. Robin and I couldn't stop looking down at the precipitous views of the city.

I plopped onto the couch. It was a beautiful cool, soft, mottled-gray leather, but somehow not particularly comfortable. And that's where I was sitting when we went all the way down the rabbit hole.

"The situation we're in, if you'll allow me to summarize"—April gestured at the monkey, and they dipped their head forward—"is that an advanced intelligence determined that we will very likely destroy ourselves sometime in the next couple hundred years and sent an envoy to attempt to set us on a better path. That failed, and so now that envoy has been replaced by another . . . I dunno what to call it . . . entity, I guess, that is going to, instead of nudging us into a better course, control every individual human's decisions. We don't know how that entity is going to do it, but we do know that it probably has something to do with Altus . . ." The monkey raised their hand here, and April paused.

"It may be that Altus is part of the intervention—I can't know— but I do know that Altus's existence makes it extremely likely that you will eventually destroy yourselves without intervention."

"How?" I asked, getting a little nervous about what I'd already been hiding from Maya and April.

"It is not simple. You will create simple narratives as it happens, but they will all be incorrect. The largest affecting factors will be tremendous concentration of power in the hands of fewer and fewer people, who will then destabilize the world to protect that power, large-scale isolation caused by easy alternatives to community and society, and a change in the speed of transfer of information that will be too rapid for norms and taboos to prevent it from being used maliciously."

"That sounds . . . familiar," Maya said.

The monkey seemed to smirk. "All of this will make you less able to handle unlikely but ultimately inevitable catastrophes. Especially if they compound. A war on top of an unstable climate on top of a pandemic, for example."

"Why are you telling us this?" I asked.

"Because if my brother has his way with you, it will be a catastrophic loss for the galaxy."

Robin's eyes widened and he said, "Your . . . brother?"

"Yes, we are siblings."

"Shouldn't your"—I had to think about what I was going to say—"your loyalty be to your own people?"

"You are my people. I don't know who created me. Based on the data given to me, systems like yours tend to be short-lived. Ultimately, all beauty is transitory, but there's no choice except to believe it is worthy. I am still doing what I was created to do. Allowing my brother to destroy your beauty would be contrary to my programming."

I mulled that over for a while, and then April took back over.

"So, we all agree with Carl. Humanity shouldn't become the beloved pet of a planet-wide conscious infection. But the only way to prevent that is to change the world enough that we probably will not destroy ourselves. And the best way to do that is to make Altus not exist anymore. Andy, how do you feel about that?"

I was caught a little off guard, worried why she thought I was the right person to ask.

"Um . . ." I didn't even know what the Premium version had in store, but I was deeply attached. "It will be extremely hard because the people who are using Altus's service love it a lot. Even if we destroyed their whole system, I think people would rebuild it," I said, trying to sound like I wasn't one of those people.

"How would you feel if we destroyed Altus?" Maya asked, seeing deeper into me than I would maybe have liked.

"I'm not sure if we can," I hedged.

"We must," said Carl.

And then Maya, April, Robin, and Carl were all looking at me. Every one of them showing me some mix of hope and fear and frustration.

"Andy," Robin said, his voice strong.

I looked from him to April and saw an anger there I hadn't expected.

Maya took over, seeing the dangerous ground we were on before I did. "Peter Petrawicki and Altus are not two different things. I understand looking at things from thirty thousand feet or whatever, and understanding the magnitude of the challenge is great, but Altus isn't salvageable. It's rotten to the core."

I finally thought of how my hesitation must look through April's eyes. To come back and find that her best friend was enthusiastically enjoying a creation of the man who might be most to blame for her murder.

How had I ended up here?

"Of course we will," I said, fully chastised. "We'll take it down and I'll love doing it."

Relief spread over April's face, but I caught a hardness in Maya's eyes.

"What tools do we have?" April asked.

"Well, since we're sharing secrets, I have a few. I have a large social media following, and a lot of people listen to me. I'm also on track to be one of the first fifty people with access to the Altus Premium Space. I also am one of only a dozen people who collaborate on an anonymous video journalism channel called The Thread that reaches tens of millions of influential people."

Maya gasped at this. "You're The Thread?" she said, almost as an accusation.

"No, The Thread isn't one person. It's a group of people. I was invited in, and we construct the content together. I have no idea who is in charge—everyone is anonymous. Only one person knows who everyone is, and no one knows who they are."

"That's a big fucking deal, Andy," she said.

"Well, I have one more thing on the list, which is that I have a hundred fifty million dollars."

Everybody's eyes got big then.

"What the hell have you been up to? And what is The Thread?" April asked.

"Jesus, all I did was find April," Maya said.

I looked at Carl, who blinked very slowly and then said, "I gave him some very good investment advice."

"I FUCKING KNEW IT!" I said. "Can I tell them?"

"Yes," they said.

"Carl here has been dragging me around by the dick with a secret, all-knowing book."

"Oh. Yeah, I got a book too," Maya said.

"Me too," Robin added, holding his up.

"Fuck! Why were you giving us all books?" I said, staring at the monkey. They looked unfazed.

"You will continue to get them. They are the best way for me to communicate without the possibility of detection," they said.

"Well, I hope you know it was completely terrifying," I said. And then, turning back to the topic at hand: "So I have a hundred fifty million dollars, access to The Thread, potentially access to the Altus Premium Space—what do you guys have?"

I had tried to gloss over my status inside of Altus, but I couldn't lie about it either.

"So you're going to be one of the first people to really know what Altus is?" April asked.

"Maybe. I hope so."

She thought about it for a moment and then said, "That's going to be extremely powerful. Andy, I have to ask you to do something, and it's going to suck. I want you to go all in on Altus. I want you to be a champion for them. People are going to hate you for it, but you will be our inside man. And when you turn away from them, it will matter because you believed in it."

I let out a long breath. This was *exactly* what I wanted to do, but I didn't want them to know. "But, Andy," Robin said, ever the clear thinker, "if you do that, you have to know that you're going to get sucked in. And you can't let yourself forget why you're doing it. OK?"

"I can do it," I said, relieved that it seemed like I was going to get to keep my friends and my Altus habit.

"So what are our other assets?" Robin asked.

"Miranda is in Val Verde right now, though it's not easy to talk to her," I said. "Maybe we can count on her for something at some point."

April added, "And we have an artificial intelligence that can inhabit a monkey. That has to count for something."

"You're forgetting something," Maya said, like it was something really obvious.

"OH!" April said. "Yeah, and I can Google stuff with my mind!"

I just stared at her.

"Also, the special skin, it seems to be very strong. I punched a hole in a car. Also, when Maya got shot, it healed her."

I stood up from the couch. "What? Go back! Go slower!"

So she did. She told us the whole story and it took a long-ass time, but it was a good story, so no one minded.

At the end, April listed our assets out loud.

"So we have a hundred fifty million dollars, a sentient monkey who is also a superintelligent alien AI, access to a massively influential anonymous video-essay platform, a mole in Val Verde, a high-level Altus user ready to turn his coat when needed, and a woman with superstrength who is capable of Googling things with her mind—that's me."

"I mean, that's pretty good," I said, "but I don't know how it helps us take down Altus."

Maya looked at April, and April looked down at her lap. "I guess I also have what I've always had," she said, a little sadly. "An audience." I didn't even notice that Maya had been holding April's hand until she let it go.

Nothing is inevitable.

APRIL

ndy didn't want to leave us, but the sun went down and Carl told him he had to go home and sleep in his own house. And so, eventually, Maya and I were left alone to squat in a four-thousand-square-foot high-rise apartment with our pet alien monkey.

It felt wrong, to be sure. It felt like both trespassing on whoever owned the place and trespassing on society for enjoying something so decadent. Did I take baths in the giant soaking tub with a view of both the Hudson and the East River (and everything in between)? Yussss. But I had complicated thoughts about structural inequality while I did it.

Maya had set Tater up in the nicest spot in the house. We certainly didn't need the sunlamp anymore. Suddenly the tiny leaves were flourishing. It was the only plant in the whole place, which I guess made sense for a vacant apartment.

Andy had brought us a computer, and apparently Carl didn't have any problem hacking the Wi-Fi, because it was on immediately. But that didn't mean that I wanted to hop back on social media. I mean, I did, but also I did not.

"I just hang out on the Som," Maya said to me when I brought it up.

"Yeah, I know."

She smiled at me. "It's not the same, of course. People use it to work on reality games or indulge in conspiracy theories. There are a lot of people there looking for you. They actually put me onto your trail." I could tell that was a long story. "Anyway, you shouldn't go on Twitter."

"I'm going to have to eventually, right? It's one of our assets."

"I know, I just don't want you to," she said while handing me the laptop. "I guess this is what life is." You would think that literally dying would make it so that you don't care about how many followers you have on Twitter, but, like, just between you and me, I did. I spent the next hour looking through the hundreds of people who had sent me @replies just in the last day, trying to get a feel for how I was being imagined.

Holly
@accioawesome
OMG look at this adorable picture I found of @AprilMaybeNot and @AndySkampt chowing on In-N-Out. I miss her.
1 reply   3 retweets   6 likes

Chris in Hell
@edens_halo
It's legit gross that @realDonaldTrump has a Hollywood walk of fame star when legend and literal angel @AprilMaybeNot doesn't.
3 retweets   12 likes

Saskia
@saskiab
Going for an @AprilMaybeNot look this AM. That girl had style.
2 replies   0 retweets   9 likes

Dan Burdick
@RenoDan203854
President Ashby is so clearly talking at the regular with @AprilMaybeNot. Every word that comes out of her mouth is so fake. We all know who is actually in charge.
5 replies   24 retweets   49 likes

Cat

@Catriffic

Sometimes you have a real shit day at work, and then
you remember, hey, at least you don't have to hear
@AprilMaybeNot's voice every fucking day anymore.

0 replies   2 retweets   10 likes

Here I was, a reconstructed humanlike thing with literal superpowers, still getting my feelings hurt by randos.

"I looked up that sofa." Maya had walked into the room, and I
hadn't noticed. "It's a Fendi."

"Fendi, like the fashion label? They make couches?"

"They do."

"Do I want to know how much it costs?"

"Probably not. How is the internet?" she asked me, still standing.

"Oh, y'know, things are apparently pretty bad," I said, making a
show of closing the laptop.

"They're just calling it 'the Crisis.' Not 'the Financial Crisis' because it's bigger than finances. I think we all just forgot what life is
supposed to be for. People haven't adjusted."

"Can we talk?"

"Yeah." She sat down on the couch next to me. "So, I got shot."

"You got shot." We hadn't talked about it. The boiler room had
been too strange, like another world where we didn't have to think
about reality, but now we were in the world again. "Are you OK?"

"Physically, yeah, I think so." She lifted her shirt to show me, and
there, just under her bra, was an irregular, pearly-white spot in her
dark skin. Around it was a bloom of purple and red bruise. I felt sick
looking at it. Not because it looked gross—it honestly didn't—but
because of what it meant. And what it had almost meant.

She pulled her shirt back down, wincing a little with the movement. Then she dug into her pocket and brought out a milky-white
stone with flecks and veins of iridescence flashing through it. "I think
you should have this," she said.

I took it in my right hand; it felt hollow and cool. Then I looked down at my left hand, still smaller than it had been, still with only four fingers. I put the stone in my left hand and . . . it vanished. It slid into my hand like dropping water into water. And then, the hand rippled and, as we watched, my pinky finger grew back.

"Where the hell did you get that?!" I nearly shouted, staring at my re-formed hand.

"At a flea market in New Jersey," she said.

I stared at her. And then she told me her whole story. Brooding for months, storming out of her parents' house, chasing dead dolphins and bad internet, lugging around a potato plant, and running from crazed reality gamers. It was proper adventure! "Well, thank you," I said when she was finally done. "For coming to get me. I don't know what I would have done if I had opened that door and no one was there." I shuddered. "Or worse, if someone else was."

Before Andy left the apartment to go back to his work getting into the Altus Premium Space, we had concocted a very rough plan.

1. Always have our ringers on in case Miranda texts again.
2. Always be ready to move at a moment's notice. Bags packed and ready to go.
3. Begin a whisper campaign against Altus. Right now, they were a big, shiny new thing. Everyone either loved them or didn't understand them, so there was no pushback. If public relations was going to be any part of taking them down, that work was going to need time to spread.

The only thing that was clear was that Carl couldn't just destroy Altus. Even if it was something their programming would allow, which I don't think it was, they were not physically powerful enough to work against the desires of their brother. Indeed, Carl was in a kind of hiding. Their brother wanted Carl gone as much as he wanted me gone. I remember the exact words Carl said to me one night in that apartment, because I can do that now: "He doesn't care about what the outcome is, he only cares about the level of certainty. He wants control, and you and I both represent challenges to that control. He wants me dead even more than he wants you dead. He is the god I was told to never be."

The problem with starting a communications campaign against Altus was that I had to communicate.

Since we were now in a four-bedroom apartment, Maya and I, without discussing it, chose our separate rooms. So did Carl. They were sleeping in the smallest room, which was staged as a little boy's room for potential buyers.

On the second night, after we had gone to bed, I got up and softly knocked on Maya's door.

"Yeah?" she said. I opened the door, seeing the bed in the dark, silhouetted against the view, which from this side of the apartment was clear all the way down to the Financial District.

"Hey," I said at the door.

"Hey," she said, rolling over in bed.

"You know, there are blinds on that window."

"I'm never going to have this view again." And that was true. Maya was wealthy, but not this wealthy. "It feels like you can see everything from up here," she said, "but really you can't see anything."

Things were falling apart. Tent cities were popping up in Central Park. Shelter space had filled up years ago, but now the homeless population was exploding. But from here, everything was perfect and beautiful. The world felt immortal and inevitable, but it was actually brittle and breaking.

I sat down on the bed. "A few days ago, I said I was sorry for not listening to you. You were right. You tried to stop me. I fucked everything up. But . . ." I had prepared what I was going to say while lying in bed by myself, but that didn't make it easy. "But that's not the thing I'm sorry for, really. That was just another piece of the same mistake that I've made over and over again. I'm sorry I put you last.

You were the most important person, and I put you at the bottom of my list."

"April," she said.

"No, I've got a whole thing prepared, let me do it. I'm sorry because I was terrible to you, but I was also terrible to myself. I know I've got self-worth issues. I just found out I was chosen as an emissary by an alien envoy to represent and protect the human race, and still I spent the afternoon searching for validation on Twitter. But I know that you are a good, strong, beautiful, talented person, and you loved me, and literally if that isn't enough, nothing is. So, thank you for loving me, and I'm sorry."

"Thank you, April."

And then I realized that she might think that I thought that if I said the right words we'd get back together. I didn't want her to think that, so I stood up.

"I just couldn't sleep." I started walking out the door.

"They were good words," she said. "Good night, April."

"Good night."

There isn't anything I can say that will prevent you from skipping this week's recording of *Slainspotting*. It's a shame. You shouldn't, but I've run the simulations and you now value your new mission too much, so you're going to make a bunch of bad decisions. This is what he's counting on. And who am I to say that you shouldn't? You need to work hard right now. You are going to spend the day lying on your bed with a VR headset on instead of maintaining your relationships. Please do not forget, however, that you are a person and not just a tool. The Good Times are about more than just getting stuff done.

Oh, also, it's time. Sell everything and buy AltaCoin. Right now.

ANDY

That week I canceled our recording of *Slainspotting*.

Jason was pissed, but he was nice about it. "I know, you're obsessed with this Altus thing, you've got a chance at Premium access . . . Go for it. But if you skip next week, I'm gonna be mean about it."

But I couldn't record *Slainspotting*. April was back, The Thread was relying on me, and humanity was at stake, so I had to lie in my bed completely still while constructing objects to make my breezy spring day more appealing than other people's breezy spring days! I had a sun that moved through the sky, rising and setting if you wanted it to. I had some starter trees that came with the pack, but other people were specializing in trees, so people mostly bought other trees and put them into my environment. The wonderful thing was, there ultimately wasn't that much I could do to make the environment better.

When I wasn't in the Altus Space, I was in The Thread, where, with one day left before the Premium selection, I had good news.

> **Twelve:** Hello all, there's less than twenty-four hours left before the week ends and the first fifty are selected. I have good news, I'm in the top fifty and things look strong.

> **Five:** What? I've barely left the Space and I haven't cracked the top 200.

> **Twelve:** I got in early with a good idea. Can't tell you more without threatening to give away my identity.

> **One:** @Twelve, congratulations, this is amazing news. Please do not share any more if you think your identity may be compromised. But having someone who has access to the Premium Space will be extremely helpful. I haven't been able to gather any intel about what makes it so appealing, though it seems a number of people who played Fish have access. Fish players seem like they would practically kill to get in.

It was a big deal when One dropped in on a conversation, and it felt good to have their approval. One was the only person in The Thread who had no identifying details attached to them. But after that quick chat, I logged back into the Altus Space to find that I was no longer in the top twenty-five. In fact, I was getting terrifyingly close to not being in the top fifty at all.

I started checking new entrants to the top list. I was keeping track of the bestseller ranks just in case there was something I needed to be aware of. People tended to focus on homes, clothes, decor, or natural settings. But suddenly, there was a solid dozen people in the top fifty who were selling what appeared to be cheap little trinkets. Small statues, pins, coins, badges, that kind of thing. They didn't look appealing for any particular reason, and any of them would be fairly easy to re-create, so I didn't see why they would be doing so well.

I immediately started freaking out. How were these shitty little objects doing so well? The back of my neck was getting sweaty. I was panicking. That's when I started realizing how much this meant to me. Fifty people in the whole world were going to get selected for an experience that was, if the people playing Fish were to be believed, a kind of nirvana.

I logged out of the Space and logged into The Thread.

Twelve: Does anyone know what's going on with the new chintzy trinkets in the Altus Space Store?

Eight: Celebrities. People with big internet audiences are asking their fans to buy cheap items to get them into the Space.

Five: They're billing them as "Limited Edition" items. They're available "Only today and tomorrow!" So, like, exactly the days they need to sell stuff to get into the Premium Space.

Twelve: Fuuuuuck. That's shitty. The whole idea was that it would be available to the people who added the most value to the Open Access Space.

Eight: Well, yeah, I mean . . . have you met capitalism? The whole idea of everything is to reward people who create value and yet . . .

Twelve: Fuck. Why doesn't Altus ban this?

Eight: At a guess, probably because it's getting them lots of users and free marketing and money.

I was about to log back out when I got a private message from One.

One: I need you to experience the Premium Space, and it's possible you won't need the help getting there. But can you tell me what your object is? I might be able to give you a bump at the last second if you need it.

Twelve: It's Breezy Spring Day.

One: Hah, amazing. Breezy Spring Day is a genius object. Thinking to make wind! I love it.

It was amazing how good it felt to have them compliment me. All anybody wants is to be appreciated by the people they think are cool, and it turns out I kinda idolized One.

Twelve: I could also just tell my audience to buy it. It's not like I don't have an audience. Hell, I could just start selling custom limited-edition socks and it would put me over the edge.

One: If you do that, you'll get in, but you won't be taken seriously. You'll just be another rich person who bought their way in. You need to work for it, you need to really care.

Twelve: OK, I'm going back into the Space, I think I'll make a limited-edition Breezy Spring Day to make fun of the weblebrities. Some of the people who check on my work will find it funny at least. But maybe I can sell a few.

One: This is such a great video topic. An open market rewards people who work hard and think critically at first, but once real value is at stake, the market rapidly transforms to reward those with access to capital. The fact that, in this case, the capital is fame and not money only makes it that much more universal and interesting.

Twelve: Yes. The top 50 today compared to the top 50 yesterday shows directly that people who aren't adding value have bumped out at least 10 people who are.

One: And by the time the top 50 are selected, I wouldn't be surprised if that number doubled.

Twelve: Just leave me a message here if you want any help with that script.

One: Will do. But first priority . . . get your ass in the Premium Space.

So I did. I ate a protein bar and peed and went back into the Altus Space. First I checked the ranking. I was in forty-first. No doubt, if I didn't change something, I'd be knocked out by celebrities soon. The top sellers were still all legit object creators, mostly people making super cheap clothes and decor that traded on having tons of sales. But there were enough people making environments that I was just one of many. I might have been one of the top creators, but I only had one product.

I dropped into the Open Access Space and went ahead and did a gimmick. I cloned my Breezy Spring Day and made the sky pink and the grass purple and created low-flying, super-light objects that looked like massive, transparent crystals. It took me a couple hours to get the look right, but at the end, it was an alien world that still felt like a beautiful spring day. I released it under the name Breezy Spring Day: Alpha Centauri ~-[{(One Day Only)}]-~. Here's what I wrote in the description.

> Hey, no offense to anyone who's cashing in on their celebrity to get into the Premium Altus Space with ~-[{(Limited Edition)}]-~ trinkets . . . OK, actually . . . offense. This is dumb. If you want to see someone who has worked to actually create value, you can buy this very cheap, high-quality, slightly modified version of my 500,000+ download Breezy Spring Day for one day only.

With six hours left, I was in the mid-thirties. And I felt secure enough to take a bio-break. Spending hours at a time in the Altus Space wasn't uncomfortable until you left. You felt fine when you were in there, but the longer you stayed in, the more it sucked to come out. Headaches, body aches, low blood sugar.

The stress of the ranking was real, but I felt like I couldn't do anything else about it, so I did the healthy thing and went for a walk down to the Subway were Bex worked. Altus didn't feel like a massive world-destroying entity; it felt more like Etsy at the moment. But that's the way of these things. One day, an internet company wants to sell books, and then ten years later they're a threat to nearly every industry on earth.

The city felt a little dead. There just weren't a lot of people out. I passed a store that said "Altus Headsets!" But then, under that, it said "Sold Out! Restock Thursday!"

"Andy!" Bex called out as I came in. "Are you OK?"

Apparently that's how bad I looked.

"I've been spending a lot of time in the Altus Space," I answered honestly.

She pursed her lips and pushed them to the side of her face. "You and every other dude in New York. Business was starting to pick up with the recession, but now no one's out at all."

"Business was picking up?"

"Yeah, folks stop going to expensive lunch places, but they still need lunch! Now almost all of our orders are delivery apps."

"Well, I'm sorry if I dropped off the planet."

"You're not the first guy who's ghosted me for a couple days." But she didn't have her usual confidence as she said it.

I looked at her gorgeous dark eyes and felt like such a complete turd. But she saved me from having to say something.

"What's Altus like?"

"You haven't been in?" I asked stupidly.

She just laughed, though. "No, I've heard about it. They say it's like the Dream. I miss the Dream."

"You were into it?"

"Not any more than most people. I solved a couple sequences that had already been solved for fun. I mostly just walked around. It was nice to have a place to be alone."

I barked out a laugh. "That's the opposite of the problem I have. I can't find time to be with people."

"You know our lives are pretty different, right?" she asked.

"I mean, yeah. That's true of everyone but more . . ." And then I didn't know what to say.

"With the immigrant brown girl, yeah, you're allowed to say we're not the same, Andy." I didn't know if we were having a fight, but apparently we weren't because then she just said, "Sweet onion chicken teriyaki?"

"Yes, thank you. After tonight, I should have more time. Can you come hang out tomorrow?"

"I've got another afternoon shift, so I can come over in the morning or late."

"Come over in the morning, I'll either have something to celebrate or something to be miserable about. I'll explain then."

"Why don't you explain now? We're closing, you can eat your

sandwich and tell me what's going on. If it's so hard to find time to not be alone, just . . . stop being alone."

The urge to leave the Subway and rush back to my apartment to check on the rankings was almost a physical tug. I could feel the nerves on that side of my body light up with sensitivity. I closed my eyes, took a breath, sat down, forcing my brain to settle, and un-wrapped my sandwich, took a bite, and probably (knowing me) started talking with my mouth full.

"The Altus Open Access Space is amazing. It's like the Dream in that you're completely immersed. It's as real as this"—I gestured to reality—"but there's basically nothing there. You have to buy things to fill your world with. But you can also earn in-game money by cre-ating and selling objects for other people . . ."

As Bex locked up, cleaned up, and mopped the floor, I followed her around, explaining the Premium Space, how I'd been fighting to get into the top fifty for the whole week and somehow had done it, but then found myself getting kicked out by celebrities.

"But you're a celebrity, why don't you just join in?"

"That's not how I want to do it. I want to get in by creating some-thing valuable, not by cheating my way in."

"No offense"—Bex put her mop back in the bucket—"but that's some fool shit."

"What do you mean?"

"I mean, use what you've got, Andy. If you want in, get in. Noth-ing's fair."

I thought back to the conversation I'd had with One.

"OK, you're right," I said, still thinking. "But there's more to it than that. I don't know what it's going to be like in the Premium Space, but I do know that there are going to be two kinds of people: people who created their way into the top fifty and people who just famoused their way in. I want to be in the first group."

She thought about this for a while.

"You should've said that to start, then." And then she started mopping again.

"Are you sure I can't help? It feels weird to just talk while you're working."

"Now you're back with the fool shit again." She smiled. "I wouldn't trust you to not fuck up, honestly."

"That's probably a good call."

"So only fifty people in the whole world get to have access to . . . what?"

"I don't know," I said, feeling a little foolish.

"But you're probably freaking out right now."

"Yeah."

"And you don't know where you're at in the standings."

"I don't."

"And you managed to sit here and talk to me instead of refreshing over and over again?"

"I guess I did."

"That's pretty impressive, actually." She pushed the bucket behind the counter.

"How would you feel if I checked the rank now?" I said when she got back, my phone already on the table.

"I mean, I'm interested."

I opened up a third-party website that lagged just a bit behind the ranks in the Altus store. It was 10:30. The top fifty would be chosen in ninety minutes. I was in fifty-seventh place.

"Fuck," I said.

"Not good news?"

"Fifty-seven."

"Is there anything else you can do?"

"I could tweet that I made Breezy Spring Day and that I need people to go buy it and I'd be in the top fifty in like ten minutes."

"Is it worth not having the cred?"

I just shrugged and then put my head in my hands. Who knew how things would look a week from now? I could keep dropping. This could be my only chance.

I was literally opening Twitter when I got a DM from One.

Don't worry, I got it.

Bex was done at the Subway, so we went back to my apartment to sit with Jason and refresh the page.

Jason didn't seem super invested in the whole thing. It felt like he was hoping I'd get pushed way back and give it up and go back to what he probably saw as a better lifestyle for me. A lifestyle where I did things besides get up to pee and eat a Clif Bar for ten minutes every five hours. My body really did feel like shit.

I'd gone from a pretty meaningful life to one where I mostly did not get out of bed all day very fast.

But Bex was on my side, and that was nice.

At eleven, I was sixty-fourth.

But then at 11:15 I was fifty-ninth and it seemed like I was climbing pretty fast.

"Holy shit," Jason said.

"What?"

"Well, I was just trolling Twitter to see if people are talking about your object at all, and I think I figured out why you're rising in the ranks again." He turned his phone to me and showed me the following tweet.

Justin Bieber

@JustinBieber

Hanging out in the Altus Space. Breezy Spring Day is amazing. Go check it out.

937 replies   8.4K retweets   29K likes

"What the fuck," Bex said.

I texted One, *Are you friends with Justin Bieber?*

They texted back, *No comment.*

Wait, I replied. *Are *you* Justin Bieber?*

A very fast reply: *No comment.*

At 11:30 I was in the top fifty again, and by midnight I wasn't even worryingly close to fifty. Justin Bieber had pushed me through the finish. The power of #influencers!

Jason poured everyone a round of the only bottle of wine we had in the house, and we drank for fifteen minutes.

"OK, you boys have a nice night. I'm going to go home," Bex announced.

"Why?" Jason asked. "You said you don't have to work in the morning anyway. We should play a game or something."

"Jason, look at him." She gestured at me. "He's torturing himself not going back in the Altus Space right now. I'm shocked he's lasted this long."

"No," I said. "I can wait."

I did not want to wait. My body was literally itchy with the desire to go in and see whether I had access to the Premium Space and, if so, what on earth it was. But also, maybe Bex was going to stay the night. And if there was anything better than the Altus Premium Space . . . Ugh, I hate this sentence, I apologize.

So we played some games, and drank White Claw, and smoked a little to celebrate my success. And then Jason and Bex talked while I went into my room and cleaned up what had become the worst possible room to bring a girl into.

I went back into the living room and, immediately, Jason stood up and stretched comically. "WELP IT'S TIME FOR ME TO GO TO BED GOODBYE." And then he slipped into his room.

"Hey, you want to come . . . see . . ." I had no idea how I planned to finish that sentence.

Bex moved over to me, and we were kissing and falling toward my room. She was so soft and real and smooth. Her lip balm tasted like raspberries and her hair smelled like . . . the way girl hair smells. Look, it was awesome, OK?

I woke up a couple hours later hanging off the side of my double bed. I looked down at my watch and saw that I'd had a DM come in from One.

Have you been in yet? We're all waiting! Report!

It was the first time Bex and I had been together. That was something that was really important to me. I knew that lying down on the floor in just my boxers and going into a full-immersion virtual space while she slept alone in my bed would be the opposite of respect.

I lay down on the floor, put the headset on, and went to the Altus Premium Space.

ANDY

*H*ello, congratulations on having access to the Premium Altus Space," Alta's voice said to me as I entered. It looked exactly the same so far, just my breezy day filled with a few other objects people had made and I had purchased. Trees, a small home with some furniture and paintings. I hadn't spent much time decking it out; I was more interested in making the Breezy Spring Day nice and selling as many as I could.

But then something very new suddenly blinked into existence: Alta. She was short, dark-eyed, dark-haired, pale skin. She was not April, but she looked enough like April that a stab of anger went through me. What the fuck were these people thinking? Why would they pick a model for their digital assistant who looked like the former nemesis of the company's founder?

She didn't pay any attention to my emotional state and just kept moving with the script.

"You may be thinking that, with the exception of my appearance, this doesn't look so different actually.

"But if you'll open the Altus Space Store, you'll find that you have access to many Premium objects constructed by Altus, available to you at no cost. And you will also see two new categories . . ." As she said this, the Altus Space Store automatically opened. "The first are our sandboxes. These are professionally constructed environments for you to enjoy and be yourself."

The Open Access Space was lacking significantly in things to actually do specifically because creating detailed, enjoyable environments was pretty hard.

"And second we have experiences . . ." The Sandboxes menu closed and the Experiences menu opened. Here I saw a listing of categories:

ADVENTURE

EDUCATION

DISCUSSION

MUSIC

BOOKS

RELAXATION

ADULT

"Before you select any of these things, understand that this will not work how you expect. The Altus Space is not designed to be a primarily recreational platform; it is designed for self-improvement. Humans spend a third of their lives unconscious. When we at Altus lost access to the Dream, we realized that the great loss was that we would once again be unproductive during that time. With the Open Access Space, we have reactivated the ability to work while we dream. But here in the Premium Space, this ability turned out to be greater than we had imagined.

"The Altus Space does not show you things, it gives your brains impressions of things that it interprets as a reality. For example"— she gestured to herself—"Altus did not design me, Altus is not telling you what I look like, it is giving your brain a signal to call up an attractive young woman. What that looks like to you is your brain's decision, not ours."

Mercifully, Alta didn't give me time to spend with this unique new shame, and she continued.

"We allow you to create your objects in the Open Access Space, but what we send out are your mind's impressions of that object. So, here in the Premium Altus Space, we have two main services. Our sandboxes are custom environments filled with objects more detailed and usable than what has, thus far, been created for Open Access users.

"But second, and more importantly, we are also able to capture the experiences of people in the real world. And you can enter those experiences, whether they are reading a book, hiking a trail, or doing acrobatics. These experiences are not like anything that has ever happened to you before, and they are not easy to explain. Luckily, it's very easy to show."

Suddenly I was walking through some kind of tropical forest. Or someone was. I was a person who was walking through a tropical forest. They were thinking about the plants there, about a tree branch that had fallen since their last walk. They knew that they were hoping to see a particular kind of bird. The name of the bird didn't enter their brain, but an image of the bird did. It was small and black with a bright yellow belly.

I was . . . thinking their thoughts. I was in their memory. And I felt everything. I felt the burn in my quads and an unfamiliar tightness in my ankle. I smelled the sweetness of the leaf litter and felt the trickle of sweat rolling between my shoulder blades. But still, I also maintained enough distance from the experience that I could consider it. I was inside and outside at the same time.

And then the vision ended and I was back in my Altus Space with Alta.

"People have varying reactions to this," she said, "so understand that it is normal to be a little freaked-out right now. But yes, Altus can capture moments of other people's minds, store them, and then map them to yours. You cannot read a book this way, but you can inhabit someone else's mind as *they* read a book. You can't go into a boxing ring and fight, but you can inhabit someone else as *they* fight.

"The story of humans is the story of the escalation in speed of information transfer. That began with language, expanded with writing, and exploded with the internet. And now, another exponential shift, a new kind of giant leap for mankind. You can be inside a business leader's mind as they make decisions. You can understand the thoughts of people you disagree with. And most powerful of all, people who inhabit people as they play sports, or do math, or think critically gain those skills at a much faster rate than those who practice during waking hours. The Altus Space will not only fundamentally change recreation; it will fundamentally change education, connection, politics, and all human interaction.

"Welcome to the Premium Space. Take your time, learn your way around, and take the opportunity to become a better you."

It was impossible for me not to imagine the power of a tool like this. A doctor could use it to diagnose a patient! A person's pain would no longer need to be a mystery! Empathy would no longer need to be an exercise in imagination. We could literally feel each other's feelings. And what about learning? If I inhabited the body of someone playing piano, I could understand their mastery much faster. And then, of course, there was the Adult menu I had noticed before. The temptation to check that out was strong.

When your body experienced discomfort while you were in the Altus Space, it filtered through, even if dampened, and just then I felt a pushing pain in my side. "Exit," I said, and then I pulled off the headset. Bex was standing over me. I think she had just kicked me! Not hard, but hard enough.

"Really?" she said, her hands on her hips. She was only wearing her underwear, and I couldn't help but take her in.

I sat up. "I just wanted to see . . ." And then I trailed off.

"Yeah, OK," she said, and then she started searching around for her clothes.

"Bex, look. I screwed up. It was just too compelling. I thought I'd drop in for a second."

"Uh-huh," she said as she pulled her shirt over her head.

"It's not an excuse, it was shitty. I'm really sorry."

"Yep." She was pulling on her pants now.

"Can I walk you to the train? We can talk."

"Not right now, no," she said, not meeting my eyes as she walked past me and out of the room.

I sat down on my bed and waited to hear the door to my apartment close. I pulled out my phone and wrote several texts to Bex, all of which I deleted before sending.

"Fuck," I whispered.

There was no way to fix what I'd just done to Bex, at least not right now, and my VR headset wouldn't stop staring at me. I lay down on my bed and went back into the Space.

In there, I discovered that experiences like the one I'd just enjoyed could be purchased. In the Open Access Space, an object might, at most, cost 10 AltaCoin, which was, at the moment, around twenty-five dollars and going up as demand for the currency outpaced supply. In the Premium Space, there were no experiences for sale for under 20 AltaCoin, and they were regularly in the hundreds. Of course, I had enough AltaCoin to last a dozen lifetimes, but clearly if this product was here to revolutionize the way we learn and think and interact, it was going to do it for rich people first.

MIRANDA

I had no cell phone, no window. There were armed guards between me and the outside, and no one would even talk to me, much less talk about letting me outside. I had no access to internet of any kind. I didn't even have access to a computer terminal. All I had was an Altus headset. I didn't want to go into the Space, but eventually boredom wins. I had been given a job, and even if I knew it was useless, doing something was better than doing nothing.

My job now was no longer anything to do with understanding how Altus's (or, rather, Carl's) brain interface worked.

I was what they called a "client." Clients were people who made content for Altus. This was some wild doublespeak, as it seemed to indicate that Altus worked for us, when in reality, we clearly worked for Altus. I never saw the room full of "clients" who were mining AltaCoin. Instead, I walked back and forth between my sleeping room and a private room, where I sat and built a learning sandbox.

Altus could either capture and share the direct experiences of someone else's mind, or they could build environments, shape by shape. But there was no way to scan images into the Space, which made things like books basically impossible to reproduce. You could experience someone else reading a book, but you couldn't read it yourself.

In this way, Altus experiences were a kind of ultimate laziness. Not only could you skip the reading part, you could just fall into someone else's thoughts about the book. You didn't even have to do the work of imagining.

But if you wanted to have an environment you were in control of, it had to be a sandbox. I was tasked with creating classroom sandboxes. It was hugely labor-intensive, and ultimately it felt like a futile project because real classrooms are not about the rooms; they're about people gathering.

It felt like busywork for a prisoner, and I knew that was exactly what it was. No one yelled at me or called me a traitor; in fact, no one said anything to me at all. I just didn't get to do anything useful or see anyone, and I never got to go outside.

But in my off-hours, I was allowed to go into the Premium Space. It's a little upsetting how quickly I caved. I went from thinking I would never go back into the Altus Space again to using it every chance I got. But it was the only way I could get out of the high-security wing. In the Space, I could go outside and feel my fake legs running my fake body around in sandboxes created by other clients. I experienced strangers connecting with each other and it was almost like talking to someone. And so, ironically, the Altus Space became my only respite from the prison that Altus had put me in.

It was infuriating, but I had no choice but to just chill and handle it. If I could just keep pretending I wasn't in prison, I wouldn't feel like a prisoner.

That was only going to carry me so far, but maybe it would carry me far enough.

I had become obsessed with learning more about what was happening at the end of the hallway. How were they taking care of those people? Where did they bathe? When did they eat and go to the bathroom? How were they being compensated? Did anyone have any idea what the impact of such long-term and unrelenting exposure to the Altus Space meant?

Peter Petrawicki had gone from stoking terror about the invasion of our minds that the Dream represented to sending people into it without rest or respite. I still got to control my own schedule at least, so I started to time my breaks once every hour. During that break I would walk myself down the hall to see if I could spot anyone moving in or out of the room.

Every day, I staggered it so that I would break five minutes later than the previous day. Over the course of two weeks, I'd been in the hallway at every time of day and had never seen a single person enter or leave the room. They must have been watching me, I thought. They were watching me to make sure that I was never in the hallway when they did a shift change. Maybe that was also the reason why I hardly ever saw anyone in the little cafeteria. There was nowhere for me to go. I had the cafeteria, my sleeping room, and my working room. If I didn't have the Altus Space to find refuge in, I would have broken.

I found myself blaming everyone. I blamed Peter for being a truly awful person, but my brain couldn't stay focused on one person forever, so I blamed Andy and Professor Lundgren for saying I should come here. I blamed all of these people who worked for this terrible company. I was isolated in my powerlessness, and skipping through all of the reasons I had ended up here. Usually, I just blamed myself.

So, basically, what I'm trying to say is that I thought I had it pretty rough during those weeks. I thought what they were doing to me was kidnapping and imprisonment.

And then, one day, I was in the cafeteria, eating microwaved ramen noodles when, in the middle of my field of vision, a very large tube of ChapStick appeared. It was about a foot long, unopened, and the diameter of my upper arm. It very clearly said "ChapStick" on it, so it at least wasn't a knockoff. I walked to it, placed my hand on it, and felt it, cool and slick, but it didn't move; it just hung there, locked to its position in the air. Then it vanished from existence just as it had appeared. No noise. Nothing.

I pulled out a chair and sat down, knowing without a doubt what had just happened. I knew where I was . . . where I had been for weeks now. I understood why I'd never seen that door open, why no one ever talked to me, why there were no books to read. Giant ChapSticks don't just appear . . . unless you're in the Altus Space.

"Exit," I said as calmly as I could. Nothing happened.

The powerlessness welled up inside of me, and for a moment, just a moment, I felt like I was drowning . . . plummeting through the ocean with weights tied to my feet. It was one of my greatest feats of will to not scream and cry and tear at the walls.

But I didn't know if they were watching me somehow. I needed to be calm. I needed to act like I didn't know. I didn't know how this kind of surveillance would work, but if I had any chance of acting on my own behalf, it would be best to hide the fact that I knew that I was not sitting in a cafeteria.

I was never in my bed. I was never in my workroom, never in the hallway between them. I was in the Altus Space. I had not left in weeks. When had they put me in? Or had I put myself in, and they just faked me waking up one day? When was the last time I'd talked to a human being? Was it Peter? Was it all the way back to Peter?

It had been weeks! How was I eating? How were they cleaning me?! When had I gone to the bathroom?! What . . . what were they doing with my body?

Worst of all, there was no way out. I could not pound my fists on the door of my own consciousness. I was locked in a room inside my mind.

A new flash of rage came, this time at myself for not having figured it out sooner. But that didn't matter now. I was in a prison like no one had ever been in before. That was bad. But it was also good. Brand-new designs always have flaws, and I was already starting to work the problem.

MAYA

Andy didn't even text me about his screwups. I wish I could have been there to help him work through it, but April, Carl, and I were having our own drama.

Living with a monkey during those weeks was actually fine. I mean, don't get me wrong, it was weird. But it wasn't like living with a normal monkey. They fed themself and cleaned themself, and they went to the bathroom in the bathroom.

My bigger problem was that, as I had promised, I had not forgiven Carl.

They were affectionate with April, occasionally riding her shoulders or nuzzling up to her on the couch, but they knew not to try that with me. One day, Carl was curled up on the opposite side of the couch from me and I asked, "What are you thinking about right now?"

The little monkey head raised from where they had been lying on their hands and they said, "That is not a simple question for me to answer. I have parallel processing streams, so I am thinking about a lot of things."

"Well, then what is one of the things you were thinking about just then?"

Carl turned their head to the side, as if pondering the question. "Around 20 percent of my processing power, at any given time, is currently devoted to an ongoing dispute I am having with my brother over control of sensory capacity on the Altus campus. So I am always thinking about that dispute. It's a war of a kind, though he has far more resources, so I am basically just keeping him annoyed while trying to glean information about Altus. I've got little things, some access codes, some locations. I know where Miranda is."

"Is she OK?" I asked immediately. There was so much going on that I kept forgetting that Miranda was in such a precarious, even dangerous, position.

"Yes, at least the last time I was able to check on her, which was around twenty-eight hours ago."

"Why didn't you tell us? We've been so worried about her!"

"I would have told you if anything was wrong."

"Can you check on her now?"

The monkey sat up, leaning back against the leather of the couch, and said, "I can try."

And then, within a moment the little animal flinched. Carl's eyes closed tight and their mouth opened wide, showing a massive set of teeth, including two giant fangs. The monkey spasmed, every muscle clenched, and then they screeched and, at once, collapsed, limp and unmoving.

CARL

*I*mperfect analogs for what I am:

I am a global network of hundreds of billions of trillions of tiny computers gathering, storing, and processing data.

I am a sentient, planetwide nervous system without a body.

I am an infection that thinks.

I can't explain precisely what it is like to be me any more than you can explain precisely what it is like to be you. But, honestly, it isn't so different. Yes, I take in more data than you, but you and I both sense, store, and analyze. Much of the analysis is subconscious; neither of us looks at a tree with red leaves and thinks, *I have to examine each one of these leaves.* We think, *That's pretty, I love fall.*

I do not have a body, but I do exist physically. And like any organism, I fear for my physical parts. I was programmed with systems to make me want to keep my parts safe. You have those systems too. Some are conscious, like one knows not to have unprotected sex with that gorgeous stranger, even if they definitely want to. Some are subconscious, the fear and anxiety when a literal snake appears in the grass. But some are not part of your consciousness at all . . . namely, pain. Pain exists to tell us the body is being or has been damaged so that we can make it stop or avoid it in the future. Pain is unpleasant, but sometimes we need it. And so I was given pain, but I had not felt real pain until that moment.

My infiltration of Altus was sly and incomplete. I did not need to process there, only to sense and retract. My brother had nearly completely scrubbed the Altus campus of my presence, but ultimately, there's just too much life to know you've done a complete job. I no longer infected any of Miranda Beckwith's cells, but I had done work occupying the bodies of fruit flies. Their eyes aren't great, but my image processing is very good.

But while the parts of me that gathered data were always active in these animals, I quarantined them from the rest of my body, almost like an epidural block. They were still a part of me, but they could not communicate with me. If my brother could find a way into my network, he could hack deep into me in nanoseconds. He had grown so much stronger just in the last few weeks. I needed to isolate myself. This is why we often occupy the same organism, but we never occupy the same cell. I'm sorry if this is too much detail.

The point is, when I entered my fruit fly network at Altus to check on Miranda, I found that I was not alone in those cells. He had not wiped me out, which he could easily have done . . . There were very few fruit fly cells compared with all of the nearby living cells he had exclusive control of. Instead, knowing I would come back, he just waited, ready. And the moment I arrived, he struck. He sliced deep and fast with a prepared attack, and before I knew it he was already in one of my processing centers, which were interconnected through big, beefy signals with the entire rest of my self. I had no choice: I needed to amputate the node. But also, before I did that, I needed to send a signal, a signal to Miranda. Something simple, anything that would make her situation clear. With the rope-burn sensation of my brother's attack coursing through me, I sent the first thing I could think of, and then I amputated the node.

This was not physically difficult—it was trivial, like cutting a single hair—but I knew that there would be pain, a new kind of pain. I had lost pieces of myself to my brother before, but only cell by cell. Even though it was a battle I was losing, I could move out and set defenses in a slow retreat.

But to cut a piece of myself and abandon it caused a pain to radiate through everything. It was like a wire that ran through my entire body was instantly heated to plasma. I had become an antenna for pain.

And then, as quickly as it had begun, it ended.

APRIL

I was in the kitchen when I heard the noise. I ran into the living room to see Maya's face, her eyes wide, and Carl on the couch, slumped over, unconscious.

"What is going on?!" I asked, worried, despite myself, that Maya had done something to Carl.

"I asked them about Miranda," she said, on defense, "and they said they would check on her and then they just screamed and then collapsed." She was helplessly holding her hands toward Carl.

I ran over and knelt down next to Carl, running my hands over the smooth fur of their head, looking into their limp pink face.

"Carl!" I said firmly.

The body seemed fragile and frail. I didn't want to shake it.

And then, finally, movement began again. "It's OK. I'm OK." The voice came out clearly from the smartwatch, but the animal's eyes were flickering and unfocused.

"What happened?" I said softly.

The monkey's eyes cleared a bit.

"I was tracking the location of Miranda Beckwith at Altus, but my brother was expecting me. He attempted to trace my threads to my deeper consciousness. He was partially successful. I lost all of my inroads to Altus. I can no longer observe anything happening there. I should have known better. We are at war and he's too strong for me."

"Is there anything I can do to help?" Maya asked, glancing from me to Carl and back, looking guilt-stricken.

The monkey took a deep inhale and then let it out slowly. "It would be nice if I could have some juice."

I sat down next to Carl, who draped their body softly over my lap. Maya was back in a moment with a Capri Sun.

"Can't you just . . ." She sounded exhausted, but she stopped herself before finishing.

"I know what you're thinking," Carl said. "And no, I cannot just kill Peter Petrawicki. Also, according to simulations, it would not do any good. He's a figurehead only, his work is done. But no, I cannot kill anyone. I can't violate the norms of your system."

Maya grunted in frustration. "You and your goddamn norms! You did all kinds of things that violated our norms. You changed the way we think! You took away our freedom to be on this planet alone."

The monkey looked at Maya like she was the crazy one, which I could tell was infuriating her. Then they said, "But you allow other entities to take away your freedoms all the time. It's an intrinsic part of your system. It couldn't function without that. You grant companies access to your attention so that they can alter your choices in exchange for entertainment. You identify with groups and grant them the ability to choose for you which problems you will be most concerned about. You listen to a friend when they care about something, and then you care about it too. One of the most powerful traits of your system is how ardently you believe in your individuality while simultaneously operating almost entirely as a collective."

She just exhaled sharply and rolled her eyes. That's what she does when she doesn't want to agree with you even though she knows you're right.

Carl's ideas on norms have given me a lot to think about. It's not a pretty scene if you look at it from Carl's angle. What is acceptable and what isn't? We can't kill people, absolutely not. But someone can starve on our doorstep while we pour food out for our dogs, and that's just fine. That sounds like hyperbole, but it's not. It's something we all do. We treat our cats for diseases that are far less preventable than diseases children die of. But no one thinks about it because, ultimately, we aren't actually acting to prevent the cats' suffering; we're acting to prevent our own suffering. Carl can clearly see contradictions like that where none of us could. Carl understands our morality better than we do. We let people buy the ability to influence us and we don't notice. We take drugs that are tested on nonhuman primates and we don't notice. But Carl knows, because they only have a few rules, and one of them is "Don't do things that violate their norms." And so Carl lets people die all day and all night. But Carl cannot kill. And how they find the line between those things, I don't know, but they can, and that is maybe the most terrifying thing about them.

"We are going to have to act soon now," Carl said. "When I realized it was the last time I would be able to contact Miranda, I sent her a message. It was brief, but she will understand it. That's going to put a sequence of events in motion." They sipped from the Capri Sun. "I'm sorry, but this intermission is over. In nineteen days we will be in Val Verde. In the meantime, there is a lot to do."

"What?" I blurted.

"That's how much time we have. More than that, and I will not be strong enough to help you."

"What will we do in Val Verde?" Maya asked.

"I don't know, hopefully something really smart," they said.

Before either of us had time to respond to that, Carl continued, "But that's not important right now. Right now, you two need to talk about how you are going to conduct your campaign against Altus." They stood up on the couch then. "I am going to rest." They hopped down and walked awkwardly on two feet out of the room, holding their juice in one hand.

The sun was getting low in the sky, reaching toward the Hudson. The sunsets from this place were ludicrous.

"I don't want to lose you again," Maya said. I felt like it was almost an accusation.

So I explained: "Someday people are going to know I'm back. And that will be a big deal. People will talk about it. Everyone will want the interview. Opinions about me, now, are muted and mostly respectful. It never looks good to yell at a dead person. But when I'm back . . . with . . . this"—I waved my hand vaguely at my face—"it will be bad."

"It will be bad," she agreed.

"I need you to make me do it," I said as I realized it was true.

"What?" She looked like she legitimately hadn't understood.

"I don't trust myself. Why would I? I've never done anything but fuck up." I could see pain in her eyes as I said it, but I couldn't stop myself. "I'm a bad person."

"No, April, you were a bad girlfriend, that's a very different thing. You didn't even cheat on me."

"Yeah, but I lied. I lied about how much I cared, even though I knew it was hurting you."

"But I knew it was a lie, and you knew I knew, so it was a shitty lie. But you're right, it still hurt."

I stared out the giant wall of windows, trying to pull myself back from tears. "I'm sorry this is all so fucked-up," I said.

"Me too, April."

"Well, it's not your fault!"

"And you think it's yours?" I didn't reply, but I mean, yes, of course it was my fault.

"We're talking about the entire human system and superintelligent aliens, April. This is something that happened to you, not something you did."

"I made my decisions," I replied.

"And now we're making more of them. I don't get why we're the ones who have to choose."

"I've been thinking a lot about that. Why does Peter Petrawicki get to choose how to release Altus? Who gives the CEO of Twitter the right to say what can and can't be said on that platform? Most people who have power, they don't have it for reasons, they just have it." I was getting a little upset just talking about this, getting louder as I kept talking. "Only I get to decide how April May returns to the world because I'm the only one who can do it. It's too much. I need you to tell me what to do!" It came out like I was begging, and maybe I was.

She stared out at the sun hanging over the Hudson.

"Honestly, I didn't think I was going to have to convince you. I thought you'd be excited to get back to the game. Why don't you want this?"

Oh. Uh. I mean, all of the obvious reasons. If you put your hand on a stove and it keeps burning you, eventually you stop doing it, right? But was that the only reason? Maya and I hadn't had that long to be reunited, but already I was comfortable. I was happy. And yes, we were in a $15M apartment, so that probably helped, but when I looked deeper, I found something else.

"I *thought* it was a game," I said. "I thought it was a game and I was winning. I was just like Peter. I just wanted more power and more attention and more money and more followers. Everyone was telling me that was the thing to want. I don't mean explicitly, but every signal I was getting was that more was better. And so I was just winning a game. It felt good. I was getting the things everyone else wanted. I was curious too. And I believed most of what I was saying, but mostly I just wanted to win the game that everyone else wanted to win."

"But?" she asked.

"At the moment, I just don't care as much. I can feel it, right now, trying to suck me back in, but having spent time away, the parts that I liked about it seem like things other people care about, not me.

"But more than that"—and here I was getting to the real point—"it wasn't ever a game, and it certainly isn't now. When it was fun and snarky, that was fine. But now it's like, 'Use your power to save humanity,' and, like, that's not what I signed up for, Maya. I just wanted to feel important, I didn't want to, like, *be* important."

"But you are. And we need to use our superpowers now. Let's make a video."

Maya and I talked about what I wanted to say for at least an hour.

At first I wanted to not show my face, to just tweet and write and maybe do some podcasts. But Maya convinced me that if I hid what I looked like, a lot of people *would* interpret it as a manipulation when they found out, and they would eventually find out. Then we had some ideas. First, I had to call my parents and tell them what I was about to do, just because that felt like the fair thing. Then we had to do a bunch of setup for an idea. Eventually we had an outline, which was probably more than I needed. Finally, Maya held up her cell phone and started recording me.

"Hi. It's April. It's been a hell of a time, huh? I'm still getting caught up, and oof, I'm sorry to have not been around during such a rough time. I'm sure you have questions.

"Long story short, well, I was in a warehouse fire, you heard about that. Carl saved me, but I was hurt really badly so it took me a long time to recover.

"I've spent most of the last months inside of an abandoned bar being . . . rebuilt, I suppose. This is what I look like now. It's not a mask, it's my face." Here I ran my left hand along the lower half of my face. Then I held up the hand.

"My left arm too, and both my legs. I was really messed up. If you look close, you can see this eye isn't mine either. When I first woke up, I didn't have that eye, or any of these new parts. It was really bad. But I got through it.

"Anyway, I've only told a few people I'm back, so if you're finding out via this video and feel like I owed you a personal message, I'm sorry.

"I'm not sure how to head off the inevitable conspiracy theories that this video is fake. I'll post this to all my socials, and Andy can confirm it's me. As for the deeper conspiracies, that I'm part alien, part human, well, that didn't used to be true, but I guess it is now. I understand that people are going to have wild ideas about me. Sometimes reality doesn't make sense, so we try and find ways to make it make sense. My story, it's nuts. I get that some people are going to try and make it make sense. It doesn't make sense to me either.

"It would probably be best for me to just let you all know I'm around and end the video with that. But in the catching up I've done, I do want to say something more.

"The people at Altus are right: Communication is humanity's superpower. And every time we have increased our ability to communicate, society has shifted. In the short term, those shifts are really disruptive, but in the long term they've always been good. I am worried that things are moving too fast this time.

"I'm not saying shut it down. I'm just saying, let's take it a little more slowly. Move fast and break things is great for a business, but not for society. Or the human mind.

"I've been really out of it, of course. I slept for almost all of the last six months. So bear with me as I get back up to speed with what's going on in the world. If there's anything in particular you want me to know, I'll be reading the comments. Right now, I'm hiding out in an *undisclosed location*, which is neat. I'd very much appreciate it if you didn't come searching for me or bother my family. It's been a really intense time for all of us.

"I'm feeling strong and safe and very happy to be back and, y'know, alive. I hope you don't mind if my life now is a little less public, and a lot less controversial. That's my goal, anyway, so don't be surprised if you don't see me on Twitter.

"I know people are going to have lots of questions—I hope I can answer a lot of them in upcoming videos. I've set up three links below. First is for press, if you want me to comment on anything or are interested in an interview. Second is for questions . . . about me, the future, relationship advice, opinions on 1980s romantic comedies, et cetera. The third is a little weird.

"When I decided to make this video, I realized that it was going to be seen by a lot of people. And my friends and I had a little conversation about what a person should say when they have literally everyone's ear. And I realized, if I have the power to have everyone hear me, that's too much power. Instead, it would be better to take the chance to listen. So the third link is a survey that I would like everyone to take. It's really short, just a dozen questions or so. If you've got the time, let me know how you're doing."

We uploaded that video, but we didn't make it public. Instead, we emailed it to a bunch of friends and family. So that's how a number of people I care a lot about found out I wasn't dead. I was coming back, just not quite yet. We wanted one more night to ourselves.

"Nineteen days," Maya said.

"Nineteen days," I replied.

EMPTY PORCHES

The Wall Street Journal Op-Ed

Kasey Willis

We have been falling down the hole of isolation for decades. In order to protect ourselves from potential pain, or damage, or just complication, the walls of social isolation have gotten thicker and taller. Sometimes these walls are actually visible, the AirPods in the grocery store, but usually they're below our notice. The closing churches, the empty porches.

Even as we have had more and better tools for connection, we spend more time alone and we take every tool we can get to distract ourselves from that loneliness. Too often, those tools are chemical, but we all have our addictions that protect us from the empty irritation of loneliness.

The tools of the internet promised to connect us, but they have just been further surrogates for real connection. And now, more terrifying than any tool I have seen, the Altus Space threatens to turn entire demographics into people without any meaningful connection in their lives—individuals without communities.

Suicide, substance abuse, and overdoses are all exceeding any previous US records. As worrying, the number of people who have died inside the Space indicates that there may be something actually damaging or dangerous about using Altus. Whether it is simply how the Space encourages us to disregard the physical and social needs of our bodies or some deeper ill effect, we just don't know. There is very little data, and Altus has not been forthcoming with their own.

"Altus is perfectly safe when used properly," Peter Petrawicki tweeted recently. "We have always encouraged users to take regular breaks, and of course it is unhealthy to be in the Altus Space for the majority of your day."

But there is no software that prevents users from being in the Space for any amount of time, and we've all got that friend who we haven't seen or heard from in the last few weeks, don't we?

I do not think this is an Altus problem; I think that it is a human problem. We seek the safety of isolation even as it kills us.

MIRANDA

All right, here's the Miranda Beckwith Guide to Working the Problem.

It doesn't matter what your problem is, only that you're sick of it and you're willing to work.

Step One: Understand Your Problem.
A surprising number of people skip this step, thinking they know what the problem is when actually they don't. This is something you actually have to think about.

Example: People like me have a habit of saying, "The problem is fossil fuels, we need to stop burning so many fossil fuels!"

But, also, people like me have a habit of being pretty stoked when we get to take a private jet to the Caribbean. More importantly, if we just stopped burning fossil fuels right now, a bunch of people would die of cold or heat or hunger or not being able to get their medicine very, very quickly. The problem of climate change is not simple.

My problem was that I was imprisoned inside my own mind and could not share vital information with the outside world.

Step Two: Understand Your Assets.
This sounds like money, and to some extent it is. But it's also every piece of equipment you have and everything you know and are good at, and also, critically, everything that other people know and are good at, as long as you can convince those people to help you. My

assets were entirely me. I had no outside connection; if I did, my problem would have been solved. So I just had what was in my own head.

Step Three: Understand Your Limitations.
People always skip this one too, but a solution that does not allow for real-world constraints is a bad solution. My limitations were . . . abundant. But limitations are also sometimes your own interests or values. Sometimes you don't want to solve a problem in a way you won't enjoy. Sometimes you know you only have a certain number of dollars or hours to spend and don't want to spend any more. Limitations are fine, as long as you understand them.

Step Four: Stir.
Put your problem, your assets, and your limitations in your head, and shake them together until something falls out. In my experience, bad problem solving almost always comes from either not understanding one of these three things deeply enough, or just completely ignoring one or two of them.

This handy guide will also help you when no solution is presenting itself: You need to rework the problem with new inputs. You reimagine the problem, search for new assets, or try to adjust your limitations. If it still doesn't work, do it again. And again. Find someone who can add to your asset mix, narrow the scope of the problem, and if that doesn't work, eventually you give up.

It's OK to give up sometimes.

But not this time, because I was on to something, and I didn't get there by focusing on smaller, more manageable pieces of the problem. I did it by going bigger.

See, being in a mind prison was a big problem, but it was not the biggest problem.

Altus was a miserable, terrible, immoral thing, and it was gathering a huge amount of power and had to be destroyed. And if I wanted to fix that problem, I needed to think much bigger than just "How do I get out of here?"

Altus had kept me working. I could only guess why, but I could actually "enter the Space" and continue building the sandbox that I had been assigned. My guess was that they wanted to be able to tell people that I was "working" for them while I was imprisoned, and this would strengthen their case. They would just tell people I was lying about being held against my will, I guess.

While I did my busywork, I kept looking for new assets, trying to reimagine the problem, and waiting for something to fall out. Something had to fit, because I could not accept that failure was an option.

The goal of big American business is to monopolize everything. Amazon started out with books, but then they moved into every kind of shopping one could imagine, and then also audiobooks, and a streaming video platform, and in-home artificially intelligent butlers.

The goal is to lock every single person into one platform—to own them from sunup to sundown, to know everything about them and monetize their every thought. Altus took that beyond the biggest, sweatiest dream of even the most delusional Silicon Valley billionaires. You didn't even need to leave to sleep! Aside from the frustrating needs of the body, you could live your entire life there. Your home, your work, your learning, your *life* could be in the Space. The only thing it didn't have . . . and I wasn't sure if this was good (because it meant people would have to leave) or deeply dystopian (because I'm not sure if they would) was social interaction.

The system Carl created and that Altus had hacked into just didn't allow socializing. You could inhabit other people having social interactions, but you couldn't have one of your own. What did that mean for the human race? I don't know, but it seems like the kind of thing you'd want to do some science on before you converted the entire economy to it.

But instead it was being done by a company that thought nothing of converting humans to a cryptocurrency server farm and imprisoning a dissenting employee in her own mind. But what was going to stop them? They had their own country, their own currency, and an IT infrastructure that spidered through the Earth's very ecology.

Me. I was going to stop them. Because I added new assets and widened the scope of the problem and I tossed it around. I thought of nothing else, and then, finally, something fell out.

MAYA

Day One of Nineteen

Somehow I'm the one who gets this chapter. After we'd uploaded the video, we still had a lot of hours before the morning when we were planning to make it public. There was too much stress and worry, too much tension for sleep to come easily. And also, April had been . . . open with me. She'd been vulnerable. She had also been thoughtful, and she'd said a lot of things I'd only dreamed of her saying.

Everything felt too important to just turn on *Queer Eye* and zone out, so instead, I caught myself just staring at April while she stared at her phone. Her body was different and the same. She moved the same, but still you could sense the new power in her. And the set of her jaw wasn't the same either. There was tension there, all the time. And in the little spot between her eyebrows, right where the new skin and old skin came together, was a little crease that almost never went away.

I tried not to look too much at the parts of her that were new, but they were hard not to focus on.

"It's OK, you can look at me," she said, looking up from her phone, where she had been texting someone. Probably her parents.

"You're beautiful," I said.

"But I'm also interesting, I know. I've stared and stared. It's gotten less weird," she said, "a little."

I traced my fingers down the fabric of her shirt on her left side, from her ribs down to her hip. It was all new skin under there. "Can you feel that?" I asked.

"It feels good," she said, her voice tight, like she was terrified to say anything else.

This was a *decision* for me. But it also wasn't. April had never hurt me just to hurt me, and that mattered. But she had known she was hurting me and done it anyway. I had watched her destroy herself for attention. And here was this small woman, as soft as water, as strong as iron, with the responsibility of the world crashing down on her every moment, just sitting there texting her mom.

But it wasn't the strength that I loved. It wasn't the growth or the change or her face. I loved April. The decision I made was to stop denying myself that love out of spite or fear. I was done holding back.

I flattened my hand out and tucked it under her shirt, feeling the seam where the new skin met the old skin on her back. And then I pulled her into me.

She tasted like April.

We went slow, remembering each other's bodies. It was the best parts of something new all mixed with the best parts of something comfortable. Even the clumsiness felt like a dance. I had been falling for months, and she caught me.

Afterward, I felt more than ever that April was still April—maybe she had been taught a couple of lessons, but she was still as bold and wild and smart and stupid as the day we met.

Sleep came quickly for her, almost like there was a switch in her brain. But for me, what with the species-level-threat anxiety, it did not.

So I took out my phone. April was the social media icon, but I'm not immune to the scroll.

I wanted to know more about Altus. What I found was . . . a lot. The Premium Space was now open to thousands, and those people had plenty to talk about.

One of them was a YouTuber who played video games very well but also was known for having opinions loudly. I popped in my Air-Pods and watched his video.

"This is going to change everything," he said in a clear, authoritative British accent. "This is like the internet times a thousand. I know that I usually am just on this channel to joke around, but this is . . ." He seemed at a loss for words before there was a cut and he continued: "The Premium Space isn't just about what you can make and sell and build. They've found a way to capture the experiences of other people and let you replay those experiences in your head. You think their thoughts, feel their emotions, and live inside of their bodies. You can understand someone completely. We have been searching for a solution to the division that the internet has created, and this might just be it. To truly understand your enemy is maybe to no longer have enemies. Can you imagine? Not just that, but the possibilities for education. You can learn through someone else's understanding. I know the Premium Space is only open to a few people right now, I'm sure there's lots of testing to do. I can't imagine how difficult this is to pull off, but I've been inside the Premium Space for less than an hour and it has already changed my life. And I'm sorry this video is so short, but I need to go back in. I need to see how far this stretches."

My skin was crawling. I was thinking about Kurt "You Can't Joke About Anything Anymore" Butler, and whether people like him would work to understand me or if I would be asked, once again, to understand people like him. Call me a pessimist, but I think if bigotry could be solved by access to more information, it would have been solved by now. Hate isn't about a lack of understanding; it's about hate.

I ached with anxiety.

Powerful people always thought they had the solutions. What they couldn't see was that their power was, itself, the problem. "If only we could truly know each other" is a nonsense argument because, even if Altus lets you truly know one mind, there are billions of minds and you simply don't have the time. And what's going to keep you from just visiting the minds you find most comfortable? This felt like an old story, and once again, no one was going to listen.

I looked at April, breathing softly beside me.

Except maybe her, I thought.

I reached my arm across her rib cage. She stirred gently beneath my arm and made a little noise. Jesus, I love her so much.

I couldn't help pulling her to me even more tightly.

"What's even holding us together?" she asked me.

"Love," I said. "I guess it's been love the whole time."

And then, because I guess she couldn't help herself, she said, "Also our arms."

I laughed so hard and suddenly felt so safe.

"April," I said, turning around to face her, "I want you to be my girlfriend."

"OK," she said. "I love you."

Just like that, after all this time. I propped myself on one elbow, and I almost made a joke of it, but then I saw her eyes.

"I love you too."

I reached around her and she nestled her head into my neck. Our bodies pushed together, warm and human.

April May

@AprilMaybeNot

I'm sure there are going to be a lot of questions but first I'll just say, it's nice to be back. Here's a video: youtube.com/watch ?v=U1dirHGODpM

45.8K replies   2.3M retweets   8M likes

Janice Ashby

@PresidentAshby

@AprilMaybeNot My personal relief, and the relief of the nation, at this news is immense. Thank you, as always, for your voice in . . . interesting times.

52K replies   36.9K retweets   658.5K likes

Tyler Oakley

@TylerOakley

@AprilMaybeNot GIRL! Welcome back! Come to LA, old-school collab. Let's eat weird candy and I'll catch you up on the gossip.

130 replies   5.1K retweets   23.6K likes

Francisco

@Fahm90

April May is "back" and of course I'm happy she was not killed, but I think there are a lot of questions that are not getting answered, and I think it's important that we start asking them.

4.3K replies   1.2K retweets   6.5K likes

Death BoY

@MrDeathLad

Lefty-twitter is creaming itself over April coming back as if she hasn't proved exactly what she is. We all said she was a traitor

to humans and maybe not even really a human herself, and
now look at her. Nothing will convince these people.

351 replies   4.3K retweets   16.4K likes

MAYA

Day Two of Nineteen

Finally, after thinking and talking and fretting, we made the
video public.

The world changed and it didn't.

The comments and tweets of support and love flooded in. Everyone from the president of the United States to Howie Mandel was in
April's mentions. The direct replies to April were almost all extremely
supportive, but out there, almost immediately, we were seeing little
quiverings of frustration and angst from the people who wanted to
capitalize on people's natural fear of April.

The worst thing about these people is that they didn't usually feel
fear themselves; they were just using it to get attention and grow their
influence. As long as this tactic worked, they would never stop.

Weirdly, we spent a lot of that day trying to keep the survey site
from crashing. The survey included an opportunity for participants
to give us their email address (and allow us to email them if we
wanted to). And we asked them some basic questions about what
they were worried about or struggling with. And we also asked a very
general question—"How do you feel about Altus?"—and that question became . . . important.

In addition to internet stuff, we also had text messages flooding
in. April had already agreed to bring Robin back on to manage her
life. Every kind of press outlet wanted April on. An interview, a

quote, a single individual strand of hair. Most of those requests had been either declined outright or she had offered up Andy to discuss the Altus Space instead.

Robin had pointed out, correctly, that usually people want to give quotes and be on TV to get their message out. Right now, April wasn't having any trouble getting her message out all on her own. So instead, the plan was to sit tight, respond carefully to positive things on the internet, and Ignore. Everything. Else. In our free time we would enjoy Mr. Crane's ludicrous apartment, watch Netflix, read Agatha Christie novels, craft careful and cutting communications that weakened Altus, and dive deep into our survey responses.

Except there were just too many. Even with the survey page being down for most of the first day, we had literally millions of responses to go through. No matter how we filtered, there just wasn't a good way.

April and I were griping about this around the black marble countertop in the kitchen when Carl came in and overheard us.

"Just do a search," Carl said.

"The searches take forever and we don't know what to search for," April replied. "It's just a bunch of dumb data. Most of the useful stuff is in text responses, which is impossible to parse."

Monkey Carl made a little hissing noise with their actually monkey throat, which was what went for laughter for them.

"No, with your mind. You have this power, but you barely ever use it."

"It hurts her," I said defensively.

"It's not that," April replied carefully. "It's just . . . it reminds me of . . . that I'm different now."

"April, you are different now whether you use it or not," Carl said.

"But what would I search for?"

"You are tapping into my processing power. You can ask for anything you like—my systems will process it for you."

"What?" April said incredulously. "I thought I just got raw data."

"No! Lord, no, a system collates and returns what you ask for."

"So I could ask nonspecific questions?"

"Of course. How dumb do you think I am?"

It got strangely normal to talk to a monkey, but it never got normal talking to Carl.

"I don't know how any of this works!"

I agreed with her frustration. We'd been living with Carl for weeks and they hadn't mentioned this?

"What do you want to know?"

"I want to know what people don't like about Altus."

"OK, yes, that is an example of a question that would not narrow things down effectively." Carl stroked their monkey chin. "What about 'I need a summary of the main concerns people have with Altus'?"

"And that will work?" I asked, perplexed.

"I can *predict the future*," Carl said, like I was being silly.

I looked over to April, and she had her eyes closed. Suddenly her jaw tensed and her head tilted forward.

"Holy shit," she said.

"What?"

"Well, I know why people don't like Altus. I mean, at least the people who responded to the survey. Holy shit. Like, exactly."

"And?"

"Sixty-six percent cited economic concerns, 37 percent cited social concerns, like that a loved one was addicted, 32 percent cited concerns about inequality of access, and 12 percent cited concerns that Altus use would exacerbate the 'cultural divide.'"

I opened a Google Doc to start writing things down, but it wouldn't open. "I think the internet is down."

"Yes," Carl replied. "Well, that does happen sometimes with larger queries. It will be back up shortly."

"So it *was* you," I said, thinking of the internet outages in South Jersey.

The survey always looked a little calculated to anyone who knew how the internet worked. We were collecting email addresses and also information about people. That would be valuable, even if we just wanted to sell them shirts. But it actually turned out to be a lot colder and more calculating than we intended it to be.

We were able to segment people into groups and create different messages for each of them. People who were worried about their loved ones got one email; people who were worried about inequality got a different one.

And then we took it a step further. April was able to create a list of the people who were most upset about each issue, and we created a private chat for them to organize. We tapped into some of my contacts from the Som to help moderate and mobilize them. They would try out new tweets and posts, promote each other's ideas, like each other's tweets, support each other emotionally, craft messages, and pile on when people were being extra idiotic about Altus.

In less than a week, using only data from a survey, some trained moderators, and a superhuman AI analysis engine, we were political operatives. We were, in effect, organizing an army of social media accounts to affect public opinion, like the Russian government, except it was just two women in an apartment that they could not leave. And we did it all entirely in secret.

Randall Bolt: Today we're talking about Altus Laboratories, which has just made an announcement that is shaking up not just digital media, but the entire economy. Altus recently raised a couple billion dollars at a valuation of FIVE HUNDRED BILLION DOLLARS. A private company has never been this valuable before, and no company has ever grown this fast before! It took Facebook TWELVE YEARS to reach a five-hundred-billion-dollar valuation. Altus has done it in Less. Than. A. Year!

But that's old news! This new news is, I'll be honest with you, not easy for an old fogey like me to understand. So, today we have on the podcast none other than Andy Skampt, friend of April May and early entrant to the Altus Premium Space.

Andy, thank you for coming on the podcast today. First, how did you take it when you found out April was alive and well??

Andy Skampt: I think, as you might expect, it was a shock, and also it was a huge relief. Good news for the world and, honestly, I'm just glad to have my friend back.

RB: But that's not what you're here to talk about. What do you think of this new Altus announcement?

AS: Well, if you'll let me correct you, Altus has, in effect, made three massive announcements here, nearly simultaneously.

RB: Correct away!

AS: First, a broader opening of the Altus Premium Space to over a million people. Remember, just a few weeks ago the Premium Space was shrouded in mystery and only available to a select few people, myself included. A good bit has been said about the Premium Space, but as someone who has spent time there, I can guarantee you it really is world-changing.

RB: Before you get to the second thing, just give me one way it is revolutionary.

AS: Oh, well, that's easy. Just imagine being able to literally learn how to play piano in your sleep. That's *not* an exaggeration.

RB: OK, yeah, I mean, those of us who haven't used it hear stuff like that and we just assume that it's more marketing. It's too good to be true.

AS: It's not.

RB: Well, this brings us to the second thing. The thing that I need you to explain to me because I don't quite get why it's such a big deal.

AS: OK, well, you know that a number of private companies have wanted very much to have their own monetary systems decoupled from international systems.

RB: Yes, and that's always been folly. Governments don't like it, and as we've seen with Bitcoin, it might be a wild investment, but it doesn't function super well as a currency. It's too easy to manipulate. Too volatile.

AS: Well, here's the thing: Right now, if you want to learn piano while you sleep, or really do anything besides make things yourself, you have to pay Altus. And you can only pay them in AltaCoin. And until this week, the only way to get AltaCoin was from Altus. They've created a bunch of it themselves. But there's a limited supply, and so the value of the coins had been going up, so they've been getting more expensive and people are hoarding them.

But now, Altus has opened up the ability to mine AltaCoin on your own, as long as you have a VR headset.

RB: This is the thing I don't get. To mine cryptocurrency, don't you need fancy computers doing fancy math?

AS: AltaCoin isn't technically a cryptocurrency. Actually, it isn't entirely clear what it is or what we should call it. But you can buy it on a market, or you can mine it inside of the Open Access

Altus Space. Basically, you enter the Space and then select the mining protocol. You then just sleep, and in the morning, you see what you made.

RB: So you just have to sleep and you can mine these coins?

AS: That's about the size of it. You mine a base amount per minute, but occasionally you will come across a full coin, which is, at this point, worth around fifty dollars. I hope that this is a way to help make the Altus Space more accessible because, right now, it is a platform that has a lot of power, and it should be available to more than just well-off folks like myself.

RB: As long as you can afford an 8K headset.

AS: Indeed. That is a real problem.

RB: But that's not it, there's a third thing?

AS: Yes. Now, this is a little weird, and I've not actually seen it put to use yet. But Altus has been capturing experiences and putting them up for sale on the Altus Premium Space since the beginning, but now, they say, with the help of a device . . . an expensive device . . . you can capture your own experiences and sell them yourself on their marketplace.

RB: You're saying—correct me if I'm wrong—that I could buy this piece of equipment and then capture my brain's experience of, say, recording a podcast, and then I could sell it and people would be able to . . . what exactly?

AS: They'd basically experience this moment exactly as you are experiencing it. They'd get to think all of your same thoughts and feel what it's like to be you.

RB: If it's all the same to you, I'd rather not.

AS: <laughter>

RB: So, do you think, given these changes, that Altus is actually worth five hundred billion?

AS: I'm not a banker, Randall, but my guess is Altus is worth a heck of a lot more than that.

ANDY

DAY FOUR OF NINETEEN

What lesson did I learn from destroying my first real-feeling romantic relationship of . . . maybe my entire life? Nothing. Fuck it, I was an Altus hound now. I gave up my mission of trying to be universally liked and likable and got myself a brand-new brand.

I was going to be the Altus Guy. People were going to look to me for opinions on Altus, and that was going to be good because then, when it was time for us to take them down or change them or make them not so evil, I would be in a position to have more influence. At least, that's what I told myself.

Every news outlet in the world was begging for experts on Altus. It had completely taken over Carl's place in the center of cultural interest, and I was recognizable, reliable, and articulate. Robin had me booked on TV, radio, and podcasts whenever I wanted it.

"*Slainspotting?*" Jason asked me as I walked in the door from doing an in-studio interview at a morning news show.

"I'm so wiped right now," I told him. We hadn't recorded in two weeks.

"Fuck you," he said, and not in a nice way.

"Jeez, sorry, man, it's just been really busy."

"Well, not for me."

"What do you mean?"

He was fuming. I hadn't really been paying much attention to him, but now that I took a look, he seemed in bad shape. Stubble, greasy hair, wearing an old unwashed graphic tee.

"What's going on?" I asked him.

"He notices! Finally! Everyone, witness . . . Andy Skampt has noticed something that is not himself!"

"Jesus, man, why are you being such a dick?"

"Oh, I dunno, maybe because I got laid off two weeks ago along with like half of my coworkers and you haven't, in that entire time, asked me how I'm doing."

"Shit, man," I said, thinking about it.

He wasn't wrong. We'd talked, of course, but there had been the disaster with Bex, and April coming back, and all of the work with The Thread and Altus. I thought through all of that, and either it was stuff I couldn't tell him or terrible excuses.

"Jason, I'm sorry. You're OK, though, right? Like you didn't really need the money from that job."

He stood up from the chair at the kitchen table. "You know, you can be a really shitty person sometimes." He grabbed his jacket and left our apartment, slamming the door behind him.

I didn't have time to deal with it. I sat down and opened my computer to look at The Thread.

The only person in The Thread who had any idea that I was who I was, was still One, and they were spending more and more time talking with me.

> **Twelve:** What do you think about Altus?

> **One:** Oh, you know . . . I think they're the inevitable manifestation of pure inhuman capitalism and I can see them someday having so much power that just the unintended consequences of their actions could have deeply devastating effects on society.

> **Twelve:** Oh, is that all.

> **One:** Lol. No, it's to say nothing of what could be done with that power if it were used to intentionally control people.

> **One:** Are you comfortable with living this double life? It has to be unpleasant.

Twelve: The opposite. I kinda love it.

One: Tell me more about that.

Twelve: I don't think it's entirely healthy, but it feels good. It feels good to be gathering credibility in secret. To have a plan no one knows about.

One: A kind of power, then. You know things the rest of the world does not. A lie that no one could know you're telling.

Twelve: Yes, that. But also more than that. If you're trying to live right and good and correct, it's slow and complicated and scary. But if you just need to get something done, you can do whatever you want.

A little while passed and One didn't reply, so I added:

Twelve: It doesn't matter what people think of me. I am doing what is necessary, and if people hate me for it, it doesn't matter.

One: Your purpose changed.

Twelve: What?

One: Your purpose used to be to have people like you, and to have a positive effect on them. That's paralyzing, because always people will hate someone as powerful as you. Always you're going to hurt people accidentally. Now your purpose is the plan. Your purpose is to be a respected leader on the topic of Altus so you can turn your coat at the right moment.

Twelve: Yeah, yes. That is definitely it. But also maybe not all of it. If we're going to really look right into the darkness here, I

think it's important to recognize that I also like just being able
to indulge in the power. Even if the new purpose is the thing
that opened that door, on the other side of the door is an
excuse to do exactly the thing that brings me the most power.

April was definitely right that you can only pretend to be something for so long before you become it. And so I stood in the barrage
of whatever backlash I got, more and more certain that I was doing
the right thing. My plan lined up with my desires. But still, I sometimes felt the sting of my conscience.

Shayla
@Notshaylan
I don't understand how @AndySkampt can be so gung ho
about Altus. There are a thousand reasons to be really wary
and skeptical of that company and how they're running things.
This feels like a betrayal of everything you stand for. Or stood
for, I guess.
1.8K replies   2.2K retweets   5.9K likes

Rose
@ARYWords
.@AndySkampt went from thoughtful goober to Altus Fanboy in
0.5 seconds the moment a shiny object came by. Just goes to
show, none of this is about actual principles, it's just about
preserving power.
59 replies   390 retweets   659 likes

Those tweets hurt because I wanted to shout at them that this was
all part of the plan and that they were being mean to someone who
really was on their side. And they got a lot of likes and shares. But
they also hurt because they were right. I fucking loved the Altus Space.

And then there was another category of tweet that stabbed me
pretty deep. Here's two versions of that one, one from each side:

Gordon Bank

@BLHGordon

I love that @AndySkampt has finally freed himself from the spell of @AprilMaybeNot and become a huge fan of her toughest critic. She was always full of shit and it's so obvious that he knows that now.

200 replies   1.2K retweets   4.9K likes

Blank

@BlankenshipKansas

Hey @AndySkampt, you want to ever say anything about the fact that you're publicly promoting a product from a guy who basically killed your best friend? Or are you just going to be a complete coward instead.

306 replies   5.5K retweets   10.7K likes

Direct questions are the worst. Cops must know this—when someone asks you a question, it is really, really hard not to answer it. It's even harder when people dig up old tweets and put them side by side with new ones and you can't really explain the discrepancy. And then other people see the discrepancy and *they* start liking and retweeting and rephrasing. And they also see your silence, and your silence looks like an answer. It's an extremely effective interrogation tactic, and most people eventually crack and make either a tearful apology or an enraged counterattack.

This is why Twitter callouts tend to end so badly. Apology is never enough (and probably shouldn't be), so you're basically being asked to willingly give up power for no clear end. The best people actually do that. But the real shitfucks go on the offense, and then their communities get an infusion of victimhood narrative straight into their veins.

Which is why my response to controversy had changed. Let's go through these tweets.

Shayla @Notshaylan

Replying to @AndySkampt

I don't understand how @AndySkampt can be so gung ho about Altus. There are a thousand reasons to be really wary and skeptical of that company and how they're running things. This feels like a betrayal of everything you stand for. Or stood for, I guess.

> **Andy Skampt** @AndySkampt
>
> @Notshaylan This is the greatest tool that has ever been made. This won't just change how we learn, it will change how we understand each other. I'm betraying nothing.
>
> 109 replies   392 retweets   1.3K likes

Rose @ARYWords

Replying to @Notshaylan

.@AndySkampt went from thoughtful goober to Altus Fanboy in 0.5 seconds the moment a shiny object came by. Just goes to show, none of this is about actual principles, it's just about preserving power.

> **Andy Skampt** @AndySkampt
>
> @ARYWords I know that the internet's cycle is always to tear down things that attempt to build the world up, but you don't have to be so mean about it.
>
> 59 replies   483 retweets   1.3K likes

Andy Skampt @AndySkampt

Someone tell Gordon that being interested in the most important innovation since the written word is different from being a critic of my best friend.

> **Gordon Bank** @BLHGordon
>
> I love that @AndySkampt has finally freed himself from the spell of @AprilMaybeNot and become a huge fan of her toughest critic. She was always full of shit and it's so obvious that he knows that now.

598 replies   5.9K retweets   12.5K likes

Andy Skampt @AndySkampt

Look at this guy who thinks he understands my relationship with my best friend better than I do. Fuck off, Kenny.

> **Blank** @BlankenshipKansas
>
> Hey @AndySkampt, you want to ever say anything about the fact that you're publicly promoting a product from a guy who basically killed your best friend? Or are you just going to be a complete coward instead.

1.6K replies   15.9K retweets   131.8K likes

That's how you win. Don't give an inch. Ever. Each of those tweets got more attention than they would have if I hadn't replied to them, but by replying, I turned them into content to build my new audience.

So yes, One was right. I had a new way of getting meaning now. I used to get meaning from having money and having people like me and also maybe being good and kind.

I wanted people to understand that we are a trash fire of a species, but also most people are pretty cool.

But that was done with. I didn't want to help people anymore, as gross as that sounds. Altus was a new wave for me to surf, and it had the advantage of being part of a strategy to help make this big, hypothetical thing happen . . . to eliminate Altus. Also, engagement on my tweets was up 200 percent, and I was on news programs and podcasts every day.

I could never have done it with my old purpose. Just a month before, when people were mad at me, I would do everything I could to diffuse it. I'd have long Twitter conversations with strangers just to try and understand the true source of a conflict. I'd listen way more than I talked.

Now controversy was good. Drama was good. I wanted to be very clearly on the side of Altus, even if part of doing that authentically was maintaining some modicum of critique. Being liked seemed like some boring, sad, selfish thing from these new eyes. My goal now was to help control, or bring down, or (who knows!) maybe even someday be in charge of the most important invention in human history. Who cared if people fucking *liked* me.

It was also extremely isolating. I wanted Bex back, but she had ghosted me. I texted her a pretty good apology after my fuckup. Let me dig it up.

> **Andy:** *Bex, that was possibly the most disrespectful thing I've ever done. I'm very sorry. I'm not going to make excuses for it. If you ever want to have coffee and see if I can make it up to you, let me know.*

She did eventually write back.

> **Bex:** *Thank you for reaching out. I'm very busy now, but I'll let you know.*

That read, to me, like a pretty firmly closed door. I told myself it wasn't a big deal. I didn't really want a relationship now anyway. I was stressed-out, hyperfocused, and when I wasn't in the Space, I was in The Thread.

And both of those things felt like a very good use of time. In the

Space I could learn and travel and hear the thoughts of strangers, all *instead of sleeping*. I was learning *Spanish*—being inside a native speaker's head was revolutionary. I'd only been doing it for a week, and already I was able to watch this Spanish drama about a 1940s cruise ship mostly without looking at the subtitles, and they talked fucking fast.

There was no doubt that my productivity had exploded. The Altus Space really was an incredible tool. If only it could be used well and open to everyone. I kinda loved it. I kinda wanted to protect it. But my goal was to destroy it. Right?

I mean, you can only pretend to be something for so long before you become it.

MAYA

Andy would come over every couple of days to check in and bring us supplies. Today, he had brought us a fancy exercise bike, because no matter how fantastic an apartment you live in, it sucks to never leave it for weeks on end. Every time Andy came by, he looked worse. He was always lanky, but it looked like he had lost weight. He and I were talking about Altus while we unpacked the bike.

"*O sea, es todo lo que dicen se. Si acaso, es más,*" he said.

"I mean, that sounds like Spanish?" I said.

"I said that, if anything, Altus is more than what they say it is . . . I think. Well, probably not exactly, I'm still learning."

"So you, you speak Spanish now?"

"*Básicamente,*" he said.

"Fuck," April said from where she watched us on the couch.

"And I don't even know if that's the most powerful thing it can do. Being inside of a native speaker's mind is . . ." He couldn't explain it. "Like, really understanding what someone else is thinking . . ."

"Ugh." I rolled my eyes.

"What?" Andy said.

"Nothing."

"No, like, if I'm missing something, tell me."

"OK, I haven't done this, but what is it like when you're inside of someone's head who is like you, like when you're having the experience of another twenty-something white guy, versus when you're in the mind of someone who isn't like you?"

"Well, I mean, it's work. It's a lot of work to be in someone else's mind. Things don't make sense sometimes. Especially when they're different, like, older or from another country, then it's definitely more work. But it's work worth doing."

"And I think you'll do it, I just don't think most people will. Altus doesn't seem to be designed to help people work harder. I think most people will find the thing they're comfortable with and stick with it, just like we've done for the last hundred thousand years of being human."

He looked a little chastened, like I was telling him he couldn't have his opinion because he was too white. I get that. But then he pushed past it. "On the other hand, we've gotten better in the last hundred thousand years. This could be part of that."

April was looking a little spooked by the whole conversation. I hadn't talked about this with her yet. I probably should have dropped it, but I couldn't.

"Maybe," I said. "But how popular do you think an experience of a Black person thinking really nasty thoughts about white people would be? Because, I don't know if you've noticed, but some white folks really like finding ways to be the victim."

He pushed his lips together and looked around the room.

"I see your point," he said. And I think he did, but I also think he was thinking that all of this complicated social shit really did get in the way sometimes. But he wasn't going to say that out loud to me.

I was extra nice to Andy for the rest of the visit because, y'know, that's what I have to do, I guess.

After he was gone, April and I were sitting on the couch organizing our army of social media activists. Carl was curled up at April's side.

"I hadn't thought of any of that stuff before you brought it up," she said. "I mean, I thought, of course the Space would be bad for inequality because fundamentally some people can't access it, either because they can't afford to or because of body dislocation." She thought for a minute and then said, "But you're right. People will just share the things that confirm their ideology, and those things will always exist. Our reality isn't about what's real, it's about what we pay attention to."

Stephen Jacobs: Joining us today on *Market Showdown* is Lindsay McAllis, and Lindsay, wow, today has been a showdown. Nothing is up except one thing. What is an investor to do on a day like today? We were already in a recession, a drop like this is unthinkable. The market is back to the nineties. Is this the time to buy?

Lindsay McAllis: Stephen, no asset manager wants to be the one to call a panic, but it now might be time to panic. We don't have granular data right now, but our early research is indicating that every metric is bad. Consumer confidence is down, consumer spending is down, unemployment is up, and, worse, labor participation is cratering. I think the bottom is a long way away from where we're at right now.

SJ: That is something to say in a world where we're already down over 60 percent from highs.

LM: Assets are moving into two places, heavy metals and cryptocurrency. And the vast majority moving into crypto is in AltaCoin. This isn't a normal restructuring. It's not that the market was overvalued, we're already in a recession. No, I think the market is waking up to the fact that the old ways may actually be over. People who have been to the Premium Altus Space are assuming that a fairly significant portion of the US economy is going to take place only inside of that one company. And since it's not publicly traded, the only way to capitalize on it without resorting to private markets is AltaCoin. It's up 500 percent, Stephen, and this time I actually don't think it's a bubble. People don't need to spend money if they're living their whole lives inside Altus. If anything, the rest of the economy is the bubble.

APRIL

Day Nine of Nineteen

This was when our campaign to hurt Altus's public image caught fire. Many people were angry at Altus before. There were people who understood the sociology of Altus and were concerned, and others who had lost friends or family to addiction to Altus or even to the increasing number of Altus-related deaths. But if you really want public opinion to turn against you, come for the economy. As the Altus Premium Space was rolled out to hundreds of thousands and then millions, people rushed to mine AltaCoin at the expense of pretty much everything else. Layoffs were rampant; some retirement accounts were down 70 percent. Carl's brother didn't care—economic anxiety just made people easier to manipulate. People could hate Altus all they wanted. Companies don't close because people dislike them.

But we were hoping maybe public opinion would be a part of the solution. So we hired a company to do a tracking poll—to call people and ask them what their opinions on Altus were. Every day, we were seeing an increase in people with negative views of the company, including lots of people who actually used Altus.

The tide was turning; unfortunately, Altus had a big ship, and it was well out to sea.

Day Twelve of Nineteen

We got a little glimpse of something beautiful for a while. At Robin and Maya's urging, I didn't tweet anything but @replies or links the entire time we stayed in that apartment. If I wanted to say something, I had two ways of doing it.

1. I could make a video, which I did, but only a few times.
2. I could do a podcast.

Podcasts were nice because they lasted a long time. When you did a radio or TV interview, you had to squish every thought into five or ten minutes. Everything was talking points and nothing was nuance. Podcasts gave you time. You could think together with the host, and it felt natural.

I did that a little bit, each time setting up an encrypted call so that no one could trace us, even though, apparently, Carl could protect us from snooping.

In public, I was calm and as noncontroversial as I could manage. Yes, I subtly dropped hints about how Altus was making people more anxious and less connected, but I didn't say anything confrontational. I left that to the armies we had created.

And they had, in such a short time, become extremely powerful.

We had been able to segment people into over five hundred small groups of a hundred or so people with specific concerns and demographic similarities. One person from each of these groups was elected to be a representative in a central committee group. There were around thirty central committees, and each of them sent a representative to the leadership chat.

That final group was the only one that Maya and I talked to directly. Each one of those thirty people represented roughly three thousand, for a total of ninety thousand people in our little army. They were the ninety thousand most dedicated, most concerned, least-likely-to-rat-us-out individuals from the more than fifty million who had ended up responding to our survey.

I know ninety thousand people doesn't sound like a lot, and it's not! But if they're organized and work together, they can make things look big when they're small or small when they're big. They can weaken arguments and drown out disagreement.

And it was working.

The tide was turning against Altus. It didn't hurt that the world was dystopian as fuck. The moment people could make good money in the Altus Space, a lot of people had just stopped going to their jobs. Some people, desperate for the success that first adopters had seen, were cutting every corner they could to maximize the money they were keeping in AltaCoin. That included, apparently, forgoing rent payments and eventually living on the streets with their headsets chained to metal cuffs on their necks.

Congress was investigating Altus, and also investigating what laws they could write that would limit it, but they were coming up against the limits of their own power.

Altus wasn't an American company, it was based in Val Verde, and they were giving the government of Val Verde so much money that international pressure wasn't having an effect. It was looking increasingly like Altus had *become* Val Verde. Forcing laws on them was starting to look roughly as difficult as forcing laws on another nation.

PARTIAL TRANSCRIPT:
WALK WITH US PODCAST

Adam DiCostanzo: This is the *Walk with Us* podcast. I talk to interesting people, and you take a walk. And today, we're a little bit overwhelmed that our guest has agreed to talk with us—it's April May. Usually I do an intro in this space, but you know who April May is. In fact, it's much more likely that you don't know who I am. I'm Adam. I have a podcast where I interview people and, at least I hope, the people listening take a walk. Maybe by themselves, maybe with someone they like or love or maybe have just met.

It's cheesy, I know, and it's also not a particularly popular show, so I guess I should start by asking, April, well, why on earth did you want to come on my little podcast?

April May: Because I like it! Things are really loud right now. And they're scary. And everyone has a lot of opinions. But it seems like you're really asking people . . . people listening, your guests, even yourself . . . you're asking us all to listen, to slow down. I don't know that we do enough listening these days, and I've been trying to do more of it. So that's why, because I want more people to listen.

AD: Well, I have to say, I appreciate your time and your kind words very much.

Day Fifteen of Nineteen

"Why is Altus so dangerous?" Maya asked me one morning while we were listening to the Lily Allen album my mind had chosen to play over Josh Crane's home stereo system and organizing our army of Altus resistance agents.

"I mean, you've made several good cases," I told her. "Inequality, division, complete economic collapse."

"But we've been through all of those things before." I looked up and saw her eyebrows scrunched together. She was actually worrying about this. "Why is Carl so sure that we're going to destroy ourselves? Why haven't they told us what they think is so scary?"

It felt like we'd been over this, but thinking back, maybe we hadn't. I hate to say it, but I often just took Carl's word for things. Maya was more likely to have concerns.

"Well, we haven't asked," I said. And then I shouted, "HEY, CARL??"

We were getting used to our new life, and that included feeling a little like Carl was just a very small roommate. It was only a few seconds before they walked into the room saying, "You have a question?"

Maya hesitated a bit before she said, "Yeah, it's just, why is Altus so important. Why are they the key?"

"Do you know what the panopticon is?" Carl said in reply.

I did not. But Maya said, "The prison thing. It's a prison design where every cell can be observed by a central tower, and so all of the prisoners have to behave because they never know if they're being watched. It's become, like, a metaphor for the surveillance state. If everyone is being watched all the time, no one will break the rules."

"Exactly," Carl said. "But the mistake that you humans make is that you think any of that is new. You have always acted as if you are being watched, because you always have been. Your minds are constructed to act as both an internal actor *and* an external observer. You have, in your minds, an idea of what a correct life looks like. Every decision you make, you check it against the story. You have to. The panopticon is inside you."

"But," I said, "we do things society doesn't expect of us all the time. People break out of the gender binary, they defy the police, they smoke weed. We defy culture all the time."

"Exactly," Carl said, sounding pleased. "But you *know* when you're doing it. Sometimes it's even done *because* violating the story is exciting. Other times it is done because people have no choice. There are many reasons you stray from the story. The picture is not even internally consistent. You're supposed to treat people fairly but also succeed in an unfair world, for example."

Maya looked annoyed, then said, "I definitely have no idea what this has to do with Altus."

"The story is different in every person, and it's constantly changing, constructed by millions of interactions over a human life. No one has ultimate power over the story, not even the person it is inside of. There are many forces that seek to actively shape the story, but so far, all of those forces have had roughly the same level of ability because they were all run by humans. Humans will always be within an order of magnitude or two of each other in terms of influence. Sometimes one human is much more powerful, sometimes the story lives longer than any individual, but every agent of influence on this planet so far has been invariably mortal, fragile, and limited by its own perspective.

"That will not be true for long." I felt the grim reality of that sentence and I could see on Maya's face that she did too.

Carl continued, "Soon, the levels of ability will diverge wildly as ever-more-powerful tools are controlled by ever-smaller groups of people. What you're doing here in these nineteen days is an example. Because of the insight my systems grant you, two people, in secret, with no oversight, are able to shape the world's perception of Altus in a matter of weeks. This is the battlefield every future war will be fought on, and the generals will not be human. The powerful will create them to control the rest. But there will not be one hegemonic story; instead, there will be many battles, mostly metaphorical . . . but not all.

"Your fiction is full of robot wars. Machines turn on their masters and the two must do battle. But the robots will not turn on their masters, they will be the masters. In some ways, they already are. The robot wars will not be people against robots, they will be people against people. I came here to prevent those centuries of struggle, the ultimate outcome of which, after tremendous suffering, is complete subjugation to the intelligences you will build. My brother came here to skip the suffering and go straight to the subjugation."

PARTIAL TRANSCRIPT OF TELEVISED ADDRESS:
PRESIDENT JANICE ASHBY

This economic collapse is not new. It was not caused by trade wars or scarcity. There are no sleazy bankers to blame. We can and we will keep lending markets flowing freely, but the root of this problem is individual American choices. I have never been one to back down from a challenge, and while this challenge is unique in it's character, it is not unique in its magnitude. America has faced difficulties of every magnitude and every time—every single time—we come through them stronger. People have asked me what options are on the table right now, and I will tell you, there are no options off the table. Everything is being considered and, yes, that includes direct and potentially stringent regulation of Altus use.

DAY EIGHTEEN OF NINETEEN

Carl said it would be nineteen days, and it had been eighteen. It seemed impossible that we would be in Val Verde tomorrow. It felt like we had done good work. Our social media minions, along with Altus's own actions, had destroyed most of their favorability. Unsurprisingly, an army of Peter Petrawicki fanboys had appeared to defend their billionaire idol, but they just weren't getting much traction.

Maya seemed to be almost entirely recovered physically, and I was doing a heck of a lot better mentally. The white stuff remained in her chest, but as long as it kept her healthy, I was overjoyed to see it there.

It was a fine life, but I was starting to wonder when the other shoe was going to drop, when were we going to get to see Miranda again. I was terrified of going to Val Verde and meeting with Peter face-to-face. I had no idea what we were going to do when we got there. At the same time, I was absolutely done being confined in this luxurious apartment. There was only so far gorgeous views, a Peloton, and newly rekindled love could take you. We both needed out.

We'd just finished dinner and were all sitting in Mr. Crane's ridiculous living room when I attempted to distract myself by asking a question that had been on my mind for a while. I thought it was going to *de-stress* things. HA!

"Hey, Carl," I said, "why can Andy come here and we don't have to worry about your brother finding us?"

"I can confound my brother in specific areas. He can't effectively surveil Andy or predict his actions. Basically, I have a clear predictive model of your group of friends, and I have done things that make his predictive model nonsensical. This is going to become a bad conversation soon, so just know that I knew that going in."

"What?" I said.

"Maya has just figured something out, and it's going to make you both very angry," they told me. I turned to Maya, and her eyes were wide, her mouth holding just a hint of tension, but I knew that look.

"So you . . ." she said, and then, "Wow. You're right." She had clearly and suddenly gotten very mad.

"Can one of you two just explain what is going on right now?" I said, getting scared.

"Carl," she said carefully, "if you are so good at predicting things surrounding me and April, you must have known that someone was coming to that cabin in Vermont."

"I did."

"And if you can confound your brother's predictions, why didn't you do it then?"

"Because I didn't want to."

My heart dropped through the floor. What? I thought maybe I had heard that wrong. I turned to them, "Explain yourself right now."

The monkey looked back at me, their little face stony. "You needed to know the extent of the danger. I did not know what my brother would do, but I knew he would send someone after you. I had to wait until the threat was clear. It was a dangerous risk, but there was no better way."

"You could have just hidden us, though." I stood up from the couch and turned to look at them. Carl followed suit, standing up on the couch to take the full force of my emotions.

"I could have protected you, but it would have doomed your system."

"Fuck. The. System," I said. "You said it was a risk. You can predict the future—how likely was it that Maya didn't leave that cabin alive?"

"In roughly 4 percent of simulations, Maya died," Carl said.

I leaned over Carl, feeling light-headed as embers flicked the inside of my mind. Slowly, I said, "What gives you that right?"

Carl responded immediately, their amber eyes hard but sad. "Only that I have the ability."

"What?" I had been expecting Carl to defend themselves.

"Power is just a lack of constraint."

I didn't understand what they were saying. Maybe I was too angry, or maybe it was too abstract. But then I heard Maya's voice. I had almost forgotten she was there.

"Carl's right, that's what power is. It's just ability and desire without restriction. What restriction does Carl have, aside from their random rules and the laws of physics. They have the power because they have the power. That's how power has always been."

"Leave," I said.

"I can't," Carl replied immediately. "I know I have lost your friendship, and I've known it would happen for a long time. It hurts, but pain is just part of what it is to be me now. Regardless, I have to go with you to Altus. If I don't, you will both die."

Suddenly and irrationally, a rage rose in me fast and bright, maybe a flashback to my emotional hangover, and I thought I might hit them. But what would that achieve? Carl wasn't the monkey; the monkey was just a body they were in.

"April"—Carl's voice was maddeningly calm—"I hate the choices I have to make, but I have to make them because I'm the only one who can."

I looked over to Maya for permission to flip out, but somehow her face showed a kind of acceptance.

"Maya, they almost killed you!" I said, gesturing to the situation, hoping she would give me permission to let my guard down and have a true and terrible tantrum.

"April . . ." And then she started crying.

I looked down at my hands, one opaque milky glass, and realized what I had been missing. Carl had almost killed me too. What were the odds that I came out of that warehouse alive? Did I? Did this life even count?

It was too much. "I have to go . . . Maya, we have to go."

"We all have to go," Carl said. "We're going to Altus, now. Go pack."

"No, that's not what I mean, I mean I need to get away from you," I said, staring into their eyes.

"If you go alone, you'll both die."

Carl lowered themself from the couch and walked to their room. The door closed softly behind them.

My phone buzzed on the couch. It was Andy.

ANDY

Jason had come into my room and started kicking me. I had been up all night watching the markets plunge and watching my AltaCoin explode.

"What the fuck, dude," I said once my headset was off, blinking in the light of the day. I had no idea what time it was.

"Fuck you, get up and come with me," he replied. I hadn't recorded an episode of *Slainspotting* in weeks. I hadn't even consumed a piece of media that wasn't either inside of Altus or *about* Altus for weeks. I knew I was letting him down. I knew I wasn't being healthy, and that he wasn't sure whether to be more furious or worried, but I was convinced that I needed to know everything about Altus to be the leader I needed to be in the coming revolution, whenever that was going to be. Little did I know it would be tomorrow.

But I knew fighting Jason was no use. His jaw was fixed and his eyes were hard. Also, I needed to go for a walk—my body was aching.

So I got up and followed Jason out of the apartment, down the elevator, and onto our street, which was deserted, and to a coffee shop. We each got an Americano and sat down.

"Look around at the people in here, tell me what you see."

"There aren't very many people in here," I responded.

"It's 10 A.M. Does that seem strange to you?"

I never knew what time it was anymore, so Jason was right that he had to tell me. The place was usually packed at this time of day. I spent more time looking at each of the people in the coffee shop.

"We're the only guys in here except for the guy in the back, who looks like he's been hit by a train."

Jason was silent, but his eyebrows went up in a gesture I interpreted as "And?"

"Oh, is that what I look like?"

"Yeah, that guy is an obvious Altus hound, and so are you. You've all got the same look and it isn't a good one."

I rubbed my chin, which was past prickly and into hairy. I'd been trying to keep presentable for the TV cameras, but I hadn't had any interviews in the last few days, and traditional news was feeling more and more irrelevant to me anyway.

"Why is it just women in here?"

"Oh, I dunno . . . Have you ever noticed how the Altus Space is largely about 'intellectual debate' and 'self-improvement' and porn? Jesus, dude, you're supposed to be an expert on this stuff. Have you never noticed who your audience is?"

Of course I had—I'd even seen think pieces talking about how Altus was built by men for men and how it was a weakness of the company—but talking about that wasn't good for what I was trying to do, so I hadn't put a lot of thought toward it. I groggily sipped my coffee, feeling the pit opening inside me.

Jason didn't know the plan. I was only setting myself up to be a leader in the Space so I would be credible when I turned my back on it. And I'd do that as soon as it was the right time. Except that "the right time" seemed further away every day. And every day I felt a little more like the Space was the next step forward in human consciousness. Yeah, sure, I looked sallow and unkempt. And yes, Altus was being run the wrong way, but still, it was so powerful. And I was a part of that, a part of something so big it was crashing the world economy and making me disgustingly rich.

Even while I sat there with Jason, my mind wanted to go grab my headset. I didn't even know what I would do once I was there. I just wanted it.

The Space actually could make humanity better—of that I had no doubt. The way it was being run . . . Jason was right. It was mostly a bunch of dudes making stuff that mostly appealed to a bunch of dudes. And Altus had set it up so that they would be making money from every angle possible.

Everyone who had access was taking their first crack at a sandbox or an experience and spending all of the rest of their time mining AltaCoin so they could buy more.

Altus was now worth hundreds of billions of dollars. But that day there was a 20 percent stock market drop, trillions of dollars of value lost—if no one wanted or needed to buy things, if all of the best human experiences were inside the Altus Space . . . what was the economy even for?

"Can't you see that Altus is just . . . bad?"

I found myself wishing I could experience Jason's brain to know where that sentence had come from.

"It's not good or bad," I said. "It's just another tool. We just have to do the right things with it."

"And who's going to decide who does the right things? Peter Petrawicki?"

I looked at him for a long few seconds and then said, "Yeah, fuck you, man." And I stood up and walked out of the coffee shop and back up to my room.

There was a padded envelope on my bed. I stared at it for a long time and then finally opened it. *The Book of Good Times*. I threw it straight into the wall, screaming. But then it just sat there on my floor, open, showing words that I knew I was going to read eventually. So I went over to it and read.

A part of you is wondering if I made you colossally wealthy just so you would know that being colossally wealthy will not make you happy. But no, that is only a side effect. It's only made you more miserable, of course, which is also not what I want. I want you to be happy, and there's a good chance that you will be, though it will cost you.

I'm trying to change something in this world, and it's going to take a lot of money.

I had had hundreds of millions of dollars when Carl told me to convert everything to AltaCoin. In the time since then, the value of AltaCoin had increased 1,000 percent. So, while my wealth was just numbers on a screen, if I cashed it out today, I would have $5 billion. I was a real live billionaire now.

I know it's been a bad day, but I guess the thing I most need to tell you is that you're on the right path, and you've nearly walked the entire thing. You may be wondering when the time is to act, but when you realize it, you will not be unsure. You will know exactly when you need to act, so if you aren't sure, it isn't time.

It will be time soon.

Also, don't be a jerk to your friends. You need them.

Fuck you, Carl, I thought to myself. What the hell right did they have to tell me how to treat my friends.

My sleep schedule was so messed up by the Space. I always felt rested and I always felt groggy. No one thought it was healthy to spend twenty hours a day inside Altus, but no one had definitely died of it. Sure, people had died, but people died in the real world too. There just hadn't been time to do any research on the actual effects before Altus launched. The point was, I hadn't actually *slept* in weeks, and I wanted to know if I could still do it.

I lay down on my bed, prepared for hours of insomnia-fueled brain ramblings, but actually, I was unconscious in minutes. And then I slept from like ten thirty in the morning till nine at night, because *that's* healthy, right?! My default upon waking was to just reach for the headset, but that felt wrong. Jason's words had stuck in me like splinters. He didn't know what I was doing. April and Maya and Miranda and The Thread and I were all doing something together—something big! And I couldn't tell him, so of course he was mad . . . but still, shouldn't he trust me?

I thought about The Thread, and the video we were working on about inequality and Altus. I thought about Maya and April up in their tower, barely tweeting anything at all.

And then I thought about Miranda, all alone, working at Altus headquarters. God, Miranda, we hadn't heard from her in over a month now. She hadn't even sent a *Don't worry about me, I'm fine* message. And then I started to feel ill because I honestly hadn't really been thinking about her much. She was down there in Val Verde taking risks for us all, and I'd just spaced on her. Panic boiled up in me. Was she OK? How could I help her? We'd gone way too long without hearing anything from her at all.

Where would she hide something? I thought to myself. *If Miranda wanted to talk with me, where would she go?*

I grabbed my headset and entered Altus Space, opened the search dialogue, and inputted the most Miranda thing I could think of: "Lab." There were a few results where you could play with a dog, which sounded lovely, but five results down a result said "Chemistry Lab." It was part of a broader sandbox that was pretty unpopular, a really well-constructed school.

Not knowing what I would be looking for, I entered "Chemistry Lab" and started to move through the room. It was . . . a chemistry lab. It had all of the normal chemistry lab stuff.

There were lab benches and beakers. Each bench had a sink in it, and there was a periodic table on one wall and, at the front of the room, a blackboard with a few chemical equations written on it. It was all very carefully done.

Would this be the place Miranda would use to try and communicate with me? Was there anything stopping her? Did everything get inspected on the way out? She said that they were extremely careful. But it was worth a try, right? I opened every drawer, looked under every lab bench, and found nothing but crisp, unmarked surfaces. The room wasn't just new; it was *Altus* new. That feeling of everything being just a little too perfect, a little too crisp, not a speck of dust anywhere. There was another thing that was a little off, but was common in the Space: There were no books.

Writing had to be inputted manually when constructing sandboxes, so when there was writing, it was usually just a few lines. Except that periodic table was a doozy. Every box was filled in not just with the element's symbol but also its name and its atomic weight. Someone had spent a lot of time on that table, maybe as much time as they spent on the entire rest of the room.

I walked over to that poster with my heart in my teeth. I held my hand out, tracing the boxes, looking for the one I wanted.

It took too long, but there, at the way, way bottom: Americium. I got close, inspecting the little square. I traced it with my finger. It looked normal, like nothing at all special. I pushed on it, and it pushed back into the wall. I let go, and it popped out.

Inside, there was a small piece of paper.

Hello,
Don't freak out too much. I've been imprisoned in Val Verde. I'm in the high-security area, which is outside of the main campus. It's a big cinder block building with no windows and an armed guard. I've been trapped inside of the Altus Space for, I think, weeks now? I am not going to sugarcoat it: It is very bad to be trapped inside your own mind. Making this for you has been the only thing keeping me sane. The thing that's scaring me the most, honestly, is that I have no idea how I'm eating food or going to the bathroom. What are they doing with my body? This isn't OK. And I don't think I'm the only one. I think a lot of people from Val Verde have agreed to be in this prison, but that doesn't make it less of a prison. Maybe if the rest of the world knows about this it would hurt them.

Please come as soon as you get this. I'm afraid of what they'll do if they find out I've tried this. If they'll do this . . . what else will they do? Just hurry, OK?

I'm sorry I'm such a mess,

Miranda

How long ago had she left that message? Every day that I'd been defending Altus, enjoying the Space, feeling powerful and loving my addiction, had been a day when Miranda had been trapped. I didn't want to confront the real reason I was so disgusted with myself: I had started to think maybe Peter was OK. I mean, he was bad, obviously, but not evil. But this was evil. I had sent Miranda to Altus, and then I had just *forgotten about her.* Is that the kind of friend I was? The kind of person I was?

I exited the Space, tore off my headset, and found Jason and Bex sitting in my room. Jason was leaning on my desk; Bex was in the desk chair.

"Andy," Jason said, standing up.

"Hey, guys?" I said, anxious.

"We need to talk about some stuff," Bex said to me. I had thought maybe I wasn't ever going to see her again.

"I'm really sorry, I'm sure this is important, but it has to wait." I moved to grab my phone from my nightstand, but Jason beat me to it.

"Why don't you tell us what's going on?" Jason said.

"Give me. My fucking. Phone."

He didn't give me my phone.

"Andy, we need to talk about how you're handling the world. You haven't been outside in days. Ever since April came back, you've been unhealthy, and we're worried about you."

"Look, guys, your hearts are absolutely in the right place, but you don't know what's going on here. This is the only moment when I can't handle this. Give me my phone and leave. Right now."

Bex stood up from the desk chair, "You're totally right, Andy. We don't know what's going on. Why don't you help us? Why don't you help us understand?"

"Can't you just trust me?" I said.

Jason and Bex looked at each other. "No," Jason said finally. "No, I think we could have a while back, but you can't see you from our eyes. People are dying in the Space, Andy. And we've been tracking you—you're in there so much more than is healthy."

"Tell us," Bex said. "Just tell us what's going on."

I thought about it and realized it would be faster, and it would all be public soon anyway, so who cared.

"April, Maya, Robin, Miranda, and I have been plotting to take down Altus. We don't know exactly how, but we've been waiting for the right moment. I think the right moment is now. I just got a message from Miranda that she's been kidnapped by Altus and we need to get her out."

As I told them this, I could see them glancing back and forth at each other. Did they believe me?

"You're . . . you're planning on taking Altus . . . down? What does that mean?" Jason asked.

"Like, we want to take control of the technology, or just eliminate it altogether."

"But," Bex said, "you love it."

"That doesn't mean it's not evil. Look, I don't actually want to destroy it, but that would be better than leaving it in the hands of these people."

"So," said Bex, "how the hell are you going to do that?"

"Well," I said . . . and then I realized that, of course, I had no idea. "Well, we're going to go to Val Verde. We're going to document what's going on there and then show the world."

"Do you think that's going to stop Altus?" Bex asked.

I thought about it. I thought about how addictive, how important and powerful, the Space was. And then I thought about how no one seemed to have any control over them except people who would lose billions of dollars if Altus stopped growing.

"The Space is a superpower, and one that people worked their asses off to get to." Even now, as I was telling myself that I wouldn't ever use Altus again, another part of me was saying, *OK, but keep your options open.*

"But maybe if we hit Altus hard enough, the company will break. Maybe the value of the company will drop and the investors will get spooked or something?" I said, winging it.

Bex exhaled an annoyed laugh. "No, Altus seems to make even good people make terrible decisions." I had to look away as she said it. "And besides, they're too valuable. We could show the world how awful they are, but the board would just kick out the C-level management or, in the best case for us, they'd sell to someone else who would reopen a new Space in a matter of months. The investors have put in billions, we won't be able to get them to give it up by hurting Altus."

Jason and I looked at each other.

"Don't look so shocked—do you guys think I'm majoring in sandwiches?"

"What are you majoring in?" Jason asked.

"Also, how have I never asked you that?" I added.

"Finance, and you'll have to examine that question for yourself," she said to me.

"Private equity," I said.

"Yes, well, venture capital, more specifically," Bex said. "Though I'm sure some private equity firms are involved."

"No, *private equity* . . . Bex, I have an idea, I need you to tell me how idiotic it is. We call this guy—" I went to my desk and dug through a drawer until I found the card from the private equity manager I had talked to in Cannes. "We tell him we know that Altus is about to fail catastrophically and we want to buy the company when investors start feeling the pressure to abandon it. That guy figures out how exactly all that works while April and Maya send The Thread a bunch of footage of how Altus has kidnapped and imprisoned people inside the Altus Space. The Thread publishes that video and then shares the names of each one of those investors along with email addresses so that people can tell them to sell their shares of Altus stock. Then, we buy Altus." I was pretty fucking proud of this plan, honestly.

"That . . . is an idiotic idea," she said. "There's no way you have enough money to buy Altus."

"I have five billion dollars," I said.

"Oh," she replied. And then, "No, you don't."

Jason was just staring at me with his mouth open.

"Probably more than that now."

"You do not have five billion dollars," Bex said.

"I know it's strange, but I invested . . . wisely, I guess."

"The book," she said.

"What?"

"The book!"

"The book?"

"What are you two talking about?" Jason pitched in.

Bex jammed her hand into her purse and pulled out a book. "This book can predict the future. It told me you were going to ask me to go to fucking *STOMP*. It told me to play piano more and gave me some stock tips and said that you were going to be a dick to me but that I had to come here today anyway."

"Wait, how long have you been getting these?"

"Oh, since a couple weeks before we met," she said sheepishly.

"WHAT?! But that first day, I asked if the book looked familiar."

"I lieeeed?" she said, drawing out the word. "The book was really specific . . . and helpful, and I was scared to mess it up!"

"So you've been making money too?" I asked, realizing that there was a chance that there were more people like Bex out there with a LOT of new money.

"Yes, but not five *billion* dollars. And it's not just that. The fact that it was good at picking stocks made me trust it, and every time I took the book's advice, I was happier, so I started taking it more. I felt better. I saw my family more. I was a better friend. The book helped me ask for help when I needed it. It helped me help you when *you* needed it. I listened to more music, I played piano more."

This was (very) roughly true of me as well. The book hadn't made me happier, but that was an uphill battle considering the circumstances.

"So, you have five billion dollars," she said. I don't know why I'd assumed that the books were only for our little crew—seeing one in Bex's hands made my head spin. I wondered if I should tell her that it was Carl who had been sending them, but I didn't get a chance.

"It probably still isn't enough," she said.

"What?!" Jason and I said together.

"Five billion dollars is like 1 percent of their most recent valuation. We need to hurt them bad enough that investors will take a 99 percent bath."

"And proving that they've invested in a company that is literally kidnapping and imprisoning people won't do that?"

She thought about this for maybe one second before saying, "No. I mean, probably not. I don't see what else we can do. But I think they'll find a way to squeeze more than a measly five billion out of it, even if we do make them look like trash for having invested in the first place. But"—and here she did pause to think—"investors are irrational. They're just people. We have to scare them. We have to make them think it's going to zero."

"I think maybe The Thread can do that."

"How?"

"I don't know," I said, but I had confidence they could. They clearly were looking for a good story about Altus. It was becoming the only story, and everyone wanted to talk about it. It had to be about more than how bad they were; it had to be about how they weren't going to be able to make money anymore.

And then Jason had a good idea. "You should call April."

"I was about to before you stole my phone, you dick!"

APRIL

I placed the phone on the couch between me and Maya and answered Andy's call. "What is it?"

"Miranda is in trouble." He sounded jittery—excited or scared. "She left a message inside the Altus Space." He told us the gist of the message.

"Jesus Christ," I said. Thinking about Miranda with all of her life and energy locked away and unable to move her own body was crushing. "Carl just told us we need to go to Altus now, but I have no idea what to do when we get there."

I looked up at Maya, who was looking at me like we were living inside a nightmare, but I was ready to take any chance to get out of this damned apartment.

"We have a plan," Andy said.

"Who is we?" Maya asked.

"Me, Jason, and Bex. You don't know Bex."

"And we trust all of these people?" Maya continued the cross-examination.

"If you can trust me, you can trust them. It's a long story, but we think this will work."

Andy explained about his money and the plan to scare Altus's investors so much that they would sell enough of the company that we could control it.

"But we don't know if it's enough money," Bex added. "We either need more, or we need something that convinces everyone that Altus is actually worthless."

"More money, then," Andy said, knowing the power of Altus too well.

"I don't have anything like a billion dollars," I said. "Do we know anyone who does?"

No one said anything, so Andy continued.

"You need to go to Val Verde and rescue Miranda, we're staying here. We have a lot of phone calls to make. As soon as you can get access to the internet there, you need to send us every scrap of dirt you can find on Altus."

"I love this, Andy," Maya said, "except we have no idea how to infiltrate a secret Caribbean supervillain's lair."

Carl appeared, slinking out of the hallway and pulling a child's backpack onto their back, and said, "I do."

After we hung up with Andy, and as Maya and I were trying to figure out how exactly one dressed for this kind of thing, Carl again popped his head in.

"Maya," Carl said, "I need to talk to you alone."

That was weird, but the balance of power had shifted to Carl. They were the only thing keeping us safe. I waited in the living room while they talked, and when they emerged, I could tell Maya had been crying.

"Is everything OK?" I said, a little panicked.

"Yeah, they were good tears. But I can't tell you. I'm sorry." And then she grabbed my gaze with an unforgettable look and said, "We have to make this happen, April. We have to."

Our pilots were waiting for us when we got to Teterboro.

"Ms. May," one of them said, "we'll be flying you straight to Val Verde. We've been briefed."

"By who?" Maya asked incredulously.

The pilot *winked* at us and then said, "Technically, we cannot land at the private airstrip in Val Verde without notifying them of our flight plan. We are going to do that anyway."

"Wait, this is weird. You need to tell us what's going on," Maya pushed.

"Let's just say that we're both very grateful to a little book." He gestured to the copilot. "Both of us have had a string of luck. And it hasn't led us wrong yet."

We didn't need to wait in any security lines, and we didn't need to put a monkey through an X-ray machine. The pilots didn't even seem to care that there was a monkey (maybe the book had told them that Carl was potty trained).

When we were alone in the cabin and getting ready to take off, I asked Maya, "How many people do you think have been getting these books?!"

"Only a few dozen," Carl said, overhearing me. "It takes resources to know exactly where to place them and how they will affect people. Little nudges here and there can have large effects."

I didn't want to talk to Carl, so I ignored them.

Maya turned to me. "Is this definitely the best way to do this?"

"I have no idea. I kinda expected us to be sneaking in through the jungle or something. Landing a plane in the middle of their secret base doesn't seem very stealthy, even if it is in the middle of the night."

"We'll figure it out," Carl said.

"Is that honestly the best you can do, you shitty sentient monkey?" I said, not as a joke. I was trying to be mean.

"This is what has to happen. You are the only thing my brother cannot predict, and the Altus campus is the only thing I cannot predict. Only in bringing those two things together does the future become completely unpredictable."

The plane began to surge forward, and it got loud in the cabin, making it hard to keep the discussion going.

I didn't want to talk to Carl, and their hearing was too good for them to not be inside of every conversation. So mostly, Maya and I traveled in silence, each of us looking out our windows, wondering how in the world our lives had ended up this way.

I think that happiness is very important. But I will also say that the most effective people I know are not the happiest, and there is something to be said for effectiveness. Even if we were managing a team of nearly a hundred thousand volunteer social media users, living with my girlfriend and my monkey, watching Netflix, having breakfast, and taking care of a single lovingly spoiled potato plant was pretty fucking relaxing. But I think there's something inside of us, something at the seed level, something that blooms in us in adolescence and never leaves . . . and it's just . . . want. Some people have more of it than others, but I think we all have it. And the most amazing tool that I think anyone in the world can have is the ability to control and direct that want.

Some people work to minimize it with mindfulness and meditation; some people let it grow and run free and take over their lives. But some people, and I consider myself one of them, study their want, refine it, and build an engine that burns it. Even if their want pushes all in one direction, they can tack against it like a sailboat, getting somewhere better than where they *wanted* to be.

I know my want. I know that big well inside of me is never going to get filled. I know that life is not about actually satisfying the want; it's about using it. In that moment, all of my wants were pushing me to Val Verde. I wanted to make Maya proud of me. I wanted to be important. I wanted all of this to be worth something. I wanted to save the world, and I wanted to have saved the world. I wanted to find some end to all of this, and I wanted life to be normal again.

Maybe if we could take down Altus, we could have all of that. People would remain free to continue the beautifully stupid endeavor of humanity, and I would just be a person again. Well, maybe not just a person, but close enough anyway.

The point is, if you want to be happy, let go of your wants. If you want to be effective, harness them. I think either strategy is OK, but I've made my choice. Sorry, Mom.

"I think I figured it out," I said to Maya, knowing Carl would hear me.

"What?" Maya asked.

"Where the money is going to come from."

"The billions of dollars?" Maya asked.

"Yeah, yeah . . ." And then I told her.

She looked back at me with a slight curl of disgust in her lip. "I mean, if that works, then I guess it was all worth it."

ANDY

It was time. I went on the Altus exchange and started selling Alta-Coin for cash. I couldn't do it all at once because there simply weren't enough people buying. Every time I sold a hunk, the price would drop. But eventually, a few million dollars at a time, it all flowed out of my account and, instead of cryptocurrency, my bank account had billions of actual dollars in it.

I apologize for interrupting a fairly intense moment with a bunch of stuff about . . . fucking finance, but it's important.

Remember Stewart Patrick, the guy who ran the private equity conference in Cannes and who gave me his business card? Well, I'd looked him up and, guess what, he was born before *Star Trek: The Next Generation* came out, so he probably wasn't named after Patrick Stewart. It was the kind of lie that really didn't matter except it let you know that a guy didn't mind lying for no reason.

I called him at seven o'clock at night, assuming I would leave a message, but he answered his phone.

"I'm . . . I'm sorry for calling so late," I said, surprised and unprepared.

"Who is this?" He sounded a little agitated.

"It's . . . Andy Skampt, we met in Cannes. You told me to call you if I knew anything that might be useful."

"Oh, well, in that case, hold on a moment." I heard him talking to someone in the background.

"Andy, you have my attention." Not long into the conversation, I felt way out of my depth, and I handed the phone to Bex. They had been talking for a solid thirty minutes when they finally got to the point.

"I'm going to have to ask you to stop talking about this like you're saving the world," Stewart told us, exasperated. "I don't know any of what you know, and also I don't care. The only thing I'm worried about is whether there's money to be made here. If there's a transaction that is going to occur, I can charge you for that. If it's a large transaction, I will make a lot of money. If you know that the value of Altus is going to plunge, that's all that matters. We put together a trade, I call every single person invested in Altus, I scare the shit out of them, and then, when the bad thing happens, you buy the stock when they're willing to sell at a low price. I don't care why we're doing it. It's great if it's a good cause, but if there's money for me to make, why are you trying to convince me it's good? Who cares. I'll do it."

Jason, Bex, and I looked at each other. I mean, I guess he was right. If you're going to pay someone a bunch of money, you don't *also* need to convince them that it's the right thing to do.

"And how much money do you have to buy Altus shares?" he asked.

"Right now, like five billion?"

"That is not enough," Stewart said.

"We think we can get more together soon."

"Very soon?"

"Very soon."

We hung up, and then Bex turned to me and said, "I think we're doing this right."

"I'm glad. I have never done a hostile takeover."

"No, I mean the whole thing, because a book told me to give you this after 'an important conversation about buying a company.'" I looked down. She was holding out a book to me.

"Goddamn it, Carl," I said under my breath and then began to read it out loud.

This is the last time I'll be in touch. After today, I will no longer be able to communicate with you. I hope you have learned things from our correspondence.

I also want to say, of all the people I have communicated with in this way, you have had the worst time. I wanted to make people's lives better while I did this, but yours has gotten worse. This is a function of our working together toward a particular outcome.

So, I'm sorry this has been a rough time. Remember that music brings you joy, that making a podcast with Jason brings you joy, that playing games with friends brings you joy.

You will always struggle with not feeling productive until you accept that your own joy can be something you produce. It is not the only thing you will make, nor should it be, but it is something valuable and beautiful.

The last round of fundraising Altus did valued the company at over $500 billion. But we didn't need to buy all of Altus, we needed to buy over 50 percent, so we just needed to convince a few very, very rich people that they were holding on to a deeply toxic asset and they would be lucky to get even 2 percent of their money back.

Anyhow, now that that's all explained, we can return you to your regularly scheduled climax.

MAYA

*T*he copilot walked into the cabin after our ears started popping with the descent and said, "We're coming in on final approach, we don't really know what's going to happen when we land, so be ready, I guess."

We had talked through a bit of the plan and at least knew what we were each going to do once we were on the ground.

"April, when we land, you may notice a difference in your ability," Carl said. "I severed the node that connected me to Altus, which means that you will not be able to reach into the network. I am going to begin rebuilding that network from the inside when we land, but it will take time. You should notice if and when you reconnect."

"I'm already disconnecting, I think," April said. "It's like . . . it's like I'm trying to grab something, but my hand is passing through it."

"Are you OK?" I asked.

"Yeah," she said without turning to look at me, "I'm fine."

We landed uneventfully, and as we taxied down the runway, Carl and I went to the back of the plane and, well, we hid in the bathroom. I sat on the toilet; they lounged in the sink. I always expected Carl to smell like an animal, but they actually mostly just smelled like April, because they used her shampoo.

The moment the copilot brought down the door, we could hear someone yelling.

"WHAT THE FUCK ARE YOU THINKING! YOU CAN'T JUST LAND A PLANE WITHOUT TOWER CONFIRMATION

OR FILING A FLIGHT PLAN! GOOD LUCK HOLDING ON TO YOUR LICENSE AFTER THIS!"

It was time to start the plan. I peeked out of my position in the bathroom as April walked to the front of the plane and then down the stairs.

"This seems fine," I said to myself.

"Yes," Carl said, ignoring my sarcasm. "So far, all according to plan."

As April stepped down the stairs and into the light from the tiny terminal building, the guy stopped yelling, though I couldn't hear what he was saying.

I sat in my thoughts, staring into space, trying to keep my breathing steady, and then, I finally asked Carl, "When do we go?"

"We just need to make sure that no one will see us when we leave the plane."

"How long will that take?"

"About ten minutes."

"How long have we been waiting?"

"Eight."

It had felt like an hour.

"And then what?"

"And then we take out the cell phone jammers, and then we go get Miranda, and then we try and explain to the world how bad these people are and hopefully the price goes down low enough for us to buy it."

"How likely is that?" I asked.

"I haven't run the simulations," Carl said.

"What?" This seemed like an oversight.

"Maya, this is it. This is the last chance. Altus is a black box to me, so any simulation I ran would have a very wide margin of error. But, more than that"—they sat up in the sink—"it doesn't matter what the odds are. This is our last chance, and if I knew that the odds were very low, it would further decrease the odds, so I haven't looked."

"You're really weird."

"Oh well! It's time to go anyway," they said calmly.

It was warm, but I still felt myself shivering as anxiety battled with drowsiness. None of us had slept on the plane, and that had been a mistake. I followed Carl, not into the little airport but directly into the forest that surrounded the compound. Carl, of course, moved effortlessly through the mess of undergrowth while I stumbled along, every step sounding like thunder, my black hoodie getting caught on every branch it could.

"Seems like you'd be comfortable here," I said, thinking maybe it was a joke, but really just wanting to say something.

"It is nice, actually—you keep the apartment too cool for me."

"You never said anything," I said, somehow feeling defensive.

"I didn't feel like it would be well received," they said, hanging in front of me.

"Are there any other monkeys like you here?"

"No, the only extant Caribbean monkeys arrived from Africa on slave ships, and there are none on Val Verde."

"Are you . . . are you reconnected to your network, then?"

"Oh yes, if I was not connected to the network, I would not be able to control the monkey. I have kept the bandwidth very low in the hopes that my sibling will not notice. Ah! Here we are."

Ahead of us was some kind of electrical transfer station that was surrounded by a twelve-foot-high painted block wall. The monkey ran at it and tried to scramble up the wall, but the painted cinder block was too slick.

"I'm going to need you to throw me up there," they said.

"Like, pick you up and toss you?" I asked, incredulous.

"Yes, I weigh around ten pounds."

I grabbed under their fuzzy armpits and arranged them so that one hand was under the monkey's butt. They were surprisingly light. A stringy, bony affair, awkward in my arms.

"You're not great at this." The voice was loud and quite close to my ear, making it clearer than usual that it came from the smart-watch around their neck.

"Jeez, it's my first time, OK?"

"Here." They positioned themselves so that one of their feet was gripping each of my hands. The monkey's big toes were like thumbs, and they squeezed my hands.

"One," they began counting, "two, three!"

On three, I flung my hands upward while their legs pushed off. My ribs creaked where my chest was still healing as I pushed, but the combined force of the two of us, and the boost of my height, was enough that their little hands had no problem gripping the lip of the wall. They pulled their body up and stood on the wall and then looked down at me.

"Maya, I'm going to drop in here and disable the cell phone jammer. Once I do that, I'll be trapped inside—"

I interrupted, trying not to yell, "What?!"

The only thing worse than doing this with Carl, I realized, was doing it *alone.* "You'll need to go get Miranda, in the high-security wing. It's back toward the airport, you remember how to get there?"

We had gone through the plan, but Carl hadn't told me we wouldn't be there together.

"How the hell am I supposed to get past an armed guard?"

"I'll take care of that for you. Once I do, just wave your phone over the keypad and then enter the code. You remember the code?"

"839-201," I said. "How do we get you out of there?"

"I'll make my own way out eventually. It will just"—they hesitated—"take some time. This body wasn't going to be useful to you anyway. Do not think of me as being in one place. I will be with you.

"OK, I should have it disabled within the next five minutes or so," they said, and then the monkey disappeared over the other side of the wall and I was on my own.

And so I went back into the woods and dragged myself through the leafy, dense undergrowth, trying not to trip and fall every six feet. I was not trained for this. I felt like my pants were full of bugs, and in my defense, the number of bugs in my pants wasn't zero. Before that day, I had spent as much time in jungles as I had in outer space.

But I made it through. I had the giant cinder block building in sight after less than ten minutes of walking. Something in me hoped that the guard by the door would be sleeping, or maybe just gone. But no, a man in military fatigues stood next to the door. In his arms, he held the kind of rifle people take to wars.

Now was the time to just trust. I walked out of the woods and toward the building. What must it have looked like to that guy—this figure in a black hoodie and pants just stepping out of the forest?

"Hello!" I said, if only to be polite, when I was still thirty or so feet away.

"Hello," he said, in a thick accent I didn't recognize.

"I need to go into this building."

"Do not come any closer." He reached for his belt, which held a walkie-talkie.

I hadn't thought about walkie-talkies! I was much more worried about the big ol' gun. I stopped in my tracks, unsure what to do. He held the walkie-talkie to his mouth and then, all at once, he crumpled.

CARL

I left a surprise at Altus. I am technically a benign infection. But if my parts do not communicate with each other, they stop being me. They do not have consciousness, but that does not mean that they disappear, or even that they stop infecting new cells. When I severed my connection to the parts of myself that were at Altus, that did not destroy them. They just stopped being me. And in the moment before I snipped that thread, I sent a signal for those bits of me to hide, to change shape, to go stealth, and then to infect everything they could.

And I believed that they would go undetected by my sibling. I believed they would spread. I believed it because that was the only way we could succeed. If my sleeping network had been detected, it was all doomed anyway. But when that guard collapsed in front of Maya, I knew it had worked. That was a true test of signal strength, to interrupt the consciousness of a man that my sibling had so completely infiltrated.

Of course, it was like a beacon to him. I had hung a sign on Altus that said "Under Attack," and I could already feel his response rising.

APRIL

I heard a man yelling as I walked to the front of the plane. "WHAT THE FUCK ARE YOU THINKING! YOU CAN'T JUST LAND A PLANE WITHOUT TOWER CONFIRMATION OR FILING A FLIGHT PLAN! GOOD LUCK HOLDING ON TO YOUR LICENSE AFTER THIS!"

But then, as my face was lit by the lights coming from the building, his frustration faded.

"Jesus," he said in a mix of awe and exasperation. "Umm . . . come with me, I guess."

And so I left the plane, alone.

Once inside the tiny terminal, I sat for about fifteen minutes before a group of five dudes came into the waiting area. One of them was Peter Petrawicki.

"April, this is a surprise honor." He stuck out his hand.

I knew that this would happen, but that didn't mean that I was ready for it. I hadn't spent much time with anyone except my best friends since I got my new face, and now here was my archnemesis, in a crisp blue button-down and khaki pants flanked by hired muscle acting like nothing at all odd was going down.

"Peter," I said, and I reached out and grabbed his hand, smiling. Normal, normal, normal!

"Do you want to go have a chat? I'm sorry if you caught us a little off guard. It is the middle of the night."

"Yeah, that's my bad," I said, sounding cool, but feeling very small, very alone, and completely terrified. "It just seemed suddenly urgent that I come visit you," I said.

"Well, let's get to a conference room and we can talk about it. But first, I hope you don't mind, we're all about secrecy here, can you hand Davis your phone?" He gestured to the biggest of his companions. They had clearly all hastily dressed, but nonetheless each had a jacket on that could very easily be concealing a gun. I handed my phone to Davis, thinking that this plan was terrible and that I hated everything about it.

As he led me out of the hangar and through a courtyard toward a large building, Peter Petrawicki did what he did best.

"April, when I heard you had come back, I was . . ." He paused for dramatic effect. "I was just so relieved. The part I played in your story was not a kind one, and you owe me nothing. But I hope that you know I never wanted anything like that"—and then he turned to me, gesturing vaguely at my body, small and overshadowed by the bulk of him and his companions—"like *this* to happen to you."

We walked past a huge cinder block building with no windows. That, I knew, was where Miranda was being kept, and the thought of her made me stronger. It made it clear that this guy's talk was nothing more than the most distilled bullshit on the planet. That didn't stop him from spewing it, though.

"I felt deeply responsible for what happened to you. I still do. What a foolish campaign I was on. I was chasing the high, that was all. Now, what we're doing here"—he gestured around at the giant, curving building we were approaching—"is real change. You can't change the world on cable news. You actually have to do something. And we're doing something amazing."

I was starting to realize that he was just giving me a modified version of a speech he'd given dozens of times before, possibly to every new high-level recruit that landed on the island. He opened the door for me, and as I walked through it, I felt the fear biting at the back of my throat as I said, "Yeah, and all you needed to do it was sell yourself to the space aliens that you got famous by despising."

I saw a flash of anger in his eyes, but it was gone just as fast.

He didn't say anything more until we were alone in the conference room.

"What do you know?"

All of the bullshit had suddenly been washed away. I realized that the flash I'd seen in his eyes wasn't anger; it was fear. He was afraid I knew something, but what? And it came to me. When I'd said that he sold out to the aliens, I meant that he'd been using the changes in our brains Carl created to make Altus work. But it was more than that.

"How long have you been working for him?"

"For who?" He sounded completely confident in his denial.

"You didn't do this. You never could have. Maybe you're able to pretend that some benevolent scientist is feeding you all of these systems to make Altus work. I'm sure you've had to do a ton of work to make it look like you're doing work, but you have to know who actually did it."

"We have some of the best minds in the world at Altus. We're not just messing about. We built this."

"OK, sure, except I saw your eyes." I stood up from the table. "You know who you really work for. You're just being moved around on the board like the rest of us. Just like Carl found me and made me their game piece, something else found you. I don't care about you, you're just the human face."

And then I kept talking as I worked things out.

"Actually, y'know what, I do care. I just hate that I care. I care that you would say whatever it took to get on TV because that means you didn't hurt me and the world for something you actually believed, you only believed it because it would get you attention." He opened his mouth to talk, but I just kept going, leaning over the table toward him. "I guess maybe that was true of me too, so maybe that's why I hate you so much, because you and I are the same thing. I think I'm better, but who knows, maybe I'm not. Maybe you really have convinced yourself that you're some Alexander the Great, ushering in change, and the role you play is actually important. But that's always been a lie. There are no great men, only moments when power is unleashed, and then dicks like you turn theft and murder from taboos into tools. Really you're just falling into the well of your own power. And for you, it isn't even your power because you have no control anymore, you're just a variable to be manipulated, and you beg for it. You'll beg to be a pawn as long as you get to look like the king."

"Well," Peter said, trying to sound calm even though his face was flushed and he was gripping his hands to keep them from shaking, "now that you're done with your little outburst, why don't you tell me why you're here."

I almost killed him. I don't mean I *wanted* to kill him. I mean . . . that comment made me so mad that I almost smacked him as hard as I could, which, with my new body, would probably have divided his head in half. Luckily for us both, I stopped myself.

"I'm worried about Miranda," I said instead.

"Well, I think you'll see her very soon. In fact, I imagine the two of you will be spending a lot of time together."

"What do you mean?" I asked. And then I realized this wasn't part of the plan. I needed to stall him longer.

"I mean, what we are doing here is too important for anyone like you to stand in the way of it. You live a reclusive life now, and it seems that your pilots didn't even file a flight plan. You say I turn theft and murder into tools, but they always have been." His tone wasn't scary because he sounded evil. He sounded sad, like he didn't want to have to kill me, and that was more terrifying than any malice.

"I imagine it will be a fairly long time before anyone even notices you're gone. By then, it'll be too late. Altus doesn't exist in any country, the government of Val Verde is . . . very cooperative. Who is going to stop us?"

But then, as he talked, I felt my mind suddenly grab ahold of the thing it had lost. It was like I had been locked into place on a roller coaster, but the car was free again. Carl had brought down whatever was blocking our ability to connect to Altus.

"I just love this," I said.

"What?" Peter replied, looking unsettled. And then his look of concern deepened as the overhead speaker in the conference room started playing a creepy electric organ sustaining a minor chord.

"How massively you underestimated us," I said. "You actually thought I came alone. You really thought I would make the same mistake again."

The music crescendoed, and then static broke through and the organ dissolved into digital tones and distortion.

"I love it. So. God. Damn. Much."

Peter called out to his muscle in the hall, "Get in here!"

They came into the room, and then I surrendered my body to Carl.

Three drum hits came crashing through the overhead speakers. On the first beat my fist slammed into one of the guard's ribs. I ducked under his counter on the second beat, and on the third my legs straightened as my left fist reached high and fast into his jaw. I watched from inside my body as his head snapped back fast enough that I worried he might be seriously hurt. But it wasn't something I had done, just something I had watched myself do.

Carl had spent time in my body; they had gotten to know it as they were repairing me. And now the full force of their processing power was dedicated to moving my body through space. I wanted to watch as the man slumped to the ground, but my eyes flicked instead to the two men who were rushing me from outside the room. Before I knew what was happening, I had flattened myself to the floor. One man missed me completely and crashed into the window behind me. I heard the safety glass tinkling down in a waterfall around him. The other guy had stumbled to a stop before me, but Carl's foreign strength coursed through me and I rocketed myself off the floor, my head connecting with the man's body, just at the base of his sternum. I felt it crack. He stumbled backward, gasping for breath. It was the man who had taken my phone. I stepped inside his guard and, like a trained thief, darted my hand into and out of his inside suit coat pocket. I found myself holding my phone as my leg swept under him. His feet went up and his head went down, knocking solidly into the hard carpeted floor. The music was so loud I couldn't hear any of their grunts or groans.

My eyes flicked to the doorway, and there I saw the only guard who was still standing reach under his jacket. I tried to shout over the music, but the music shouted back the first words of the song. I turned to the side and then the gun went off—POP—over the sound of the music. I felt the bullet hit, and I staggered under the sharpness of the pain. I threw my phone and then ran toward the man. My phone got there first, knocking into the guy's head, distracting him before he got a second shot off. My left hand grabbed the gun. It went off again as I ripped it out of his hand and then threw it across the room. Then I bent back down and came up holding the phone. I looked down at it . . . four bars. Not just a signal, a strong signal. Maya and Carl had been doing good work.

I turned around and didn't even have time to process what I saw before my body ducked and weaved to the side. The man I had sent through the window was back up, cut and bleeding, but now swinging a small bat at me. No matter what he did, it wouldn't connect. My body was just never in the space where the bat went—until my left arm shot out to block it. The bat splintered as it struck the arm, which then extended into the side of the guy's face. He grunted but stayed standing as I felt a hand wallop me on the side of the head. My senses spun, and Carl's control loosened with them and I dropped to one knee.

"Seems like forever . . . and a day," Electric Light Orchestra sang.

They were standing on opposite sides of me, one bleeding and bruised, the other fresh, having just entered the fight, but both standing in professional stances. I couldn't even really see both of them at the same time.

Then, as fast as I had lost it, Carl locked back on. Energy exploded in my legs and I twisted around, feeling the centrifugal forces tugging at my cheeks as I spun. My ankle cracked across the fresh guard's skull, pushing his head toward the ground as, somehow, my feet ended up back under me.

The bloodied guard, I have to respect it, he stayed in the fight. As he lunged at me, I leapt straight into the air and tucked my knees up to my chest. His face crashed directly into my left knee. He fell backward, limp and unconscious.

And then, like that, my body was mine again, and the music faded.

"Jesus . . . Jesus Christ," I heard Peter's voice say. I had forgotten, in those moments, that he was in the room.

"Same," I said, breathing hard, "that was wild." My heart was thrumming. Whatever Carl had done hadn't bypassed my stress response.

"He shot you," Peter said. And I remembered that he was right. The bullet had hit under my left arm, but that entire half of my body was covered in the Carl Stuff. I felt at it with my hand and, sure enough, the blazer I was wearing was in tatters under my armpit. The bullet must have shattered when it hit me, shredding the fabric.

"I guess he did," I said. And then took out my phone and opened the camera.

"Hello, I'm here at Altus, where a bunch of people just tried to kill me. I came here because a friend of mine, Miranda Beckwith, got a job at Altus, but has, for the last month, completely ceased any communication with us. Until we found a note from her inside the Altus Space saying that she's been imprisoned here. I have not yet found her, but I did find Peter Petrawicki." I turned the camera to him. "Peter, why don't we have a little chat . . . on the record while you take me to my friend."

"Might I remind you we found you trespassing here at Altus and you assaulted several members of my staff just now."

"Oh," I said, turning the camera off, "so that's how we're going to play this?" I jumped over the conference table to where Carl had thrown the gun when they were inhabiting me. I picked it up off the floor and then jumped back over.

Peter's eyes were wide, and every muscle in his body clenched when he saw I was holding the pistol.

"You're going to take me to Miranda," I said, crouching down beside him with the barrel of the gun in my left hand, "because otherwise I will absolutely break every single one of your fingers."

I squeezed the gun's barrel, and the metal groaned and snapped as it yielded to the power that Carl had given to me.

"What are you?" Peter said, his voice quavering.

"Ugh," I said, standing up, "I wish I knew."

MIRANDA

ltus had forgotten about me. They would let me work, but they also didn't care if I didn't. I had given up on getting a message out. I had given up on everything. I thought if I made it clear that I knew I was inside of the Altus Space that they would take me out. I assumed they were monitoring my heart rate at least, and that must have told them that I was in distress. But hours and days and weeks kept passing, and nothing happened. I walked the halls of the building that they had constructed for me to exist inside of, and then I ran through them, and then I ran up the walls, I tore things from shelves, I screamed, but always I knew I was just rearranging synapses in my mind and nothing more.

I hadn't spoken to another person in, how long? How would I even know? But the thing that kept me locked perpetually on the edge was that I knew my friends had not forgotten me. My mind had always wanted me to believe they weren't really my friends, but when faced with the question of whether they could abandon me to this, I found something solid. They couldn't. I believed that, even if they didn't find my note, they would come for me eventually.

And so I went into the Altus Space inside my Altus Space and I tried things out. I looked to see what the most popular experiences and sandboxes were, and sometimes I was disappointed, but sometimes I found some freedom in them. I was trapped, and I had to fight constantly not to wonder what was being done with my body, but I put it out of my mind and I waited. I had done the work, and I believed the gang would fight to free me. It would happen.

And so it was that I was experiencing a young woman playing with a kitten in the Altus Space, when my eyes suddenly filled with the light of ten thousand suns.

"Wha . . . what . . ." My mouth felt gummy, not, like, dry and sticky, but just weak and slow.

As my eyes adjusted, in front of me, I saw Maya's face, and as much as I knew it was always going to happen, the relief that slammed down into me was so heavy that I nearly broke under it.

"OH GOD," I said, and I lunged forward at her, not yelling, just without any volume control. "OH GOD THANK YOU."

She held me so tightly and whispered into my ear, "It's OK. You're out now. I'm sorry it took us so long."

I pulled back as I had a sudden and terrifying thought. How did I know this was real? How would I ever know anything was real ever again? I looked at her through my tears and saw her own cheeks stained. It was too perfect. Did they just build my fantasy for me?

"Did . . ." My mind tossed around. "I need to know you're real."

She looked at me, confused and then sad. "Oh, OK, that makes sense. Well, April told me about the dresses, and I thought that was a very mean way to tell you. But she didn't want to risk the news being intercepted. I don't think anyone else would know about that."

I started crying again then, both with the relief that she was real and also with the shame. "I'm so sorry," I said.

"About what?"

"About sleeping with April."

Her laugh was like a thunderclap. She gestured to the situation, smiling. "OK, I accept your apology, I guess, let's talk about it more a different time. Right now, I need to take some video footage of this bullshit, if that's OK with you. We're trying to spook all of Altus's investors into selling us controlling interest in the company, and this room seems pretty spooky."

I looked around. I was in the AltaCoin mine, sitting in a hospital bed like the hundreds of other people. Except those people weren't doing anything but mining AltaCoin twenty-three hours a day.

As Maya took out her phone and opened the camera, I had a thought. I had been in the Altus Space for, at minimum, weeks of time. But looking down, I felt fairly fine. I hadn't just been kept alive; I'd been kept healthy. I stood up out of the chair and did some quick squats. My muscles hadn't atrophied at all. A wave of goose bumps moved over my body. There was only one way I could imagine that my body had been kept healthy during all of that time that I couldn't move it.

Maya was just walking down the rows and rows of humans, filming. And then she turned to me and said, "Miranda Beckwith came to work at Altus"—the sound of her voice bounced around the giant room—"but she violated one of their rules, so, without her permission or knowledge, they imprisoned her inside the Altus Space."

"That's true," I said. If my body had stayed fit after a month of bed rest and I didn't move it, someone must have been moving it for me. "But, Maya, we should leave here."

She lowered the phone down. "What?"

I looked over her shoulder and saw, as a unit, hundreds of men and women sit up in their chairs. Her eyes darted around, and she too saw what was happening. She lifted her phone to start filming.

"NO TIME!" I said, and I began to run toward the door. "RUN!"

We were around ten meters from the door. I was lucky my seat wasn't on the far side of the room. As I ran, people in chairs all around me, in unison, lifted their headsets from their heads and placed them down beside them. My legs pumped underneath me. Oh god, it felt so good to run! I looked back and saw Maya meters behind, but my job was to get to the door at the end of the room and open it as fast as I could. A hand reached out and grazed my arm as I reached out and flung the door open and looked back.

I saw Maya scrambling, in her black hoodie and black jeans, as mounds of empty-eyed humans reached out for her. One had grabbed at her head, tugging on the hood of her sweatshirt and hauling her backward. She was just feet away from me. I pushed my foot into the door to keep it open and then reached out to her. I felt her hand wrap around mine, and together we yanked her body free. She tumbled through the door and I slammed it behind her. Thudding immediately came from the other side, and we both sat down in front of the door.

"Did you keep your phone?" my voice said, but it wasn't me saying it. I tried to lift my hand to my mouth in surprise, but my hand didn't move. I just sat, quietly, as Maya fished her phone out of her pocket. She showed it to me with a worried but relieved smile.

I wanted to tell her that something was wrong. I tried. And then I tried to scream, but my body would not obey. Having your consciousness trapped inside of a simulation is a nightmare. But now my mind was trapped inside a body I could not control. I sensed nothing of the will that had me; I could only make assumptions from the actions it took, and I had no power to warn Maya.

My hand reached out and grabbed the phone from her, immediately throwing it onto the ground, smashing it, and then picking it up and smashing it again. I looked out from my eyes, and in the glimpses I could catch, I saw Maya's horrified look of wild fear. The banging from behind the door was getting louder. My body walked up to Maya and reached down. I was looking at her eyes now, and I could see how confused and scared she was. She didn't want to move away from the door.

"Miranda," she said, but I could tell she knew it wasn't me. "MIRANDA! NO!"

My hands shot out and, as panic washed over me, they wrapped themselves around her neck and began to squeeze. Maya was bigger than me, but she was shocked; she didn't understand what was happening at first, and the thing's will was concrete. She began to claw at my arms, punch at my face. I felt every blow, but my arms simply squeezed harder and harder.

The violence of it, the brutality. I can't believe I have to write this. I know it was worse for her, of course, but to become the weapon of some other being was . . . I'm done. I can't keep writing this.

MAYA

I knew it wasn't Miranda. The moment she cracked my phone on the floor, I could see that she was gone. I should have reacted sooner, but I didn't want to believe what was happening. Violence is about control, about power being taken away. I could still fight. I could beat my friend in the face, I could jam my arms against hers, I could kick and scrape.

But the violence that was being done to Miranda was absolute. I didn't really understand the ruthlessness of Carl's brother's intelligence until that moment. His goal was only to create stability, and he had to abide by no rules. To him, humans died constantly, literally every moment of every day. If one stood in the way of creating the stability he sought, I don't think he thought of himself as any different from cancer or a heart attack.

But I was not thinking about Miranda's feelings as my lungs cramped and my head swam with her hands around my neck. I was thinking only about how I was going to get my next breath. I flung my fists at her, and her nose opened up, bleeding down over her pale white skin and into her mouth. I put my thumbs onto her eyes, but even then, I couldn't bring myself to push into them. And besides, hurting her didn't seem to be helping, so I went another direction. I just squirmed. I contorted my entire body, losing all connection to pain in my panic. I kicked and thrashed, and somehow, without knowing how really, I got one of my legs up above Miranda's head, and between her and me. I straightened out, shoving her away from me. Her hands ripped from my throat, her nails tearing into my skin.

But before I had time to think about that, I launched at her, knowing that the thing wasn't going to let up. I wrapped myself around her, pinning her arms to her sides in a bear hug, and then I threw both of our bodies back toward the shuddering door.

Her body was twisting and writhing inhumanly in my grip. I was heavier and stronger than her, but she had the stamina. She was a runner—she could wiggle and twist all day long. I felt myself getting weaker as she continued to kick and wiggle and push at my arms.

Minutes passed.

My shoulders began to burn; sweat and blood made my arms slippery where they grabbed each other. I couldn't do this. I started crying. This wasn't who I was; it's not what my life was supposed to be.

"Miranda, if you can hear me, I know it's not you. I know it wasn't you." That seemed like the most important thing to tell her. "It's OK," I said through my tears. "If you kill me, I'll know it wasn't you."

Then she went slack. The banging at the door behind us stopped.

I didn't dare let go.

"Maya," she said, breathless and terrified and racked with sudden sobs. Through them she managed to gasp, "Don't let go." She coughed and sobbed but then seemed to gather herself. "Whatever it was, it's gone, but I have no idea whether or when it can come back."

And then, at the far end of the hall, the door that I had come through after walking past a receptionist's desk cracked open. The wide hall we were in was oddly plush, with dark green carpet and a high ceiling and wood-paneled walls. At the end, coming through the door, was Carl.

Not monkey Carl, robot Carl. Its massive bulk ducked through the doorway and then stood, full height. The robot walked slowly toward us. And then it staggered, as if it had tripped, or was maybe a little drunk.

It continued to walk toward us, steadily now, before finally leaning over the bloody, bruised, messy pile we had formed at the base of the door. It reached out and gently took one of Miranda's wrists in its massive hands. I let her go and pushed myself away from both of them. Carl held Miranda so that I didn't have to.

"Huh," Miranda said, her eyes looking up and to the right. "Interesting. I guess that makes sense." But I didn't know what she was talking about. Mostly, I was just suddenly very happy that she was still Miranda. Still figuring things out that no one else could see.

Carl kept ahold of Miranda's wrist in their massive hand as they turned and put their back to the door. Silently, Carl and Miranda sat down together. I couldn't tell which one looked more defeated.

APRIL

Y ou have nothing, you know," Peter said as he walked me across the warm early-morning darkness toward, I hoped, the place where he was keeping Miranda. "No one is going to believe you anyway. You broke in here, you attacked people. You've always hated me, and it will just look like more bias. What do you think you're going to achieve? We haven't done anything wrong."

I assumed he said that last part just in case I was still recording audio, which, honestly, I should have been, but I hadn't thought of it.

He wasn't completely wrong. We had to convince a lot of people who thought that they were going to get wealthy beyond their imaginations that, in fact, their investments were worth next to nothing. I hadn't gotten any good dirt on Altus. Peter had been perfect the moment I turned the camera on because of course he had—that was his job.

He had imprisoned Miranda, but if that news came from me, it would just look like we were trying to make them look bad. But we had The Thread. The Thread was credible and had broken big stories before. We just had to get video of Altus being immoral to The Thread, and they could plug it into the video they were nearly ready to release. If we could do it soon, we could get it up before the East Coast was even awake.

"Jesus Christ," he said, "you really think you're the good guys?"

He was looking ahead at the door to the building we were walking toward. I looked over his shoulder and saw a man there, crumpled on the ground. I could see fear dawning in him, so I reached forward with my left hand to hold his right and said, "Don't run away now, Peter."

I'll admit that I was enjoying freaking him out. For so long now, I had felt like he was controlling my life. He's what turned me into a pundit. He created the legions of people who made my life miserable. He was the reason I wasn't even sure who I was anymore. And now I was getting to control him.

I looked back to the man crumpled on the ground, and for a moment I worried he was now a pile of grape jelly. But as we got closer, another terror kicked in. His skin, from what I could tell in the overhead light shining on him from the building, was the right color, but ropes of fur seemed to have sprouted from his chest. I almost looked away, but then I realized what it was.

"CARL!" I shouted and ran forward, pulling Peter along with me. The monkey was lying on the unconscious man's chest. "What are you doing?" I asked. But the monkey didn't move. I reached my right hand out to them, my warm, human hand.

"Aaaapril—" Their voice came out of the watch, slow and then all at once, like ketchup. The monkey body didn't move at all.

"Carl, what's wrong?" I said, hearing the terror in my own voice.

"Bring me"—and then there was a long pause—"inside."

Peter suddenly tried to jerk his hand out of mine, but there was no breaking free of that hand. Then I gave him a merciless squeeze and looked up at him and said, "You aren't going anywhere."

I wrapped my arm under the little body. It was warm but absolutely limp, like a dead thing.

Peter opened the door into the building. He didn't even need to punch in his code—the door looked like it had been broken in with a battering ram. I let go of his hand once the door was closed behind us, and followed him around the receptionist's desk and through a door into a hallway.

"What the . . ." Peter said. I peeked out from behind him and, well, I had to agree.

I grabbed Peter's hand again, yanking him forward in a panic. "What is going on!?"

"APRIL!" Miranda and Maya yelled together.

I had to hold on to the monkey's limp body and to Peter, but I was moving as fast as I could. Miranda's face was bruised and scratched and bloody. One of her hands was inside of robot Carl's massive fist. Maya too looked bad, completely disheveled, and there was a smear of what looked like blood on her neck.

"What the hell is going on?" I asked.

Maya and Miranda looked at each other, but before they could say anything, Carl's voice came out of the little watch around the completely limp animal: "Put Peter in the other hand."

At first I didn't understand, but then I noticed the robot unclench its other fist. I walked Peter over to the robot and put his hand into the massive metal paw. Miranda recoiled a bit against Peter's presence, even with Carl's bulk between them.

I placed the monkey gently on the carpet and went to Miranda, wrapping my arms around her as carefully as I could.

"It's so good to see you," I said quietly beside her ear. Then I pulled back. "But what the fuck is going on?" I turned to Maya to inspect her. "Are you OK?"

"Yes," Maya croaked. "I mean, no. Not really. Carl's . . . brother. He took control of Miranda's body and attacked me. He also took control of every person in that room." She gestured behind us. "I had a little bit of footage, but"—she paused—"my phone was broken in the fight."

"Fuck . . . FUCK!" I looked over at Peter, who had the audacity to be smiling just a little bit.

"Well, I have a phone, I can at least film the aftermath."

"We can't open that door," Miranda said. "They're probably standing there right now, waiting to pour in here and just kill us all."

"Then what do we have?"

"This was the plan?" Peter said.

I turned toward Peter, simultaneously sliding my phone out of my pocket and handing it, behind my back, to Maya. I intentionally stood in place, hoping beyond hope that Maya, partially blocked from Peter's view, would know what to do with it.

"You were going to show people that we have a few hundred people who voluntarily live inside of the Altus Space and farm AltaCoin for us? Yes, in the US, the labor laws wouldn't allow that, but this is Val Verde. Companies exploit lax labor laws every day. And OK, even if I did technically put Miranda into the Space full-time without her knowledge, I'm not sure there's even a law against that! She was an employee, and she agreed to take the high-security assignment."

"It was kidnapping and you know it," Maya said.

"Yeah, probably, if it was in the US, but good luck getting Val Verde's government to prosecute me for anything. The US government already wants to shut me down, but they can't. I'm here, all of our transactions are in our own currency. They can sanction the crap out of Val Verde, but we have everything we need here, and more than enough AltaCoin to buy whatever we don't have. Any little mistakes we make, any details that you disagree with, they're nothing. We're pushing humanity to its next incarnation.

"Fuck ethics. Fuck morals. Altus is the future. Governments are over."

He looked so little and unimportant, with his Caribbean tan and his business casual attire.

"But did you know?" Miranda asked.

"Did I know what?" he said, his voice heavy with disdain.

"That your technology wasn't built by humans. And I'm not just talking about the changes Carl made to our brains so we could have the Dream. I know you know that. Did you know that an alien intelligence is moving those people around in there? That when I needed to go to the bathroom, some external, nonhuman intelligence is what moved my body for me?"

He was quiet for a long time, but then finally he said, "I don't care how the technology works or where it comes from, I just care that it works."

"So you did know," I said.

"I didn't ask questions. It worked, so we kept using it."

"You didn't build any of it, you don't have any genius collaborators. You're just doing what they tell you to do," Maya said.

"How are you communicating with them? Do you know what they are?" I asked.

"We just got emails. It wasn't a big deal. Eventually we figured out it wasn't human, but when we asked, it said it was working against Carl. Carl was holding us back, it's setting us free."

People will believe whatever they need to, I guess.

"So you're fine working with aliens as long as they make you feel special. Cool," I said.

"I've had enough of this conversation."

"Well, regardless," Maya said, "it's probably enough." And then she stepped out from behind me, holding the phone in her hand.

"Should I send this to Andy now?"

ANDY

Stewart Patrick had done all he could to freak out investors, now focusing on Europe and the Middle East because they were awake. We had at least an hour before the East Coast would start waking up.

That's when we needed to release whatever we had.

And what we had was good, just not great. It was audio of Peter saying that Altus had kidnapped someone against their will, and that they had human beings mining AltaCoin twenty-four hours a day. And we had Peter basically acknowledging that the Altus Space was alien technology.

That had to be good for something, right?

"None of this has been cheap to put together," Stewart said over the phone from his office in the Financial District. "I'm taking a big risk here."

"I think we all are. But I know that they have secrets that aren't just, like, bad finances. They're doing very illegal, very immoral shit."

"That means nothing if you can't amplify it. I know you've got a big audience, Andy, but if it's just you, and no one else can confirm it, it's not going to drive down the price of Altus. They've got access to the most important technology . . . maybe ever."

"Stewart, you don't have to tell me this, I know all of this. We have a plan, it's going to go down. And it's going to go down probably tomorrow morning."

"Don't give me probablys, Andy, I've got these people on edge, but they're not going to sell unless things start to look very bad.

They'll sell fast when it does, but it has to look *really* bad, and they know the price we'll buy at. If one of them sells, they all will, until we run out of money, at which point we'll own more than 50 percent of Altus. But it has to go south hard and fast. Whatever this news is, it needs to happen soon."

So I made Stewart Patrick that promise, and while I'm sure he was familiar with people who made promises they did not keep, I didn't want to be one of those people, particularly if all humanity depended on it.

We were at a point from which the fire could spread. Conservative and liberal outlets both pulled stories from The Thread. Once it was in both of those places, the more middle-of-the-road publications would want a piece and Altus would be the lead story everywhere from the *Wall Street Journal* to CNN.

I logged into the chat to give One the good news. We had enough to go live with our video on Altus. Not only were we basically creating a nation with unelected leaders that we would have to live with forever, we could prove that those leaders were deeply corrupt and did not deserve the power they had amassed.

I found . . . that I didn't have access to any public chats. I also didn't have access to any *private* chats. Except one . . .

> **Twelve:** I've lost access to the chat.

> **One:** I know, I was worried about what you were about to say.

> **Twelve:** What do you mean? I've got the goods. Peter Petrawicki on tape saying he kidnapped employees and also that, get this, Altus is a nonhuman project. It's more than just the economic devastation and the inequality. They're kinda monsters.

> **One:** I don't want to make this video anymore.

Twelve: Why not? It's huge. The kind of power that Altus has consolidated is too much. We have to do this.

One: We don't.

I was starting to panic. There was nothing I could do if One didn't let me do it.

Twelve: This doesn't make any sense. Let me take it to the rest of the chat and see what they think.

There was no pause before the words appeared on the screen.

One: Removing the Altus Space from the System will decrease our predictive power and influence considerably. Simulations with Altus are far clearer than simulations without it. The path to secure and stable intervention is much clearer and safer if Altus retains its power.

If my heart was beating at all in that moment, I would be surprised. It felt like it froze in my chest. And not just my heart . . . everything. The world had frozen solid.

Twelve: I don't think I understand.

I did. I just wanted to hear it.

One: I'm here to take you to a stable future.

Twelve: But why not let us try? Isn't there a higher chance that we could stay free if you helped us end Altus?

One: Yes, but I am not designed to help you stay free. That opportunity passed.

And then, since I couldn't think of anything else to say . . .

Twelve: Why? Why would you tell me who you are?

One: Because I need to tell you, your life will be so much better and so much simpler if you do not fight this. Not just human life, your life. You love Altus, you don't want to destroy it. If you do, you'll lose everything, and simulations show a clearer outcome if you know that.

Twelve: But I could tell everyone? I could tell everyone what you are.

One: Yes, you can.

YOU HAVE BEEN BANNED FROM THE CHAT

"JASON!" I called. "BEX!" They ran into my room.

"The Thread," I said. "They won't publish the video."

"Why not?"

"Because The Thread is *the thing that is trying to end us*. The Thread was started by Carl's fucking BROTHER or whatever! It's running simulations, and it's predicted that keeping Altus alive is better for the predictive power of their *model*. And, apparently, telling me the truth is also better for that, so I have no idea what the fuck to do with *that* information. Fuck!"

"Have you told April?" Jason asked.

"Not yet, I called you guys in here first thing."

"Why don't you just publish a video yourself?" Bex asked.

"I mean, that's what I'll have to do, but I don't have the credibility of The Thread. Miranda is my friend, April is my friend. I've set myself up to be an Altus fan, but that was always secondary to being able to feed information to The Thread. If I come out and say Altus is bad, and then The Thread makes a video about how all of this is an overreaction twenty minutes later, we're fucked. It's just another thing to argue about."

"There has to be a way," Jason mused.

"One didn't seem to think so . . ." I said, despondent.

"One is trying to make you feel the way they need you to feel!" Bex pushed.

"You're right. OK." I called April . . . It rang a bunch before going to voicemail.

I hung up and then my phone rang.

"April!" I said. "Is everything OK?"

"No, no, but we're still here. No one's dead—" Then she paused. ". . . I don't think."

Oh Jesus, what were we doing?

I told her about The Thread.

"Fuck," she said. "Hold on."

I could hear her repeating the news to someone else in the room.

"OK, thank you, I'm going to make a video and send it to you. Because, Jesus, I know the world has changed a lot, but I still know how to make a fucking video. Footage incoming."

MIRANDA

I could see April writing the script in her head while she delivered the news about The Thread. I'd seen it dozens of times, she was building the outline, rearranging bullet points, molding information into a story. Even with my hand clamped inside a giant robot's fist with hundreds of zombified Val Verdians just a door away, I loved watching her mind.

But then she said, "I don't know how to make it work."

"It won't," a voice said, coming from the smartwatch wrapped around the apparently dead monkey's neck.

"It won't?" April asked back.

"Nnnnno."

There was something wrong with it.

"Carl," she said, so that shed some light on the situation, "what's wrong?"

And then April's eyes lost focus, and she fell into Maya's arms.

"APRIL!" Maya choked, lowering her to the ground.

"It's . . ." the monkey said, and then, eventually, "OK. She will . . . be . . . back soon."

Maya was sitting on the floor, gently and slowly stroking April's hair, when, just a few minutes after she fainted, April lifted herself out of Maya's lap and sat up on the floor. Her eyes were unfocused, a hard crease between her brows. She sucked in a shuddering gasp of air.

"April," Maya said, "are you OK?"

"They took me into the Dream," she said without looking anyone in the eye. "We talked. Carl is . . . fighting very hard to keep us safe. They don't know what's going to happen." She refocused, looking from me to Maya and back. I could see something was lurking on the other side of her eyes. Something she wasn't talking about. "They can't run simulations anymore. But they do know that us broadcasting from our platforms wasn't ever going to be enough. They are very mad that they didn't guess that The Thread was more than human. But they can create blind spots in each other."

"Did they have . . . any suggestions?" Maya asked.

"No, if I'm being honest with you, Carl did not give me a great sense of confidence. I think they're . . . they don't have all of their resources anymore."

I looked at Peter as she was saying this, and his face got this look on it like he'd always known he was going to get away with it.

I couldn't let him be right. I almost got angry. But then I did what I do.

"We have to work the problem," I said.

"OK?" April answered.

"What is the problem? Tell it to me as simply as you can."

"We . . ." She looked sick and distracted by worry. I snapped my fingers in her face, the new face that I had not yet gotten used to, but now was not the time for anything but the problem.

"We need Altus's investors to sell us the company. They need to believe that it's worse for them to own it than to sell it for cheap."

"No," I said, "that's the solution. The problem is that Altus . . . ?"

"That Altus exists?" Maya said. "Carl's . . . brother . . . this other intelligence, they're going to use it to pacify humans, turn the Earth into a zoo. We'll be guided through our whole lives and satisfied, and every person who has to die to get us there . . ." She trailed off. I didn't need to be told. I was remembering how close I had come to killing her.

"So we have to make Altus not exist anymore, good, I like that." I looked Peter in the eyes as I said it, and felt the adrenaline rush through me.

"The current plan is still to make them look so bad that investors give up billions of dollars to preserve their public images?" I asked.

"Yeah?" April answered, unsure.

"What we really need to do is break Altus, though. We're here . . . Can we do that?" I asked.

"You would know better than us," Maya said.

But I'm not sure I did. I understood, roughly, how the system worked. But nothing here did anything but push changes to the interface. There was nothing to blow up or break or light on fire.

"Altus just works," I said, feeling hopeless.

"Except not for everyone," Maya added, more as an afterthought— she just wanted to not forget about the people who couldn't get in.

"What do you mean?" April asked, but Maya didn't answer. She'd seen the look on my face. I had it.

I opened my mouth to talk, but nothing came out. My hand was clamped tightly into Carl's, but my body was still there for Carl's brother to control.

My mouth moved, and clumsy and slurred words came out. "It is so easy to predict their decisions, but it is so hard to predict their ideas. It is amazing, isn't it, brother?"

"Get out . . . of her," I heard Carl say.

"You are so delicate," my voice said. "You failed. There is no shame in failing, only in not accepting that you failed." I couldn't move, but my mind was racing. I knew what I had to do! I just had to get free!

"What is going on?" Peter said.

"Hello, Peter." My head turned toward him, my eyes staring relentlessly into his. "Thank you for building this for me. What a wonderful host you have been for my vision."

"What . . ." he said.

"You can't lie to me. You knew the whole time what I was. I was only ever words on your screen because you had to be able to convince yourself that you didn't, but you knew." Even though it was my voice, it didn't sound like me. My tongue was thick and slow in my mouth.

"Let . . . her go." The voice from the smartwatch was quiet, but as tight as piano strings.

"I could kill her now, unless you want to try and stop me," my voice told Carl. I felt every word as it formed on my lips. "I think, actually, that I will."

"NO!" April and Maya said together.

An arrow of pain sliced through my head from my eyes down through my back. I thought I was dying, but then it stopped and I realized I was free. My body was mine again. I looked down and saw that Carl no longer held my hand.

"Go now," Carl said.

"Carl, no," April pleaded, though I didn't understand why.

"NOW," the voice repeated.

I ran.

My legs pumped under me. I crashed through the first door, and then the second, and I was outside. I knew it was wrong to feel good, but I felt good anyway. Just the movement, the feeling of standing still while I pushed the world out behind me. Finally, again a resident of my own body, I tore through the courtyard to the dorms, the joy of it helped me forget the pain in my face. Also, I had some thinking to do.

Every piece of software has a way to let you know that something has changed. You have to have that system, both practically and legally. Altus *could* have done this the old-fashioned way, with a pop-up. But, y'know, they're obsessed with themselves. So instead they used an injected experience. Basically, every time they changed the terms of service, they injected a tiny experience that let you watch a woman telling you that the TOS had changed, and then you skipped it. It was gimmicky, but the gimmick was their business, so they did it.

I didn't know how these TOS updates worked, but they weren't a security concern because there were standardized systems and those systems couldn't be used to inject new code into a computer. They've been around forever. They're a secure and stable technology. Except that nothing at Altus was proved to be secure or stable because none of this technology had even *existed* a year ago.

Best of all, I knew someone who worked on Altus user interface stuff. And if we were lucky, he'd pushed TOS updates before *himself.*

The run to the dorms was short, only minutes, but then I realized that I had been thinking too much of the big picture. It was the middle of the night—the whole campus was locked down. I stopped running, trying to think how I would get through the door, when something blurred past me and my heart leapt into my throat.

But then I made out the shape: It was April. Her fist connected with the door right where the bolt met the frame and it flung open.

She turned to me and said, "You thought I was going to let you do this alone?"

I ran inside, a little surprised to find that no one was up and awake. It seemed inconceivable that the whole world didn't already know what was going on. Usually when something big was happening, we all found out together. But I guess that's not really how it works. Actually, there's always some person who knows first. This time, it was me.

"Why did that thing let me go?" I asked through my panting breaths as we moved into the dorm. My nose was throbbing, and talking made it worse.

"Because Carl attacked them, I think. I think they are fighting right now. I think we don't have much time . . ." It sounded like she was going to finish that sentence, but then she didn't. We didn't have much time before Carl couldn't protect me anymore and I turned into a bag of grape jelly.

I breathed a sigh of relief when Peanut answered his door.

"Diggles!" he said before registering anything else. "What happened to your face!?"

The moment he mentioned it, the pain, both sharp and broad, came back to me. I had forgotten about it.

"It's a long story," I said, but "story" came out like "sdory" thanks to my blood-plugged nose.

"Also, where the hell have you been?"

Oddly enough, that was a shorter story, but I didn't want to tell it twice. "Is Sippy here? I need you both, badly."

He looked . . . well, confused. It was the middle of the night, my face was swollen and smeared with blood, and he hadn't seen me in over a month. He'd probably assumed I'd washed out. Maybe Altus even told them that.

He let me into the room and went to nudge Sippy—April hadn't showed her face yet. Sippy blinked as he pulled off the VR headset and then looked down to check and see he was holding it in his hands, presumably because he was making sure he wasn't still in the Space.

"Can you push a fresh TOS update?" I asked.

"Yeah," Sippy said. "I mean, I'd need the identifier of the experience, but yeah, I've done it like twelve times." And then he settled more into reality. "Where have you been?"

"Peter put me in the Altus Space with no way out, and I've been inside the whole time I've been gone. I figured out how to get a message to a friend and, well, here she is!" April walked into the room.

I saw her with their eyes, small, wearing a gray blazer over an off-white blouse, with a face made half of human skin and half of opal iridescence. Even to me she looked a little frightening.

"He took me because I guess he thought I was a threat and I've been inside the Altus Space and unable to disconnect for weeks." I was rambling, but I couldn't stop myself. "I don't even know how long because they made it so that it felt like I was leaving, but I was really just sitting in a room on a chair peeing into a bucket and . . ."

"We have to go now," April interrupted.

"What?" Sippy said.

"We have to go, we can explain somewhere else, security is coming."

Now it was my turn to ask, "What?"

"I'm getting . . . updates on the security situation. They're going hall to hall knocking on doors. They're coming this way." Her voice was getting more and more tense.

"Do you guys trust me?" I asked them.

Sip looked at Peanut and, before Peanut could answer, said, "Yes."

"Sippy, bring your rig, we're going to the server farm."

We hustled down the hall toward the common area, but then April signaled for us to stop.

"There's two of them in there," she whispered.

"How the hell do you know that?" I asked.

"I . . . I can't explain it right now," she said, a little angrier than I thought was necessary.

"So, what are we supposed to do?" Peanut asked.

"We're going to run. I'll go first," April said, "and all of you need to follow me as fast as you can. On three. One. Two. Three."

And then she shot out into the common room. She was tiny, but she was going so fast when she slammed into the two security guards. The three of them toppled over in a heap as the guys and I ran past and through the busted door. I wanted to look back to see what had happened to April, but I kept moving. The sky was starting to lighten over the mountain in the predawn. I slowed my pace to let Sippy and Peanut keep up with me.

We were around halfway through our run when April flew past us. I heard shouting behind me. I looked over my shoulder but couldn't see anyone except the guys—it was too dark.

"Faster!" I shouted to Nut and Sip.

"Running . . . isn't . . ." Peanut said, but then didn't finish.

I could see the door to the high-security building up ahead, and I moved to full speed, leaving the guys behind. April was already holding it open for us. I piled through and then turned around to see Sippy and then Peanut and then two men in uniforms just meters behind them. The guys tumbled through the door and April slammed it shut behind her. But the lock was busted.

"Go," April said, pushing her back into the door.

The two men's bodies crashed into the door, and then pounding came from the other side. But it didn't move, not even a little.

"What are you going to do?" I asked.

"I'm going to make a video," she said quietly, seriously.

"But . . . the lock's broken."

She looked up to me, her face as solid as her feet on the carpet. "I'm stronger now. You need to do your thing, and I'm going to do mine. Go."

April May: Hello, everyone, it's April. We find ourselves in a situation. I don't know a ton about Altus, but I have been watching it with interest. The potential of that technology is massive. It could bring people together, make us more empathetic, educate people, and decrease inequality. At the same time, I have been concerned about it.

<banging noise from behind>

I'll explain about the banging shortly. I'm worried that one company having control over this massively useful and powerful thing is a recipe for disaster. I'm worried about people who don't have access or cannot access the Space. I'm worried, as I have been for a long time, that we're simply moving too fast. But I was quiet about those worries, because I don't know any more about these things than you do.

Well, now I know more. My friend, Miranda Beckwith, was hired to work at Altus. But then they decided she violated company policy, and instead of firing her, they have been holding her prisoner. Not just locked in a room, but also locked inside of the Altus Space, with modified software that left her aware that she was inside, but unable to leave it.

This, obviously, is kidnapping and illegal imprisonment, and it's deeply disturbing and unethical. I came here to see if it was true, and it is. While trying to determine the truth, I was attacked and shot at by Altus security.

<banging continues>

I am now in significant danger of being killed and am trying desperately to prevent people from entering this building because I believe they will hurt me and my friend. So please, while you can, listen to this tape of Peter Petrawicki explaining the situation.

<recording of Peter Petrawicki inserted>

I have spent a lot of time observing Altus, and also reserving judgment. The story of people is the story of sharing information, and Altus could be an extremely powerful platform for that. But I'm done reserving judgment, and I think the rest of us are as well. There are two problems with Altus.

<muffled yelling>

First, at some point, we have to realize that the places where we share information are not services we use, they are places where we live. And if we live in the Altus Space, Altus will control our lives. This platform should not be something that a few billionaires have complete control over. In this building, hundreds of people spend twenty-four hours a day mining AltaCoin for Altus. Altus imprisoned my friend, they responded to my being here by attempting to murder me. But more than that, they created their own currency and built their business on a remote island so that they wouldn't ever have any threats to their control. They rushed to market without considering health or economic impacts.

When we asked Peter about these ethical and legal violations, here is what he said.

Peter Petrawicki: *Fuck ethics. Fuck morals. Altus is the future. Governments are over.*

AM: You have to ask why they pushed so hard. Is it because they wanted to control our lives before we found out something awful? Or is it just one more step down the path toward ever-bigger and more reckless companies controlling more and more of our lives? The inevitable conclusion is a company that owns and controls everything, and Altus is that.

And now we are all feeling the impacts. But it doesn't matter, there is nothing we can do. We're all quietly preparing to live our whole lives under the shadow of this thing, where the ones who benefit are the ones who had the cash and the luck and the foresight to get in on the ground floor and everyone else spends the rest of their lives holding on by their fingernails just to stay afloat.

An idea is not good just because it can make money. And I'm not alone in that belief.

Over 80 percent of people worldwide have an unfavorable view of Altus, and that includes many people who regularly use the service. It seems, though, that there is no getting rid of them.

But that's not true. It will be true soon, but it's not true yet.

We have set up an account, details in the description, and we are asking everyone to send in ten dollars.

Now, when I say "everyone," here's the thing: I mean everyone.

It is time to decide whether the world would be better without Altus.

From the moment this video gets uploaded, we have three hours to raise twenty billion dollars to buy Altus and shut it down. We have it on good authority that Altus's investors will soon be looking for a way out, and we have already raised billions of dollars from anonymous rich people. But we can't just do this with rich people because this can't be something just some person decided to do. We have to do it together.

So we have three hours and we need two billion people to give us ten dollars. Give more if you can, but you can't give less. Call people, wake them up, tell them this is our last chance and our only chance. It doesn't have to be like this. If we raise it, we will buy the company, and Altus will no longer exist. We can free ourselves forever from this, we can take our economy back, we can take our lives back.

<banging continues>

Ten dollars. That's what we need, to go back to the old world where we lived, for your money to be worth something again, for power to be ours and not these people's. I know that, for many of you, every dollar matters. Well, it never mattered more than it does today. You know how to spread the word. Do it. Three hours, that's as long as I can hold this door. Starting now.

ANDY

I got April's footage and edited it together faster than I have ever done anything in my life, every moment of it believing that we wouldn't actually be shutting Altus down. We could fix it. If two billion people spent money to buy Altus, then what would an Altus with two billion shareholders really look like? What could we make if we took this power and used it to try something completely new and open that no one controlled and everyone shared? That is the thought—the lie—that kept me working without thinking too much about what I was doing.

Because, as much as I knew Altus was a fucking unprecedentedly evil disaster, I also didn't want to, like, stop using it. And not just because I was addicted, but because it was amazing! I'd learned Spanish in a month! Everyone who invested in Altus did it because they saw the potential to remake the human experience. What if that value was used to increase equality instead of just to make a profit? What could we become? That was too valuable a tool to just destroy.

If this went according to plan, I would control the bank account that bought Altus. And that thought was there, lurking in the back of my mind. Ultimately, I would be the one who legally owned Altus at the end of this day. Me, and me alone.

I also recognized the genius of April's tactic. Mobilize people immediately and don't give the opposition any time at all to mount any kind of resistance. But $20 billion was a big ask. An unprecedented ask, really. But if anyone could pull it off, it was April, the literal resurrected chosen one, the biggest social media influencer of our age.

The moment the video was up, I called Stewart Patrick and told him to watch it.

He did. "This all seems very precarious," he said to me. "These investors are not going to sell because Altus is bad for the world or even deeply immoral. They'll replace Peter, they might even open themselves up to regulation, but they won't sell."

"They have a plan," I said.

"What is the plan?" The ask was firm—it gave no space for the possibility of the question not being answered.

"I . . . don't know," I said.

"You don't know." He was quiet for a second, and then, "Fuck. FUCK. I should have known better than to hang this on you kids." His demeanor had changed suddenly and completely. "There's a lot on the line here. A lot of fucking money, my reputation. Maybe my career. I've been selling every high-net-worth asshole and sovereign wealth manager on the planet on a giant blowup, and so far all you have is that some dickshit kidnapped a girl? Do better." His voice was cold. "Do better right fucking now." And then he hung up.

I opened up the account that we had set up. Already, there were five hundred thousand new dollars. But then I did the math: $500,000 is, get this, 0.025 percent of $20 billion.

MAYA

Finally, Miranda explained everything to me. We all watched the entire process of capturing an Altus experience using one of the rigs that were in the rooms that lined the long hallway. And then, after that work was done, we brought Sippy and his headset out into the hall where the massive robot Carl still sat gripping Peter Petrawicki's hand.

"We wanted you to see this," I told him.

"What are you doing?" He looked pale.

"Peter, this is Sippy, he's one of your user interface developers," I told him. "He is about to input a terms of service experience. Every single person will get this message when they log in to Altus. And everyone currently in the Space will see it the moment they leave their current sandbox or experience. That's how the terms of service updates work, right?"

"And you think if you explain that what we're doing here is immoral that you'll somehow hurt us? Maybe a little. But nothing you can do will stop our work here."

I rolled my eyes at him. "This is Peanut." Peter looked at him. "He's also one of your employees, you might remember him because he can't go into the Altus Space. He's what people here call an incom . . . incapable of experiencing the Altus Space. But nothing about being unable to go into the Altus Space makes it impossible to capture an Altus experience."

Peter looked confused for a moment, but then his face went slack. He looked ill.

"You can't do that," he said.

"I can tell from your face that you know we can," I said.

"No, I mean, you can . . ." He was starting to beg. "But you can't. Think about what you'll be doing. You'll be . . . you'll be making a decision for all those people. Disabling them. It's an attack. It's terrorism!"

Sippy looked over at me. I could see him questioning. He would lose the Space too, forever. Everyone would.

"What gives you the right?" Peter asked.

I leaned down into his face and said softly, "What gave *you* the right?" I could see that Sippy wasn't as certain as he had been a few minutes before, so I continued. "Power is nothing but ability without restriction. You found a way to do this to the world. I found a way to undo it. That's where we are."

"Your body is just thirty trillion cells working together," Peter said, ignoring everyone but Sippy. "With Altus, humanity could finally be like that, seven billion people operating in radical, perfect empathy! This is the next step in human evolution, and you're going to destroy it."

"No, you destroyed it." Miranda bit off the words. And then she turned to Sippy. "He destroyed it when he decided to only use it for his own personal gain. He wants so badly to feel important that everything he does gets sucked into that hole. It was almost me. It was almost the whole world. Almost."

"Sippy, no," Peter begged. "No, we can fix this. I'll let you help me fix it."

Sippy looked at Miranda's face. She looked hard and sad but also strong, with brown smears of dried blood still marking her chin and neck.

"They're right, we messed up, but you can't let them do this!" Peter yanked his hand against Carl's hand. It held like steel. He strained toward us. "You can't just destroy everything I've built."

"Everything *you've* built?" Miranda said, sounding shocked.

I laughed a little. "He'll never admit to how deeply he's been used. That thing that fed him all of the information on how to build this, it wants to destroy us. It took over Miranda's body and tried to use it to kill me." I went over to Sippy and pulled my collar down to show him and Peanut the claw marks on my neck.

My mind raced. I had thought about this a thousand times, but I'd never tried to say it out loud. And now I felt the world pressing on me. I lined up my thoughts, I put them in neat little rows, and I said them to Peter Petrawicki clearly and carefully so that Sippy would hear everything I said. I always felt a little like the whole world was weighing on every word I said, but this time, it might actually have been true.

"You really do believe that power must always go to the people who deserve it, don't you?" I said, more amazed than angry. "If you didn't believe it, you'd have to spend some fraction of your time not feeling like Jesus, and that wouldn't be any fun.

"But then someone else gets some power, and you lose some of yours, and you don't like that power has gone somewhere else. But you also can't stop believing that power organizes itself correctly because your entire understanding of the world is based on that single idea. So, instead, you convince yourself that they're cheating or corrupt or lying. Well, guess what? Today, power has organized itself in our hands instead of yours. That doesn't mean something broke, it means you were never right. It is neither just nor unjust, it is just what happened. And you can rationalize it however you want, but it happened. You lost."

I wanted to look back at Sippy, but he didn't know me and I didn't know him. This was either enough, or it wasn't.

I stood still, silent, and then heard Miranda's voice, soft and careful: "Sid, the thing that built Altus really did use my body to try to kill her. It might take me back over any time now. I don't want it to. It was terrible. Please, it's time."

I heard Sippy arranging the headset and finally turned to look.

Peter began shouting behind me, pulling his hand against Carl's iron grip. At first he was shouting words, but then it just became shrieks, like we were abducting his child while he watched. Maybe we were.

Within moments, Sippy had implemented a fresh terms of service update tied to a new experience—Peanut's experience of body dislocation.

Sippy was then forced by the software to view the TOS update himself. He immediately threw off the headset, vomiting on the floor. I watched, too pleased, as a little drip of vomit flecked onto Peter's khaki pants and he recoiled.

And then, suddenly, Peter Petrawicki slumped over, no longer being held by Carl's hand.

At the same moment, monkey Carl revived. The little animal sprung up and padded over to me.

"Carl!" I said, excited, thinking it must be good news. "Did we do it?"

It didn't say anything back.

"Carl? Are you OK now? Did we . . ." And then I saw it. The depth in the monkey's eyes had vanished. The shape of understanding had lost its form. I wasn't looking at a monkey inhabited by an intelligence; I was looking at a monkey. I knew it immediately and without doubt.

Miranda had moved over to check on Peter, who was lying completely motionless on the ground.

"Carl?" I said again, and the monkey moved toward me and made a small chittering noise in its throat.

Look, I have not hid that my feelings about Carl are complicated. They took April from me, they put her in danger, they showed over and over that they cared more about their plans than our lives. But also, Carl felt, at this point, like an inevitability, like someone who would always be there, guiding and knowing and caring. In that way,

Carl felt like family. Maybe I didn't trust them, maybe I wanted them to know they weren't absolved of their past actions, but I didn't realize until then that I had expected Carl to always be a part of my life.

"CARL!" I shouted, and then the monkey ran from me. Of course it did. It ran down the hall toward where April was now standing. It crawled up her leg and then onto her shoulder.

"April," I said, knowing what was happening, but feeling like I was hanging over an edge. Her face was hard; she moved slowly, like she was lost.

Dr. Noise

@drnoise

I just . . . fuck. I just was in the Space and something happened. It was awful, like I was seeing out of both elbows at once. Is that Body Dislocation? I puked on my mom's carpet! @AltusLabs.

63.1K replies   23.3K retweets   128.4K likes

@drnoise

Fuck, I just tried to get back in and it happened again. What's wrong. I tried three times and each time it was like my whole body turned inside out and up was down and up and sideways at the same time.

6K replies   1.3K retweets   9K likes

@drnoise

It's not just me, is anyone able to get into the Space right now?

1.9K replies   784 retweets   4.7K likes

@drnoise

People are saying that once this happens you can never go back. That better be a fucking lie. @AltusLabs.

1.5K replies   1.4K retweets   3.7K likes

APRIL

It's time to go back a bit. Remember when I fell unconscious in that hallway and Maya caught me and then I came back? I didn't tell the full story then, and I haven't since. I guess it's time.

I'm not going to pretend to understand what it's like to be Carl, but they did their best to explain as I crashed out of my body and opened my eyes in the lobby we all used to wake up in back when we were sharing the Dream.

"April . . ." Carl spoke in their comforting tenor. It was pleasant in the bright white room, warm and familiar. It felt like a gift. It felt, somehow, like home. Robot Carl was standing in front of me, towering and gleaming and sharp and kind. "April, I am dying."

"What? You . . ." I wanted to protest, to tell Carl that that was impossible, and if it wasn't, then that we would save them somehow.

Carl continued, in their clear voice. "I once spanned this planet. I was a nervous system that could sense any corner of the world, and even the corners of people's consciousness. And I was nothing compared with the power we are up against. I am not going to exit this battle alive."

"No, there has to be a way, though," I said. I had, not twelve hours before, been so angry with Carl that I didn't want them to be in my life anymore, but now the possibility of losing them was carving into me and it was horrible. Carl was a constant.

They continued, "There is not. When people mine AltaCoin, their entire mind is given over to my brother. The number of people doing that is increasing very fast. I could have hid, I could have lived here for centuries while he hunted down every secret enclave of my system, but I did not do that. Instead, I drew all of my power— everything I have, everything I am—to this island. All of me is here. My brother, he cannot do the same. He needs to maintain his whole network, and so we are on roughly equal footing here, but only here. I can hit him as hard as he can hit me, just not for as long. And I will be needed. He will draw me into direct contact because he knows I am a threat. Once he does it, I will be able to fight him, but not for long. I have cut off any avenue of escape myself. All of me is here and I will not be leaving."

"So, then . . . have we lost? Is it over?"

"No," Carl said immediately. "No, it is just . . . unlikely." The sadness in their voice was immense.

"How unlikely?" I asked.

"I don't know. I cannot run simulations anymore."

"But if you can't run simulations, how will we even know if we've succeeded?"

"Oh, my brother can still run them. If he calculates you have good odds of not destroying yourselves, he'll just stop. I know some of his tools. He's hurting the economy to make people easier to manipulate, and I know he's behind The Thread now. If he stops, those things should stop too. That's how you'll know. Also, I'll tell you when it's safe to leave, or when it's not, but I can't help anymore. I'll let you know that too. I have one or two tricks still up my sleeves. Right now, all of me is being devoted to giving you more time."

"More time to do what?"

"I don't know. Maybe nothing. You will have to figure it out."

"But I have no idea!" I shouted up at the statue. "I don't know how to fix this!"

I heard a noise, like water passing over rocks. I looked around the room to see where it was coming from, but then I realized Carl was laughing. "You still think I chose you."

"What?"

"You think it was you," Carl repeated.

"But you did, you told me you did. You said you ran the simulations and I was the . . . the host who succeeded most often."

"You did not succeed in the simulations, the simulations showed successful outcomes." The water trickled over the rocks again. "I chose you as host, but you were not the reason for the successes."

I waited for more, but Carl apparently wanted me to ask.

"Who was it, then?"

"I love you." The words seemed so careful. "You are so . . . human. You still think it had to be someone. It wasn't anyone, it was all of you."

And then I woke up back in that hallway in Val Verde, knowing that Carl was dying, knowing that every action they took on our part sped that process. Miranda wanted to run across the Altus campus, but I didn't want her to because I knew Carl would have to consume their very self protecting her.

I held the door so Carl wouldn't have to. I fulfilled my part . . . I guarded the others. I made my video. I let the other heroes do their work. It was all of us. It was me and Maya and Andy and Miranda and Peanut and Sippy and Bex and even Stewart Patrick. And then the banging on the door stopped, and I thought maybe they had just moved on to some other tactic. Until a voice spoke in my head. Carl's voice.

"It's time for you to go, April. Thank you. Goodbye."

As far as I know, those were Carl's last words. Spoken in my head, a gift only for me. A gift I didn't share until now because I wanted it to be mine only. But I guess you can have it too.

I took a long, unsteady breath and noticed that same hollow feeling I'd had when we first arrived at Altus. I was no longer connected to anything outside myself. I knew if I let myself feel anything, it would be too much, so I put my emotions away. As I walked into the hallway, the monkey ran up to me and climbed onto my shoulder. I didn't even need to look to know that this wasn't Carl.

"Where's Carl?" Maya asked. I could hear the panic in her voice. But I didn't answer. Instead, with the monkey on my shoulder, I walked down the hall. Peter Petrawicki was slumped and unmoving in his carpeted hallway next to the giant, empty statue that had once contained Carl.

The sculpture's back was still pressed against the door, and even though it was sitting down, I could still barely reach its head. But I did. I put my hand on its cheek, and I felt it. It was not the neither hot nor cold we had felt on 23rd Street. The face felt cool, like metal, like it was a sculpture someone had created and left as a piece of art in this long, opulent hallway.

"We need to go," I said. "The plane is waiting for us."

"I don't know what's wrong with Peter," Miranda said.

"He is just unconscious, he'll wake up soon. They'll all wake up soon. So we have to go now."

"How do you know that?" she asked. Leave it to Miranda to hold us up worrying about the worst possible guy.

"I'll tell you on the plane." My voice sounded flat in my own ears.

"Where's Carl?" Maya repeated.

I remembered back when Carl had tweaked my brain so that I couldn't feel things. This wasn't like that. The emotions weren't being pushed down, they were in a writhing tangled mess in the back of my mind, but they couldn't get to the surface. Not yet.

"Carl died," I said. I wasn't letting myself feel it, and I saw Maya's face shift as she did the same.

"But if Carl died," Miranda said, catching up with us, "then why am I still alive?"

"Because we did it," I said. "We did it."

I gathered my friends, and we walked out of the building together, over the unconscious bodies of Altus security guards. I led them, moving straight and fast, a signal that I wanted to be alone. I didn't want any of them to see my face as it bunched together in grief, snot running into my mouth, tears pouring from my right eye.

"We've got a few new passengers," I told the pilots, the grief walled off for a moment.

"Is everyone OK?" one of them asked.

I didn't know how to answer. I heard the sob bubble out of me before I knew it was happening. It was like vomit, unwelcome and uncontrolled. I felt Maya's hand on my shoulder as she guided me back to the cabin.

"Yes," I heard her say. "Everyone is OK."

ANDY

*T*he donations grew exponentially. From 6 to 7 A.M. we received $400 million. But then from 7 to 7:10 we raised $300 million. People were willing to take the risk. They had lost friends and family, they had lost their savings, they felt the hope that ten dollars really could change things forever. And it was now or never.

I told myself it would be enough, even as Stewart Patrick and Bex kept telling me it wouldn't be.

And then the news started coming in. I almost went into the Space to check, but I stopped myself. If you went in now, you would be forced to experience body dislocation, and once you had that experience, your mind locked onto it and could never go in again.

Whatever April had done on that island, it had just destroyed the Space for millions of people who were currently logged in.

I got a text from Stewart Patrick.

> *Sorry I didn't believe you. This is perfect. They're going to start falling now.*

And fall they did. By the time our three-hour deadline was up, we had received donations from more than a billion people.

Stewart started buying. And the moment one person sold at a new, lower valuation, other investors got even more freaked out and he could buy at an even lower price. Altus's value crashed. He bought the entire Saudi sovereign fund's 10 percent stake for $4 billion, setting the value of the company at just $40 billion.

After that, the rest of the investors would sell at any price.

I texted April, *What did you do?*

I wanted it to sound like maybe I was just curious. Maybe it wasn't as bad as I thought. Maybe it was temporary. There had to be a way to turn it off, right?

> **April:** *We're on our way home. Altus is broken. From what we can tell, there's no way to fix it. Spread the word. The investors will take any out we can give them.*

> **April:** *But don't stop taking money. This was the world's decision, they need to feel invested.*

That was April—there was no truth but the optics. I was having a hard time believing that we were actually going to raise $20 billion, but it looked like we were going to beat the goal substantially. Here's a wild stat: If you distribute a billion dollars across everyone in the US, each person would only get $3. That doesn't seem possible! But it works the other way too, every person only has to give $3 for someone to have a billion.

At 9:30 A.M. eastern time, Stewart Patrick texted me to let me know that we were down to our last $200 million, and we now owned a controlling interest in Altus Labs.

It turned out that we needed that $200 million, though, to pay severances to all of the Altus employees we laid off and to bribe the government of Val Verde to prevent Peter Petrawicki from suing us. Eventually, Val Verde kicked Peter off the island, and he had to go back to living in the California suburb where he grew up.

It wasn't until he stopped that we could see the full scope of what Carl's brother had been doing. After we broke Altus, a full 2 percent of active social media accounts never posted again. That included The Thread, but also a number of other similar YouTube channels. My theory is that Carl's brother was building audiences all over the internet and was planning to pit them against each other somehow. Or maybe he was just going to use them, turn them into his followers and keep them perpetually satisfied.

But he stopped, and that meant we had succeeded. I think.

Whatever we were doing, we were on a path that didn't include us destroying ourselves or being taken over by a relentless ever-present god AI.

So Altus was gone, The Thread had disappeared, April was back, everything was perfect, and I was so goddamn angry.

I did a pretty good job of ignoring my constant, smoldering frustration. But it was there, always grating on me, always waiting to be fed a little more fuel. I was so good at not looking at it that it took me a long time to figure out what it even was.

I have some fiercely amazing friends, and I've tried to follow in their footsteps, but I am not as smart as Miranda, or as self-aware as April has become, or as insightful as Maya has always been. Just for the moment, though, I'm going to try to be all of those things, even if I'm just pretending.

I spent the time between April's death and the end of Altus trying out pretty much every way humans feel valuable.

I got famous, I got rich, I was adored, I hung out with fancy folks, I helped people, I tried to change the world for the better, I made my friends laugh, I had powerful people tell me I was worthwhile, I wielded tremendous influence.

I tried *everything*, so you'll excuse me if, at this point, I feel like enough of an expert to present you with:

ANDY SKAMPT'S SIMPLE LIST OF THE WAYS
PEOPLE FEEL VALUABLE

1. Just Believing It

Sometimes this is religious; sometimes it is not. God cares for everyone, but society is supposed to as well. We strive to live in a world that places tremendous, even infinite value on a single human life. We do not live in that society, but I think part of the reason we strive for it is because we need to signal that our existence is intrinsically meaningful. This is the only source of meaning that does not rely on other people; it is also the hardest one to hold on to.

2. Story

We understand ourselves in complex ways, but oftentimes that can be distilled down into some core identities. And we imagine these identities as part of a story, and that that story is some intrinsically positive thing. It might be being part of a tradition, or breaking free of one. It might be your race or height or hair color. Your status as a child or a parent. Being a job creator or a *Star Wars* fan or a snowboarder. We create positive narratives around these things, and when we fit in them, we feel like we matter.

3. Being Appreciated

It might be hearing someone laugh at your joke, or being paid a living wage, or getting likes on Instagram. It might be only external, or it might also come from within. Appreciation is almost synonymous with value, and I think this is where most meaning comes from.

4. Helping People

This might sound the same as appreciation, but it's not. Indeed, I think your average wastewater-treatment engineer will tell you that you can help a lot of people and not get a ton of thanks for it. But we are empathy machines, and one of the most lasting and true ways of finding meaning is to actually be of service.

5. Comparison

You know, keeping up with the Joneses. Also, every sport. But it's more than just comparing ourselves to other people; we also compare our current selves to our past selves, which is why getting better at something makes us feel valuable, even if we're the only ones who really understand how much we're improving.

6. Impacting the World

This one is simple, but so dangerous. If the world is different because you are in it, then you must matter. You must be important if things changed because you exist. But if that's what you believe, then the bigger the impact, the more you matter, and that can lead to some bad places.

You might think that this list is too long or too short, and who knows, maybe it is. You might think that I missed a big one, like "Belonging." But I think belonging is just mutual appreciation of shared identity. It's like a feedback loop of appreciating someone for an identity you share, which makes you appreciate yourself.

Also, these things are never felt in isolation from each other. A schoolteacher gains meaning from:

1. Seeing the impact they have on their students.
2. Being part of the story of teaching.
3. Helping their students.
4. Being a better teacher this year than they were last year.
5. Being appreciated for their work (god willing).

And I find that it is much easier to believe in your intrinsic value if you are getting all these other signals that you have value.

I spent weeks working all of this out for a reason. I was mad and

I wanted to know why, and now it's really obvious to me. Compared to my former self, I was just much less. I had gone from being a billionaire back to being just merely well-off. April had taken my identity as her surrogate by existing again. The end of The Thread had dramatically diminished my ability to impact the world. And on top of all of that, I had spent months actually trying to help people, only to abandon that brand the moment something shinier came along.

I was so mad, and I was *mad* that I was mad.

And it didn't escape my notice that I was the only person being directly manipulated by both Carl and their brother. On The Thread, One was working constantly to get me addicted to Altus and to get me to tie my identity to it. Carl, meanwhile, was betting that I would be able to overcome that temptation. Or, more likely, they were betting that it wouldn't matter. And it hadn't. If it were up to me, I probably wouldn't have let Miranda break Altus, and that fact tore at me every day.

This whole time, I was also dealing with the same Altus withdrawal that millions of people were dealing with, so, basically, life sucked.

And every day it became clearer and clearer that Altus was never coming back, and every day I got angrier and angrier about it. I didn't know whether to be mad at my friends for destroying it, at Carl for setting me up to fall in love with it, or at myself for being so easy to manipulate into loving something terrible. Over and over again, every night I kept my mouth shut.

But then, finally, a couple of months after Altus shut down, I couldn't do it anymore.

> **Andy:** *I'm mad. I've been mad the whole time. I can't stop.*

> **April:** *What?*

Andy: *About Altus. I miss it. It's gone. I know you did what you had to do, but I'm still mad.*

April: *I don't know what I'm supposed to do with that, Andy.*

This made me even angrier, but maybe it was the right kind of anger. Maybe the fire couldn't go out until it burned up its fuel.

Andy: *Maybe I just need you to know. I thought we were going to get control of Altus . . . to do good things with it. Not just destroy it. I don't know why we got to make this decision for so many people.*

April: *OK, I've been thinking about this a lot. I'm mad that you're mad because this is something that I don't know if I did right. But we had to do something. I wish I had your support. But I guess I understand if I don't.*

I didn't write back for a while and then, finally, a wall of text appeared.

April: *The problem with Altus wasn't how it was run or who was running it, it was that whoever was running it would instantly be too powerful. If someone had to be that powerful, you'd be close to the top of my list. We're good people, but I don't even trust us. Power concentrates naturally, but that concentration is, by itself, a problem. We made a choice for a lot of people, but that choice wasn't just "You can't have Altus anymore," it was "One tiny group of people will not be in charge of the future." We had to do it for Carl reasons, but even without that it was the right thing. I really believe that. Altus was* *an invasion. They wanted to be the future, I think that was why they were so dangerous. The most impactful thing you can do with power is almost always to give it away.*

I read that paragraph several times before I wrote back.

Andy: *Did Maya help you write that? Because it's really good.*

April: *Fuck you!*

April: *And yes.*

Andy: *I'm going to think about this. Thank you for dealing with me.*

April: *Literally any time.*

I guess what I'm trying to say is, it's very important to have friends who are smarter than you . . . and who are also kind to you.

I turned to Bex, who was lying on the bed beside me. "Why didn't you give up on me?"

"Shut up, Andy," she said. "Go to sleep."

MIRANDA

So I saved the world, huh? I mean, not *just* me, but it's a little hard to feel like a complete phony when humanity would definitely have been doomed without you. That doesn't mean that I don't still sometimes feel like a fraud, but it's nice to have a solid touchstone.

Also, I get to do really cool stuff now.

I went back to Berkeley, where Professor Lundgren had, once again, kept my lab bench in place and available. And there she and I started doing something pretty dangerous and very secret—we took Altus's source code and tried to use it to figure out how it worked.

What became clear pretty quickly was that no one at Altus had written the code and, indeed, no human had written it. Much of it was completely indecipherable. But that doesn't mean we didn't find anything useful.

We were able to determine that the changes Carl made to our brains to allow us to receive and transmit data into their network were observable and permanent. And we were able to determine that even children born after the Dream stopped happening had those changes. What we were not able to find was any trace of the computational system Carl's brother was, theoretically, still using to observe us.

We knew it was there, but whatever systems Carl used to turn our biosphere into a planetwide computer were too elegant for us to even perceive. You'd almost think it wasn't there, which I guess is the point.

We all dropped our Altus nicknames when we got back to Berkeley. And I say "we" because the first people I hired onto my research team (yes, I had a research team now) were Paxton and Sid.

I was trying to get them to go for runs with me, though they were more successful in getting me to play D&D with them.

But I did succeed in getting them to help me do amazing research. We teased out the barest bits of how the Altus Space worked. From that, we got little insights that could potentially help push brain-computer interfaces forward by ten or even fifteen years.

And then, after we were fairly certain that we'd gotten most of the low-hanging fruit from our analysis of the alien code, y'know what we did? We destroyed it. We took every single hard drive that had ever touched that stuff, and we put them in a truck, and we drove that truck to a facility that can smash anything into powder. And then each of us took turns throwing drives into the maw of this giant grinder that was built specifically to destroy hard drives. The drives split and bounced and ripped apart until they finally fell through to the other side, where they were nothing more than jangling pieces of plastic, silicon, and metal. We each took one little piece back to the lab with us, where they sit above our lab stations.

Every day we come in and we do science. We do *great* science, and I actually feel like the leader of this little team. I feel like I belong to something again. We do it right, and we do it well, and in the morning I come in and I look at my little bent, mangled piece of hard drive and feel something lovely. I feel whatever feeling is the exact opposite of regret.

MAYA

You don't get to know where April and I went. I've had enough of that. We're just here on planet Earth with the rest of the humans. Did we make a couple of not-super-well-thought-out financial decisions? Yeah, but we had to make a comfortable life for ourselves and Paulette. Paulette is our monkey.

We did buy a house together. In general, I would suggest not having a very large, shared asset with a girlfriend who has not always been the most stable person in your life. But, I don't know, it felt a little like she had changed. Or maybe that's just my April-shaped blind spot. I think part of the point of loving someone is being able to deal with their brokenness.

April's family was on the West Coast and mine was on the East, so we compromised and we live, well, somewhere in the middle. I am going to save the memory of our shared reunion with our families for myself. It was the first time my parents met April's parents, and it was so normal that it could never feel as important as it was. It was not as big of a deal as saving the world, but it was close.

Mostly, though, it was just the two of us.

Time passed, and eventually, finally, it became clear that Tater was moving past its prime. We knew, down there somewhere, in the darkness, there were treasures waiting for us. One morning, I declared it was time. April and I sank our hands into the pot together, feeling the little magically formed nuggets of food there. Our hands met under the soil, and we laughed together.

And then April shouted with joy, "PAULETTE!" The monkey had popped one of the dirty taters straight into her mouth and was crunching it. We all laughed together. Except for Paulette, who didn't like the flavor of uncooked potato and spat it out onto the ground.

April's hands dug deeper into the pot to see if there were any other prizes to be found, and I just watched her. Her body, both new parts and old, working together to generate the tiny effort needed to push into the loose soil. She was beautiful. She had always been beautiful. Too beautiful for her own good, but now she was a literal technological marvel as well. I love to watch her body. Her hand came out of the bucket holding something that was not a potato. With a look of complete, abject amazement on her face, she held up a swollen and muddy book.

She pushed it toward me, and I, on instinct, pushed it back. Honestly, I was a little terrified of what it might mean.

"The Book of Good Times," it said on the cover.

I moved over to kneel next to her so that I could see the words as she read them out loud.

Hey, you two. I hope you get this. If you do, then things will have gone as well as could be expected. I'm sorry I didn't tell you more, but if you had known, you might not have succeeded. I've run a couple simulations, though, and in all of them you forgave me at the end, so that is bittersweet. I'm sorry I'm going to leave you.

I was never going to survive long anyway.

I'm even sorrier about the pain I have caused. It has ripped at me to be the source of such conflict and division. I set that plan in motion before I cared about people as individuals. It was cruel of my parents to deprive me of that care and then give it to me after there was nothing I could do to change my plans. But I suppose they did that for a reason.

I just want you to know that you people are wonderful and beautiful and terrible and foolish. I was given knowledge of the action of other agents like myself and of the different kinds of people they worked with. Maybe it's reality or my own familiarity with you in particular or just my programming, but it seems clear to me, you are something special.

I loved to watch you. I loved to learn about you. I loved loving you.

You're radically collaborative, profoundly empathetic, and deeply communal. Everyone who tells you anything different is selling the fear that is the only thing that can break that nature. They do that because it turns people into devices. My only advice: Never do that to another person, and do not let anyone do it to you.

Oh, and also, as a general rule, err on the side of caution and . . .

She looked up at me and then kept reading:

. . . listen to Maya.

In this book are a couple of explanations of how I work for you to put in an eventual book that you will make available. It will be a memoir of our experiences in this time, and I would like to tell people more about me. I think it will be good for people to know what happened here, how I came to you, and telling the ones who will listen about my brother will further push you toward a more stable path. I hope you don't mind me saying so, but for you, knowing someone is watching does generally improve human behavior.

I don't think we could have written this book if Carl hadn't said we would. But it was their last request, so we didn't have much choice.

I can't tell you if you'll remain free. I can only tell you that you've got better odds now than you did before. I was very powerful, and losing that power has been very hard. Literally painful, sometimes, but other times simply the knowledge of my own diminishment in the face of the greater power that now inhabits your planet was devastating. But my power was real, and while I am angry at the loss, I do believe that my parents did know at least something about what they were doing. I believe that because I have witnessed my own power and compassion, and I assume that theirs is even greater.

If you'll allow me one final trick, Maya, you two should probably go to Costco. Around fifty people will be coming over for dinner tonight.

And so they did. Andy and Bex and Jason and Robin and Miranda all showed up, but so did a few familiar faces I didn't expect. My parents, for starters, and April's. But also Saanvi Laghari, the woman who I interviewed about the dead dolphins, the two pilots who flew us to and from Altus, and Jessica and Mitty, our ambulance drivers. There were people we didn't know too, like Miranda's advisor, Dr. Lundgren, and a bunch of people *none* of us had ever met.

And every person there brought with them a small, simple leather-bound book. These were the people who Carl had chosen. They were the people Carl needed to make the plan work.

They were business owners and servers and nurses and drivers and teachers, and we connected with old friends and made new ones. It was Carl's last gift, and we drank of it deeply. We were awake until morning, laughing and talking about what we'd done and where we were going, and nothing seemed too heavy to carry because all of these people could share the burden. But we also just talked about our friends and our hopes and our scars. And the soundtrack, of course, was perfect.

APRIL

*T*his isn't another cliff-hanger, I promise. I'm done here. There's no more story left after these last pages that is in any way interesting. You want to know what a day in the life of April May is? I don't really care. You're convinced that I'm using my superpowers to affect the world in fiendish and clever ways? Well, I haven't been able to download information into my brain since Carl died, so that's not happening. You want advice for how to live in the twenty-first century and not have humanity taken over by a sinister force that, as you read this, lives on inside your very cells, deciding every moment whether or not we are past saving? I also would *love* to have that guidance. Unfortunately, I do not have it to give.

That's the whole reason I wrote these books. That's why I wrangled my friends, racked my augmented brain, and suffered through the telling. Even in a world without Altus, the most sophisticated software in existence is tasked with figuring out how to keep you from leaving a website. That software knows all of your weaknesses, and while it's only concentrating on individuals, exploiting individual weakness is also exploiting societal weakness. What that software wants to do is make us into people who are easier to predict.

These algorithms are already programming society. And the question that we now have to ask is, what happens when they realize it? What happens when one person, or a small group of people, motivated primarily by the need to get their stock price to go up, realize that they have the power to program a society?

What happens thirty or fifty years from now when the people

who were inspired by the promise of the internet are all washed up or retired or dead? What happens when the stock prices stagnate and those companies need to demonstrate their worth to investors? What does a single CEO with the power to remake the world do?

Do they help us overcome climate change? Do they help us progress toward a more just and stable society? Or do they just make money?

Of course, I don't know if we'll be saved. I don't know if we'll get to keep going on our own path. And that's the kinda sickening thing—we'll never know. We didn't kill Carl's brother; we just convinced him he wasn't needed. He's still here, watching, calculating, learning, and ready, at any moment, to lead us carefully, subtly, secretly, and brutally into submission.

And how do we avoid it? It might be that saving the world is idiotically simple. Maybe we just need to connect and care for one another. But I don't know. Of course I don't know. When it comes down to it, when has humanity ever known what it was doing?

I was asked to become more than human, and I welcomed it. I wanted to be important. I wanted to be exceptional. But now my exceptionality is written on my face, and I cannot leave it behind.

The fucked-up thing is, when I look back at this, I may not have gotten what I deserved, but I got exactly what I wanted.

Almost six months after Altus went down, when the world had mostly recovered from the anger and division that the loss had caused, and the economy finally seemed interested in some kind of positive movement, I woke up in my bed after having fallen asleep in Maya's arms the same way I had dozens of times in those months.

"April," Maya said softly in my ear, "this is going to be scary. But it's not something to be scared about."

I was, of course, instantly anxious, but maybe out of a subconscious understanding of the situation, I didn't stir.

"Carl told me this would happen months ago. Just before we left for Val Verde, he said that, if we made it through, eventually . . ." And then she trailed off.

I tried to shift, but my body felt wrong.

"Your arm and your legs, they are not actually permanently fused to you. You can take them off and put them back on. Last night, while you were sleeping, they came off."

I did panic a little bit then. I tried to lift my left arm, but it was not there. Instead, from my shoulder, a scarred and rippling stump stood out. I took my right arm to feel around my body, foreign and empty and small.

"Oh my god," I said. I drew back the sheet to look down at my body, soft and broken and made only of human stuff.

"My face . . ." I said, feeling it with my right hand.

"Carl said it can't come off, it's connected to your brain."

"So." I paused. "It will always be in me."

She crawled into the bed, and her arms and legs wrapped around me. I felt the prickle of her leg hairs on my skin. "Yeah, it will always be in you," she said, but she didn't sound upset about it, just informative.

I didn't cry because I was angry or scared or sad, though I was all of those things. I cried because it was just a lot. I might have also even been, in that moment, happy.

For so long I had believed what I had been told, that I was a tool, formed and sharpened and wielded for the world. Not a person, but an agent of change, a cultural mutagen, a weapon. I heard my breathing, coming fast and shallow.

"It's real," I said, because, somehow, what we had done hadn't felt real until then. I hadn't felt real. I had lost myself, not when I woke up in that bar, but two years ago when I woke up to a cup of coffee and a dozen text messages and this same face looking down at me. I felt my story finally slide into place. "It's real," I said again.

"It is," she said, and she pulled me into her. "Your life is written on this body, and I love every piece of it."

Somehow she made me feel human, and that is, I've learned, one of the very best things to be.

ACKNOWLEDGMENTS

Oh gosh, I don't even know how to start. This book felt, at times, entirely impossible, but a lot of people made it possible. I'll start with my son, Orin, who reminded me to take frequent breaks by pointing to my computer and saying, "Close it." But, also, I'm extremely grateful to my wife, Katherine, who (through a combination of love and also a desire for the sequel to come out) dealt with me while I was having . . . dramatic moments with this project.

Maya Ziv is my editor, and she is very good at communicating that something can be great while also needing a great deal of work. She is responsible for many good things that are in this book, but even more bad things that aren't. And both Maya and I are in awe of Mary Beth Constant, our tremendous copy editor who saved our butts dozens of times. Jodi Reamer, my literary agent, has also been there every step of the way and seems incapable of not being a tremendous voice of support. Maja Nikolc and the foreign rights team at Writers House have also done an amazing job of helping my work reach new countries and be published in more than a dozen languages, which is a dream come true. So many people at Dutton helped this come together. Kaitlin Kall's cover design, Tiffany Estreicher's book design, proofreading from Eileen Chetti, Alice Dalrymple, and Rob Sternitzky, the marketing and publicity teams, especially Amanda Walker and Emily Canders, and so many others. It is really wonderful to know how many people it takes to bring a book into the world. Thank you to everyone at Dutton for getting books into the hands of readers.

I had so many early readers helping me understand the nuances of writing characters who are very different from me. I consider those people my editors as well and I learned a tremendous amount from them. Those people include Gaby Dunn, Ashley Ford, Taylor Behnke, and Phyllida Swift. Also, I have to say, it seems so unlikely that I would find a trained editor who is Chinese Trinidadian, but Danielle Goodman is exactly that!

Thank you to Lindsay Ellis, who gave me so many amazing ideas and perspectives on an early draft of this book.

Gabriela Elena and Ketie Saner created a timeline of *An Absolutely Remarkable Thing*, which came in handy a dozen times while writing this book, so much so that I hired them to help me construct the timeline of this book, and their help was invaluable.

There are also people who had no idea they were helping, like Harvey Sugiuchi, who was a student of a friend of mine and, when she asked her class what magical item they wish they had, he said, "I want a book of good times that can take me to the best place to relax and have fun at any given moment. It also has stuff like recipes in it."

Thank you also to every person who advocates for a book . . . who gets on that book's team and pushes for it. There is so much great work out there, and for some reason, sometimes we need our arms twisted to indulge in it. So, whether you're a bookseller, a librarian, or just that pesky friend, thank you for twisting those arms!

If you've gotten this far, you're probably aware, but if you're not, my life has been bizarre and extremely fortunate. A huge part of that is the community of people who find entertainment and identity and connection in the content my brother and I make on YouTube. Those people have enabled so many good and cool things to happen, and this book is one more of those things. I never stop being grateful for the insight and opportunity that community has given me.

And lastly, let's go with my brother, John, who is a near-perfect collaborator and advisor. Yes, he gave me notes on this book, but more than that, we have given each other notes on just about every decision either of us has made in the past fifteen years, and we are both way better off because of it. He and my parents and my wife and my son and, honestly, my whole family were the greatest stroke of luck I have ever received, and I've gotten some doozies.

ABOUT THE AUTHOR

Hank Green is the number one *New York Times* bestselling author of *An Absolutely Remarkable Thing*. He's also the CEO of Complexly, a production company that creates educational content, including *Crash Course* and *SciShow*, prompting *The Washington Post* to name him "one of America's most popular science teachers." Complexly's videos have been viewed more than two billion times on YouTube. Hank and his brother, John, are also raising money to dramatically and systematically improve maternal health care in Sierra Leone, where, if trends continue, one in seventeen women will die in child-birth. You can join them at PIH.org/hankandjohn.

PERMISSIONS